THE
FOREVER
SEA

THE
FOREVER
SEA

Joshua Phillip Johnson

TITAN BOOKS

The Forever Sea
Print edition ISBN: 9781789093377
E-book edition ISBN: 9781789093384

Published by Titan Books
A division of Titan Publishing Group Ltd
144 Southwark Street, London SE1 0UP
www.titanbooks.com

First Titan edition: January 2021
10 9 8 7 6 5 4 3 2 1

A CIP catalogue record for this title is available from the British Library.

Printed and bound by CPI Group (UK) Ltd, Croydon, CR0 4YY.

'Sing, memory,' the storyteller says, the words low and quiet, a dirge for the darkness. His skin, the few stretches of it not covered by patchwork clothing, emanates a faint glow illuminating his steps and casting shadows of the fractured, broken buildings surrounding him, jagged outlines of the old world.

'Sing,' he says again, perhaps to himself, perhaps to the darkness, perhaps to the history running through and held forever by the shards of the broken buildings.

He steps carefully. He has walked this path many times before. The storyteller keeps his eyes ahead and fixed on the two burning pricks of light giving challenge to the totality of the darkness. They are shrouded, protection against attracting predatory vines and wild animals, but the storyteller is not just a creature prowling the ever-night. He is something more, and something much less, too.

Slowly, step by meditative step, the storyteller nears the camp. His steps need not cause sound, but he strikes his heels hard on the ground all the same. His lungs do not need air, yet he gulps it in noisily anyway.

In truth, he needs nothing, not anymore, but he remembers well enough the brash existence cultivated by needing.

'Sing, memory.'

This time, he imbues the words with their true weight and import. Those around the fires knew someone or something approached through the darkness. Now they would know who.

He hears the satisfying shift, confusion and fear resolving into peals of delight as memory sparks and catches, and suddenly, voices unused to joy are raised in it.

The darkness holds little of mystery or fear for the storyteller – save the one question dreaming in the still caverns of his heart – but these people see nothing but monsters and terror in the dark. They are both hunted and hunter, searching for the water and food they need to survive; their hopes are like their small fires holding back the forever darkness of this world.

But they know of the storyteller, have heard from parents and grandparents about the one who wanders the world, telling tales of what used to be, of what still is, and of what just might be again.

They know, too, that those beasts that move in shadow and hunger for light and life do not trouble the storyteller. Where he walks, the dangers of the world do not follow.

The people of this camp know, as he approaches, that they will be safe for at least the length of his stay.

'Sing, memory,' he says again, near enough now to see the faces ringing the fires, a mix of young and old. In the last camp, maybe some thirty or forty miles behind him, the storyteller felt the echoes of something that might once have been sadness when he saw how much the population had diminished since his last visit some years before. It is a reminder of the inevitable decline of things, and the storyteller wished he could have felt more of something in response.

But he is happy – or at least aware that he might have been

happy once – to see that this place has grown. Forty-two, he counts, each one looking hungry and thirsty, dirty and tired, and *alive*.

Twist, this place is called, or it was the last time he passed through, and he starts with the sudden realization that he can't remember why it has this name. More and more, the world and things of humanity feel fleeting to him, like so much noise carried away on the wind, empty and purposeless.

'Storyteller!' a voice from the darkness shouts, and then they are appearing around him, offering hands to aid his steps, torches lit and held aloft to light his way. These people, terrified a moment ago of what the black might hold, now turn raucous and joyful at the gift the darkness has given them. So it goes.

Children clap and giggle, able to play loudly for perhaps the first time in their lives. The charred flesh of a vine and a cup of water are produced and offered to the storyteller, and though he has no need for either, he accepts both with a smile and a word of thanks. It would do no good for these people to know the truth of him, not yet, anyway.

'I am the First here,' says a woman who steps forward and nods at him. She is short and lean, with a hard face and arms braided with taut muscles. 'Welcome back to Twist.'

He nods back. To be named First in this camp is both a statement of power and of determination. She is the leader here, that much is clear. But in an attack – either from one of the other camps or the more-likely invasion by one of the creatures that hunt in the darkness – the First should be the first to fight and the first to die.

'Thank you,' the storyteller says, looking around at all that has changed since his last visit here, most of which is lost to the slow fog blanketing his memory. Buildings in further disrepair, more and more stripped for wood to burn and stone for weapons. Caught in the flickering light of the fires, more bridges than the storyteller can remember weave from place to place, each one a strand in the spider's web that is Twist. Bridges spanning vast chasms where the ground has fallen away, arching high to the homes built above, nestled among the splaying, crisscrossing branches.

This close to the ground, the branches are enormous, mighty things, wide around as a person is tall and springing from central stalks three or four times wider than that. The effect, here as everywhere the storyteller walks, is of a vast and mighty arcade. Great pillars rise from shattered ground to a ceiling vaulting too high to ever see, lost in the infinite darkness.

People from those homes above are descending now on bridges that angle up and away, quickly scuttling down to join the other people of Twist. The storyteller is not to be missed.

'I am happy to return,' he says. 'Your numbers have grown since I was last here.'

'We have been lucky,' the First says, her smile big enough to nearly disguise her curiosity at the storyteller's wandering attention.

Time has become a fluid, smudged thing for him. More than once, he has come back to himself on the path as if from a trance, one foot raised for a step he had taken some unknown time earlier, his body totally still, his memory offering no hint as to how long he had been like that.

He is going, that much is clear, losing more and more of the world, of himself, each day. And it takes every bit of willpower he has left to care at all.

'Can I stow your things?' the First asks, gesturing to the pack slung over his shoulder.

'No!' he says, a strange flood of panic overcoming him suddenly. His glowing hand, the skin nearly translucent with age, clamps possessively on the bag he carries.

He imagines the speculation behind the polite looks of shock at his sudden burst of possessiveness. They imagine he hides some powerful weapon or secret power that might change the world. A weapon to kill a monster. Or a map of water.

Or perhaps they imagine his bag to be full of bones, the dry clacking of them his only companion, the grain of each one slivered with memory and magic.

But no. These are the fantasies of a world long gone, and there are none left living who know the magic of burning bones.

He leaves them to their wild imaginings. Better that than the truth of what hangs swaddled in his pack.

'Of course,' the First says, holding out her hands as if she might smooth away any offense she might have caused.

The storyteller takes a noisy slurp from the cup of water he has been given. It feels like sand sliding down his old throat.

'I am grateful for what you have already offered,' he says, holding up the cup. 'I don't want to ask any more of anyone. Besides!'

He smiles, wide and mischievous. Finally, the reason he is in Twist. The reason he *is* at all.

'It is I who have come to offer *you* something.'

A joyful cry erupts at that. These people clearly have not had anything to celebrate in a long time, perhaps for some the entirety of their ragged, shadowed lives.

Between the two fires, a small dais is cobbled together from bits of buildings and a section of wood that looks achingly like a scrap from an old ship hull. Even as the storyteller slides his bare feet across it, he can feel the slight bend in the wood, echoes of voyages past traced across the panel in dents and divots.

A chair is brought for him, but he sends it away. The story he has to tell – the same he has been telling in every camp and settlement since Before turned into After – is long, but he has not felt the quicksand pull of fatigue since... well, since before he can remember.

More water is brought, too, and this he accepts. Let them imagine him as impossibly powerful and full of unending stamina but still, at his core, dependent on those necessities that define human life. Let them love the object of curiosity he is for them. Let them build stories and myths on this myth of him.

Better that than the truth.

The people of Twist circumscribe two fires before him – one, two, three rings deep, faces turned expectantly toward him. Children grow still and slow their perpetually manic breathing. Adults, meanwhile, feel their hearts beat quicker, not with fear or worry, as they are used to, but with anticipation. With expectation. With wonder.

The storyteller allows the stillness to grow and draw every face toward him, until the only sound is the low, endless sighing of the wind moving through grass. He looks at the buildings barely illuminated in the darkness, old husks that once held and housed so much more. The largest of them, despite its shattered frame and stones blackened from fire, shelters both fires from the darkness beyond. It is diminished, a shadow of what it once was, but the bones of it remain in the shape of drying halls and display galleries, hallways once walked by those with few concerns and money to spend. In times of old, when such things mattered.

'Sing, memory,' he begins, giving the words weight and power and *magic*.

'I have come to tell you the story of Before. Before all was darkness. Before the Sea became monstrous. Before.'

Beyond the flicker of firelight and rising behind and above the remains of buildings, he can see the great stalk-like pillars holding up some celestial world far above. The world waits for him, and he speaks from memory.

'Once, the people of this world lived in a land that was bathed in light each day. They moved through their lives without fear of what the dark might hold, and one could hope to spend a full life pursuing their pleasure before dying of old age, surrounded by family and friends.'

'I thought you were telling us a story of Before, not today!' a man shouts, smiling broadly. He is met by waves of laughter.

It is good they can still joke and laugh. It offers nothing to the storyteller. But in the face of the inevitable, defiant joy is effort and reward both. It is how to survive, and it is why.

'There once was an island in this mythic, sunlit place called Arcadia. On all sides, Arcadia was surrounded by a Sea of grass, miles deep, and on this prairie Sea, *boats* would sail.'

He cuts one luminous hand through the air: a ship cutting across an endless field of green.

'On land, the people lived out lives full and mundane, lacking imagination and wonder. But on the Forever Sea . . .'

The storyteller trails off, lost in his own thoughts before offering a bright smile to those watching with wide eyes, already caught in the web he spins.

'Imagine it with me. A Sea so deep that none who walked above had ever seen its floor. A Sea reaching so far east that none who had set sail for its end ever returned. Well, *almost* none. As large as it was unknowable; that was the Forever Sea in those days, and those wild enough, or mad enough, would sail on it.

'But these were no ordinary boats, for nothing – or almost nothing – could float on the Forever Sea. In the center of each ship, set into the wood of the deck, a great fire would burn in a metal basin, a fire much like yours here, giving power and lift to the vessels.

'Some harvested the plants that grew in this Sea, and a vast system of trade grew around these harvests. Plants could be burned to release the magics trapped within their flowers or stems. They could be used for the healing of diseases or injuries. They could be eaten for nourishment or turned into clothing or fed to animals who might later be eaten or used for clothing or craft. The world of Arcadia was defined by the Forever Sea, and no one moved through their life without the gifts of the Sea.'

He has them now, he can tell. Faces rapt with wonder and imagination, caught in the litany of myth that feels at once impossible and strangely true. Not just a fantastical history, but *their* fantastical history.

As it is.

The storyteller lets his eyes rise to the darkness pressing in before continuing.

'For many generations, the sailors of Arcadia made their lives on the Sea, plundering the prairie of its riches, only to have it all grow back again, ready to be harvested once more. They were parasites living on the body of the world.

'And eventually, the world began to take notice.'

A child, her face showing no more than ten or twelve years, sucked in a breath.

'But I'm getting ahead of myself. This story – your story and mine – begins with a young woman on a ship. See her now, if you can. Tall and lithe, with the careless ease that only youth can offer. She is twenty-two and seeking her place in the world, a sailor wanting to make a name for herself. Dark hair cut short to stay out of her face, skin darkened by soot and grime and sun.

'She is about to lose everything, this woman, though she doesn't know it yet. And it might be equally true to say, too, that she is on the precipice of finding everything. And more.

'Her name, the most famous this world has ever forgotten, is . . . was . . . Kindred Greyreach. And right now, as this tale begins, she is singing.'

KINDRED threaded her hands deep into the fire and sang a quiet song.

Around her the ship was chaos: boots pounded rough tattoos over the deck as crew members rushed to secure and tie and pull and coil; shouts – panicked, angry, excited – shook the air, threatening to break Kindred's concentration. The captain's voice was a silver bell amid the turmoil of *The Errant*; Kindred couldn't make out her orders ringing through the noise, but the toll of authority was recognizable nonetheless.

And amid and above and below and through it all, the threat that had *The Errant* hurtling fast across the Sea, bearing hard for port.

Pirates.

Kindred's hands spasmed in the fire as she thought of the ship pursuing them, of wild, jagged predators' smiles.

'Focus in, *girl*,' a voice hissed in Kindred's ear. Rhabdus, the senior hearthfire keeper leaned over her shoulder, supervising with a sneer Kindred felt without needing to see. 'I don't fancy sinking into the deeps because of your incompetence and *creativity*.'

Kindred took a breath, stilling her thoughts and trying to ignore Rhabdus's wheezing sighs and the play of her imagination. She focused on her present: the hearthfire blazing indigo before her, the rustle-touch of flames arcing around her wrists and fingers.

And her song.

The whispered words countered the fearful storm on deck and staved off the fear slinking sideways along the alleys of her mind.

'A litany for the fire.

Burn bone, ay lay, burn bone to black
sing white, ay lay, brand bone to black
for ship and Sea and crew, ay lay,
to sail the green, to sail the grass, ay lay.
A fire, ay lay, a prairie flame
a blaze, ay lay, a blaze of bone
for ship and Sea and crew, ay lay,
to sail the green, to sail the grass
ay lay, ay lay.'

Kindred's song stilled the fire, changing the color from a dark indigo to a cloudy grey and revealing a tree-like structure of bones at the center of the flames. Kindred monitored the interplay of air and flame and bone there at the center, the rush of heat swooping and rising through the tendrils of bone and winding amid caverns made of air and flame. She noted breaks in the structure, bone branches drooping from where she had set them earlier.

Rhabdus scoffed, her derision nasal and low.

'Inefficient and idiotic,' she said, leaning in, nails digging deep into Kindred's shoulder. 'You're the hearthfire keeper, girl. You own it, you control it – now start acting like it. Enough with the *imagination.*' Rhabdus snarled the word. 'Quit messing with my build and follow the shit-spitting rules.'

Kindred swallowed her indignant response – Rhabdus knew her name, had been mentoring her some time now, but still refused to call her anything other than 'girl.'

Your *build was ugly and plain*, she wanted to say. Your *build had no spirit*. Your *build will kill us*.

'Understood.' Kindred released a calming breath and examined the fire and bone.

Somewhere in that phantom movement of flame and air was mystery, pure and awful. Despite Rhabdus's shortsighted insistence on the rules, Kindred felt no urge to challenge the fire's mystery with clumsy attempts at misguided logic – that was for the scholar-stylists on Arcadia and the Mainland, and for those hearthfire keepers like Rhabdus who felt a need for control over everything natural, everything untamed.

Such a need to possess the flames was distasteful to Kindred, and wrong, like a child given a palette of beautiful colors and mixing them all together into a muddy, monolithic brown.

That the fire demanded a captain's bones to burn, Kindred knew.

That it kept a ship afloat, gave it lift and speed on the grasses of the Forever Sea, Kindred knew.

That it spoke a language unwritten and inscrutable, a language like rain, like the changing Sea itself, Kindred knew.

The whys and hows were the flames' mysteries to keep, and it was to them Kindred sang.

As melody slipped from her lips, Kindred reached farther into the flames, lifting the structure where it drooped, sculpting the supple, malleable bones to better articulate Rhabdus's vision of speed, of escape.

She found and eliminated her own improvisations – extra branches plucked from here and twining vines carved there, each meant to offer more speed to the ship, each one *almost* there, if only Kindred could have had more time without Rhabdus leering over her shoulder, following her every movement, criticizing her every decision.

Pirates.

The word echoed again in her mind, threatening to pull her down into the chaos and anxiety of the ship. She fought the urge to stand from where she huddled amidships next to the hearthfire. Perhaps she could leave the hearthfire to Rhabdus and quickly climb to the quarterdeck, get an update from the captain, allow her eyes to follow the disturbed grasses tossed about in their wake, to see the pursuing black sails, the scarred hull, the jeering, leering pirates flinging forth their unnatural magics, their broken grins –

Kindred cursed, breaking her song and pulling her hands back from the hearthfire, which grew hot and nipped at her wrists, punishment for losing her connection to the flames.

She felt the drop in *The Errant*'s speed and saw it in the disarray of the flames.

'Idiot child!' Rhabdus wheezed, pushing in to kneel next to Kindred on the deck, her veined hands mottled with old burn scars and age marks, plunging into the fire as she sang her clipped song. In the swirl of flame, she slapped Kindred's hands away, giving her a hard-eyed look despite the relative softness of her song.

Rhabdus moved quickly, her motions practiced and perfectly efficient, brutal in their precision. Her hands were tools that ordered and owned, demanding where Kindred had appealed; where she molded soft curves, Rhabdus imposed hard lines.

The words of Rhabdus's song were mostly nonsensical. Every

keeper Kindred had ever met – save one – sang to the fire in this way, with some measure of gift for the language of the hearthfire but no real understanding of it. Like a child mimicking her parents.

It was what set Kindred apart, what gave her the edge over every other hearthfire keeper she'd ever met. She not only sang to the flames; she *understood* what she sang, and what's more, she understood what the hearthfire sang in return. When Kindred kept the fire, she was not breaking a wild animal to her will as Rhabdus sought to, singing thick-tongued nonsense; when Kindred worked, she worked *with* the fire.

'Keeper!' Captain Caraway shouted. 'What is going on? We need more speed, not less!'

Kindred turned to see the captain standing fore on the quarterdeck, her wild hair tossed by the wind, her eye ablaze with a gallows light. She wore the black of her station, the only concession to color a dirty white strip of cloth covering one eye. She grinned into the wind.

Gods, she's enjoying this! Kindred thought with a start.

Since Rhabdus was engaged with the fire and couldn't yet break her song, Kindred responded.

'My fault, captain. Apologies. It won't happen again.'

Before joining up with the crew of *The Errant*, Kindred had asked around about the ship and its mysterious captain. Most knew nothing other than the stories: wild, dangerous, insane, and protective of her crew beyond all else. But she had heard other rumors, little bits and fragments of gossip: Captain Caraway sailed too far; Captain Caraway took crew members aboard who had not been sanctioned by the ruling bodies on Arcadia; Captain Caraway liked her crew rough and strange and just as wild as herself.

All of this flashed through Kindred's mind as she shouted at the captain across the madness of the deck – between them, the crew moved in a chaotic dance to adjust and coil and pull and climb and *sail*.

Captain Caraway nodded, her smile predatory and gleeful.

'See that it doesn't,' she shouted, and turned her attention to the frenzied activity of her crew. 'Quartermaster! Aft defenses!'

Kindred saw Little Wing, the quartermaster, tall and powerful, lope across the deck, moving aft to follow the captain's orders.

Each to her place; each to her power, Kindred's grandmother had always said about the hierarchy aboard boats.

A pair of red comets sailed high and wide over *The Errant* before bursting into a shower of sparking magical energy. She tried not to think about how close the pirates had to be to start hurling their magical assaults. Too close.

The fire had returned to a calmer shade of red, and still Rhabdus wrestled with it, her hands moving in ugly straight lines, devastating the imperfections that continued to appear in the bone structure, making out of the bones and the fire a ruled thing. Kindred had let the bone tree in the heart of the fire flourish, pulling bone blossoms into existence and etching creeping vines along the trunk. She had envisioned the build and the hearthfire as a piece of the world, as something blending with wind and sky, the grasses of the Sea and the long-cut line of the horizon. Not solely the pure source of energy Rhabdus saw; not an unruly beast burning in the center of *The Errant*'s deck, brutish in its power and possibility.

Rhabdus let her song wind down, her voice ragged even after so little singing.

Kindred tried not to rub at her wrists where the fire had burned her. Hundreds of tiny, furious bubbles had broken the surface of her skin. She would deal with it later.

'Always these *flourishes* with you, girl,' Rhabdus said, voice raspy. She slapped the deck with one hand. 'Feel how *The Errant* sails steadier now that the build isn't burdened by your *nonsense*.'

'But we were going *faster* with my changes,' Kindred said, raising her voice enough to be heard over the tumult on deck. 'The textbook build has a limit on speed! If only we could try –'

A shout of alarm warned Kindred a moment before *The Errant* was rocked by the impact of a spell slamming into the aft defenses. Kindred was thrown to the deck. Rhabdus spilled onto her side, cursing in hoarse syllables.

Only Captain Caraway, it seemed, held her feet. Kindred looked back and saw the captain holding tight to the great wheel, shouting orders and encouragement to the rear guard who maintained their meager magical defenses.

'Piss and nonsense,' Rhabdus said, righting herself and settling in before the fire. 'The textbook builds are textbook for a reason, girl. They *work*. They're *safe*, which is more than I can say for your nonsense. Now get over here. I need a melody.'

This had been Kindred's primary role since coming aboard *The Errant*. In theory, she was the junior hearthfire keeper, training to keep the fire on her own someday. In practice, she served as a replacement for Rhadbus's tired, dying voice.

'Keepers!' Captain Caraway shouted. 'We need a push!'

'Sing speed,' Rhabdus ordered as she jabbed her hands into the blaze.

Kindred took a breath, stilling her mind, pushing away thoughts of pirates, of bitter senior hearthfire keepers, of wild and mad captains.

Speed, she sang to the flames as Rhabdus broke and reformed the bone structure, making it stronger, funneling the fire and air up and out.

Speed, she sang, as her melody moved and pitched with the fire's delicate dance.

Speed, she sang, listening to the crack of bones releasing their ancient power, a force Kindred felt in the abyss of her stomach, tasted on her tongue, bitter and overwhelming.

'Arcadia, ho! Land and port, ho!' Ragged Sarah called down from the crow's nest.

Kindred spared a glance above, seeing Sarah perched atop the mainmast, surrounded by a corona of winged shapes – birds, come to offer advice to the crow-caller. Sarah's frayed clothing and many-colored hair, so distinct when she walked among the crew, made her resemble one of the birds, each flap of torn cloth or whip of raggedy hair like the flair of a wing on the wind.

The Errant pushed forward, the fire obliging Kindred's request and Rhabdus's enforcement, and Kindred felt hope rise in her chest for the first time since that first cry of 'Pirates!' came from Ragged Sarah. Hard sailing for nearly two full days, coaxing more and more from the fire without breaking it, an exhausting marathon as the pirates neared and neared, first a flutter of black near the horizon, then sails, then hulls, more and more, and Kindred bound to the hearthfire and subjected to Rhabdus's constant insults, insulated from the danger and acutely aware of the way it grew in echoes across the deck.

Unbidden, a fragment of a conversation with the captain from the previous morning came to Kindred's mind, a conversation between Rhabdus and Captain Caraway during which Kindred had stood silently in the corner of the captain's quarters, listening to these two women who had sailed together for nearly forty years.

'We've pushed out too far, captain,' Rhabdus had said. 'Aren't we too near the Roughs, to pirate grasses?'

The captain had smiled up from the maps and diagrams and correspondences littering her table.

'Aye, I would think so, Rhabdus. But those grasses nearer Arcadia are harvested to nothing. And look at the bounty we've already cut.' The captain tapped a ledger on which she'd marked their harvest thus far. 'Ninety bundles of lie-leaf and twenty-two of prairie smoke – both much desired by the medickers for their herbwork and cures. Another seventy-odd bundles each of bluestem, thrice-root, giant stalk, and coneflower – all wanted by the mages for their battle magics, the cooks for their creations, and the schools as they teach the next crop of hopeful sailors how to burn a plant to release its magic. I expect we will sell at our best prices yet.'

'Aye, captain,' Rhabdus replied, snorting, 'it will be a mighty payday.'

'It will,' Captain Caraway said, fierce suddenly, her smile sharp and wide, 'enough to keep us sailing free and out from under the Collective's grip for many years to come.'

Now, sitting before the fire, coaxing as much speed from this particular structure as it would give, Kindred wondered what really drove the captain – money to sail and harvest freely or the ever-increasing need to push at freedom's boundaries, to sail into danger, not for money or independence or fame but to define freedom itself.

A great shock sent tremors through the ship, and Kindred nearly lost her seat again.

'Hit! Hit!' came a cry, and Kindred looked around to see one of *The Errant*'s sails badly damaged, the sheet caught in the spread of a wicked flame that reminded Kindred of paintings she'd seen of the old prairie fires that used to sweep across the Forever Sea. Those fires, she'd been told, burned with abandon, with purifying and rejuvenating vengeance, and she saw some of that now.

'Quixa! Cora! Gwen! Get on that fire!' Captain Caraway shouted, and Kindred saw Long Quixa, Cora the Wraith, and Stone-Gwen leap to take care of the blaze.

'And dammit, Rhabdus, we need more speed!' the captain said before turning back to survey the defenses. Kindred could just hear Little Wing's shouts, low and authoritative, ordering and motivating the defenders.

'Aye,' Rhabdus muttered, turning back to the flames, though how she was going to get more speed from the fire, from this build, especially with *The Errant*'s mainsail no longer aiding them, Kindred had no idea.

Again Rhabdus worked, pruning and perfecting, seeking maximum efficiency, following every rule of keeping the fire taught in the schools.

Again Kindred sang, aiding Rhabdus with her voice.

Kindred inspected the structure as Rhabdus worked, looking for any sign of inefficiency, any break in form or unnecessary extension of bone – searching for any remaining bit of flourish.

It was an old design, a structure of bone named simply *Shal-El-Shep*, an iteration of the Mainland term for a horse, and like a horse, if coaxed and allowed to build in intensity, it could provide great power and speed over a long distance, though not quickly, and not in short bursts.

'More, you fiend,' Rhabdus growled at the fire, at the structure. 'Give me more speed.'

But Kindred saw the plain truth now: *Shal-El-Shep* had no more to give. Its structure was perfectly maintained, the flow and release of air, the sinuous smoothness of heat, all of it balanced, efficient, effective.

Kindred grimaced at the perfection of it. They had traded in the wild wonder of the flames for contrived, purposeful motion.

Mastery over mystery.

'There's nothing more,' Kindred said, whispering to herself. *Shal-El-Shep* provided speed with minimum safety, and Kindred wasn't sure she knew of any other builds that could give more speed, not with so little time and the conditions – winds, temperature, light, Sea character, all of it – as they were. Rhabdus had been forcing her to memorize all of the known structures, and Kindred thought through some of them now, dismissing each more quickly than the last.

Heaven's Knot: No good with a tailwind.

The Red Flash: Too long to build, not nearly enough speed.

Rhizome, Fragmented: Totally unpredictable this long after noon.

Shadow Wright: Hearthfire basin too large, temperatures too high.

On and on she thought, cursing more and more under breath as she dismissed every build she knew, which, given her recent studies, was probably just as many if not more than any other sailor on the Forever Sea, her grandmother not included.

Her grandmother.

A memory caught at Kindred as she glanced up to see Quixa and Cora scaling the mainmast, scurrying up the single powerful length of wood, its runes glowing a hazy blue amid the creeping fire. For a moment, Kindred was a young girl again, ten or eleven years old, sitting on her grandmother's ship, *Revenger*, taking her turn at the hearthfire, still learning the rules, still earning her keep. Young and brash and stupid, she'd ignored all of her grandmother's indirect attempts at teaching Kindred how to keep the fire.

The old woman talked too much about the Sea, Kindred had thought at the time. Always the Sea, how it moved and swayed, how it held secrets ages old. She talked of old myths as if they were true, told children's stories as if they were fact. Kindred had often found her grandmother staring down into the prairie grasses, leaning precariously over the gunwale, murmuring to the waves of green, muttering to them.

Other sailors feared the depths of the Sea. With the magic of a hearthfire burning and a mainmast carved with the correct runes, a ship could sail over the grasses. But a person falling in would be lost forever, falling to the beasts or the Sea floor some impossible distance below. The Forever Sea was a surface to be crossed and a field to be harvested for every one of its sailors.

Except the Marchess.

Kindred had thought her grandmother crazy – still did often enough – and had ignored every shred of lucid advice she'd given.

Instead, that day, Kindred had followed the first rule of keeping the hearthfire – a rule she had found herself, her own guiding star – had whispered it under her breath as she took a single bone, long and straight and painfully bright white, and impaled it into the coal bed at the bottom of the hearthfire.

Kindred had almost destroyed her grandmother's ship and killed everyone aboard that day.

Her grandmother, the Marchess, had been furious and then shocked and then, for the first and last time Kindred could remember, frightened. It was her quick thinking that saved them all from Kindred's stupidity that day so long before. They had shared a silent meal at port that night, her grandmother's burned cloak piled between them on the table as a reminder.

'Speed in tenuous length.' Kindred whispered the rule to herself now as she left Rhabdus at the hearthfire, still trying to coax more speed from a build that had none left to give. Kindred lurched toward the bone closet.

'Speed in tenuous length.'

Long before on the deck of *Revenger*, Kindred had listened as the hearthfire sang in her mind, had watched as it described in its fiery dance a complicated and beautiful world governed by only a few rules – five in all. Four offered freely by the fire, and one given to her by the Marchess. It would be years more before she understood how strange, how unique it was that she could hear the fire so well. So young, and under the tutelage of the Marchess, who also understood the flames, Kindred had just assumed all keepers heard the song of the fire, spoke the language of the flames.

And so she had listened as the fire sang of its rules. They were not the ones, Kindred would later come to learn, that were found in books meant to teach young keepers how to tend the fire. The fire did not sing of efficiency, of builds easy to replicate, of words to break a hearthfire to your will – all things Kindred had learned during her short, unsuccessful time in the schools that were supposed to train hearthfire keepers.

Once, in her first class, Kindred had asked why a particular build was placed facing aft in the hearthfire basin, and the teacher, her expression caught between annoyance and rage, had simply said, 'That is where it is placed because that is where it *must* be placed. This is how it has always been done and how it *will* always be done.'

Kindred had not lasted long in the schools. She had already received her education on the deck of her grandmother's ship *Revenger*, where there were no prescribed builds, no words spoken to the fire without understanding, no rules about bone market value or breaking an unruly fire to your will.

Kindred's rules came from the fire itself, and she had paid particular attention to the first.

Speed in tenuous length.

As more pirate magics arced over or slammed into *The Errant*, Kindred ripped open the trapdoor set seamlessly into the deck to reveal the storage bin containing their wealth of bones, the fuel to keep them afloat and moving across the Sea.

Amid the shouts and flurried movement aboard, the bone closet was a pocket of peace. Bones in rows of white held down with carefully secured straps, still and calm as time itself. The chaos of the deck was muffled in this space, and Kindred took a breath of dry, dusty air, filling her lungs with this silence and reverence, letting it calm the hysterical fear beginning to well up inside her.

'Tenuous length,' she whispered to the bones, letting her hand slide over the rows of white until she found the one – a rib bone, describing a slender arc. Not the longest bone in the body, Kindred knew, but both long and tenuous, just a thin ray of white meant to protect a beating heart, billowing lungs. Like a strand of spiderweb, calcified and fragile.

The swaying cut of *The Errant* through the Forever Sea, the shouts of the crew and even the threat of the pirates – all of it faded in the bone closet. Kindred thought she could hear Rhabdus crowing for her, but even that sound was muted by the peace in the bone closet. The world became dust catching stray rays of sunlight, dust becoming constellations in the late-afternoon light angling in around Kindred, dust from before this day that would last well beyond.

Another explosion slammed into the ship, and even in the relative quiet of the bone closet, Kindred felt it.

She was needed.

Her crazy, insane, nigh-suicidal plan was needed.

She climbed out of the bone closet, letting the trapdoor slam shut.

The captain was shouting for more fires to be put out, and crew members clustered starboard aft, fighting the blaze. Cora the Wraith clung to the mast, cutting away the remnants of the mainsail fluttering from the yard.

Long Quixa, though, lay on the ground, one arm bent at an unnatural angle beneath her, blood trailing from a head wound.

Relieved, Kindred saw Ragged Sarah, the crow-caller who normally spent all of her time in the crow's nest communing with birds, tending to Quixa's injuries. Stone-Gwen knelt beside her, helping as she could, her face a picture of calm despite the madness.

Ragged Sarah looked up as Kindred moved back toward the hearthfire, and even with everything going on – the pirates, the fires, the captain's shouts, the too-slow rise of land on the horizon

– even with all of that, Ragged Sarah looked up at Kindred as she passed, and smiled.

It was a small thing, quick and then gone, but like the bone closet, that moment existed outside of the chaos.

'No time,' she told herself, muttering the words under her breath and forcing her feet to continue moving, forcing her mind away from the way Ragged Sarah angled her head to one side when she smiled, the way her cheeks dimpled just slightly, the way –

'Get over here, girl!' Rhabdus shouted. 'You don't just get up and leave when we're running this hard.'

Rhabdus still had her hands in the fire, though for what reason, Kindred couldn't see. *Shal-El-Shep* was perfect. It looked exactly like the drawings in the manuals. Rhabdus had been forcing her to read them to make up for Kindred's lack of schooling, the pages full of diagrams and arrows, charts and tables, turning the magic of keeping the fire into a fearful science.

'Keepers! Either get us moving or send us to the deeps now and be done with it!' The captain's voice rolled over the deck, eliciting a grunt of anger from Rhabdus. Kindred thought of the length of bone she held hidden behind her back.

Speed in tenuous length.

Rhabdus slapped the deck by the fire.

'*Sit*. And sing speed.'

Kindred sat down and began singing, the bone hidden beneath her thigh, and waited for her chance.

And soon enough, it came.

Kindred sang, asking more from a fire and build that were spent, while Rhabdus's hands were plunged into the fire urging on *Shal-El-Shep*, when a great explosion slammed *The Errant* forward.

Crates and rope and spare tools scattered about the deck and sent any detritus not tied down in a whirligig dance around the ship and, in some cases, overboard.

Rhabdus was flung back, and she cried out in pain and frustration as she careened into the ladders leading aft toward the quarterdeck. Kindred rolled the other way, right into the mainmast, and despite the pain of her collision – a sharp shot through her shoulder – she immediately looked down and breathed a sigh of relief.

The rib bone remained whole and unbroken.

'Speed!' Captain Caraway shouted. 'Speed!'

Kindred launched herself toward the hearthfire, already letting the music tumble from her mouth, letting the blaze know she was coming.

Her song was different this time, more urgent. She chewed out the sounds, letting them fall from her mouth in blocky, low bits. It was a song for breaking, and she did its work with her hands as she sang, reaching into the flames and collapsing *Shal-El-Shep* as quickly and brutally as possible into a thick bed of hot coals. From nearby where she lay, Rhabdus let out a cry of rage and disbelief.

'What are you doing?' Rhabdus shouted.

Every moment the fire burned without a structure, the ship lost speed.

The breaking song done, Kindred looked at the still-smoking mainmast. She thought again of that day so long before on her grandmother's ship, the only other time she had tried this dangerous maneuver.

'Speed in tenuous length,' she whispered.

She sang then, a song without form, a single note really, wavering and high, high enough for her voice to splinter slightly, to fray at its peak. It was a song, Kindred thought, for high hopes, for a structure without a name, so basic and simple and dangerous that no keeper sailing the Forever Sea would consider it.

Kindred brought down the slender length of rib bone through the flames and buried it, planted it in the bed of coals. She let her voice unravel completely into a single, wordless call for the fire to burn, for flame and speed and power.

And the hearthfire answered.

Flames roared up around the bone, reaching into the sky, challenging the majesty of the sun's dying light. The hearthfire became color, shifting sickeningly from wild violet to blinding whites and yellows and back again to violet, flames the color of freshly watered mud growing with the promise of harvest, blues as sacred as a cloudless sky, oranges the color of clouds caught too early in the morning. On and on the fire shifted and roared and grew, and as it did, *The Errant* picked up speed.

'Hold on to something!' Kindred called out, pushing away from the fire, until her spine collided with the mainmast. She heard her call echoed by the captain, who sounded, if anything, joyful, ecstatic with the sudden speed and danger.

Rhabdus hooked an arm around a post and stared at Kindred. Her eyes full of a murderous rage that nearly blanched Kindred's adrenaline, she shouted, 'You've killed us all, girl.'

'Help us with her.' Stone-Gwen called Kindred's attention away. She crawled over to where Sarah and Gwen struggled with Long Quixa's still-unconscious form. Between the three of them, they dragged her to the mainmast and tied her tightly to it.

'I, for one, am glad we're getting back a little sooner,' Ragged Sarah shouted over the roar of wind and fire, grinning again, as she tied herself to the mast next to Quixa. Stone-Gwen offered Kindred a nod before crawling away, staying low to the deck.

The Errant raced over the Sea.

'Oh?' Kindred kept her eyes on the approaching landmass of Arcadia, trying to juggle their speed, their distance, her worry about the pirates potentially still following them, the likelihood of this all ending in disaster.

'Yeah. The sooner we get back,' Ragged Sarah shouted, 'the sooner you can take me out for dinner.'

Kindred turned back, her mind suddenly a smooth wheel spinning in space, catching nothing, touching nothing, simply spinning.

Still smiling, Sarah nudged her with the remains of the rope. 'You'd better tie yourself up.'

Kindred shook her head. 'I can't. Someone has to stop us.'

'Land, keeper!' came Captain Caraway's voice, and Kindred angled around the mast to see the captain still at the wheel, the only one aboard still upright, her hair a tangled trail behind her head, laughter on her lips. 'Land! Slow slow slow, keeper!' The wheel spun in her hands as she curled *The Errant* away from the island, an arc not sharp enough, Kindred saw when she looked up at Arcadia. Not nearly sharp enough.

Arcadia loomed large. Too large. Too quickly.

Kindred pushed away from the mast and lumbered toward the hearthfire, ignoring Rhabdus's shouting over the torrential winds. Her knees felt like blocks of wood, and every step was a mountain.

She fought forward on a collision course with the hearthfire even as *The Errant* raced on its collision course with Arcadia.

The lighthouses on the island were clearly visible now, the guards standing at the top framed by the blaze of their own casting fires. This close to the island, no pirates would dare approach lest they feel the wrath of Arcadia's mage defenders.

Kindred stripped her black cloak from her back, flaring it out in front of her, the velvet night catching in the wind and becoming its own sail, though the fire had grown tall enough to be visible even above the cloak.

Kindred sang into the wind, her voice caught and thrown away immediately, though she knew the fire heard her. It always heard her.

'*Enough, enough, enough*
Rest, perturbed spirit
Rest now, flame
Enough, enough, enough'

Kindred fell forward onto her cloak, shifting her body so she wouldn't impale herself on the single, tenuous bone but rather depress it, push it flat onto the bed of coals. Releasing every strained muscle, every tensed tendon, Kindred became a mass of fluttering cloth and heavy flesh falling.

For a moment, the fire wrapped around her, reaching blue and red arms around the suffocating cloak and embracing Kindred. She felt its warmth, heard the low susurration of its song, and for just that moment, Kindred was weightless, somehow supported by the fire's embrace, as if she didn't fall but flew over the deck, over the hearthfire.

But the moment was gone in an instant, and Kindred crashed down, her cloak covering the blaze. The hearthfire gasped as it reached for air, begged for it in the inky black of her cloak, but Kindred continued her refrain – *enough, enough, enough* – and held fast.

The Errant groaned and pitched, velocity vanishing as the hearthfire choked and suffocated.

And still Arcadia loomed, impossibly large now.

Colossal scrapings rent the air, sounds like the world falling apart.

Yes, Kindred thought, *the cradle*! The scraping noise grew, and Kindred could see in her mind the chains strung along through the Sea, meant to hold up boats docking at Arcadia, meant to protect from the danger of the deeps.

The ship pushed forward, quaking as it caught on the chains of the cradle, its speed dying but not yet dead, accompanied by the great rasping noise. Kindred tried not to think of the damage, the cost as the ship's hull scraped and ground against the huge metal links below. Ahead, Arcadia's buildings, the streets, the smoke from fires were all too close. The chains pulled and slowed, but maybe not enough, maybe too late.

The hearthfire beneath her was now nothing more than a haunting, a ghost of flames and heat pushing the ship forward.

'Come on.' Kindred's whisper was buried in the world-rending noise of the cradle. '*Enough* now.'

The Errant lurched, stuttered to a stop, the chains of the cradle below the ship creaking, straining, pulling.

And holding.

The Errant had stopped, only a few lengths from the shore of Arcadia.

Kindred rolled onto her back, letting the breath rush from her lungs. Her body felt weighty, her mind thick, and it took a few moments for her to register the flares of color racing above her through the quickly darkening sky framed by the damaged sails.

Spells, she realized. The mages atop the lighthouses were raising the defenses, hurling their magics into the grasses behind

The Errant, pushing back the pirates, reclaiming their portion of the Forever Sea.

Kindred could feel the coals of the hearthfire beneath her, keeping their heat like misers, sullen in the darkness.

Ragged Sarah appeared over her, smiling, and then she scaled the nearest mast, moving quickly.

'Pirates away,' Sarah said, her words floating down to the deck like a cool breeze.

Above them, the spells of the defenders continued to light up the sky, flaring riotous.

2

KINDRED'S head still echoed with the grinding of *The Errant*'s hull on the great chains of the cradle, and her body felt weightless with exhaustion, as though she might release her claim on the patch of deck where she sprawled and become air, ephemeral and ethereal.

But a ship's deck was meant for activity, for bustle, for getting ahead or clawing back to equilibrium. The captain's voice spiked into Kindred's dullness.

'Quartermaster! Damage report!'

'Aye.' Little Wing's response sounded as though it came from the other side of the Sea, but Kindred angled her head back and caught sight of Little Wing already moving over the deck, pulling a few crew to help her assess the damage from the pirates.

And from their arrival.

As the captain continued to order crew members here and there – 'Begin stacking the harvest and make ready to move,' 'Check water stores and give me an exact measurement,' and so on – Kindred rolled back over to the hearthfire, peeling her smoking cloak away.

The rib bone had snapped under Kindred's weight and lay in three pieces over the turf of black coals.

'I'm sorry,' Kindred whispered, gathering up the fragments of bone. 'It was the only way.'

The hearthfire's pull, normally a constant in her mind, was gone. Or nearly.

Kindred reached a shaking hand toward and into the coals, letting her fingers slip deep into the furrowed darkness until she found, just at the bottom, a last lingering of warmth, like that on a pillow abandoned for a day's work. Kindred released a short sigh.

'Idiot child,' came a husked voice just a moment before Kindred was wrenched up, a hand closing around the back of her neck. She turned, hissing in pain, to find Rhabdus, angrier than Kindred had ever seen her, teeth bared, jaw clenched. She spoke quietly, murderously, eyes wide and mad.

'Do you have any idea how dangerous that was? How close we were to wrecking? You nearly ruined the ship, nearly killed me, killed us all.'

'I'm sorry,' Kindred gasped, angling her body around, anything to lessen the pain as Rhabdus maintained her hold, digging her fingers deep into the skin of Kindred's neck. 'It was the only way. We needed more speed. I thought – '

Rhabdus cut her off with a slap that sounded like a tree branch cracking drily in the air. Rhabdus yanked her so close that Kindred could smell the older keeper's hot breath, could feel the waves of heat and anger radiating from her. Her face burned from the slap.

'The builds are there for a reason, girl. That uniformity you're always bemoaning? It means results you can count on. It means knowing how fast a boat will go, how to slow it down, how to keep it in one fucking piece. The builds keep the sailors on board the ship alive and keep the ship whole, which is more than I can say for whatever piece of *creativity* that nearly killed us all. What kind of damage do you think those chains holding us up right now did to the hull? Are you going to pay for the repairs? Are you going to tell the captain why the underside of her boat is beaten up? Are you?'

Rhabdus's questions cut into the bit of glory Kindred had been holding close. She had brought them in safely – *she* had done that. Not Rhabdus. Not anyone else on board.

But she couldn't forget the sound of *The Errant*'s hull scraping over the chains of the cradle, which were meant to support boats after they'd been brought into port, but only after a slow, careful docking, after a measured extinguishing of the hearthfire, an easing of a ship into the support of the great, looping chains cutting through the grass below them.

They weren't meant to slow a ship. They weren't meant to check a reckless, out-of-control vessel pushed to breaking by a keeper working outside the known and expected rules.

Kindred's victory turned to bitter dregs in her mouth, and she felt suddenly like she might throw up.

'Not our most graceful arrival to port.'

Rhabdus dropped Kindred to the deck, and both turned to find Captain Caraway standing there, a single eyebrow raised. The captain offered Kindred a hand up.

'Apologies, captain,' Rhabdus said, before casting a disgusted look at Kindred. 'Had I been in control of the fire, things would have been different.'

Kindred listened, her stomach churning with unease. She

had hijacked the hearthfire, damaged the ship's hull, and nearly killed everyone; she would be lucky if the captain only kicked her off the ship.

Kindred felt waves of nausea as she stared down at the deck, trying and failing to blink away the onset of tears. All of her actions suddenly felt foolish – her fight with the Marchess, her storming off the deck of *Revenger*, shouting back that she'd find a new boat, something of her own. Kindred's certainty that she would make her mark, that she would find her place, that she would be loved and lauded, all of it felt like a fantasy now.

'I couldn't see what was happening with the hearthfire there at the end. You're telling me Kindred was in charge of it?' Captain Caraway asked, looking between them.

'Aye, captain,' Rhabdus said, stepping between Kindred and the captain, cutting her out. 'She stole control from me after one of the pirate volleys. She can't be trusted.'

Rhabdus paused a moment – a single intake of breath that set Kindred on edge.

'She can't be trusted, captain, if you're asking my opinion. She's no good for the ship and no good for the crew. I don't care who her grandmother is; she's a reckless child.'

Every muscle in her body hurt from putting out the fire. She had saved them, this crew she was only truly beginning to know. She had saved them *and* the ship.

But had she saved them from a mess of her own making?

'Captain, if I – ' Kindred began, but Rhabdus turned and kicked her, viciously silencing Kindred.

'You've done enough, girl,' Rhabdus said.

The crew continued to move about the deck, each one pushed

by a singular purpose and a singular task, too busy and focused to pay attention to Kindred's world falling apart.

'She's been trouble since we took her on, captain,' Rhabdus said. 'Too young, too little experience. Yes, she's the Marchess's granddaughter, and I grant that she has some natural skill with the fire. But this is what happens when we take on a keeper who failed out of school, who couldn't follow any of the damned rules, who couldn't be bothered to learn like the rest of us.'

Rhabdus looked back at Kindred, disgusted, before continuing. Memories of her time in the Arcadian school flashed through Kindred's mind – teachers talking about the fire as if it were an unruly animal needing to be broken, a puzzle to be brutally solved. Kindred hadn't known then how to square their ideas about keeping the fire with what she'd learned from her grandmother: a bloodless, heavy-handed method from the bookmavens and an imprecise, instinctual approach from the Marchess. She wasn't sure she had the answer now, but Kindred was clear that it wasn't Rhabdus's style.

'Her *recklessness*,' Rhabdus sneered, 'with the fire might have been cute once, but look where it's gotten us. The girl is a menace, captain, and she doesn't belong in this crew.'

The captain grunted and looked around Rhabdus at Kindred, her expression unreadable, her eye holding Kindred, intense and searching.

'If I could, captain,' came a voice, and Captain Caraway and Rhabdus turned, revealing Ragged Sarah, who still knelt beside Quixa, wrapping her arm in a thick, black gauze. 'Without Kindred's work there at the end, we would have been caught up by the pirates, that's for sure. They were gaining until Kindred took over.'

Silence took hold for just a moment, and Kindred thought she might kiss Ragged Sarah then and there. Sarah smiled over at her before returning to her work.

Captain Caraway turned back to Rhabdus, her eyebrow arced into a question.

'At what cost?' Rhabdus wheezed, her hands clutched into fists at her side. 'A damaged hull this time, captain, but what happens when she docs it again? Do we have deaths? A full wreck?'

'Whose cloak is that on the fire?' Captain Caraway asked suddenly, pointing a finger down at the splay of black still obscuring the hearthfire basin and the still-warm coals nestled in it.

Rhabdus licked her lips, flashing her yellowed teeth in a grimace.

'This girl is trouble, Jane,' Rhabdus said, leaning in close to the captain. 'We've sailed together, you and I, for more voyages than I can count. This girl is trouble for the ship, I know it.'

Captain Caraway turned her enigmatic stare to Rhabdus.

'She's unpredictable,' Rhabdus hissed. 'She doesn't follow any of the rules. No seal of accomplishment from the schools. She's too wild to sail.'

Captain Caraway's eye – a brown so dark, it was almost black – held Kindred in a gaze more intense than any she'd ever experienced, including that day not so far back when Kindred had approached her, fresh from the last argument Kindred would have with the Marchess, desperate for a place on some vessel, any vessel that wasn't *Revenger*.

Kindred took in the smooth slope of Captain Caraway's nose, the crooked slant of her mouth, the unkempt mane of hair that looked unnatural not caught in a prairie wind.

'Wild,' Captain Caraway said, nodding. 'I like wild.'

Rhabdus sucked in a breath and looked around, taking in the eyes of those few who had stopped to watch, taking in the captain.

Kindred stood.

'You gave us that speed? You stopped us up at the end?' Captain Caraway asked.

Ignoring Rhabdus, who had finally turned to glare at her, Kindred nodded.

'Aye, captain.'

'You can't be serious, Jane,' Rhabdus said, her voice like steel now, all anger and rage. 'This fucking *girl* almost destroyed your ship, almost killed every single sailor aboard. She's not fit to be on this deck. You have to –'

'Don't,' Captain Caraway said, stopping Rhabdus's fury with a single word. She shook her head once. 'You don't give orders, not on my boat.'

Rhabdus inhaled through her nose, nostrils flaring, lips pressed into thin parallel lines.

'*Fine*,' she said after a moment of grinding silence. 'But that girl will be nothing but ill luck for this ship. She'll bring us all down, and that's true as the green.'

Rhabdus stomped off, every movement singing with her rage. Kindred heard her cursing all the way down the dock. If her last few stays at port were any indication, she would spend the next few days in a lie-leaf house, chewing the dream-inducing plant and blissing out on whatever joyful madness it called forth.

'Thank you, captain,' Kindred said, pulse jumping like lightning in her veins.

'Don't thank me; thank Sarah,' Captain Caraway said, watching Rhabdus go before turning to regard Kindred. 'And don't ever pull something like that on my boat again without consulting me first.'

Kindred thought her spine might bend and tear through

the skin of her back as she shrank from the sudden chill in the captain's voice.

'Have you ever seen a boat boarded by pirates, Kindred?' Captain Caraway stepped closer and regarded Kindred with one wide eye. 'Ever seen the damage, the killing? Don't misunderstand me, Kindred: I like that you take risks, and that you don't follow the rules that have grown old and stale. But this remains *my* ship, *my* crew, and if anyone is going to make the decision to risk lives or livelihoods, it isn't going to be my junior keeper. Do you understand me?'

Kindred felt sick, and the feeling only deepened as she realized Ragged Sarah still hung close enough to overhear what the captain had said.

Revenger had never been boarded while she'd been on it, but she had experienced a few terrifying flights from pursuing pirate vessels. And she had seen ships make it out of a fight with pirates, either after being boarded or in an open-Sea skirmish. Dead and dying sailors, wounds cut jagged into flesh, masts battered and scarred and broken, hulls the same. Her second year sailing with *Revenger*, she had watched a ship, *The Cracked Crown*, sail into port with a bare crew, the rest dead in the skirmish, the decks still painted red and telling a grisly story.

The hearthfire keeper had survived the attack, but the pirates had taken the captain, one of the Marchess's friends, for her bones.

The funerals for those lost had been simple, plain things.

'Understood, captain.'

After a moment, Captain Caraway spoke again, her voice softer now, a lift after the weight of her anger.

'Rhabdus is a good keeper, Kindred. And once not *so* long ago, she was the best on any boat sailing out of Arcadia, maybe any boat at all. You can learn something from her.'

'Aye, captain,' Kindred said, dipping her head.

'Now get this mess cleaned up and the hearthfire squared away.'

'Of course, Captain. And about the damage to the hull. . . I'm sorry. I . . .' Kindred trailed off, unsure what she would or could do. She could guess at the damage to the hull, and a shiver tripped down her spine as she imagined climbing down the side of *The Errant* to repair the rents in the wood, climbing until she was below the surface of the Sea. It had been several years since she had felt the grasses of the Forever Sea cover her, since the Marchess had taken her below.

'I don't want your apologies, keeper,' the captain said. 'The material for repairs will come out of your cut. Despite Rhabdus's suggestion, I'm not kicking you off my boat.'

'Thank you, captain.'

'But you will be sitting out our next harvesting voyage.'

Air drained from Kindred's lungs.

'You can work on your land legs and think about your role on my ship, and when we come into port next, I expect you to be there, helping unload cargo and occupying your spot on the ship. You're still part of this crew, Kindred. You just need time to cool off.'

'Aye, captain,' Kindred said. 'Of course.'

'Grab anything you need from the ship before we sail again. I expect we won't be docked more than a span.'

A span. Ten days. And then Kindred would be sitting on the shore, watching the ship – and her role on it – sail off, the fire kept by Rhabdus again.

Kindred couldn't help but think of the last time she had stayed behind at port as her ship sailed off. Had it been two years already since her fight with the Marchess? Since her last day aboard *Revenger*? Since the hard words she had traded with the Marchess?

That had been a different time, and this was not the same situation. Kindred *would* be back aboard *The Errant*. She had worked too hard for that spot, for the belonging that she had only begun to find among the crew. Two years of pushing to find a place among this crew, listening and watching, searching for how and where she might fit in.

'Cantrev,' the captain said, pulling Kindred back from her memories.

'Come to complain about the pirates or our entry?' Kindred asked, looking up to where a pack of people were walking down the dock toward *The Errant*.

'I imagine we'll soon find out,' Captain Caraway said, turning back to her. 'Though between the two of us, I'd take the pirates over that sack of shit.' She nudged her chin toward Cantrev's approach.

He stumped in the middle of his retinue, a weak man emboldened by the weaker men around him. Sweat glistened on his face, illuminated by a flickering torch carried by one of his servitors. Night fell quickly upon Arcadia's streets.

'Looks like he's gained even more power since we last saw him,' Kindred said, noting the blue paint on Cantrev's face.

Captain Caraway spit and walked over to meet the new senator of Arcadia.

'Jane! What an entrance! My gods, we all thought you were finished. I've been saying it about these pirates for years and years. Menaces and monsters. I've been saying it, haven't I?'

Kindred bit down hard to keep from correcting Cantrev. The

captain was too well respected and too senior for anyone – including a senator – to use her first name so casually without permission.

Cantrev turned to his retinue, who nodded like a pack of obsequious dogs. He snatched a waterskin encrusted with gems in swirling patterns from one man and drank noisily.

'Aye, I suppose,' Captain Caraway said, her humor and wildness gone.

'Jane, listen, we need to get you under the Collective's protection.' Cantrev neared *The Errant*'s gangplank and looked as if he would step on it, and then thought better of it. 'The dew boats and half – more than half by now, I think – of the harvesters sail under my flag. Think of it: cheaper water *guaranteed* for Collective members, and that's not even to mention the protection! Everyone, *everyone*, gets outfitted with two of my mages. And a Collective mage is worth at least ten pirates.'

He turned again for agreement, his sagging, doughy cheeks following the movement of his head with some delay. The blue senator's paint shone on his face, pebbled with sweat.

'Maybe even twenty of them, eh?' he said, eyebrows jiggling up and down in excitement. He tapped his chest, which bore the symbol of his Collective – a clenched fist, white on a black background.

Cantrev's gaggle laughed and sneered in response, and he turned back to Captain Caraway.

'Eva Golden and her ship, *The Nettle*, said no to my offer of protection, and you don't see *The Nettle* anymore, do you?' Cantrev gestured around, as if everyone on Arcadia hadn't heard about *The Nettle* getting taken by pirates. Captain Golden had made it close enough for those on shore with longsights to see *The Nettle*'s harried flight, but not close enough for Cantrev's mages in the towers to help once the pirates caught up. The whole thing had been over by the time any of the ships at port had pushed off and sailed out.

'What do you say, Jane? My boys have already saved your ship once tonight.' He gestured up to the lighthouses towering above and the men – his men – standing next to the roaring casting fires, serving as both waypoint for sailors in the night and an iron fist for pirates venturing too close. 'You don't want to go the same way as *The Nettle*, do you?'

'My answer hasn't changed,' Captain Caraway said. 'My crew and I sail under our own flag; we harvest where and when we want.'

Kindred watched Cantrev's smile twist slightly so that his teeth were no longer perfectly aligned, a grind instead of a grin.

'Soon you'll be the only one, *Jane*,' he said, biting down on the captain's name. 'Those damned, filthy pirates are sailing closer and closer and *you don't get it*.' He hissed the words and flapped a hand of stubby fingers at the crew, catching Kindred's eye as he did. 'We need to be unified. *One* Arcadia. *One* complete defense against the pirates. The old ways are going, Jane, and you'll be going with them if you don't shape up.'

'The old ways are best,' Kindred said, speaking without thinking but glad she did. It was something her grandmother had always said, something Kindred believed in.

She shivered when Cantrev looked at her again, the darkness of his eyes puckered in by the pouty flesh of his face, hiding something, some secret or knowledge that turned her insides.

'The old ways are *done*,' Cantrev said, smiling, before taking a single proprietary step onto the plank, leaning on his knee. 'Kindred? Captain Jane's new junior keeper?'

About to respond, Kindred realized suddenly that she wasn't sure. Was she still the new junior keeper? Could she be if she were about to sit out a whole voyage?

'She is,' Captain Caraway said, fiercely. Whether from protectiveness or hatred of Cantrev, Kindred didn't know, but either way she was glad of it.

Cantrev chuckled and held up his hands in mock apology.

'Of course. My congratulations. And condolences.' Cantrev leaned in and nodded at Kindred. 'So sorry to hear about the Marchess. Speaking of the old ways.'

Kindred blinked, unsure of what that might mean. Sorry about the Marchess? Sorry for what?

'I'm not interested in your Collective,' the captain said, cutting into the man's laughter. 'And we have work to do.'

Dismissively, the captain turned back to her ship and clapped her hands, setting the crew to work.

Heartbeat loud and with a dry mouth, Kindred, though, stood like a statue watching Cantrev, who stared furiously at Captain Caraway's back before storming off, speaking quickly, venomously, to those keeping pace beside him.

'That man is truly a shit,' a voice said from beside her, and Kindred turned to find Ragged Sarah watching Cantrev storm away. 'I don't understand why he has to be such an enormous *shit* so much of the time.'

Kindred nodded, though she wasn't so sure. The greatest problem with a man like Cantrev, she thought, was that there was nothing mysterious about him at all. He was rotten in the most obvious, boring way. A man after power, a child after praise. Kindred could see ten lengths into him and he was only three lengths deep.

But what had he meant about her grandmother?

'Ragged Sarah,' Captain Caraway said, interrupting Kindred's thoughts, 'you're on mail duty. The letter-pass should be open still if you hurry.'

'Aye, captain,' Ragged Sarah said, nudging Kindred and tipping her a wink before hopping from the boat and moving off down the dock, in toward the rancid thrive of the city. Kindred watched her go, feeling again the strange swirl of something inside her chest.

'Before your *break*, Kindred,' the captain said, emphasizing the word, as if calling it a break instead of a punishment made it go down easier, 'I want you to get us fixed for water.' She passed over the paper detailing their stores and showing their need.

'Aye, captain,' Kindred said, taking the paper, glad to have something clear to focus on. 'I went with Rhabdus the last several times she was on water duty. I can get it done.'

She scanned the numbers, trying to get her mind back under control. Sailors took time away all the time, some to see family, some to get some rest, some to spend their coin. It meant nothing. Even the captain didn't seem to think it was a big deal. She would be back. It was her spot. She was part of the crew. This meant nothing.

What had Cantrev meant?

'Try Low first before the Zero twins or – '

'Mick, right,' Kindred said, nodding, her mind everywhere else. *So sorry to hear about the Marchess*, he'd said. *So sorry.*

The captain's silence brought Kindred's attention back to the present, and she realized with some horror that she'd interrupted the captain.

'Sorry, captain,' she said, shaking her head. 'I'll get it done.'

Captain Caraway put a hand on her shoulder.

'Don't let him into your head, Kindred,' she said. 'Cantrev thrives on trouble.'

'There's *Revenger* right there.' Captain Caraway squinted down the harbor and pointed. 'You can go ask the Marchess for yourself what that blowhard is talking about. In fact, why don't you stop over there before you see about the water. There's plenty of time to get it done before we leave port.'

Kindred could just barely make out her grandmother's ship, the smaller, older craft tied off. Two years since she'd shared a word with the Marchess. Two years of nothing more than glimpses in the few instances where both boats were docked at the same time.

Kindred felt the beginnings of tears sting at her eyes.

'Aye, captain. Thank you,' she said, turning back, but the captain was already off, shouting orders, moving her crew toward their tasks and moving among them with ease, once again the calm, confident woman in charge.

Kindred leapt up onto the plank bridge and walked down to the dock, the grasses of the Sea reaching up to the wooden walkway as she set off, whispering around her, giving voice to her fear.

Revenger lay still as Kindred approached. The wind, chill in the sun's absence, cut across the clean and carefully stowed deck. A single ghost light hung, somehow articulating the darkness aboard her grandmother's vessel instead of dispelling it.

So sorry to hear about the Marchess.

Standing on the dock, darkness and silence cultivating her fear, Kindred saw the scars.

Runnels like rivers cut through the old, old wood of the ship. Splaying this way and that, running parallel and perpendicular and crosshatch and every which way, the slashes ravaged *Revenger*'s hull, marking it in a language of violence and destruction.

Kindred stepped close and ran a hand over one of the cuts, tracing it all the way up the hull. She thought of the beasts and plants moving below the waves of the Forever Sea that could do this, the great roaches and wyrms and scathe barbs. Shadows collected in the cuts, a thousand still, dark streams giving weight to Kindred's unease.

So sorry.

She climbed aboard, leaping over the gunwale, the old wood solid beneath her hand. Familiar. As if it had been only a few days since she'd left *Revenger*.

'Grandmother?'

On the morning of her last day aboard *Revenger*, Kindred found her grandmother walking the deck, muttering to herself. The rest of the crew remained in Arcadia, getting their last thrills in before *Revenger* set sail later that day. For some reason, the Marchess had always preferred setting out for journeys in the evening.

'Kindred, good. Pace with me,' the Marchess had said, as if she'd been expecting her granddaughter's early rising. The sun had just begun to stain the sky an aching, foggy cobalt.

'Have you decided on our course?' Kindred fell in step beside her grandmother. 'North for the veins of bluestem or east to see if any of the thrice-root has survived the other harvesters?'

With so many boats harvesting Arcadian grasses in recent

years, it had become more and more difficult to find untouched patches of matured, harvestable plants. But somehow, the Marchess always managed.

'No and no.' The Marchess shook her head curtly.

'Where, then?'

The Marchess leaned over the gunwale, her greying hair dangling as if it might mix and dance with the grasses below.

'What moves beneath us?'

Kindred closed her eyes and focused on holding back the frustrated sigh screaming for release in her chest. More and more, this had been the way of things. *Revenger* charting stranger and stranger courses, no longer to harvest plants or rework old maps for use again but simply to satisfy some brooding curiosity inside the Marchess.

And always it began with these nonsense questions.

Kindred, the only crew member without grey in her hair, felt more and more caged by this vessel and their meandering voyages, more and more like she was idling her time away, chasing nothing, accomplishing nothing.

'It's just the Sea, Grandmother.'

The Marchess squeezed Kindred's arm, her grip like iron.

'There's no *just* about it, child. You understood that once.'

Kindred eased the Marchess's hand from her arm but did not let go of it. She took a deep, steadying breath.

'Grandmother, please, can we stop this? There's nothing below but plants, the beasts that live in them, and everything else is just children's tales. The Sea is simply the Sea. And we are harvesters, so can we please set sail for a patch of something to harvest?'

The Marchess, her brown eyes wide in concern and curiosity, peered into Kindred's face.

'Is it money you long after, Kindred? You can have mine if it is. I care nothing for coin; you know that.'

'It's not money,' Kindred said, frustration snapping her syllables. 'It's respect! The other ships are laughing at us. They watch us sail in and out with the same empty hold, the same empty list of accomplishments. We're a mockery, Grandmother!'

'Those other crews,' the Marchess said, rolling her eyes and shaking her head. 'They wouldn't recognize respect if it slapped them in the face.'

'It's fine for you and the rest of the crew,' Kindred snapped, aware that her voice was climbing. It felt good to finally release the frustrations and anger she had been growing so long. 'But I have a career to make still, Grandmother! I'm at the beginning of my life, not the end. I'll have to get my own boat at some point, or find a place on another one. All of this might be enough for you, but I have to find something more, and I can't do that if the only experience I have is wandering around Arcadian grasses!'

'When did enough stop being enough?' the Marchess asked, her face close enough to Kindred's to share the same breath.

'Grandmother,' Kindred said, steadying her voice and speaking slowly. '*Please*. Can we do what we're meant to and harvest some plants? I could try my hand at plotting our course for once? You once promised to show me your secret of mapmaking; why not this voyage?'

But the Marchess was staring out at the Sea again, lost in her thoughts, and when she spoke, it was as if Kindred had said nothing at all.

'More and more, the Sea is threaded by dying patches of grasses, Kindred. Boats cannot sail through them. Plants cannot grow through them. Something is killing our Sea, and the answer must be below. It must be.'

'Dammit!' Kindred shouted, slapping the smooth wood of the gunwale with her open palm, the sound and the immediate pain both gratifying in the moment. 'Can't we just do our jobs? Can't we follow the rules and do what we're supposed to for once?'

A few of the other crew had begun to arrive back on *Revenger*, and they stood nearby, looking uncomfortable.

'There's a child in there somewhere,' the Marchess said, speaking quietly. 'You've locked her away deep down, tied up with her curiosity, but I know underneath this nonsense about bringing in coin and having a respectable career, you want to know what's happening to the Sea just as much as I do, my girl. And *that's* why you're in such a foul mood.'

Kindred stormed off the boat, vowing that she would find something better, that it was time to grow up. She found *The Errant* two span later.

That had been almost two years before, and it had taken the better part of that time to come to bitter terms with the fact that the Marchess had been right.

Kindred moved through the near-darkness of *Revenger* by memory, calling out a soft hello as she went. Her grandmother's words on that fateful morning two years before lingered in the soft pull of rigging flexing in the wind, in the endless shush of the Sea, the grasses whispering and colluding.

You've locked her away deep down, tied up with her curiosity.

Revenger was a small ship and old, built in the days when a single mast and sail were enough. Boards ten times as old as Kindred's twenty-two years creaked below her feet as she moved toward the center of the deck and put a hand on the mast, thinking of how much this little ship had done, how many memories she had burrowed deep inside her from days sitting on the deck, long afternoons experimenting with the hearthfire, trying to steal her grandmother's techniques, to learn what the older woman would only ever demonstrate with few words and fewer explanations.

Like Kindred's grandmother, *Revenger* was part of an earlier age of harvesters, smaller than the more modern ships, crudely built, angles over curves. It was a ship from a different time, small enough for a crew of five, maybe four instead of the twenty-plus aboard *The Errant*. Kindred sometimes marveled at how many crew members it took for a single operation aboard *The Errant*. Six deckhands to lift that sail, nine or ten to extend those harvesting planks, three or four to coil the piles of mast ropes. Kindred's role in keeping the hearthfire, Sarah's work in the crow's nest, and the captain's role in commanding the ship were the only tasks better completed by a single person.

So sorry to hear about the Marchess.

Kindred pushed back against the memories rising to the surface and focused on her task, walking toward the steps leading belowdecks. She felt strange walking this deck, coming aboard as she had so often but now without permission. The wood of the deck, the gunwale, the mast was at once familiar and foreign, warm and alive in her memory even as it all looked cold and distant in the darkness.

More than anything, she felt her grandmother there, could practically hear her commands ringing around the small deck, shouts to tie that line off; to hold, dammit; to steady the ship, Kindred; to pull your eyes skyward, Kindred; to *feel* the Sea, Kindred.

For a moment, Kindred felt herself surrounded by ghosts, her grandmother's and her own from so long before.

So sorry.

So sorry to hear.

"S a right shame, what's happened to the Marchess,' came a voice from the darkness, and Kindred stumbled, nearly toppling over. She twisted to see a man standing on the dock next to the ship, a light held above him in one hand, a cudgel in the other. One of the dock guards.

'What have you heard?' she asked, stepping forward enough that the man might see her fully, take in her garb and know her for a harvester instead of some petty thief.

'Terrible, jus' terrible. Awful indeed,' he muttered, his eyes roaming through the darkness, never lingering on anything. 'Jus' jumped right in, they say. Jumped.'

'Jumped in where?' Kindred asked, knowing already somehow. She heard her grandmother's voice in her mind, could almost see her leaning over the edge again there in the darkness, her deep-lined face describing in relief the Sea she so loved. So often she had stared down into the endless stalks of grass, searching for a deeper, truer dark than anything the sky might offer.

'Well, she leapt inta the Sea, a'course,' the guard said, shaking his head slowly. 'Went an' killed herself, she did. Jus' terrible.'

What moves beneath us?

'Killed herself?' Kindred said, in a voice quiet enough to be swallowed up by the low evening wind.

'A great cap'n gone.' Still more head shakes, slow and somber and like he was enjoying it somehow. 'And takin' her bones with. Terrible. Selfish, might be. Her whole crew, I seen, headed for the rocky shore, they were. A funeral, I suppose.'

The man stood in that darkness for a time, and so, too, did Kindred, seeing in her memory's eye her grandmother leaning toward the Forever Sea, always speaking of the Sea, demanding Kindred feel it, really feel it, sense it, understand it, be it. She asked what moved beneath, and finally she went to find out.

'Well, on with it,' the guard said and continued walking out toward where some of the other ships were docked, his light held above him.

So sorry to hear.

Arcadia stank.

The island city proliferated before Kindred, streets stretching and winding through darkness, covered in the refuse of its people and its refused people. Prairie dwellings bulged from the ground like pockets of inflamed, infected flesh. Lights flickered in windows and on streets, suggesting what lay in darkness even while bringing homes and shops into existence in the night.

Odors bright and sharp attacked Kindred. Boiled-fat stew and the acrid tang of unwashed bodies, smoke from plants burned too soon and the distinct, gorge-tickling smell of piss. All of this and a thousand other wretched stenches clogged Kindred's nose and throat, pummeling at the strange cocoon she found herself in, at once aware of and distanced from the world.

'The putrefying bouquet of us,' her grandmother used to say as

Revenger sailed into port, and something deep twisted in her gut as Kindred heard those words in the Marchess's voice, a voice silenced now, lost in the forever of grass and wind and the darkness below.

The steady, slow drumbeat resonating from the city center was the only sound, the pace always seeming to slow down slightly, always hanging back slightly. No nighttime revelry cracked the air, no drunken shouts cawed into the star-strewn sky. Workers toiled with an almost lazy pace: a builder stepped with deliberate sluggishness up the rungs of a ladder laid against the side of a house; a pair of scholars from the school walked lackadaisically ahead of Kindred, their voices low and soft, like lovers sliding without hurry from word to word, caught in the slow rhythm of exhaustion.

All set their feet and their words and their work to the sluggish beat of the drum sounding through all. It took Kindred a moment to realize she had done the same.

Her first day in Arcadia, Kindred had listened to the Marchess describe how a city gripped by perennial water shortages functioned. Work at night. Sleep during the day. Keep any sort of physical activity to a minimum whenever possible. Waste as little water as possible on bathing. Eat the most liquid-heavy bugs and plants you can find or buy; don't overcook anything. Why buy wine when you could buy a cup of water and a finger of lie-leaf, which would numb the world without dehydrating you? Listen to the drum and let it slow you down. No need for speed.

The city shuffled; it did not run. It longed to slink through the night and skirt the edges of the day.

Energy was a luxury. There were no fights, no drunken brawls in poorly lit alleys. Such anger required blood singing with water. Rage was for the rich and not to be wasted.

Only sailors paid reduced prices for water; only sailors could buy water outside of the rationing requirements. Without harvesting ships bringing back plants, Arcadia would be left defenseless and hungry, stripped of the plants that filled the medickers' bags and lie-leaf lodges.

Kindred stepped into the low flow of people milling about the outskirts of the city and became just another drip of its sluggish lifeblood, trickling toward the center, always toward the center. The pain in her gut continued to twist as she passed storefronts and streets wrapped in memories of the Marchess.

A fight with a man in that store that had resulted in Kindred and her grandmother racing back to *Revenger*, the Marchess cackling with laughter, Kindred screeching in fear.

A foodcart that haunted that street, Kindred's favorite as a younger girl, a treat from the Marchess whenever they arrived back at port.

That bench where she and the Marchess sat one evening, talking about nothing, watching the world move around them and feeling contended to simply sit, simply be.

That store. This alleyway. That church and those statues and this street and these windows and . . .

Arcadia was a house haunted by a woman who had left it behind, and Kindred saw her shade everywhere.

She put her head down and walked, focusing on being nothing more than a pair of feet stepping one at a time.

The streets evolved from shadow-soaked corridors to lantern-lit thoroughfares filled with the slumping, mostly silent mass of Arcadians walking to or from their jobs, the pulling rhythm of the drum like a heartbeat behind it all.

Kindred walked and walked, letting the distraction of the city do its work on her. She passed through a bazaar. At each stall, sellers sat comfortable, sometimes calling out softly to attract the passersby, sometimes silent. Riddles and songs, terrible tales whispered over shared drinks, mysteries and fantasies given, spells sold, maps drawn and redrawn: all of it for sale in the uncanny quiet of the bazaar.

She paid a few coins for a riddle from a man who spoke in soft four-word sentences. He pulled her close and whispered the riddle in his halting idiolect, breath hot and hoarse against her ear. Into her hand he slipped the answer – a tiny scroll of paper, no bigger than her little finger.

'Little-light, fallen from above. Sun sight without eye. Young, I follow dawn. Old, I drop young.'

Kindred turned over the riddle in her mind as she walked, prodding and pulling at it, working it around like a piece of desert toffee in her mouth, wanting at once to devour it and prolong it.

The answer sheet she crumpled into a fist and let fall, leaving it behind as she turned a corner and continued on into the heart of Arcadia.

She saw more silent bazaars as she walked and purchased a few more oddities: herbs, a new map of the Forever Sea – surely as imperfect as the rest – a small set of crescent-shaped throwing knives. She should have been saving her coin, she knew. *The Errant's* next journey was likely to last a few span, and the reduced cost for water only extended to active sailors. Otherwise, every waif and thief would go to one of the water authorities, singing about their voyages.

A sudden memory of the Marchess paying out their journey's wages: bags of heavy coin passed from hand to hand. Low, excited talk of what new delights Arcadia might offer. A beggar boy came forward, shaking hand outstretched.

'Please, captain,' the young boy had whispered, voice paper-thin and dry as dust.

Pain coiled Kindred's heart as she remembered the kindness in the Marchess's eyes, the way she parted with her heavy coin, the smooth movement as she pulled out her own waterskin and held it for the boy, dribbling the water past the desert of his lips.

'Go easy, sailor,' came a nearby voice, shocking Kindred out of her remembering. It had become both greeting and cautionary note in Arcadia: Go easy. No need for speed. Or heart-racing fear. Both cost water.

She was walking too fast, her steps pulling her through the flow of people, kicking up dust. The steady beat of the drum lagged behind her heartbeat, and it took more than a few steadying breaths to bring herself in line with the funereal rhythm of the city.

'Go easy. Thanks,' Kindred said, raising her hand to the bookseller who had called out.

Split-Seams Way wound through the city, splintering smaller roads off occasionally and absorbing smaller roads just as often. It was onto this thoroughfare that Kindred eventually stepped, skirting the city center, where great crowds moved back and forth like Sea grass in a slow, rolling wind.

The farther she got from the city center, the quieter the road became, with only the occasional person passing along. She saw one of her crew members, a young girl named Scindapse, still in her first year aboard *The Errant*. She stood outside the aviary, her face pressed against the bars, her words quiet and not meant for human ears. Kindred pushed on.

She found Low outside the Temple of the Water Wight, sweeping the steps. Even as Kindred approached, the old woman continued her work, head down, muttering to herself.

On the steps of the temple, heavily armed guards stood like statues, armor glinting in the moonlight, blades picked out like crescent moons.

Low wore a grey habit adorned with the red raincloud sigil of the Water Wight.

The temple was one of the few buildings in the city that stood tall and wide at the top. The law prohibited the collection of rainwater for all but those deemed fit to collect and distribute water stores. The Temple of the Water Wight was one of those. Kindred had always thought its architecture looked like hands opening joyfully to the sky, widening at the top, stretching out as far as possible to collect as much rain as it could.

'Hello, Low,' Kindred said, stopping a short distance away, not wanting to startle the woman. She thought back to the last time she had followed Rhabdus on water duty and the bucket that had been hurled at her head when she'd surprised the Water Wight Priestess.

'And may the Wight keep you, keeper,' Low said, her mutters surfacing to the level of recognizable speech.

'I like your habit,' Kindred said, pitching her voice high and slow, a conversation with a child. 'It looks new. Praise the Water Wight.' Though not religious herself, Kindred believed that the best way to deal with someone was to see with their own world view.

Silence and sweeping.

'Captain Caraway sent me to – '

'Sweeping,' Low continued as though Kindred had not spoken. 'Horrible task. Moving dust and grime and filth around, putting it in piles so it might be blown back on the steps. If the Water Wight demands it, though, of course. Of course.'

Low continued muttering, nodding to herself or to whatever ghosts she spoke to every now and again. Kindred let her gaze move to the stately building behind Low, the Water Wight's catacombs.

After a moment, she tried again.

'Low, I've come to – '

'That's enough, keeper,' Low said, the scrape of her sweeping a constant murmuration in the night, somehow giving the darkness body and spirit.

sweep sweep sweep sweep

'I know why you've come. Always the same, a breath of the Wight's body, a sip of her soul. It's bad news this time around, I'm afraid. Bad news.'

sweep sweep sweep sweep

'Bad news?' Kindred asked, thinking but no, not thinking of the news she'd received amid the darkness of *Revenger*, pushing it back and away.

'Bad, bad news,' Low said, pushing and pulling the dust on the stairs. 'Water only for those who have signed. Only for those in the Collective.'

sweep sweep sweep sweep

Kindred felt a shiver break through her numbness. She thought through past conversations she'd had with Low, past negotiations and purchases. The priestess was always odd, always grumbling to herself about this or that, but Kindred had always explained it away by Low's ascetic existence. Priestesses of the Water Wight were not allowed to talk to one another, and so Low only spoke to sailors seeking to fill their water stores, and Kindred couldn't imagine that happened more than once or twice a day at most.

And so Low was odd. But never this odd.

Something was wrong there, something about the Collective.

'Cantrev's Collective? What have they to do with independent water purchases, Low?' Kindred felt confusion and, beneath it, anger. It felt good. Purposeful.

Low shook her head.

sweep sweep swe –

Kindred grabbed hold of the broom, jerking Low's movements to a rough halt. The guards shifted, like springs coiling, but did not move. The temple, like all temples, was a business, and it needed coin like any other. Its worshippers offered a pittance every week to praise the Wight within Her halls and sip from Her fount, but it was common knowledge that the vaults of the Water Wight filled with gold only through the business Her priestesses conducted with sailors. They drew up barrels of water – what believers imagined to be parts of the Wight's soul itself – from the great, deep well on which the temple had always sat.

'I'm here under Captain Jane Caraway's orders to purchase water stores, priestess,' she said, pitching her voice from the lungs, the chest, giving it force and power. 'Will you deal?'

Low looked up then, a ragged spirit quivering there. She shook her head and grinned.

'Fine,' Kindred spat, shoving the broom back at the woman, 'if you don't want *The Errant*'s coin or Captain Caraway's favor, I'll deal with another.'

Kindred turned and walked away, trying not to rush, trying to maintain her anger, to let it keep at bay thoughts and worries she couldn't yet consider.

'Go easy, keeper.'

sweep sweep sweep sweep

Kindred pounded on the greasy wooden door. After a time, a slot opened and a pair of eyes peered out at her.

'Agent of *The Errant* here under Captain Caraway's orders. I'm here to see Mick.'

The eyes – a dark blue she didn't recognize, though she dealt with Mick far less frequently than Low, so that was no surprise – considered her for a long moment.

'Where's Rhabdus?' a voice asked as the eyes squinted in consideration.

'It's just me tonight,' Kindred said, hating how young her voice sounded. Rhabdus had always spoken with such confidence and authority – a tone that neared derision – when dealing with suppliers, and Kindred wondered when, if ever, she could speak so. She remembered a phrase Rhabdus loved to utter. 'I speak and deal with Captain Caraway's authority.'

Did she? It took everything in her to maintain eye contact with those searching blue eyes.

The slot closed for a moment, and Kindred heard the undertones of a discussion filtering through the thick door. Kindred couldn't make out what they were saying, and so she simply stood, trying not to look like a fool. The night around her was watchful, almost predatory.

Finally, the door opened, and Kindred felt a surge of relief as she stepped through and listened to the door close and lock behind her. She had been considered and found adequate.

'Keeeeee. Perrrrrrrrrr.' Mick's wheezy voice rose and fell like the wind, like bellows, pushed out on air in long, earthy blasts.

He reclined in the corner, a small man whose body seemed elementally opposed to the great, sweeping voice whooshing out between his thin, wet lips.

'Hello, Mick. It's good to see you.' Kindred sat in a high-backed wooden chair and glanced around the low-ceilinged room, taking in the five – no, six – tall men and women standing around, each one a piece of hired muscle, fists, teeth, feet, swords, and knives all connected to Mick's voice, like extensions of his body, like his body itself. His small, knuckly fingers became gnarled, massive things with these hired goons; his thin arms and diminutive stature grew and expanded with these bodyguards.

'It. Is. Gooooooooood. To. Be. Seeeeeeeeen.' Mick wheezed laughter out into the room, at once breathless and full of breath, and Kindred chuckled along. Captain Caraway demanded they deal with Low first, preferring to buy through sanctioned and legitimate channels, and certainly Rhabdus had preferred Low as well, but Kindred liked Mick. They had only been forced to deal with him a few times since Kindred had come aboard *The Errant*, but she had taken an instant liking to the little man with the big voice. He seemed a good soul to her.

Mick grew somber for a moment and leaned forward, the movement clearly a pain for him.

'Myyyyyyyyyy. Connnnnnnnnnn. Dooooooooooo. Lenceeeeeeeeees. Fooooooooooor. Yoooouuuuuuur. Loooooooooosssssssss.'

She bowed her head once and said nothing. She would not think of that. Not yet. She could not.

The table between them was a battered and scarred and burned thing that dominated much of the room. Mick sat on one side, his back to a wall, two guards standing near him. The others were arranged throughout the room, leaning casually against walls or standing near the door, each one a violent and dangerous possibility.

On the table, books full of graphs and numbers and charts lay open, and scattered around and atop these were notes and letters of all types. She longed to rake her eyes over and through this written chaos, to wriggle through the tiny nettles of the pages and lose herself in them. Words, when written, were a labyrinth she could wander forever.

'New friends, Mick?' Kindred asked, gesturing to the bodyguards. 'The last time I was here, it was just you and – what was her name? Lita?'

Mick nodded slowly. Ponderously.

'Leeeeeeee. Ta.'

Mick lifted a thin, veiny hand, one finger flicking at a few of the guards.

'Daaaaaaaaaaaaaaaaaanger. Oussssssssssss. Tiiiiiiiiiiiiiiime. Sssssssssss.'

Kindred had no idea who would threaten Mick. True, he provided water outside of the church's, and now the Collective's, purview – though he wasn't even close to the only one – and true, his dealings had never been especially legitimate, but Mick had been in operation for more years than Kindred could remember, and it was well known that he was both fair in business and not a person to cross.

In addition to stories about his few clandestine wells, it was an open secret that Mick had a network of water catchment systems that would spring up during the rare rainstorm that blew across the Sea, each one set up and taken down by the myriad people in the city on Mick's secret payroll – politicians and the poor alike.

Mick's roots were as deep and wide as the Sea itself, it was said.

Growing up on the deck of *Revenger*, Kindred had learned plenty about the water merchants of Arcadia, how they held power and privilege unimaginable, and Mick was no exception. The Marchess had told Kindred stories about his kindnesses, his tendency to offer free water to those who needed it, but she also told Kindred of those foolish enough to challenge or wrong him. Kindred had no interest in being one of those people.

And now, here he was, speaking of danger, his eyes betraying a nervousness, his normally steady hands shaking a little as he moved. Something was not at all right.

But Kindred kept her composure, her mind still pulling at the odd encounter with Low. This was a concrete problem, a confusing mess but one she could solve, one she could push and pull at.

'I'm here on behalf of Captain Caraway,' she said, sitting forward in the chair and placing her open hands on the table, palms down. 'She asks for a refill of *The Errant*'s water stores.'

Mick nodded.

'Yeeeeeeeeessssss. Buuuuuuuuuut.' He gestured to one of his bodyguards, who said, 'Our rates are higher than they used to be.'

Kindred cocked her head, suddenly aware of how warm and close the room was. A prickle of sweat picked its way down her back.

'What's the problem?'

'Cooooooooooo. Leeeeeeeeeeec. Tiiiiiiiiiive.'

Mick gestured at his table, and Kindred followed his finger to a letter stamped with Cantrev's sigil and name.

'Cantrev?'

'Seeeeeeeennnnn. Aaaaaaa. Tooooooooor. Caaaaaaaaaaan. Treeeeeeeeeev.'

The Cantrev she still had in her mind was a small-timer, a midlevel agitator who was best known for his bawling, fatuous speeches delivered along Rickshaw Square every morning. Kindred had only seen him a few times, but she had heard it was always the same: a black, polished box was brought out into the square – Rickshaw being the epicenter of Arcadia's wealthier, resource-rich population, the square was better taken care of than most of Arcadia.

Cantrev would wait for one of his lackeys to place the box onto the ground and quiet passersby. Once he was satisfied he had everyone's attention, Cantrev would step ponderously onto the box and begin holding forth, the spittle exploding from his lips giving form and movement to the vitriol of his words, evidence of his wealth. Only someone well hydrated could produce such eruptions.

'What does Cantrev have to do with you giving us water?' That feeling of tension and anger, wild and rabid, began to pulse within her again, and she fed it.

Mick gestured to one of his guards, flicking his fingers. Speaking was difficult for him, a slow, breathy task, and his throat became quickly parched. While he slurped at a bowl of water from the table, the guard nearest him, a woman with close-cropped hair and swords angling up from either hip spoke.

'Cantrev has convinced the councils to form an economic partnership with all who sell water.' She counted them off on her fingers: 'The Church of the Water Wight, Carlus Canker, the Zero twins, the Misters, Tula, and Winders. The order is to not trade with anyone who hasn't joined the Collective. And Cantrev wants those who haven't joined or won't join reported immediately.'

She paused before continuing.

'And *The Errant* is not on the list of vessels who have joined the Collective.'

The strange meeting with Low, Cantrev's smug sneers, the blue of his senatorial face paint: it all began to chime clarity in Kindred's mind. Cantrev had gained the power to give his Collective teeth; what had been a loose association of lackeys pulled together by a small-time politician was now a web threading over all of Arcadia, its sticky pull angling closer and closer to *The Errant*, to Captain Caraway, to Kindred.

This was trouble.

And yet Kindred needed water.

'And you?' Kindred asked, turning back to Mick. 'Have you joined with Cantrev?'

'Fuuuuuuuuuuck. Caaaaaaaaaan Treeeeeev.' Mick's eyes were hard things, and his fingers curled into bony, shaking fists.

'No, we do not support Cantrev or his calls for unification. But the bribes we pay are now much more expensive. Many of our water sources have been compromised as well, and so our rates have increased.'

Mick raised both of his hands, palms up. *What can be done?*

Kindred might have protested, but she thought of their huge payday, the bundles and bundles of plants they'd harvested. It would do.

'We can deal,' Kindred said, leaning forward.

WITH Mick's promise that his people would have *The Errant* filled soon, Kindred set off again into the city. She walked without much purpose, not yet having decided whether to report back to *The Errant* right away to tell Captain Caraway about the change with the Collective or go about finding a place to sleep once morning arrived.

More than anything, though, she wanted to crawl back aboard *Revenger*, to scour it for – what? Her grandmother, stowed away in some closet, laughing herself silly at her joke? Some evidence that she was still alive somewhere in the world? Some hope to bury deep in her gut, to smooth out the clench of pain there.

Kindred just walked.

The night wind was reduced this far into the city, stoppered up and cut off by the steady rise of buildings, but Kindred could still feel it stirring her hair and playing across her neck and face, and suddenly she was remembering her grandmother's favorite practice while out on the open Sea, a wind like that one stirring the grasses.

'Let her take us, sailors!' she would call out, and all plans for harvesting or reaching this or that stretch were gone, replaced by the Marchess's insane desire to go where the wind would take them. *Revenger*'s single square sail would crack and flex and bloom as it caught the full wind.

'Blend with it, Kindred! Let it move us! Let it move you!' her grandmother would call from the helm as Kindred struggled to readjust the hearthfire, to shape the bones into something that might capture the flighty spirit of the wind, at times gusting, at times slipping, a few degrees this or that way and then not.

'Let her take you, Kindred! Let her take you!'

Kindred had spent much of her childhood there on that deck, sailing about the Forever Sea, learning to move across it and be moved across it.

And so she walked, letting the wind guide her into the city and along streets that wove and grew and shrank before her, lights dispelling and being consumed by darkness. With each step, Kindred felt the wave of memories and surprise and horror and deep sadness growing, and with each step, she felt her defense against that wave faltering.

So sorry to hear about the Marchess.

She had been walking away from the city for some time before she realized where she was going, where she had been going all along. The dock guard had told her exactly where she could find her grandmother's crew, those women under whom Kindred had learned everything: how to sail and how to curse, how to listen to the prairie wind and love its song.

'Headed for the rocky shore, they were,' she mumbled to herself, imitating the dock guard's deep-cheeked idiolect.

Kindred left behind the last bits of city and emerged onto the rocky shore.

It was – had been – one of her grandmother's favorite spots.

After so long at Sea, while her crew were indulging in any number of vices, the Marchess would go to the rocky shore and simply sit – day or night, cold or rain or sticky heat – and stare out at the Sea. She could have just returned from a hundred-day harvesting tour in the grasses to the west, that long stretch of safety between Arcadia and the Mainland, and still, her first act in stepping on solid ground would be to walk through the city – the rocky shore being on the opposite side of the island than the docks – and stare out into the ever-moving mass of the Forever Sea.

'It exposes you,' her grandmother would tell Kindred after dragging her along to the shore. 'That pit back there,' she would say, gesturing to the city behind them, 'is about shielding yourself from the world. And I don't just mean physically. *Stone*,' she would say, slapping the great slab on which she would sit, 'exposes. It protects nothing, hides nothing.'

Kindred stepped off the path and onto one of the enormous stones that made up the interlocking face of the rocky shore. As a younger girl, Kindred would run across the stones, counting a hundred steps, two hundred for a single great slab before leaping the crevice and racing across the next.

Even before she saw them, she heard them.

Laughter came through the dark night like an old friend, at once warming Kindred and reminding her what she had lost.

So sorry.

She stepped onto the rock face, its surface worn smooth by an eternity's relationship with the wind, and as she went, Kindred took off her boots, feeling for a moment a child again, her bare feet slapping on the cool surface, her toes feeling and knowing the real shape of the gargantuan stone.

Tears welled in her eyes, and an ache pulled at the back of her throat as Kindred let the memories settle over her, each one well worn and satisfying in the way only something painful can be: the Marchess playing hide-and-seek with her on those stones over there; Kindred riding on the Marchess's shoulders, singing at the top of her lungs; the Marchess telling her stories of her parents and holding Kindred when the tears came.

That old woman, so unknown to Kindred while her parents were still alive, had become her keel, her spine, her *home*.

And now she was gone, and the last thing Kindred had ever said to her were words of anger and spite.

She swallowed hard and swiped her face with one sleeve before taking off, running despite the dehydration and the drumbeats still dribbling out of the city center. She ran for light ahead.

Across one, two boulders that gripped at her toes, and then Kindred saw them, a clutch of figures in the darkness, upright shadows articulated by the wood fire they surrounded. She heard their laughter again, uproarious and defiant against the night, somehow bigger than and part of the wind, the Sea, the whole world.

As she neared, a loud voice, practiced at being heard across a ship's deck, bellowed, 'A little ghost approaches, come to haunt us from the past!'

Kindred felt herself smile despite everything, and then the owner of the voice detached herself from the night-shrouded figures and walked to Kindred, surrounding her in a bone-grinding hug.

Kindred thought of herself as a tall woman, with arms like far-reaching tree limbs and legs corded with muscle from too many years kneeling and squatting before the hearthfire. She held her thick hair out of her face with a red headband, and long-healed burns scoured her hands and arms. When she saw herself in the occasional mirror, she did not see a person easily tussled with.

But Red Alay, her grandmother's next hand and the woman who would inherit *Revenger*, had always made her feel slight in comparison. Red, a towering woman, swallowed Kindred with her hug, devoured her, and Kindred let herself be devoured by this woman who had, on Kindred's first day aboard *Revenger*, called her 'little ghost' for the way she had lingered just outside of conversations, too quiet to join them and too curious to leave them alone.

'It's good you came,' Red Alay said, letting Kindred go, and then the others were there, the crew members who had served with Kindred's grandmother since before Kindred was born: Felorna, Maggie the Tall, Three-Hearts, and the others. Kindred greeted them all, hugs and smiles and tears all around, and they returned to stand by the fire, ringing it, and Kindred became part of that ring. She was given a mug of liquor, and soon they settled into telling stories of the Marchess: the battles she'd won and avoided, the politicians and council members she'd snubbed and fucked and hated, her tendency to greet the morning sun fully nude on the deck of her ship, the odd songs she sang and the dead languages she was always trying to resuscitate.

And of course, her love for the Sea, always.

As the crew of *Revenger* remembered, Kindred felt herself lulled into the memories, or she might have been, but something seemed off. She looked around the circle of firelight and saw a strange happiness; she listened to the stories and heard a spirit and fire she had not been expecting. These women sang a song discordant with Kindred's own, and she couldn't figure out why her grandmother's death – their captain's death – wasn't impacting them more.

She listened as much as she could, smiling through the memories despite her growing confusion. And when it became her turn to speak, to share something of her grandmother, she didn't.

'How did it happen?' she asked, looking around the circle at the smiling faces. 'Why didn't any of you stop her?'

There it was again, that anger she'd been feeling. It was the wrong emotion, she knew, but it was powerful and purposeful nonetheless.

'Ain't a person alive who could stop the captain,' Red Alay said, taking a swig from her mug and smiling. 'She was a woman with an iron will, she was.'

'But why did she do it?' Kindred asked, raising her voice now, giving her anger its head, letting it fill her lungs like a sharp wind filling out a sail, pushing it on. 'You weren't attacked? She wasn't driven to it? Coerced? Forced?'

'Attacked? I think I might have remembered that,' said Maggie the Tall, chuckling into her mug.

'But what about the tears in the hull? I saw the damage there. Was it wyrms? Or pirates? Or . . .'

Kindred trailed off, realizing what she had missed. The damage to the hull never extended onto the deck. Even in the darkness, she would have known if the deck or the mast or the rigging had sustained that kind of assault, which meant that whatever had happened, it had only happened to the hull.

Kindred could only think of one thing that could have such an effect on a ship's hull.

'The Roughs,' she whispered, and those around her nodded.

'Aye, we went into the Roughs,' Red Alay said. 'And even with it being pirate territory and all, we didn't see a single one.

Must be you all attracted them.' Red lifted her mug in mock salute, laughing.

The Roughs. Kindred saw them twice in her mind, first as the edge drawn on most maps of the Sea. The prairie mages of Arcadia had flattened and tamed the grasses around Arcadia, making the Sea easier to traverse, easier to harvest. But their magic only extended so far, and beyond it were the Roughs – often depicted as an encroaching flurry of dashes on maps, meant to symbolize the wild plants, thorns, and nettles there. What the maps didn't need to depict were the pirates who sailed those chaotic grasses and the beasts who moved below them.

And yet, at the same time, Kindred saw the Roughs from just a few days before, when *The Errant* had pushed out so far, too far. Kindred had looked beyond the magically enforced flatness of the grasses around Arcadia – she'd looked out at the rise in the Sea, the strange, impossible, outrageous *rise* of it. Mountains of vegetation colored by plants she'd only ever read about articulated variety in impossible arrangements, a wonder of change and diversity in the face of Arcadia's flattened, predictable grasses. Thorn reefs cut through the green dangerously, spined and sharp. Slopes broke the level of the Sea, and Kindred had imagined giants below the waves of grasses, their shoulders garlanded with strange flowering vines and nettle patches wicked enough to carve up a ship's hull if the sailors weren't careful.

If, in fact, they were sailing back through the Roughs without a captain.

Kindred saw all of it and then she was shaking her head, confused and angry still, sadness held at a distance by the fire in her stomach.

'I don't understand,' she said through clenched teeth. 'You went into the Roughs? You went into the Roughs so my grandmother could commit suicide? Why would you do that? Why did none of you stop her?' Her words became hard metal pellets dropping from her tongue, weighty and myriad. She was crying, she realized, the tears warm in the wood fire's heat.

Her grandmother used to tell her that silence didn't exist on the prairie Sea. 'We cover the real conversations with our useless talk,' she would say. 'The wind, the grass, the beasts from the depths of the Sea and the birds in the air. There's too much life happening here, too much for silence.'

And so, the silence that fell after Kindred's outburst was not complete. Like the rocks, like the Sea itself, Kindred's silence served only to reveal, to expose.

Wary looks crossed the faces of those around the circle, and then Red Alay spoke.

'You've got it mistaken, little ghost,' she said, putting a heavy hand on Kindred's shoulder. 'The cap'n – your grandmother – didn't commit suicide. We were out near the edge, near the Roughs, and she's been quiet most of the day, just staring out at the horizon, and then she orders us to go in, and so we went, and somehow she's guiding us through the worst of it, sailing deeper and deeper in, thorn reefs and nettle patches coming near us but never cutting into the hull and we don't know what's going on but the cap'n has that look, like all is right in the world – you know the look.'

Kindred nodded, tears falling fresh now. Her own captain, Captain Caraway, had once said Kindred had inherited the Marchess's expressions, and though she never knew if it was meant to be an insult or compliment or both, Kindred had been surprised at how good it made her feel.

'Well, she's got that look and we're sailing further into the Roughs than is healthy, and we keep scanning for pirates or forged flowers or anything else but there's nothing and the wind is steady and we're sailing and then all of a sudden she calls for a stop. Maggie stifles the hearthfire and the rest of us are furling the sheet and soon enough we're slowed to a near stop and, well, and . . .'

Red Alay stumbled into wordlessness, the first time Kindred could ever remember, and when she looked up at Kindred, she, too, had tears in her eyes.

'The cap'n, well, she comes to each of us and gives us a hug and looks into each of our eyes and tells us something, something secret, some parting message,' Red said, wiping at her eyes. Kindred couldn't think of a time she'd seen Red Alay, one of the most notorious brawlers in Arcadia, this emotional. 'And then she gives the ship one final look and just steps off into the Sea, not falling down into it, not like that. She just walked away into the Sea, slow and purposeful, like she was walking down stairs. And the whole time, she was just smiling and smiling; you know how she smiled.'

And Kindred did. Her grandmother's smile had been a fierce thing, guileless and honest and mad.

The story didn't make any sense – the Sea couldn't hold up a person, it just couldn't be done. Kindred had seen sailors fall in before, and they slipped through the endless grasses like a pebble falling through air.

And yet.

Something in the telling pulled at Kindred. The Sea was wide; it stretched on to forever, or so everyone assumed, but if it was wide, then, too, it was also deep. The myths – the ones everyone knew but no one believed, the little stories that sparked the air between children up too late – rose in Kindred's mind. A hidden world, full of wonders and wilds and people and beasts and magic, all forgotten and waiting deep below the waves of prairie grasses.

'What did she say to you?' Kindred asked, wanting to know more, wanting to know it all.

But Red shook her head, smiling through the tears.

'That's not something I can share, just like I don't expect you to share yours.'

Kindred paused.

'Mine?'

'Your letter. I delivered it to the letter-pass myself, still sealed, just as the cap'n left it. If I'da known you'd be coming into port today, I would've just waited and given it here.'

In a distant part of her mind, Kindred heard Captain Caraway giving Ragged Sarah orders to go pick up the mail from the letter-pass.

'My letter,' Kindred said, her voice quiet.

'Aye, little ghost. She wouldn't leave without saying goodbye.'

Kindred looked around the circle once, eyes wide, heart beginning to pulse in anticipation of running, of racing to find that letter.

'To the Marchess,' Red Alay said, holding up her mug. 'May she find peace in the deeps.'

'To the Marchess,' Kindred said along with everyone else, holding up her mug, thinking of a woman stepping from a boat and walking away into the Sea, thinking of her grandmother telling her to blend with the Sea, with the wind, with the fire, always to blend.

Thinking of a letter waiting for her.

4

KINDRED moved quickly through Arcadia, traversing where she oughtn't go, pushing against and through the tide of nighttime workers going about their business in great droves.

She searched for Ragged Sarah, who should have already been to the letter-pass and rounded up all the mail for sailors aboard *The Errant*. For *her*.

But where would Ragged Sarah go, Kindred wondered, anxious.

As her feet pounded the ground – sometimes dirt, packed and hard and bone-like; sometimes rough stones aligned like the jagged language of civilization – Kindred realized she should be tired, should be emotionally and physically exhausted.

But she moved with energy, blood and bone and muscle and mind drawn together by the promise of words on a page.

Kindred ran along Stolon Lane, the street with all of the best bars and taverns, but she found no sign of Ragged Sarah in any of them. She moved on to the bazaars, thinking about what she knew of the crow-caller.

Ragged Sarah had joined *The Errant* a short time before Kindred had, coming to them from the cesspit of Arcadia. *The Errant* had been in need of a crow-caller, a mage capable of calling and speaking with birds in order to pinpoint a ship's location, to aid in navigation, even – depending on the skill of the caller – to ascertain the site of any harvestable plants not yet discovered by other vessels. Ragged Sarah had answered the captain's call.

And since then, she'd proven herself a contradiction among the crew. Kindred thought of the stories she had heard about Sarah: kneeling before Captain Caraway the first time she'd come aboard – 'no one kneels on my ship,' the captain had said, only a little embarrassed – telling strange and clever and crude jokes over late-night drinks on the deck under the stars, fiddling with *The Errant*'s long-defunct medical supplies cabinet and declaring to everyone, with the captain's permission of course, that she would get the cabinet in order and fit to use. She would chew lie-leaf with the other sailors and laugh wildly into the night; she wielded a pair of wicked silver blades that Kindred had seen her throw once with vicious, deadly accuracy, flicking her multicolored hair as she sent the blades spinning into the air. Tattoos covered her arms and legs and neck, and Kindred had spent more time than she would admit imagining those lines of ink and color winding their way beneath Ragged Sarah's rough shirts and pants, tracing the line of her shoulder or flourishing along the curve of her hips.

Sarah was remarkable. From the deck, Kindred had watched Sarah cast her spells and called her birds, their winged shapes appearing from the clouds and flocking to the crow's nest. Afterward, she would climb down with a map bearing for a vein of plants overlooked by the other harvesting vessels.

It had been Sarah, just the day before, who had alerted the

captain of pirate vessels bearing hard in their direction. Without her, *The Errant* and her crew would have been dead at the bottom of the Sea.

In many ways, Kindred felt a connection with Ragged Sarah; they were both isolated members of the crew, both tasked with solitude, with watchfulness. Sarah spent her days in the crow's nest alone, monitoring the horizon and calling birds to guide the ship toward more promising grasses. No one else aboard *The Errant* could call the birds, and so Sarah lived and worked in a world of her own.

Meanwhile, Kindred busied herself at the hearthfire, set in the very center of the deck, near all the activity but removed from it, too.

They were the same: sailors with tasks and skills too specific to truly be full members of the crew, working in spaces misunderstood or downright feared by everyone else aboard. The crow's nest, the hearthfire – both pockets of space aboard *The Errant* set apart from the ship's orders and commonalities.

And Ragged Sarah was certainly elusive. She hardly ever spent much of her take from their harvests, and when Kindred once asked what she was spending her money on if not drinks or brothels or weapons or treasures, Sarah had smiled that secretive smile of hers, the one that pulled at a part of Kindred she hadn't known existed, and said, 'Home.'

There were times where Ragged Sarah's laughter with the crew, the hardness of her as she climbed the mast or sharpened her blades or told stories of her past sailing experience – never mentioning specific captains or ships, just the exciting stories of fighting through the pull of forged flowers or Antilles roaches – there were moments when Kindred thought all of that was a show. Ragged Sarah playing the part of rough sailor.

Yet there was another side to her. A truer side. Kindred had seen Ragged Sarah in her quieter moments, those times when many of the crew slept, when she thought herself alone and free from observation.

Kindred remembered seeing the crow-caller leaning out from the nest one morning, dawn still just a barely lit candle on the horizon. Rhabdus had hated keeping the fire in the early morning, and so it was often Kindred's job to wake early and check on the blaze, to organize the bone closet, to sweep up any ash. At first, Kindred had hated those pre-dawn mornings, but soon enough she grew to love them. The cool air waiting to fill lungs and sails, the hushing movement of plants swirling together and whispering along the hull of the boat.

Ragged Sarah had been humming quietly while braiding grass. She'd drawn together the strands of prairie grass until they had formed a circlet of green that she nestled into her hair, a gesture at once simple and childlike.

Kindred had popped open the bone closet and stomped around a bit, letting Ragged Sarah know she wasn't truly alone anymore, and when Kindred looked up again, the circlet was gone, and Ragged Sarah gave her a wave before she focused back out to Sea. Later on that day, Kindred had found the circlet placed on her bookshelf.

Kindred searched each of Arcadia's three brothels: The Iron Whip, Rain's Home, and The Lily. Ragged Sarah was nowhere to be found in any of them, and as Kindred walked out of The Lily's thick, spice-scented wooden doors, she felt a strange measure of relief to not have found Sarah there.

As she walked out into the night, she thought again of Ragged Sarah leaving that circlet of grass on her bookshelf. She hadn't slung it on Kindred's bed or set it on the writing desk, and she hadn't just dropped it down on Kindred as she worked at the hearthfire.

No, Sarah put it on Kindred's bookshelf, amid her most prized possessions. She had shown some sense that she understood Kindred, that she could think from Kindred's perspective.

And there, Kindred realized, was her problem. She'd been running around Arcadia, trying to think from Ragged Sarah's perspective, to see this city from Sarah's eyes, to let the indulgences of Arcadia draw her as they would Sarah.

And somewhere out there, Kindred thought, Ragged Sarah was probably doing the same thing, asking where Kindred would go, asking what indulgences would draw her.

'Of course,' Kindred said, though with a smile. She moved now, sure in her steps, running back where she'd started, back to her berth, to her bed, to the Sea.

To her letter.

She found Ragged Sarah pacing the dock beside *The Errant*. Kindred's heart clutched in her chest when she saw a small cut of white in Sarah's hand.

Anticipation roiled in her stomach, but Kindred's steps faltered as she looked up and caught sight of shadows moving around Ragged Sarah. It was hard to make out in the low light of the dock, but after a moment, Kindred saw wings and beaks articulated in the impossible movement of the shadows.

They were birds – two of them, flitting around Sarah's shoulders, each the size of a fist. Their plump feathered bodies cut through the darkness, wings like sails catching a wind all their own. They arced around her head in dangerous swoops too wild to calculate or follow. As Sarah paced, her head down, the birds accommodated her movement, as if they were an extension of her.

Kindred had never been this close to Sea birds. Sure, she'd seen their shadows outlined against the sun as they approached the crow's nest above, and like any other sailor who had ever stood on the deck of a ship parting the green grasses of the Forever Sea, she'd cast her eye through a longsight to glance off a line of pelicans dizzying themselves higher and higher in the sky.

But this was something else. Kindred had seen Ragged Sarah call birds for information, for guidance on the Sea, for a greater picture of the grasses waving on the horizon. That was business, function.

Here was Sarah, the colored strands of her hair pulled into a tail at the nape of her neck, her forehead creased with worry, her mouth forming whispers only meant for herself, with birds like familiars haunting her.

She stepped nearer, until she caught Ragged Sarah's eye.

'Kindred!' Relief smoothed over Sarah's face as she came forward, her smile rejuvenating something in Kindred despite the exhaustion that slid through her body, pulling her down. The letter was in Sarah's hand, held carefully.

The birds settled themselves on the crow-caller's right shoulder.

'I was looking everywhere for you,' Sarah said. 'But then I remembered that you spend most land stays on the boat anyway, so I just waited here.'

She said it, Kindred realized, as some sort of apology, an unspoken *sorry* floating in her words, filling the interstices. She must have heard what happened with the Marchess, Kindred thought. Or at least one version of what had happened.

'It's all right,' Kindred said, her eyes drifting to the birds, which regarded her with intense curiosity, heads cocked to one side, inky black eyes ringed in imperfect white, beaks closed and solemn. Up close, Kindred could see the subtle articulation of their coloring: hazel shading into white or grey, with dashes of black that looked inspired by some mad artist. Their plump bodies hung suspended over legs too thin to hold them up, and yet there they stood, somehow perfect.

Dazzling lines of white traced back from their beaks and across their heads, giving them the look of royalty, crowned and regal.

'Oh, right,' Ragged Sarah said, following Kindred's eyes. 'Don't mind them; they were just keeping me company. Off you go.'

Sarah shrugged her shoulder, as if stretching out a tight muscle, and she whispered a string of words Kindred couldn't understand, could barely make out.

In a flash of movement, the birds took off, making their round, soft bodies into whirrs of wings and stretching feathers. As one, the birds launched from Sarah's shoulder and skimmed the grasses of the Sea, curving and angling in terrifying tandem before disappearing into the darkness, neither down into the Sea nor up into the sky but simply out, toward a horizon lost to the night.

'What kind of birds were they?' Kindred asked, as she strained her eyes to see farther into the black, to catch any last glimpse of the winged shapes.

'White-crowned sparrows,' Sarah said, chuckling a little.

Kindred tried to hold their movement in her memory, their cut and swirl still dancing across her mind's eye.

'I didn't know you could call them in the city,' Kindred said, trying to keep the awe from her voice. Of course, Arcadia saw its share of birds, but Kindred couldn't remember ever seeing a calling bird on land. As far as she knew, calling birds could only be found on the prairie Sea – and only then through whatever magical means crow-callers used.

Ragged Sarah grinned.

'We're not really supposed to, but' – she gestured around at the nearness of the moon-silvered grasses – 'the docks seem more a part of the Sea than city.'

'Where will they go now?' Kindred asked, trying and failing to find their winged bodies in the darkness. 'I know common birds nest among the trees here, but do calling birds, too?'

Sarah shook her head.

'No, no. Did you never learn the difference between common and calling birds in your time at school? Common birds live on land, calling birds live in and among the Sea – nesting out in the Roughs beyond the tamed Arcadian grasses. Common birds give the gift of their presence to all; calling birds are fickle, refusing to be seen without being called, without the intervention of fire and magic. Do the bookmavens in their fancy schools not teach their young prodigies such things?' Sarah's smile was bright in the moonlight as she poked Kindred's shoulder, her eyes mischievous.

Kindred coughed out a laugh, surprised.

'I failed out long before the bookmavens began discussing other roles aboard a ship. I didn't even make it through the core instruction in hearthfire-keeping before I was dismissed.'

Sarah's smile grew wider somehow.

'What a scandal. No wonder Rhabdus has been such an almighty ass to you. You know she was a guest maven at the schools, right?'

Kindred nodded, rolling her eyes.

'She never shuts up about it.'

Their laughter filled the darkness for a few moments until Sarah held up a hand, cutting Kindred off.

'Do you hear that?' Ragged Sarah's eyes were wide, her breath held. Kindred held hers, too. Waiting.

There.

Rising above the constant noise of the city, sharp and piercing, came the cry of a bird, part scream and part song, all wild, all untamed. Kindred might not have even noticed it without Sarah, who stood motionless, her body angled toward the noise, a smile held on her face.

'A jay,' Sarah said after the birdsong had died away. 'Sometimes, I feel like I spend more time talking with birds than I do people. It can be a lonely job.'

Kindred nodded, thinking of the tiny pocket of stillness that surrounded the hearthfire. The blaze was set in a metal basin in the center of the deck; no walls or ropes blocked it off, and a crew member might walk near enough the fire to feel its heat any time of day.

But none did. Instead, Kindred – or sometimes Rhabdus – sat there, trying to sing peace in the eye of the storm, alone, surrounded by the crew.

A moment of silence, full and comfortable, passed, and then Sarah stepped closer, handed Kindred the letter, and then, tentative and careful, she gave Kindred a hug.

It was a quick thing, Ragged Sarah's arms around her for a moment and then gone, the smell of her hair, a rich, heavy oil Kindred couldn't place – there and gone.

'I heard about the Marchess; the news is all over Arcadia. I'm sorry.'

Kindred never considered repeating what Red Alay had told her, though whether it was because she didn't fully believe it or didn't think Ragged Sarah would, she wasn't sure.

Instead she said, 'Thank you.'

Kindred took the letter and walked down the dock until she was clear of *The Errant*, the deck dark save for a few lights coming from the captain's quarters, and nothing stood between her and the Sea. She sat, letting her legs dangle over the edge, feeling the rustle and caress of grasses shaping themselves around her legs, and she let her legs sway in their movement in return.

Blending with the Sea.

'Will you stay?' Kindred asked into the moonlit darkness, staring down at the letter in her hands, feeling the weight of it and wondering if she could open it.

And Ragged Sarah did, sitting beside Kindred without a word, near enough for their shoulders to touch just slightly if Kindred shifted or moved at all.

The prairie wind sighed and the moon hung like a lantern and the Sea whispered encouragement.

And Kindred opened the letter.

Kindred.

An old scribe once wrote that the prairie is a daydream, and if that is so, then I go to lose myself in it.

I will not miss this surface world. Every day we strive more to break the environment to our will. Flatten the Sea. Sell the water. Chain the animals and order the plants. In our arrogance, we have forgotten ourselves to be a product of this place. A participant in it. One star in a grand constellation.

The blight is in us, moving our arms to destroy the rhythm of the Sea, closing our eyes to the sight of a sunrise, turning our ears from the wind.

And now the Sea has begun to die. I have looked beyond our grasses, into the wonder of the Roughs, and the sickness is there, too. I am going below, Kindred, to find the source of the Greys or die trying. Something moves below us, and it calls to me. As it calls to you, I suspect. If you seek me, look beyond. Look below.

Some will think me dead. And perhaps they are right. Every attempt to go below – for the crassness of wealth, for the stink of power – all have ended in death. But I have given myself to the Sea, have become the sail to its wind, and it pushes me down now. If I don't answer this call, Kindred, I will wither and die more profoundly than ever I could by falling into the darkness, if falling is what I will do.

I will not miss this surface world.

But you, my child, I will miss. Remember, the prairie holds worlds, and the wind beneath the Sea is unceasing. Listen for me in the grasses and listen for me below.

My love for you is.

Kindred let the letter rest in her lap for a moment, open to the moonlit night. She listened to the grasses, closed her eyes, and let the prairie wind fill her.

But she could not hear her grandmother's voice, not outside of her memories, no longer out in the world.

She sat with the letter in silence before passing it to Ragged Sarah. Maybe she should have kept it private like Red Alay and the others had with their letters. Maybe she should have hoarded it as her grandmother had hoarded so much: forcing Kindred to watch her build the hearthfire and shape the bones without ever actually telling her how to do it. 'You have to steal my techniques, Kindred,' she would say when Kindred complained. 'I have worked hard to gain them, and so will you.'

Over time, Kindred had developed her own techniques, her own approach to keeping the fire: equal parts technical and artistic, equal parts mind and spirit. Of course, when she had tried that approach at Arcadia's seafaring schools, the teachers had laughed at Kindred's intuitive approach and her claims that she could hear the song of the fire clearly, followed soon enough by mockery and then anger. The Marchess had taught Kindred to listen to the flames, to blend with them, but the teachers and bookmavens at the schools demanded total domination over the flames, and Kindred simply couldn't – or wouldn't – obey. It had always been about spirit, about curiosity, about finding something within herself.

While Sarah read, Kindred pulled a small coin from her pocket, barely big enough for a slice of bread, and flicked it out into the Sea, watching the moon's light catch and release it over and over as the coin turned in the air. For a moment, Kindred thought the coin might stop on the surface of the Sea or slow its descent among the grass.

But it dropped through.

'She writes like one of the poets,' Sarah said, handing the letter back to Kindred.

'Yes, she does. Did.'

'Why didn't she finish the last line, though?' Sarah touched a finger to the final line. My love for you is.

'She did,' Kindred said, trying to blink away the tears filling her eyes. 'That's how she ended all of her letters to me. She told me once that love didn't have to do anything other than exist. You don't have to dress it up or compare it to something else; when it is, it's miracle enough.'

The wind blew, gentle.

'Do you think she's alive down there?'

Kindred choked out a strangled laugh through the suffocating weight of her grief. It felt good, a stolen sip of joy.

'Yes. No. I don't know. She can't be; no one could be. But ...'

How many times had the Marchess done the impossible? How many times had she proven that she was always two steps ahead of everyone else, craftier, smarter, better than anyone imagined she might be?

So sorry.

'No,' Kindred said finally. 'I don't think so.'

Maybe.

'I'm sorry she's gone.'

Kindred could only nod. She felt heavy with exhaustion and sadness and confusion, as if a slow weight were pulling her down, to sleep or to the deeps, she didn't know.

And yet she heard Red Alay again, speaking in reverent, drunken tones, perhaps not to be trusted or perhaps to be trusted all the more – speaking of her grandmother walking into the Sea. Walking and not falling. Just walking away into the Sea, with the Sea.

Sailors saw the Sea as a plane to be traversed, nothing more. To think of the deeps led to madness, for how could one sail across so vast an abyss and consciously attend to its emptiness, to the forever below? The harvesters – those who crawled out along the beams and were lowered into the Sea, held up with their harnesses and ropes – were the only ones who seemed able to comprehend what might be below, and Kindred had yet to meet a harvester who was not at least a little mad. *Touched by the Sea*, other sailors said of this madness. *The Errant*'s harvesters – Cora the Wraith, Long Quixa, Stone-Gwen – were just as touched as any Kindred had met.

But harvesters never dove deep, never fully submerged themselves in the Sea. Half in and half out was their method, far enough down to let their silver blades cut away valuable harvests from the stalks and far enough up to see sky and ship.

They dipped toes into the question of what lay below.

Kindred dove in, thinking of all the stories she had heard, the tales and myths of a Sea full of monsters coming to gobble up bad children, a prairie hiding secrets and wonders if only one could dive down, could find her way below.

She shook her head, feeling the weight in her mind, too. It was all too much.

'When will the captain get back?' she said, struggling to stand up until Ragged Sarah helped her, sliding arms beneath her own, lining her own body up with Kindred's. 'I have to tell her about the water. And then find a place to sleep.' She was remembering anew her exile from *The Errant*.

'I don't know when she's getting back, but you're not going anywhere. That berth is yours, even if you're missing out on this next voyage. You're not in any state to go wandering off into the city.' Sarah helped her aboard and across the deck and, after lighting a small taper, down the steps and along the hallway and into Kindred's berth, her tiny room with its hammock strung between the walls and its small desk and its bookshelf.

'Just a quick rest,' Kindred mumbled. 'Wake me when the captain gets back. I have to tell her . . . something.' The world had turned fuzzy, and even though Kindred knew there was something she had to tell Captain Caraway, she couldn't remember it. The sound of the wind outside was like a broom sweeping, moving dirt and grime around with no purpose, but Kindred lost even that thought to the exhaustion.

Ragged Sarah helped Kindred into her hammock and, moving slowly, reminding Kindred of careful hands braiding strands of grass, Sarah kissed her forehead and left without a word, Kindred swaying ever so slightly in her hammock.

She woke in darkness.

Held in the fibrous cradle of her hammock, Kindred felt suspended in the black. The only sound was the wind stirring the Sea.

She knew herself to be in her berth aboard *The Errant*, knew herself to be waking as she had so many times before at port and out at Sea.

And yet the darkness felt charged, the emptiness around her significant.

Kindred slid a hand into one pocket, feeling her grandmother's letter there.

I will not miss the surface world.

There in the place between – between dreaming and waking, between the Sea and the shore, between one voyage and the next – Kindred imagined herself falling down through the Sea, falling and fallen to the bottom, where not even her imagination could paint the darkness with colors vivid or powerful enough to change it. Her eyes opened or closed, Kindred saw nothing but blackness, heard nothing but the wind and the ghost of her grandmother's voice.

Listen for me in the grasses and listen for me below.

In that black in between, with only herself and the ship as witness, Kindred made a promise to find her grandmother, to trade in the known bounds and exploited mysteries of the world above for the unimagined impossibility of the world, of the worlds, below.

If you seek me, look below.

'I will.' Kindred's whisper to the darkness was both a mantra and a covenant. 'I will.'

Heavy steps and whispered voices pulled Kindred from dreams of dropping through darkness. She had a last fleeting image of herself falling and falling through the Sea as Red Alay and the others sailed beside her, yelling at her to blend with the grasses – just blend! – their boat somehow able to sail below the waves. Kindred couldn't decide if it was a nightmare or not.

When she walked out into the hold, she saw four men having a whispered conversation, their voices like little storms. The near-dawn light cutting in through the portholes was tinged a soft pink.

'Lift it, damn you, lift it!'

'Oh, fuck you, I am lifting!'

'Shut it, all right, and just move the fucking thing.'

'There in the corner now, easy you bastard, easy, and there.'

'Dickwhistle! That was my fucking toe, oh shit, that was my toe.'

'That may have been my fault.'

Kindred watched them, a smile pulling at the sleepy weight still holding her face tight. The events of the previous night waited for her, held still until the moment she reached inside and lifted them to the light, but she let them be for now and watched as Mick's workers moved in the water.

'No need to whisper,' she said, causing more barrels to be dropped on more toes and more swearing to fill the hull's open enclosure. 'I'm the only one down here as far as I know, and I'm already awake.'

The men turned to her and smiled, though they seemed nervous. They couldn't be more than twenty years old, probably only in Mick's employ for a short time. She would be a little nervous working for him, too.

'Sorry about that,' one of them said, 'we were just finishing up. This is all of it.' He slapped one of the barrels of freshwater, the sound thick and meaty, and began moving toward the ladder to go above.

'Excellent. Captain Caraway will be pleased with this. I'm surprised she's not down here supervising.' The captain wasn't one for sleeping much at port. Kindred had several times heard Captain Caraway talk about how the only place she could really get a full day's sleep was at Sea.

The man shrugged and kept walking.

Kindred pulled out a few coins. 'Has anyone given you a tip yet?'

'We're good,' one of the men said as he climbed the ladder, followed closely by the others.

'And hey, when did Mick start using bigger barrels?' Kindred asked just before the last man had made it to the ladder. He turned, caught by her question.

'I don't know? I think it's, hey guys, is it, oh they're already up there, I think it's the same? The same as it's always been?'

He was speaking in fragments, and his eyes kept slipping over to the barrels and then down to Kindred's feet, back and forth, as though tracing a line between them.

'I guess I must be mistaken,' Kindred said, mostly to let the nervous young man go. After they'd stepped ashore, she went above. While she waited, she counted the barrels, and yes, she was sure of it, they were larger than normal. She wondered if it had something to do with what Mick's guard had talked about – new difficulties in obtaining the water or something like that.

Kindred popped the cork out of one barrel, just to verify, and sure enough it was cool, clear water inside, enough to support *The Errant* on a long trip.

Up on the deck, she knocked on the door to the captain's quarters but got no answer. A quick scan of the deck, the forecastle, and the quarterdeck showed no one else aboard, and even the crow's nest was empty.

In the east, the sun was a promise soon to be delivered, a shower of reds and pinks and golds staining the night sky.

Kindred did a complete circuit of the ship just to be sure and found no one, which was odd. Kindred even climbed partway up to the crow's nest, hoping she might find Ragged Sarah, but that, too, was empty. The memories of the previous night – finding Sarah after her search, the birds, reading her letter, sitting there on the dock together in comfortable silence – seemed like a dream, their significance evaporating in the bright morning light, the smooth emptiness of the deck.

She clutched at the letter in her pocket like it was a talisman against the forgetting.

Every other stay at port aboard *The Errant* had consisted of her listening to Rhabdus's orders and carrying them out. 'Take these coins and buy a pack of thrice-root essence' or 'clean out and arrange the bone closet' or, if it was a longer stay, 'empty the ash from the hearthfire basin and scrub it 'til it shines.' And once she was finished carrying out Rhabdus's whims, Kindred had gotten a little time in the city – time to chew lie-leaf with the crew, time to haunt the bookstalls or walk the city.

Once, during a particularly long period of shore leave, Kindred had sat in the amphitheater in Arcadia's Wind District for an entire night, listening to the music-mages play their requiem, a piece of music without end or pause, an ever-shifting blend of notes echoing forever in that sunken theater of stone. The mages sat around a great fire, feeding it with plants, which, unlike the battle magics that raised defensive walls around a ship or formed into coruscating bolts of power to be hurled at pirates, emitted great curls of smoke illuminated by uncanny flickers of light. The mages wove the smoke, holding and handling it as if it had substance, and as they did, great waves of music rolled out into the theater, sounds rising and falling.

It was one of the hundreds and thousands of strange, and at times wonderful, bits of life in Arcadia.

But Kindred felt no real urge to move into the city, to surround herself with every unwashed body and petty squabble that filled the streets. Every good thing in Arcadia seemed a temporary solution to the eternal problem of the city itself.

Daybreak neared, too, and soon the city would close up, waiting out the dry heat of day for the cool of night.

She wound her way around the deck before spending some time at the bone closet, going over their stores, arranging and rearranging. She should be out finding a place to stay, some pit that she could survive in until *The Errant* returned to port.

A wild thought crept up on her: why not go back to *Revenger*? Kindred had forgotten to ask who would captain the ship now, but she knew each one of them, had sailed with them all, grown up with them.

What was the point of rebelling against her grandmother now that she was gone?

No. It would be a step back – comfortable and wrong. Before, Kindred had wanted a career of her own, a reputation and name earned by her own work, a shadow of her own that stretched outside of her grandmother's.

And now? The Marchess's letter was a fiery weight in her pocket, burning up her ambitions and leaving behind something harder, something stronger.

If you seek me, look below.

Kindred walked the deck, reading and rereading her letter, thinking of her grandmother stepping off *Revenger* and simply walking away into the Sea. There were stories, of course – hints and myths and tales whispered to naughty children: monsters and the monstrous living in the darkness below the waves. Sailors drunk enough or young enough might whisper of Antilles roaches, bodies like smooth red stones rising in a pestilence, a plague from the grasses. Some said they rose every ten thousand days; others claimed they would only attack a ship with a broken-hearted sailor aboard.

There were myths of the crook'd jaws, a beastly man, all as one might expect except for his teeth, longer than they ought to be, always bared in a slant smile. He was said to climb out of the deeps and cling on to a sailing vessel, eventually getting aboard and pretending to be a member of the crew, charming and wonderful and cheery. Until someone realized, and by then it was too late.

The silver throwers. Rank folds. Light dusters. Two-toed derrigans. The seventh troop. Root sisters and rot mice and the wide-eyed thresher and on and on, endless stories of endless monsters.

The Forever Sea was a wild expanse reaching beyond the horizon, deeper than anyone knew, and though sailors spent entire lives trying to chart its surface and understand how to best harvest its produce, the only stories – the only consideration – of its depths were better saved for bedtime, to haunt the dark and bring mischievous, fearful smiles to children fighting sleep.

And even then, the stories were often about what rose from below, what shattered, horrific things crawled or flew or slithered to the surface. No sailor – even those under the thick weight of a deep and profound lie-leaf trip – would talk of what lived beneath the grasses. Only fanciful whisperings of smudge-faced kids crowding around a game of dice, trading stories of beasts big as ships with fiery skins and a never-ending hunger, of people who swam through the eternal darkness and eked out a living, of whole cities burrowed into the ground, of the Queen Who Laughed and the Running Ones. Children, it seemed, could hold such truths in their minds, could know and understand and *believe* in such a different world without it destroying their own.

Kindred thought of the few ill-fated attempts to bring practical knowledge to bear on the deeps.

The Vinsayd Family – 'too rich to be,' the Marchess always said – had long before begun extending a rope down into the Sea, its end weighed down with several fist-sized metal anchors. Every new generation of Vinsayds would add more rope to the thin, snaking line disappearing over the edge of their personal dock extending from their estate on the edge of Arcadia. Thrill seekers and adventurers were invited to climb down the rope, to let their bodies disappear into the rustling green waves, and for a time, many did, hoping to claim the prize – a fortune for any who could return with evidence that they had reached the bottom of the rope: a chip from the anchor.

Many tried.

All failed, either returning too soon, mad and empty-handed, or, more likely as the length of the rope increased from generation to generation, never returning at all.

None had ever successfully sounded the bottom of the Sea, but estimates of the Vinsayds' rope put it at or above four miles in length.

Four miles and still no bottom, no slack in the line. Even if the stories of rich water sources cutting across the Sea floor were true, who could climb down so far? Even if Red Alay's story of the Marchess were true, she would be walking for a long time to reach whatever moved below.

And that didn't even begin to account for the beasts of the Sea that made the grasses their home.

Others angled for the deeps in stranger ways. Kindred had met a man a few years earlier, back when she was still sailing with *Revenger*, who was convinced great civilizations lived at the bottom of the Sea. He had been one of the Number-Children, those tasked with the calculation and maintenance of great, complex sums from an early age. Children, it was theorized, were naturally nimbler with numbers, and so they were plucked from homes early if they showed particular talent, placed in dark basements with unending writing materials and blank rooms to aid in their calculations. Businesses, politicians, theorists: they all made use of the Number-Children. But, as often happened with them, this man had gone wild as he aged, had never given up his hold on imagination the way that others did.

He had been shouting in the streets about these civilizations, about how his calculations had assured him, had *promised* him that many people lived at the bottom of the Sea. 'The air is cool and water flows freely there,' he had said.

The man had been begging for money to help him build a contraption with which he might – Kindred shook her head in disbelief at the memory, still so odd this many years later – catch a wyrm and then ride it down to the deeps.

He had sailed off onto the Sea one day on a small boat – big enough for a single person, its tiny hearthfire barely bigger than a torch's flame. Barely fitting on the deck of his boat was the contraption, a tangle of stone and metal and rope.

He never came back.

Even Kindred's bookshelf held a few tomes filled with the myths: right next to the books about the Supplicant Few and their search for land at the end of the Forever Sea were old, equally impossible tales of undersea rivers lined with speaking stones; herds of strange, five-legged creatures that spoke in colors and dreamed their young into existence; the great graves of the Sea Lords, rising like mountains below the Forever Sea.

Kindred had read those stories, had loved them as a child. And she felt a surge of something like excitement every time a new, crazy plan was laid to discover something below the Sea.

But all of that had always seemed a fool's errand, fun to consider and pointless to attempt. Anyway, the depths of the Sea were likely a trash heap – all of Arcadia and, as far as Kindred knew, all of the Mainland dumped all of their refuse – every bit of excrement and cast-off material – down into the Sea.

Kindred climbed the mainmast, ignoring the ship laid out like a game board below her, and instead stared out at the Sea where lashes of green caught the dawn light and ignited in golds and yellows.

But veins of decay cut through the Sea like a rash striping across healthy skin, scarring the living Sea with dead and dying plant mass. An unnatural, withered mess of ash-grey plants unaffected by means magical or natural.

The Arcadian shipping authorities had sent a warning to all vessels to avoid these 'Greys,' and after a few stories of captains with too much bravado badly damaging their ships, everyone else had complied. None had yet figured out the cause, but Kindred secretly thought it a product of hubris, the Sea's response to Arcadian magics that had flattened and tamed the prairie grasses.

It was clear that the Sea was sick – dying, maybe – but it had not yet become a cause of any major concern on Arcadia; why worry about a few veins of dead plants when the Sea went on forever? The senators were already talking about expanding Arcadia's territory of flattened, easily harvestable grasses, pushing its border farther north and south. Those with any sense knew that expanding any farther east would cause even more pirate attacks, put even more strain on the already-straining Arcadian defenses.

Yet the Senators planned anyway. Mapmakers were brought in to redraw the lines of Arcadia's reach, to reimagine the wildness of the untamed Roughs as more flattened Sea.

Kindred shivered at the thought. 'I will not miss this surface world,' she whispered, quoting her grandmother's letter.

'Morning,' a voice said from the dock, and Kindred was so startled that she nearly fell. Clinging to a rope, she saw Little Wing come aboard, her broad shoulders laden with bags carrying supplies of all sorts.

'Morning,' Kindred said, climbing down a little too quickly and landing hard enough to send a shock of pain through her feet. She set about helping Little Wing with the supplies.

'I thought the captain set you to cooling your heels on land.'

Kindred flushed. Little Wing had always been nice to Kindred, had always treated her like a fellow sailor as opposed to the know-nothing child Rhabdus had considered her. But whatever change was going on inside Kindred's head and heart was too fresh, too much *hers*, to share with anyone, and so she simply said, 'Just not ready to be land-bound yet, I guess.'

Little Wing grunted and continued unloading the supplies.

'The ship's empty,' Kindred said. 'Any idea where everyone went?'

'No one around?' Little Wing set the last of the bags down and stretched her arms up and up into the sky as though she might pull the blue of it down around her. 'Not even the captain?'

'No,' Kindred said. 'I don't think I've seen her since we docked. You?'

Little Wing cocked her head and considered for a moment.

'Last night, I guess. Late. Nearly this morning. Said she had an early meeting with that fucker Cantrev.' She rolled her head around, stretching out her neck, which emitted a series of popping sounds. 'I'd love to punch that man. Don't you think he would be a better person if someone just punched him once, really hard?'

Kindred laughed and nodded.

'I guess the captain still ain't back from that meeting.'

'Did you get good prices from Legate?' Kindred asked as she began storing away the various supplies Little Wing had brought back.

'Good enough,' Little Wing said, taking a few practice swings with a pair of new curved swords like silver crescent moons. 'He was so excited to see someone had harvested some giant stalk and prairie smoke that he about started blubbering. You know how he gets about plants, on and on about how beautiful they are and how powerful they can be and all that. He gave us some serious coin, even with the new taxes from the Collective.'

There it was again, Kindred thought. Cantrev's shadow organization that used to be nothing more than a few blowhards blowing. She really needed to tell Captain Caraway about the strangeness with the water purchase before *The Errant* set sail and left her wasting away the time on Arcadia.

'I had the same thing happen with Mick,' she said. 'Cantrev's even reached him. Mick charged me more for water and – here's the really strange thing – he was acting weird about it all, like he's terrified of Cantrev and mad as hell about it.'

Little Wing cut the air with her swords, slicing a low hum into being with each cut.

'Cantrev. He's going to be running this whole damn island soon. I say we relocate to the Mainland and start harvesting there. They have almost triple the space of flattened grasses to harvest. Sure, there's worse prices and those damn barons to deal with, but a place without Cantrev pays for itself quick enough. And we wouldn't have to deal with the pirates always waiting, getting closer every year. Fucking inhuman monsters.'

'We kill them, too,' Kindred said, not sure why she was defending pirates, but feeling like those words – *inhuman monsters* – smacked of Cantrev's grease and sweat.

In Little Wing's hands, the swords described complex, dangerous patterns in the air.

'You remember *The Blue Sky*? Big boat, one of the newer ones. Pirates hit it a few years back. My best friend growing up was the boatswain. The crew fought off the pirates that boarded, but in the fight my friend lost an ear, an arm, and got stabbed twice in the stomach.'

Little Wing jabbed herself in the stomach with her thumb, twice, hard. Her face was stony.

'I didn't know that, Little Wing. I'm sorry.'

'She died as *The Blue Sky* made it back into port. I was there. When I finally saw her, the blood had all dried and she was cold.'

Kindred swallowed and looked down at her feet.

'A couple of years back,' Little Wing continued, her tone flat, 'pirates attacked a dew-skimmer crewed by a family with six kids, three sisters and three brothers. The pirates killed the parents, sailed the boat out into the Roughs, and then left the kids to starve or sink. By the time a rescue boat found them, only two of the kids were left alive.'

Silence filled the deck.

'We don't do that,' Little Wing said after a moment, her tone softer. 'We do our fair share of bad shit, but we don't do that.'

Kindred nodded, and as she thought of how to respond, she saw a few guards in bright, new uniforms walking down the dock, marching with purpose. She didn't know what was so familiar about their uniforms, at least not until she thought again of Low, her habit brand-new, which was an oddity for priestesses of the Water Wight.

Except maybe not an oddity when a senator like Cantrev had you on the payroll.

'Those are Cantrev's guards,' Kindred said, turning around.

Little Wing looked over and squinted down the dock.

'Yeah, so what?'

Kindred opened her mouth but shut it just as quickly.

Odd.

She considered the other oddity of that morning: barrels too large, workers terrified and acting strange.

And her stomach dropped away into nothing.

'No, no, no, no.' She rushed to the ladder and climbed belowdecks with Little Wing following her. 'No, no, no.'

She slapped at the first water barrel she found there, pushing at it to pull it away from the others, but it bore no markings on its edges or top.

'Help me with this,' she said, and with Little Wing's help, pushed the barrel up on one rim, enough for her to peek underneath, to see the name burned into the wood.

She heard Mick's wheezy bellows in her head. *Fuuuuuuuuuuck. Caaaaaaaaaan. Treeeeeev.*

'He must have stolen it, that idiotic bastard.' Kindred looked up at Little Wing. 'Mick gave us water from Cantrev's private stores and Cantrev knows.'

Back up on deck, Kindred looked down the dock. The guards were getting close, eight or ten of them in all, each one armed and ready for a fight. Swords flashed in the morning light like promising smiles.

Had Cantrev discovered Mick's theft? Or had Mick willingly turned *The Errant* over? Kindred tried to push away the suspicion burrowing through her. It didn't matter either way – the guards were coming, and they obviously knew.

'They must have already picked up the captain at that meeting,' Little Wing said, her voice dropping low, a predatory growl. Her new swords moved with purpose now, their hum a constant thing.

Kindred tried to think, but the strike of the guards' boots on the dock was loud now, and she could hear them talking. Which, Kindred realized, probably meant they didn't know she or Little Wing was aboard.

'We need to get off this boat,' Kindred said, pulling Little Wing portside, away from the dock, their movements still shielded by the rise of the forecastle.

'Yeah, but how?' Little Wing asked. 'There's only one dock and they're on it.'

Kindred looked around the deck for anything she might use, for any bit of inspiration. They had weapons, but two of them against so many of Cantrev's guards would not end well, especially given how little time Kindred spent swinging a sword.

They could hide, Kindred thought – belowdecks was full of shadowy spaces that might conceal them. Even the crow's nest might be left unsearched if they could scale the mainmast without being seen.

But what then? Even if they successfully hid, Kindred realized, they would only have succeeded in trapping themselves if the guards were going to occupy the ship, unable to help the captain – just as useless as giving themselves up to Cantrev's guards.

No, they needed to get off *The Errant*.

'I can take four of them, maybe five,' Little Wing muttered as Kindred shook her head in frustration. 'I'll do my best to draw them to me and you make a run for it.'

Little Wing was shifting back and forth, foot to foot, readying herself for a fight.

'There has to be another way,' Kindred said through clenched teeth, eyes moving around the deck, for something, for *anything*.

A wind cut across the deck, bright and chill, pulling at a few loosely tied ropes, and the Marchess's words whispered through Kindred's mind, a gift from her grandmother.

'The prairie holds worlds.' Kindred spoke as if in a dream, her mind suddenly wild and chaotic. Beasts below. A rope extending forever down. Graves in the deep and rivers running in the darkness.

A woman, walking out into the Sea, out and down.

An idea too dangerous, too fanciful to consider.

And yet, what else was there?

'What?' Little Wing asked, leaning close.

'We can't get off this dock, fine. But what about the other one?' Kindred said, pointing toward another dock extending into the Sea some way away, a few larger vessels stopped at it.

'Okay, but how . . .' Little Wing began, but she followed Kindred's finger as it fell, pointing not at the dock anymore but down, to the Sea, to the darkness there.

To the cradle strung through the Sea like a great, interconnected web, the giant chains holding up *The Errant*, the docks, every other boat. The cradle, which connected all of the docks from below the Sea.

'No,' Little Wing said in a voice that gave Kindred pause. It was not the strong, reserved voice of the quartermaster.

It was a woman afraid, her confidence shattered by fear of the deepest, purest kind.

'It's the only way,' Kindred said, dropping her voice to match Little Wing's. The guards were nearing, and Kindred's heart had begun to beat with a frantic energy in her chest.

Little Wing shook her head, looking like a child confronted by a world she suddenly couldn't understand. What Kindred was suggesting went beyond the madness of harvesters, their bodies cinched tight in harnesses, roped back to the ship, touching the edge of darkness without ever diving in, playing at freedom without truly letting go.

That was a hazard of harvesting, a danger that harvesters took on and other sailors ignored. Though they cut across the Sea day and night, those who lived and sailed on the Forever Sea would not – could not, it seemed – look square into its depths. It was an abyss to be forgotten when possible and ignored when not.

To fall into the grasses of the Forever Sea was to fall *through* them. The grasses were like hair, capable of holding nothing up on their own. Whatever magic gave growth and body to the Forever Sea, whatever magic the beasts of the Sea had also been granted in order to ascend and descend – none of it extended to humanity, who dropped through the Sea, dead weight falling without slowing.

'Little Wing,' Kindred said, leaning in close, dipping her head to catch Little Wing's gaze. 'It's the only way.'

A moment of silence, and then Little Wing huffed out a breath, fear and all.

'Fuck,' she said, buckling her swords in hip sheaths and spitting once.

'Yeah.' Kindred nodded.

As the boots neared and the voices grew distinct and articulate, Kindred and Little Wing climbed down the side of *The Errant*, lowering themselves to the grasses and then in, slowly through the blades until they were fully submerged.

The early sunlight filtered through the grasses at that depth, giving Kindred the impression of floating in a Sea of homogenous green, the individual lengths of grass glowing so brightly and filtering so much bright sunlight that the distance between them disappeared.

It was beautiful.

They had found the nearest chain of the cradle, though it was not directly below them. This far down the hull of *The Errant*, there was only the one ladder attached.

They would have to jump, Kindred realized.

She heard the guards reach the ship above them, heard their boots on the deck, their voices pitched. Bastards.

Kindred held a finger to her lips and pointed above, and Little Wing nodded back, her eyes saying precisely how much she hated this situation. Kindred pointed at herself and raised up a single finger. *Should I go first?*

Little Wing spit and shook her head, jabbing herself in the chest. *No, I will.*

And she did, her breath huffing in and out before stopping altogether. Kindred saw tears welling in Little Wing's eyes, and she thought to say something, confident words or a quip to ease the tension, but then Little Wing was in the Sea, truly in it, weightless and hanging suspended in the green, her powerful arms no different from the strands of prairie grass.

She hit the chain, which had links as big around as one of Kindred's legs, and hung on. After she'd righted herself on it so she could crawl along its length, she gave Kindred a shaky nod.

Kindred paused, seeing the fear behind Little Wing's affirmation. Above, Cantrev's guards were denigrating *The Errant*.

'Can you believe the senator wants this shitty old wreck?' one of them was saying.

Kindred felt herself pulled and stretched between these two worlds: the terrified eyes of Little Wing below, the condescending snarl of Cantrev's lackeys above.

And then a line from her grandmother's letter moved through her mind, silencing her fears, soothing her worries.

I go to lose myself in it.

Kindred leapt, and as she pushed off from the ladder, her foot caught on the last rung, just slightly, just enough to dampen her momentum, and she saw she wasn't going to hit the chain with the center of her body as she'd hoped. Terror flooded through her. She was dropping too fast, was approaching it not nearly quickly enough. She stretched her arms and flailed at the chain, her fingers pulling at their tendons, her sockets straining as she reached and reached.

In the moment before she made contact with the chain, the terror disappeared – just for a breath, just for half a breath – and a singular life of pure stillness overtook her, as if the Sea itself suddenly existed not around her but in her, and Kindred could feel its peace, its forever.

She understood something of what her grandmother had said, could feel a force below the Sea, in the darkness, like a wind or a movement, one that coursed through the deeps of the Sea and never broke the surface.

When she hit the chain, she did so with her hands, and despite the pain and strain of it, she tried to hold on, somehow, gritting her teeth, feeling her fingers slipping from the thick links even as she kicked her legs and wrenched herself up, or tried.

She was falling, she couldn't hold on, couldn't exist in this peace, and then Little Wing had her, the quartermaster's powerful hands wrapping around Kindred's wrists and lifting her up to the chain.

Kindred clutched the metal until her heart had slowed and she felt somewhat able to move. She gave Little Wing a nod.

'Thanks.'

'I fucking hate this.'

They crawled.

THE Sea, Kindred understood as she moved along the chain behind Little Wing, was not a thing, static and unyielding. It was a happening. It moved and changed around her, with and against and because of and without her.

Ahead, Little Wing angled her head toward the sun filtering down, a reminder that she was not yet too deep, yet Kindred found herself looking down, through the links of the chain and into the dark depths. It was a subtler forever than the horizon cutting a line in the distance between Sea and sky; this forever was quieter, deeper. A part of the Sea instead of just a product of it.

Kindred saw, too, that the Sea's terror and its joy were personal things, inconsistent somehow. The vastness below – the uncertainty and unknowability of it – was a bone-deep fear for Little Wing even as it soothed something in Kindred.

Having soaked in the morning sun, the grasses expressed the heat and light as a scent, so pure and instinctive that Kindred forgot for a moment that Arcadia slouched so close. The scent filled her nose – dry and simple, like nothing other than itself – and Kindred simply existed for a moment there, cocooned from the world by the grasses bending and shushing around her.

It was the smell of memories. Of sailing with the Marchess, learning to love this flat expanse of green, learning to hear music in the wind, to see beauty in the cut of bluestem or the clutched orange of butterfly hair.

Held in that liminal space, not on the surface of the Sea but not yet truly below it, Kindred felt weightless and connected, and memory took hold of her, pulling her to another moment of quiet, another sun-soaked day. Cantrev's guards, the question of Captain Caraway's whereabouts, the letter from her grandmother: all of it blew away in a wind rustling through the world, and Kindred was back aboard *Revenger*, her parents only recently killed in a coup on the Mainland. She stood on a strange boat, sailing a Sea she had only ever seen from afar before, numb to the world.

'Come over here, child,' the Marchess had said. Red Alay held the wheel, and *Revenger* ran in the wind, sails full and perfectly curved.

Kindred had been in mourning then, unable and unwilling to even mumble or mutter. Every part of her felt absent from the world, and so she welcomed the required period of silence. She had nothing to say. Speaking was a way of being in the world, and she wanted nothing more than to let everything – this boat, these people, her grandmother about whom she had only ever heard stories – slide by, leaving no trace on her or she on them.

Her steps unsteady, Kindred walked across the deck to her grandmother, still trying to get used to the slight sway and sweep of a ship on the Forever Sea.

'Do you have everything you need? Are you hungry? Thirsty? Is your bed all right?'

In later years, Kindred would think of how strange it was for the Marchess to have spoken in such a way – speaking in such short bursts.

Later, much later, Kindred would realize that the Marchess – the mighty Marchess who was an impossible force wherever she went, a scourge to her enemies and a bastion to her friends – was worried. Worried and anxious for this child she had never known and who was her responsibility now.

But that day, Kindred simply let the Marchess's anxious questions fall away in the wind, unanswered.

'Or maybe you would like to try your hand at the wheel? You could steer the ship, take us wherever you want! There's bound to be adventure out there somewhere. What do you think?'

Kindred looked out at the mass of green, just green, forever. She couldn't even bring herself to not want to be there.

The Marchess had eventually stopped, rebuffed perhaps by the absence Kindred had become. They stood there for some time, looking out at the Sea, Kindred letting her eyes unfocus as more of the monolithic grass slid by.

'Come to!' the Marchess shouted, causing Kindred to jump in surprise. She nearly fell over at the roar of her grandmother's voice, so loud, so commanding, a roar not even the wind could strip away.

The crew, many of whom had been lounging about, leapt

into action, hauling hard on ropes, cranking on winches. Red Alay echoed the Marchess's order, recirculating it around the small deck, until everyone was saying it.

'Come to,' the crew said as they acted together.

Revenger cut hard, the ship describing a curve through the Sea, pulling into the wind, and Kindred nearly fell over – might have, if the Marchess hadn't stepped in close, putting an arm around her. And though the deck tilted, and though the wind went from a constant push on her back to a whirlwind whipping across her body, Kindred stayed on her feet, held as she was by the Marchess.

Revenger slowed as it turned into the wind, and Kindred heard the low, beautiful voice of Felorna, who was on hearthfire duty that day, her hands moving in the flames. Unlike bigger, newer ships, with their necessarily more specialized crews, *Revenger* carried a crew who all took turns at almost every task.

The mast groaned and the sails sloughed as the ship settled, slowing and slowing.

'Full stop, Felorna,' the Marchess said.

Revenger held, rising and falling gently in the Sea. Felorna pulled and twisted at something in the hearthfire, and then the flames moved in accordance with the wind and the waves, rising and falling, too.

'Come with me, Kindred,' the Marchess had said as she climbed onto the gunwale and then over, lowering herself down to the Sea on one of the ladders attached to the side of the ship.

Kindred stood still for a moment, suddenly aware that everyone on board was looking at her, waiting for her to act or not act.

The Marchess popped her head back up, smiling at Kindred.

'It's all right, child. Come on.'

Kindred approached the gunwale and looked over, carefully angling her body so as not to touch the wood of the railing. She saw her grandmother below, waist-deep in the grasses. She held a rope in one hand, offering it out to Kindred.

'Don't worry. I'm not going to let you fall. I'll tie you to the ship just to be sure.'

Kindred felt dizzy looking down at her grandmother, the susurration of the grass lulling her into a different kind of state, pulling her ever so slightly out of her cocoon. Grasses and wind and darkness and light all moved together around her grandmother, speaking a quiet language, whispering to Kindred.

Come in, it said.

Relaxing, Kindred let her hands slide over the railing, feeling the thousand different dents and divots written into the wood. Moving as if in a dream, Kindred pulled one leg and then the other up and over, feeling a brief moment of fear as she felt for a ladder rung with her feet.

But there, one foot brushed against the rung, and then she was climbing down, letting herself sink closer and closer to this infinite floor of green.

As Kindred came level with her, the Marchess reached out to encircle Kindred with the rope, but Kindred pushed it away, shaking her head once. Her hands, two quiet, clasped things for the last few days, felt strong clutched around the ladder rung, and her feet stood firm below, out of sight in the green.

The Marchess chuckled, a sound Kindred would come to love, and nodded. She turned out, facing away from the gentle curve of the ship's hull.

'Here we are, face to face with forever,' she said, and Kindred looked out, too, nearly on eye level with the magically flattened plane of the grasses.

Breath stopped up in her chest as Kindred let her gaze roam farther and farther and farther out, sailing and skimming over endless dancing blades of green tickling the sky. It was a beauty she'd never known before, and she felt on the verge of something great and enormous. The smell of the grasses surrounded her, describing growth, articulating simplicity.

Wind blew through the grasses, stirring them, roiling them about, and Kindred sucked in a gulp of air, letting her wonder and grief speak in that breath.

The Sea sang to her and she sang back, without music or words, breathing in time and tune with the wind as it moved and gave life to this world that only a moment before had seemed flat, empty.

Tears filled her vision and Kindred let them, the Sea already a moving, blurred thing before her.

'Look at this, right here,' the Marchess had whispered, pulling Kindred's attention away from the enormity of the Sea's sympathy to its immediacy, a single stalk held in the Marchess's hand. She pulled it close, holding the wrist-thick stalk just below the point where it branched, tripling into three fuzzed reaches populated with arrowed grains. Lower, bands of brown bulged from the stalk, like knobby elbows punctuating its length, resetting the coloring and dividing the plant into segments of beauty.

'See the shading of colors, not just the green that you can see out there but a red like the sunrise, a blue like the sunset. This is called big bluestem,' the Marchess said, and Kindred mouthed the name, heard it in her mind even if she still maintained her silence. 'Here, you can touch it.'

Kindred reached out and curled a hand around the stalk, surprised by how it felt at once solid and supple, as if it could bend in any wind, could move against any hull, but would not snap, could not be broken. It was smooth against her palm, and she could not imagine ever letting it go. The Sea stirred around her and Kindred felt something like magic in the quiet chaos of the grasses working on her, asking her to see differently. To know differently.

What had been before only an unremarkable throw of green, monotonous and monolithic, became more for Kindred. She saw the rise and wave of more big bluestem around her, and other plants, too – each one articulating radical existences in the spaces between light and dark green, between yellow and gold, between stalk and stem.

Every blade a doorway and every shadow an entrance to a life Kindred had never known but which called to her all the same.

'A bundle of this – its harvested seedhead and a portion of its stalk – goes for something like eighty heavy coin in the Arcadian market right now,' the Marchess said, and Kindred's eyes widened at the thought of so much money. 'Valuable, right?'

Kindred nodded.

'It can be used for medicinal purposes and burned aboard a ship for defensive magics.' The Marchess watched Kindred closely while she spoke, as if searching for something. 'The price is well warranted, perhaps even low for how relatively rare it's gotten.'

Kindred continued to study the plant, marveling at the slow shifts in color, the way the curled hairs sprouting from the seedheads shivered in the wind.

'But here is the true value, child,' the Marchess had said, putting her hand atop Kindred's, atop the stalk. 'This plant reaches further down than anyone understands, into and through a world we have never seen, and every bit of its height is mirrored below the Sea floor. Its root system extends deep, deeper than you or I can fathom, down to where – some say – the old beasts still roam and the old tongues are still spoken. It reaches down into a different forever just as it makes up this one. It connects sky and wind and Sea and stone and dirt below, and for this moment, it allows you to be part of that chain. This is not coin waiting to be harvested or a method of travel.'

The Marchess leaned in, pulling the three of them close – grandmother, grandchild, and plant, like friends in close conversation, heads bowed together.

'This is connection, my child; this is the world – every good bit of it – reaching out. You have lost much, and you are right to mourn. But remember.'

The Marchess gently squeezed Kindred's hand, and the bluestem she still held.

'*Here* you are connected. *Here* you are allowed to be.'

Kindred had learned to love the Sea with her grandmother during those first few years aboard *Revenger*.

Or, truer perhaps, she had found the love of the Sea already there inside her.

'Keep moving,' Little Wing said, jarring Kindred loose from her reverie.

Kindred crawled, but she looked down and thought of stepping into the Sea, walking away into it.

'Finally,' Little Wing said as they reached the hull of another vessel.

'Do you know whose this is?' Kindred asked as she stopped behind Little Wing, looking at the sweep of the hull rising up and out of the Sea above them.

'Captain Fox's ship, *The Aster*,' Little Wing said, without any pause. 'It's a harvest vessel, like ours. Twenty, twenty-two years old.'

'You know her?' Kindred didn't want to climb aboard a vessel and find it full of its very angry and suspicious crew.

'No, never met captain or crew,' Little Wing said, reaching for the ladder extending down the outside of the hull. She could just barely grab it.

'But you know this ship?'

'They make you know every ship, its captain, and its primary purpose for the captain's exam,' Little Wing said, pulling herself up to the ladder and then extending her hand for Kindred.

'Captain's exam? You're going to be a captain?' She pulled back on the chain to look at Little Wing, who only nodded and extended her hand.

Kindred didn't know many other quartermasters, but that did not stop her from thinking Little Wing was perfect for the job; she was focused, hardworking, good to the crew, and intensely loyal. Kindred had once seen Little Wing beat the absolute shit out of three lie-leaf addicts who made insulting comments about Captain Caraway's eyepatch.

'What do you think that bitch Caraway hides behind that eyepatch?' one of them had asked amid laughter, eyebrows raising and falling suggestively. Kindred had been sharing a chew with Little Wing and a few of the other crew members at a nearby table.

'That's probably where the stick up her ass comes out,' one responded, laughing.

Another opened his mouth to respond, but he never got a chance. Little Wing was gone from their table and, quicker than Kindred would have thought possible, Little Wing took care of business without the frill and frippery of excess language.

She beat them. Badly.

And so there, on the chain, Kindred felt surprise and some betrayal at the news that Little Wing was going for her captaincy.

'Have you passed already? Have you gone through the ritual?' Kindred had never actually seen the ritual to make someone into a captain, to enrich her bones so that, upon her death, she might offer life to a hearthfire.

But it also came with dozens of other requirements. A captain needed at least a basic understanding of almost every part of sailing a ship, including a rough education on hearthfires and a basic ability to call a few birds for things like emergency messages and basic navigation. Kindred didn't know all the specifics, but that it was an immense and terribly complex amount of work was clear.

'Aye,' Little Wing said, just a hint of embarrassment in her voice.

'And have you purchased a ship already?'

Little Wing paused for just a moment, her normally placid, closed face suddenly opening just the tiniest bit, a single ray of sunshine lancing through a cloud-swaddled sky. She smiled and nodded.

'My cut of this last haul was big enough. She's waiting for me on the Mainland.'

'Gods,' Kindred said, pausing on the ladder, thinking how strange it would be to see Little Wing sailing out of port on her own ship, how strange it would be to walk around the deck of *The Errant* without her.

A curious thought leapt into her mind.

'Wait, did the captain push us out so far to help you buy your ship?'

Little Wing smiled again, this time with teeth.

'I owe the captain everything. Now let's go find her.'

As they climbed, she rolled the words around in her mind. *Captain Little Wing.*

The Aster was empty when they emerged onto its deck, and soon they were running down the dock, slouching down to avoid being seen by any of the guards climbing over *The Errant*.

As they ran into the city, the roads were clear, and the early-morning light made them look almost peaceful, though the city would always stink to Kindred. Most had retired for the day, seeking the dark of shaded rooms, water allowances saved for a long, slow drink before going to bed.

Kindred and Little Wing debated where to look first but settled on the Trade building, where the captain had gone the previous night to sell their goods to Legate and where, according to Little Wing, the meeting with Cantrev had been taking place.

And as they approached it, Kindred knew they were right.

She smelled the smoke before she saw it, and she felt the fire before it came into view – a raging, writhing blaze that devoured without limit or restraint. Kindred felt the fire in her gut like a deep need for more, more, more.

'Fire,' Kindred said, shock and fear catching in her voice.

A blazing hearthfire aboard a ship was one thing – not only a necessity for sailing on the Forever Sea, but carefully managed and fed, contained, and – by keepers like Rhabdus – brutally controlled. Even Kindred understood the potentially ruinous power a hearthfire could have if it were ever allowed to burn beyond the confines of the basin.

But a fire on land was *wrong*. Burning away the moisture in the air. Easily spread among the drought-stricken paths of Arcadia. A hunger that could only be quenched by water.

And a fire during the day, when so many would be sleeping, unaware of the danger?

It was folly to burn on Arcadia.

Legate's building, once tall and magnificent, a towering, ramshackle artifact built and maintained for generations, burned. The flames devoured the building with an unnatural hunger, huge tunnels of heat and fire leaping out from windows only to dive back in, crashing through crumbling walls. When she was close enough, Kindred saw Cantrev's mages – manipulating the fire, pulling and pushing it like an old man at a loom.

Kindred sensed the fire beyond just seeing and smelling it; the blaze pulsed behind her eyes. Its power coursed through her hands, her muscles. She was no caster, no spell-slinging guild mage, but Kindred understood fire, felt a kinship with it. Its song – caged and chaotic – played in her mind.

And so, she saw the web of the prairie mages' magics, saw the violet push of their assertions on the fire. She saw their power and she saw their mistakes – the places where the fire pushed back or lost articulation or went rogue. In their attempts to focus and direct the blaze, they had lost sight of its scope, its power, its uncontainability.

The sight of a magical fire so wild sent shivers along Kindred's skin. The flattened Sea surrounding Arcadia might have been made magically immune to the once-regular burns that reimagined the prairie Sea, but a magical fire like this one – given more power, more hunger than a natural fire – would devour the dried, aged grasses around Arcadia without care for any magical protections. And that would be after it had consumed every dwelling, every building, every person on the island.

A crowd had gathered before the Trade, surprising for so late in the day. The sun had already crested the horizon, and all of these people should have been turning in. Kindred was about to push forward when Little Wing held her back. She pointed to her eyes and then her ears.

Watch and listen before you act.

Kindred took a breath and nodded.

A call for quiet sounded and then a slick-faced man, thin hair puffed and wild in the fiery winds stood before the burning building, boosted, no doubt, by a polished black box. He was sweating already, the trickling slickness making his painted face shiny in the harsh light of morning. To sweat so carelessly was a sure sign of the water-rich.

Cantrev.

He faced the crowd, buoyed up by an invisible power Kindred had not known Arcadia possessed. When he spoke, Kindred saw him as nothing more than a bawling child, impotent fists waving in the air, unintelligible words vomited forth with little concern for audience or message. Cantrev was emotions made manifest, and like most emotions, he did not care whether or not he was understood. He simply existed.

'This morning, we strike a great blow for freedom, for liberty, for our Collective!' He held a fist into the air, a great meaty, fleshy bolus quivering in the perverse adulation of the crowd. The cheers of joy, of joyous rage, exploded around Kindred, the sound ubiquitous and unending.

'Legate was a known pirate sympathizer, my friends,' Cantrev continued once the shouts died away. 'Him and his clients are all in arms with the pirates, believe me; I know about these people – murderers and monsters. Legate was trading with them!'

The crowd jeered and sneered, and Kindred bit back her desire to shout out her disagreement. But she wasn't the only one who dissented.

'How many of us have lost someone to those pirate bastards? *The Nettle? Canticle?* Some are even saying pirates had something to do with our great captain, the Marchess, taking the green dive.'

Anger filled the air, hot and dry, and Kindred felt it like a tight fist in her chest. This monster was going to gain some advantage off of her grandmother's death, which had nothing to do with pirates. She had hated Cantrev, and he had hated her, but here he was, casting a somber glance around in her memory.

'Legate was on their side! Legate was working for the pirates! He took from you what you can never get back!'

'That's not true!' The words were quiet despite being shouted, as though the man were in a great cathedral or arena, as though the majority belief there could silence even the attempt at insurrection.

'Look at this fool,' Cantrev said, smirking and flicking his hands toward the man who had shouted, dismissing him before he could even start. 'He has no idea. Legate was born on the Mainland, and it's the Mainlanders who keep driving up prices and stealing from our businesses. They don't care about Arcadia; they're nearly as bad as the pirates!' He jutted a stubby finger toward the Sea. The crowd roiled in excitement, mimicking the sinuous writhe of the fire still consuming Legate's building.

'I don't want to hear from him again,' Cantrev continued, turning away from the dissident, who disappeared in a swirl of people and then was silent, absent. Cantrev gestured once to a bodyguard standing nearby, and the man moved into a nearby shed, one of Legate's, a drying shed for casting plants.

Kindred was remembering a time when she'd walked through that shed with the captain, Little Wing, and Rhabdus, picking out casting plants for their journey, stocking up for a long campaign on the Forever Sea – plants to burn in the casting fires for defenses or for Sarah's use in the crow's nest. She was remembering exactly how the captain had been discussing prairie smoke, how it could be found in only a few regions of the known Sea and even then not often, not regularly.

Kindred was remembering Little Wing's insistence that they could just harvest their own plants on the journey and the captain's stubbornness in claiming Legate's drying techniques were superior to those possible on *The Errant*, that Legate's plants were far more powerful than whatever they could harvest and dry while at Sea; she was remembering Legate entering the shed and asking if they would be buying that day or just selling what they'd harvested; she was remembering his bigness, his height and girth and spirit, the sense that he could hold up the world just fine; she was remembering the captain saying they were buying and Little Wing's sullen sigh and Legate's laughter, big and wild, and the captain's laughter, sharp and high.

Cantrev's bodyguard emerged from the shed with four people following him, each one chained and restrained. Legate stood out, a head taller and much wider than the others. Harder to spot was the captain, last in line, her head down, dried blood spattered and drooling onto her chest.

The crowd surged and Kindred surged with them, moving forward before realizing what she was doing, hands dipping into her robes for the single knife she always carried with her. In the pulse of the crowd, though, she lost track of Little Wing. Looking around herself, Kindred realized she was surrounded by strangers, all of whom looked like angry, confused children.

She stretched on her toes to look at the captain again. What could she do? What would she do?

As Cantrev began speaking again, she pushed forward little by little, moving toward the front of the mob.

'Look at these traitors. All Mainlanders trying to take over Arcadia, trying to get their people on the councils, trying to get their hands on our water.' Cantrev slapped Legate's head as the crowd roared. Legate stared at the ground, shoulders like twin slopes. 'This traitor has most of the plant-trading business on Arcadia. *Most!* We're letting a man born on the Mainland get our money, and for what? So he can have a big house and give his coin back to the Mainland?

'Well,' Cantrev said, holding his hands up, veiny and shiny in the light of the blaze behind him. 'He doesn't have such a big house anymore.'

Kindred stared at the captain, waiting for her to turn, to find her eyes. Her temporary dismissal was over, as far as Kindred was concerned. This was her captain, her crew, her ship at stake. She wasn't going anywhere.

But Captain Caraway seemed to see nothing but Cantrev. She had been stripped of her sword, and Kindred saw bruises blossoming on her face from what she could only imagine was the difficult and dangerous process of taking the captain's weapon. Her eyecloth hung loose around her face, barely covering her eye socket.

'And then there are the filthy vermin – maybe even more traitorous than the Mainland traitors – these people who give their money to known Mainlanders. They've betrayed their home and their families. Some of them – this one here, Captain Caraway – she uses unlicensed dealers and steals my water, *mine*, fills up her ratty boat with it, and then tells me she has no idea what I'm talking about while she's sitting with this Mainland trash, trading with him.'

The people around Kindred shouted their rage. Kindred thought of Mick and his laughter, his wheezing, whooshing, vengeful laughter. Did he mean to betray her? Or was Kindred, were Captain Caraway and *The Errant* simply unhappy victims in Mick's hatred of Cantrev?

Kindred thought the second, but at this point, she didn't think it mattered much.

'These are not the people we want in Arcadia. These are not the people we want dealing with our coin, our plants, our trade. Arcadia rejects them. They are no longer sons and daughters of our island.'

While the crowd jeered and roared and bellowed, their rage gluttonous with water so scarce, Kindred reached for her knife.

A hand on her shoulder made her freeze.

'Don't. Not yet.'

Kindred jerked her head around and saw Little Wing.

'But – '

'Attacking now gets you dead, and it probably gets the captain dead, too.'

'So? He's going to kill her.' Kindred noticed some of the people in the angry mob around them had begun to notice their conversation and were glancing their way with growing interest, perhaps wondering what these two women could be talking about; perhaps wondering whether either one of them was a Mainlander, a pirate sympathizer, a pirate, even. Kindred thought of growing up near the Floodplains of Eth on the Mainland, of being orphaned before she had found her feet in the world, of sailing to Arcadia for the first time on a boat that skimmed across a Sea made of grass that went on beyond the edge of every map ever made.

She refocused on Cantrev, trying to look in every way like a dissatisfied, angry citizen.

Cantrev's speech rolled on, and Little Wing pushed close behind her.

'Most of the crew is here. On my signal, we're going to cause enough chaos to get the captain out and make for the docks. I can't find Rhabdus, though. You know the songs?'

Kindred's mind was frantic as she thought over what Little Wing asked.

But yes, she did; she thought she did.

Kindred nodded and clapped, shouting with the rest of the crowd. A man standing close by who had continued to stare blearily at them, swaying with a lie-leaf rhythm all his own, moved close and slurred, 'Where are you from?'

It was unclear whether he was speaking to Kindred or Little Wing, and Kindred had no intention of finding out. In the next roar of the crowd, she pushed over, wedging her body between the sweaty, stinking ranks of Cantrev's puppets. She pulled Little Wing with her, and when the crowd had again fallen quiet to Cantrev's bawling, they were away from the drunk.

'What's the signal?'

'I was thinking I'd shout "now" just before I killed Cantrev,' Little Wing whispered.

'What did you say?'

Kindred felt a tiny stillness in the chaos of Cantrev's speech. The sweat she'd built on her run there and in the heat wash of the flames suddenly froze on her face, her neck, her body.

The woman who had asked the question grabbed at Little Wing's robes. She was large, this woman, broad-shouldered and wide at the waist. Little Wing was tall and powerful, but this woman made her look like a doll to be played with.

And yet Little Wing did not shrink back. She considered the woman who pulled her close, looked into her face before turning to Kindred.

'Here's the signal.' The thick, meaty sound of Little Wing's head colliding with the woman's was audible even over Cantrev's shouting and the low sounds of the crowd. It was a finality, and the woman fell to the ground in a heap.

A single breath of silence followed, impossibly tranquil – no air, no movement, no sounds. Only eyes looking, forever looking in that single, unbroken moment.

Kindred broke first. She drew the knife beneath her robes in a single smooth motion. But it remained in her hands, held defensively in front of her. Keepers did not contribute blades to battle; she did not contribute violence except as a final defense.

As those around her stopped looking and began moving, Kindred sang.

As Little Wing pulled crescent-shaped blades from her belt, Kindred sang.

As Cantrev shouted alarm and fell back from his box, Kindred sang.

As other crew members from *The Errant* stepped to battle, Kindred sang.

As chaos broke out among the crowd, Kindred sang.

As Little Wing's blades cut a silver loop through bodies, toward the captain, Kindred sang.

Perhaps it was just an illusion – the energy and terror and excitement of the battle setting her heart beating too fast – but Kindred felt in that moment as if she was truly, was *finally* a keeper of *The Errant*, an actual member of the crew relied on for a job she could do.

And she did it.

Her words became the flash of a blade, her fricatives the friction of knuckle on jaw, her plosives the explosion of muscles launching forward to fight. Kindred became her crew's beating, battling heart.

In battle, as in all things aboard a ship, a crew moving and acting in concert was best. Keepers were not to fight in battles except in the direst situations, so instead they sang, offering a rhythm and melody to join their crew together. In the haze and flurry of a fight, a keeper's song could act as guiding light and stirring speech at once, a tune to guide the dangerous dance of violence.

It was the oldest kind of magic: words and melody knitting together many into one.

Crew members from *The Errant* leapt from the chaos, setting their bodies and blades into the dangerous rhythms Kindred sang into being. Ragged Sarah roared into battle nearby, her long knives cutting a bright counterpoint to Kindred's melody. Stone-Gwen moved, too, calm despite everything, her face placid even as her strong arms lashed out, a cudgel clutched in each hand. Near her, Long Quixa danced into the fray, one arm still bound up from her injury but the other clasping an axe, swaying like a tree branch in an unseen wind – rising and falling, rising and falling. And as it fell, so, too, did those before her.

The crew pushed out, creating a protective circle around Kindred, letting her song move them out and forward.

Beneath this violence, thrumming along below it like a blaze, were Kindred and her battle song.

'*Now rise and stand*
for day breaks hard
this heart this hand
a whole, a shard
We push, we rise
those 'fore must fall
our foes' demise
fight on, fight all'

Through the maelstrom, Kindred watched Little Wing cut forward and reach the prisoners and the guard still standing beside them. He'd drawn a chipped, rusted blade, wicked and malicious in its disuse and disrepair. Little Wing closed, her crescent-shaped blades flicking toward the man.

Around them, the crowd had retreated. Cantrev's faithful remained, caught in the clash with the crew of *The Errant*, but the majority had no true stake in the fight and were not water-rich enough to back up their angry words with real violence. Even as Kindred's song rang out and the sounds of fighting spiked the air, these people hung back, silent and still, perhaps aware how thirsty they were, how thirsty-making the work of anger could truly be.

Their stillness uncanny, the crowd stared, a ghostly antithesis to the chaos and activity of battle.

Kindred was focusing so hard on her song and on Little Wing's progress that she nearly missed the man who slipped past the crew and attacked her with a short spear.

The rudimentary knife-work she'd learned aboard *The Errant* evaporated from her mind as the man approached, grinning like a demon. The knife in her hand felt suddenly awkward and obtuse, at once large and too small, far too small to protect her.

What was she thinking? What was she doing? As the man neared, she was just a child again, just the know-nothing novice worthy of Rhabdus's scorn, the mad protégé of a suicidal captain.

Fear pulsed through Kindred's song, which faltered as she backed away. The crew nearby heard the break but were all already engaged in battle, and so would not, could not help.

The chaos of the battle flattened into background movement as Kindred and her attacker circled.

He lashed out with the silver, leaf-shaped blade bright in the firelight, and Kindred stumbled back, twisting out of the way just in time. The knife hung from her hand, clenched tight but forgotten.

The spear whirled, blade and shaft cutting complicated patterns through the air as the man drove Kindred back. Her song gone,

Kindred realized that a low shout was now filling her throat and spilling from her, as every muscle tensed in fear.

She stumbled back into someone and turned to find Little Wing engaged with two attackers, her arms like snakes striking and striking, forcing her opponents' defenses up, keeping them occupied.

A *sssiiip* of air was all Kindred had to prepare before she was struck viciously in the head by the butt of the man's spear. Her mind went suddenly and blissfully blank for a moment, the battle disappearing as she fell, her eyes tracing the slow route from Little Wing's powerful shoulders to her attacker.

She hit the ground, dimly aware that the knife was no longer in her hand. A moving forest surrounded her – the legs of those fighting and fleeing, and Kindred tried not to focus on that. The man stepped over her, his spear held in both hands, blade arrowed down at her chest.

In her panic, Kindred reached out for what was familiar, what was home.

She reached out for the fire.

While still new aboard *Revenger*, Kindred had watched the other sailors tie knots, all of which looked the same to her at first but began, after a time, to take on nuanced identities and shapes – curls and whorls became distinct names: Illian's Tie; under-under knot; the leveler slip; two, three, or four-fingered knots; fool's knot. There were an impossible number of knots for an impossible number of situations, temperatures, wind speeds, heights, moods.

The fool's knot, in particular, had always fascinated Kindred. It was an immensely complicated knot – a bolus of tight curls and festering confusion, the kind of knot one might sit on deck and pull apart for days.

Unless that sailor knew where to look. The fool's knot, Kindred learned after a particularly long afternoon of picking and pulling at random bits of the ropy morass, could be undone by a single pull of the rope at a very specific spot in the mess. Pulling anywhere else would cause the knot to tighten and lock up, but finding this particular loop buried deep within the knot itself, lodged in its heart – that would undo the entire mess instantly, painlessly.

Kindred thought of the fool's knot as she reached out for the fire, deep into its wild heart, and pulled.

The fire became.

It became an inferno. It became a blaze. It became *wild*.

It became a whirlwind of heat and destruction and anger. It lashed out wildly, leaping to different buildings, swirling with joy as it devoured dry wood.

And the fire offered its thanks to Kindred.

The leering man didn't have time to feel the rush of heat before the blaze consumed him. It was as though the fire had reached out a single finger of writhing oranges and blues and pinks, and squashed the man as one might squash one of the micro-bugs found in Arcadia. The man was there one moment, and the next, he was only a bed of ash covered in the smoking remains of a few bones.

Little Wing shouted and leapt away, just as several others did, arms and faces and backs singed by the fire's gift to Kindred. The prairie mages, no longer in control, fled – or tried to. Some made it away; some, though, were caught by the now-free flames.

The fire, having paid its debts, raced along the buildings nearby, spreading with abandon, the constraints placed on it by Cantrev's mages made foolish by Kindred's small act.

This was true chaos: shouts collated in the air to form a single wall of ubiquitous noise, and bodies hurtled through the smoke.

Kindred stood, wavering for a moment as her head throbbed, wracked by the knowledge that she had just killed a man. Vomit rose in her throat and she threw up on the ground in front of her.

Nearby, Little Wing's attackers lay motionless on the ground, and among them Kindred found her knife. How it ended up there, she had no idea. She pushed forward through the haze, dodging around small skirmishes, looking for the captain, for Little Wing, for any member of the crew.

She wound her way around a particularly nasty fight between several people, all of them wielding axes, and it was only as one shouted in victory – his axe buried deep in the chest of another – that she recognized Mick's workers. He must have been ready for the battle, planning on it, even.

But Kindred had no time to consider Mick's plans: she saw Ragged Sarah in a desperate fight with one of Cantrev's lieutenants, the man wielding a great mace in one hand, a dented shield in the other. The head of the mace cut a low rhythm in the air before him, keeping Ragged Sarah at a distance, making her long knives worthless.

Kindred watched as Sarah feinted to the left, drawing a wild swing from the man, before cutting in on his right, eliciting a high-pitched scream as one of her knives found flesh behind his shield.

But Cantrev's lieutenant was quick, stepping forward and slamming his shield into Sarah's face, drawing a stream of blood from her nose and forcing Sarah back into a dazed stagger. She barely avoided a blow that would have pulverized her shoulder.

Kindred moved forward, stepping over fallen bodies, the knife heavy in her hand.

Sarah flung up her blades in time to block the next strike from the man, deflecting the mace head, but that was only the distraction. Kindred stifled a gasp as Cantrev's man stepped forward again and slammed his shield into Sarah's chest, the blow hard enough to send her sprawling, knives spilling from her hands.

Cantrev's lieutenant moved to deliver the final blow, his mace cutting an arc above his head.

Kindred was not as mighty or fierce as some, not born for battle and death as others so clearly were, but in that moment, Kindred wanted to kill. The glitter of the metal was a comet in her hand as she darted forward and stabbed, high and fast, just under the man's jaw. The force of it pushed his face up and away, as if he were trying to watch the movement of the smoke above.

But he would see nothing, ever again.

He toppled over, and Kindred let her knife go with him.

It was done, and Sarah pulled her away from the body quickly enough that Kindred didn't vomit on him.

'Are you okay?' Sarah asked as Kindred wiped her mouth and stood. She nodded. She wasn't, not yet, but she would be.

They moved forward together and found Little Wing with the captain, helping her shuffle out of her chains.

'Was that you? With the fire?' The captain jerked her head back toward the blaze, which had abandoned Legate's building – now a charred husk – and moved on.

'She' – Kindred gestured toward Little Wing – 'said we needed a distraction.'

Little Wing grinned, her teeth sharp and bright against the smoke and the soot coating her face.

'Where's Cantrev? Did anyone see him?'

'Gone. He is gone.' These words in a voice that might have

been deep and rich but had blanched itself on smoke. Legate stood there, a rough approximation of the giant Kindred was used to seeing. 'I saw him run away through the smoke to the citadel.' Legate raised an arm like a tree branch and pointed toward the wooden spike of the city's center, visible even through the smoke.

'If we cut through the Dowager's Quarter and then follow the path of silence toward – ' Little Wing had begun when the captain cut her off.

'No.' The captain cut her hand through the air, final. 'We flee.'

'But – '

'We will not be crushed beneath the foot of this Collective. Arcadia is dying from the inside, and I do not plan on being here when it finally goes.'

The captain turned to Legate.

'You're welcome to come with us.' She said it in a way that implied she knew Legate would say no, and he obliged her.

'This is home. If Cantrev wants to take it from me, I will fight. Others will fight.'

Kindred thought of Mick, of his workers ready for this battle, and nodded.

'Good luck.'

'And you.'

As they moved back through the smoke, Captain Caraway whistled into the chaos, pulling her crew to her, and they emerged, some bleeding, some injured, but they emerged.

And for the second time that morning, Kindred ran through the streets of Arcadia. She could only imagine what those pulled awake must have thought: smoke from a fire beginning to poison the sky, city-wide bells only beginning to ring. And the crew of a ship –

or most anyway; some had not made it, and for that, later, there would be a reckoning – racing through the snaggle-angled streets, bloodied and soot-covered and running for their lives.

The blaze would cost the city a heavy price – or it would have before the Collective, Kindred reckoned. Now, with those in charge of the water in their pockets, the councils could probably get the water to put out the flames for nothing, for the low cost of not putting chains around hands, for not throwing bodies in jails.

They would put out the fire, Kindred was sure. Some might even haul in sand to smother the blaze, but for something as lithe and quick as this fire? It would need water hauled fast from wells and rolled out in barrels, private stores appropriated for the public good. But how many more would go thirsty because of it? How many rations would be quartered, halved?

Cantrev's guards were still clustered on the deck of *The Errant* as Kindred and the rest of the crew returned. Little Wing was first to the deck, and with the rest of the crew right behind her, she made short work of them.

As she leapt aboard, Kindred felt a hand on her shoulder.

'For saving our collective asses,' Captain Caraway said, her bleeding, swollen face straining to smile, 'I officially revoke my order to stay back.'

Kindred felt a flash of something like joy as the captain left her to the hearthfire.

'Prepare to set sail!' Captain Caraway shouted.

Kindred cast a glance back toward the city, but apart from

the smoke and the now-distant alarms, she saw no evidence of pursuit. At least, not until she looked at the towers and saw the mages there frantically preparing their fires.

'The mages, captain,' Kindred said, running for the hearthfire, feeling its weak call, the tiny remnants of heat and spirit left in the bowl. She didn't know whether Rhabdus had fallen in the fight or was still rushing back, but there was no time to find her. The ship needed to sail, and for that to happen, Kindred needed to light the fire.

'Right,' the captain said, 'once the hearthfire is up, light the fore and starboard casting fires! And hurry up!'

'Aye.'

Kindred tossed aside the hearthfire cover, exposing the ash and splinters of nearly cooled bone to the air. From the bone closet she pulled out the lengths of white with little thought. They needed to move, only to move. This would not be precision work.

She sang as she worked, stilling her spirit, calming her shaking hands, forcing her actions into music and forcing music into her actions. It was a children's song, a silly thing she'd stolen from the Marchess, but it was how Kindred learned to stoke a nearly dead fire, how to begin a voyage: in innocence, in purity, in honesty.

'To light, to light, to light the fire,
First ash, then bone, then flame,
Stir the ash, stir and stir,
Grey on fingers, grey on hands,
Ash on tongue, ash on teeth.'

Kindred raked her hands through the ash, covering her fingers, her hands with it, feeling the grains pack hard under her fingernails. A gentle rain of grey fell as she lifted first one hand

and then the other out of the rich bed, touching tongue and teeth, tasting the bitter dregs of their previous journey, seeing the images of their travels as the ash caught in her saliva and disappeared into her body.

'Now bone, oh bone, a gift to burn,
Let captain's words alight, arise,
For wind, a gift, a flame,
Now bone, oh bone,
Light, light, light.'

Her hands stilled, motions smoothed by the music, Kindred took two of the bones – long and thin, probably bones from an arm – and crossed them in the now-disturbed ashes. She pulled the knife from her robe and poked a finger, eliciting a tiny bubble of red.

A ghost wind stirred the ash, swirling it into a tiny whirlwind dancing around the crossed bones. The fire called, desperate to flare into being, and Kindred obliged.

As she sang the final words – *light, light, light* – she touched her pricked finger to the bones, to their convergence point, bloodying the perfect white.

For a moment, the red of the blood paled, as though it were taking on the color of the bones, leeching from them instead of into them, becoming bone-like.

'Burn all, burn all,' Kindred sang, voice low and haunting.

The circle of pale red caught, blossoming a viridian flame that spread greedily along the lengths of bone.

'Hello, old friend,' Kindred whispered.

The Errant rose from the chains of the cradle.

A cheer came from the crew as they rushed about the deck, tying and untying, pulling and pushing.

The captain rushed past Kindred.

'Take us back, away,' she roared. 'And where is Rhabdus?'

A high-pitched whine cut through the jubilatory sounds on deck, and then Kindred was pulling herself up from the deck, which was pitching in the grasses of the Sea. She looked up at a great gash in the foredeck mast. Blue scintillas of arcane energy still burned in the wood where the spell had struck.

The mages had begun their assault.

'Casting fires!' the captain shouted. 'Little Wing, Stone-Gwen, Cora, to me!'

Coals from the hearthfire were the easiest and safest way to light a casting fire, but this hearthfire had no coals yet, at least none hot enough. It would have to be the fire itself.

Before doing that, though, Kindred reached into the hearthfire, now crackling in a merry blaze and lifted the cross of bones at its center, just enough so the bones were off the bed of ash. She sang an old song, its rhythms and melodies rough, tangled things, a technical song with little spirit, little music, no soul.

To sail was to explore, to push on, ever on; going backward was unnatural for a ship. The hearthfire was a force and it, too, longed for more, for what lay ahead.

Kindred left the bones hanging in the fire, floating, held up by her magic, her song – as unnatural as *The Errant* going backward. The toll on her, though, was massive; her tongue and teeth felt thick, the words of the song harder and harder to enunciate. The cross of bones hung heavy in the air.

This should have been a job for two keepers: one to stay with the hearthfire and another to bring the flames to the casting fires. Kindred cast a wild look around for Rhabdus, but the senior keeper, her presence so hated every other moment but this one, was absent.

With a flick of her wrist, Kindred spun the cross widdershins, and *The Errant* began sloughing backward, sullen and bitter. Kindred could feel the prairie grasses beneath them pulling at the hull with long, whispering fingers.

'Casting fire!' the captain yelled as another blast from the mages struck the ship, sending everyone not steadied or holding on to something tumbling to the deck.

Kindred picked herself up again, checked to make sure the bones were still spinning, wrenching the ship back, away from Arcadia. She leaned in and scooped some of the fire, the actual, flickering, ephemeral fire, feeling its warmth on her skin, closer to heat now that the exhaustion of pushing them backward had begun to set in.

She rushed along the deck, running with abandon, still singing her uncomfortable song, feeling herself split into two just as she was doing with the fire.

The captain was waiting with the other crew members when she got there, and the plants – their meager stores of defensive plants not bolstered or refilled by their time at port – were already in place as well.

Kindred dropped the flames, which had begun to bite at her hands. They trickled onto the dried plants.

And vanished with only a sizzle and a spot of smoke.

'Shit,' the captain hissed.

Ragged Sarah shouted from her nest above, warning of another incoming volley. It crashed into the hull, and though Kindred couldn't see the damage, the jolt that threw her to the deck suggested it would be massive.

Kindred had begun to sweat, the effort required to keep the

hearthfire burning, to keep the bones hovering, to keep them spinning – all of it too much, too much after running through Arcadia, after watching the devastation of Legate's, after her grandmother's death, her disappearance, her departure. She was thirsty. And tired. And scared.

She tried to rise from the deck but found she could not. Her legs were ghost-things not meant to hold.

The captain and the gathered crew stared at her, confused, but Kindred could not stop the song, not without stopping *The Errant* dead in the grass. Once a ship was sailing in the open Sea and all had been set right within a fire, a keeper could take time away – a few hours sleeping or eating or reading. But for a situation as this, tenuous as pressure on a knife point, she could not stop singing.

She slapped a weak hand against her chest and then mimed picking something up. It took a few times, but eventually, Little Wing understood. She scooped Kindred up and ran, somehow staying upright and moving even as another spell slammed into the side of the ship, rocking them sickeningly. In all of the chaos, Kindred focused on her song, on the spinning bones, on their retreat.

At the hearthfire again – the blaze was a jerky, stuttering thing; flames flared and died on the lengths of crossed bone – Little Wing lowered her, and Kindred reached out a shaking hand to scoop up more of the flames.

And nearly shouted at the heat of them. She was pushing herself too hard, too far – she was losing her connection to the hearthfire.

Another blast from the mages, though, reminded Kindred of her other options, and she steeled herself, singing juddering melodies through clenched teeth. She reached into the flames and scooped out a handful of fiery pain.

She watched the skin beneath the swaying flames begin to heat and bubble, her palm turning into a moving landscape, lit by a burning sun, transforming too quickly. Kindred might have been running or staying still – the world, the ship, Rhabdus, the crew, Little Wing, the mages, her grandmother, Ragged Sarah's kiss, Mick's treachery, Cantrev and his Collective: all of it disappeared and Kindred stared, lost in body and time, at the slow immolation of her hand.

The world returned as Little Wing set her down – roughly, with enough force to jar her teeth and make her realize she'd begun to slow in her singing, winding down toward the inevitable rest. She corrected with a massive effort of will, feeling as though she were being pressed between two boulders rolling slowly closer and closer, crushing her bit by bit.

'The flame, Kindred!' Captain Caraway said. 'Light the flame so we can get some defenses up!'

She dropped her hand to the bundles of plants and released the flames, which filtered down through stems and leaves, leaving only smoky trellises reaching up until finally, finally a hungry flicker spread, and then several stems were burning, and then. And then.

Kindred lay back, holding her burned, raging hand to her chest, singing, singing, until she blacked out from pain, from exhaustion, from keeping the fire.

'Time for more wood on the fire?' the storyteller says, sensing the need to stand and stretch among those listening. Some children have fallen asleep, while others are coiled springs, barely containing their excitement.

A murmur of assent ripples through the listeners, and then they are alive, stretching limbs and asking their questions in quiet tones.

He can hear it all, for he has heard it all countless times before.

'A land bathed in light? Can you imagine?'

'So much and they fought over so little?'

'How have we never heard this tale before?'

The storyteller quirks a smile at these questions, thinking of his last time in Twist, the same questions, the same story. The darkness takes much – and the storyteller certainly will do his part in the taking before his visit is up – but this is perhaps the greatest theft. Memories, even the ones the storyteller will leave, have a way of disappearing without the daylight to give them substance and shine.

When he began so long ago, the storyteller spoke to a sea of nods and communal remembering.

Now he tells the world its history as if it's a myth meant to frighten children and tickle the imagination.

The questions continue spreading, growing in scope and reach with each passing moment. But it's the quiet ones the storyteller pays most attention to, their careful calculated looks, their silence. It's these few who see him not as an object of curiosity, not just as a temporary reprieve from the horrors of the darkness.

In the glimmer of their eyes and the troubled fidgeting of their hands he sees the thing he most hopes for: the beginnings of belief.

'Can I get you anything?' The First again, her hands full of food and drink. An old man, disappearing behind his enormous grey beard, stands behind her, waiting.

'Water, thank you,' he says.

'Hard to believe it was ever so hard to get this,' she says, handing him the cup.

'Yes,' the storyteller says. 'You get yours from wells, I suppose?'

The First nods.

'It's one of the few things we don't have to worry about here,' she says, and the storyteller nods and thinks about the difference between a meager population like Twist's and the massive throng of people that was Arcadia at its peak.

He is about to ask if they still draw from the old well in the basement of the ruins when the old man steps forward and coughs.

'Oh, right,' the First says, turning aside to let the man forward. 'I should not take up all of your time. This is Praise, the oldest member of our community. He's the closest we get to memory here.'

'It's a great pleasure to have you here,' Praise says, shaking the storyteller's hand. 'I wish I had been around for your previous visit, though I'm afraid I wasn't yet born, or not yet old enough to remember it, anyway.'

The storyteller nods, thinking of how he had this exact

conversation with Praise the last time he was in Twist. Praise's beard was shorter and thicker then, and the First had been different – a man with long, strangely blond hair and a bravado that almost certainly had both got and lost him the position.

But the storyteller says nothing, only smiles and thinks about what Praise told him last time about his difficult childhood.

'I had a difficult childhood, of course,' Praise continues, musing. 'As did many here, I suppose. I can't remember my parents well, but I have distinct memories of hard days toiling away at the well, too slight and weak a boy to do anything else. I was quite small.'

People are beginning to return to the fires now, turning their eyes again toward the dais, letting their conversations drift toward silence.

'I don't suppose you know a place I might rest and sleep while I'm here,' the storyteller says, cutting into Praise's monologue. 'You look like a man who knows this place well.'

Praise exchanges a look with the First, a quick flash of surprise before returning to the storyteller.

'I suppose I am,' Praise says, mollified by the compliment. 'And wouldn't you know – I was just getting around to offering you a place in the old building where I live. You can rest, sleep, and relax there all you like.'

The storyteller does, in fact, know, but he widens his eyes and smiles in happy surprise all the same.

'Many, many thanks,' the storyteller says, as if he needs to or could do any of those things anymore.

'I'll show you there during the next break.' With that, Praise turns to go back to his seat, though not before giving a clandestine nod to the First.

It's so human, this need to scheme and plan and profit. He

offers them safety with his visit, and so they sniff at the edges of his offer and seek a longer visit, a longer stay, more safety. Who can blame them?

So human, and yet, the storyteller thinks, feeling the steadying weight of the pack on his shoulder, it doesn't have to be. There have been those to seek and find another way.

The old man wanders back to his seat at the bigger of the two fires, where he sits and begins thinking through what he must do. It will begin with kindness and invitation and end in apologies and chains.

And forgetting. Always forgetting.

'He was most excited about your approach when the scouts first gave word of your approach,' the First says by way of apology, and the storyteller cannot bring himself to hate or even dislike this woman. Like all those who have come before her, she is doing all she can – even that which she finds distasteful or wrong – to keep her people safe. She is just another plant breaking itself in the striving for the sun.

He puts a hand to his pack, still slung over his shoulder, before turning back to his waiting audience, the First moving back down to join them.

All of this inevitability, written on each face, in the fold of each hand, saturated in the words he has heard before and the actions he has undergone and will again before his visit is finished.

But maybe in the crush and press of inevitability, hope might finally flower.

For just a moment, the storyteller hears those long-ago words, full of a new-dawn belief that all might be well: 'I'll see you after.'

'Forget this interlude and return,' the storyteller says to his audience. 'As she leaves it for the last time, let me say briefly how it was that Kindred came to the island city of Arcadia.

'She was born on the huge continent of the Mainland, home to great powers and warring nations. Kindred grew up in a quiet house, daughter to parents who died young in service to a king hungry for more. An orphan with little left to her name, her closest family was her grandmother, strange and estranged, a ship captain on the Forever Sea to the east, a thing of mystery that she had only ever heard of.

'Kindred's first time on a ship was the voyage that carried her away from the pieces of her old life and to something new, something different. Something *wilder*.'

The storyteller pauses and closes his eyes and holds his open hands out, palms up, as if he is holding open a book, one he knows so well, he doesn't need to even look at the pages.

'At first there is nothing but the Forever Sea and the breath of business on the boat. Kindred spends the voyage on the deck, standing fore, eyes trained on the horizon ahead. She eats and drinks little, communicates with no one. She has brought nothing of her old life with her because there was nothing to bring.

'While the ordering of the ship goes on behind her, Kindred Greyreach lets the wind score her face clean of tears and fill her lungs like sails, as if each breath might be the push she needs to move in this new direction. And always, she looks to the horizon, holding it like an anchor, something stable and unchanging and impossibly far away. She wants something she cannot grasp, something impossible, something infinite.

'When she sleeps, it is there on the deck, and none have the heart – or mind – to move this young orphan who has lost everything. And they know the might and temper of the one who has paid her fare.

'Days of travel pass before Arcadia grows on the horizon like a tumor distending its clean line. Lookouts shout and preparations are made, but Kindred does not move. She watches as her new life rises from a field of green and golds, a field that Kindred will come to learn and love in ways most never do. Did.

'Gradually, the city grows from a lump on the horizon to a hive of activity, ships resting at port like the skeletons of huge insects, bare masts and taut lines waiting to be filled with cloth and wind.

'And beyond? The island and its city, not yet gripped by the water shortages that would come to define it. The buildings at the coastline crowd close to one another, like children, small and ungainly, gathering together against the insistent press of the Sea. But further in, as if gaining in confidence, the roofs of homes and businesses and temples rise, giving the whole city the look of sitting on a hill even though it was flat as a windblown rock.

'Everything is the washed-out brown of mud left too long in the sun . . .'

He trails off for a moment, aware of the confusion in the audience.

'Like that bit of wall there,' he says, pointing to the remaining wall of the huge building nearby, most of it a ruin of black, but still a large patch of light brown is visible in the firelight.

How malnourished these people look, how underfed in color and light. He is never sure if the events of his story or the colors and tastes and pleasures of it are hardest for them to imagine.

'Like a mound of dirt-colored rocks swarming with mindless activity, Arcadia rises before this young Kindred. Her life – her new life – is all there waiting for her. A grandmother who will teach her to love and sail the Forever Sea, who will raise her.

'See her there, a youth sailing into promise. And see her now, grown and still growing, fleeing from Arcadia with her crew, toward a different promise.

'Hear again the melody of memory. Her hand burned, her ship and crew put to flight, her destiny tied to a world below, Kindred Greyreach dreams. Remember her now. Remember with me.'

KINDRED raveled and unraveled. Dreams of fire and wind. A world beneath this one. A foundation of darkness holding up a world of endless light. Forevers lining up, one after another.

All was darkness and fire and terror.

Kindred woke in her swaying hammock. Ragged Sarah stood near her, worry and concern on her face, looking down.

Kindred moved to sit up. Ragged Sarah said something, but her voice was a distant bell, and a rising throb in Kindred's head peaked, blanketing her vision and roaring gustily in her ears, and she was again on her back and in darkness.

She woke again, unsure how much time had passed. Kindred found herself alone in her berth, a waterskin in her hand. Instead of trying to sit up again, she took a long drink of water and looked around the room, her eyes feeling like marbles stuck in honey, thick and slow.

Something was wrong, something she couldn't quite see or remember yet. The books on her shelf were where they ought to be and her small chest of possessions still attached to the wall, tied to stave off the roll and rollick of the Sea.

Above and around her, she could hear the sounds of the ship: boots on the deck, voices calling for this or that, wood creaking and singing in the wind. *The Errant* cut through the Sea and –

Kindred felt a pain that was both there and not there as she remembered – all at once, all in a rush – their escape from Cantrev, the fire at the Trade, the damage the ship had taken.

The hearthfire.

Her hand.

She remembered the pain, could almost feel it down in the core of herself, and yet Kindred felt surprise because in that moment, her hand did not hurt.

She also found she couldn't move it.

Slowly, carefully, she lifted her arm from where it hid below her tattered blanket and found her hand swaddled in black cloth, a glove of it, thick and insulated.

This was Ragged Sarah's work. Kindred had seen her use the same black strips of cloth a hundred times, covering wounds large and small. 'A dab of medicine,' she would say, applying gobs of the sunshine-colored stuff she kept in dusty, squat bottles in the medicker's closet. 'And a wrap the color of night,' she would finish, wrapping the dark cloth around the wound with a deft hand.

Kindred tried to flex her hand, to wiggle her fingers, to assert its existence in any way, but nothing happened. The only hint that a hand lay curled or uncurled beneath the black wrap was its heaviness occupying her mind.

A slow scream began to puncture the fog of sleep clouding Kindred's mind as she waited for her hand to move, to flex, to feel something, anything. She pushed and prodded and pinched as best she could through the cloth swaddling. . . and nothing.

A sound like the wind roared in her ears as she sat up too fast, panic driving the blood along her veins, flushing her face with terror. Kindred stood, wracked by waves of nausea, and nearly fell over. Everything spun, and she could barely keep her feet. A single step brought her crashing into a wall, and it was all she could do to right herself and take another step.

Walking was a slow process, but the growing scream in her mind pushed her on, out of her room, and up the narrow, worn steps, stumbling the whole way. She leaned hard against the wall as she went, grimacing at the roil of nausea in her stomach and the clustered storm of a headache.

As she stepped onto the deck, a gust of fresh prairie air caught her hard in the face, and she saw the discord aboard *The Errant*.

'Finally.'

At the helm, the captain leaned into the cock-eyed slant of the quarterdeck. Behind her, Little Wing stood next to the mast, her long body angled with *The Errant*, which rode through smooth grasses at a sharp angle far beyond the comfortable lean sailors were used to, tipping everything on the deck starboard-way. Some crew had simply sat down on deck to avoid contending with the slant – others had hooked themselves to masts or rigging or the gunwale. Still others walked the deck, pretending as though they weren't traversing the side of a great hill or a shallow mountain, striving and failing to keep spines straight, heads up.

'It's about time you woke up. We're in a mess here,' Captain Caraway said. She bore the bruises and cuts of her encounter with Cantrev.

She gestured, and the fog in Kindred's mind finally relented enough for her to understand. Moving carefully along the tilted deck, she clambered toward the hearthfire, which burned chaotically, spastically.

'Those rudimentary hearthfire studies they require for captaincy are piss-poor, it turns out,' Little Wing said as she and the captain both joined Kindred at the fire.

'I tried to get us going forward again after we were out of the mages' range,' Captain Caraway said, the confidence normally found in her voice gone. 'But I couldn't understand your build, Kindred. It was like nothing Rhabdus ever used. Little Wing even pulled out the book of builds they give to every new captain, but we couldn't make sense of what you had done. If it weren't for the strong wind, I don't think we'd be moving at all.'

Anger floated on the surface of the captain's voice, and a kind of accusation, too. Some part of this – perhaps a large part – was her fault.

'Where's Rhabdus? Why couldn't she fix it?'

A beat, and then the captain said, 'She's back on Arcadia, best we can guess. She didn't make it on the boat before we fled.'

The captain was silent a moment, her eye far off on the horizon, as if weighing some heavy decision.

'And so, it's you now,' she said quietly, turning back to Kindred. Next to her, Little Wing nodded, serious.

'What . . .' Kindred began, but the fog in her mind and the nothing that was her hand and the drunken angle of the ship were all too much, and she couldn't understand what the captain was saying.

'You're the senior keeper on board now, Kindred. You're in charge of the fire,' Captain Caraway said, without a hint of a smile, before looking down at the swath of cloth on Kindred's hand. 'Assuming you're up to it.'

Was Kindred, on her first journey as the sole keeper, capable of keeping the hearthfire with only one functioning hand?

'Aye, captain.' It was the only response.

A tiny breath slipped from the captain's lips – it wasn't a sigh of relief, not really, but it was the closest Kindred had ever seen to an admission of fear or worry from her. Fierce, she had seen – relentless and steady and even wild. Behind the wheel, the wind living in her hair, Captain Caraway was a figure cut from stone, jagged smile etched into her face, always a step ahead of the other harvesters or the buyers at the Trade, always ready with a soft or hard word for those who needed them.

But here she was, her stony facade cracking, and Kindred wondered with a chill how bad things needed to be for that to happen.

'Good' was all the captain said. Behind her, Little Wing gave Kindred a grin.

'Now get this fire in order. I expect to be sailing clean soon.' And she was back, the captain in control of her ship, her crew, herself.

Kindred checked on the hearthfire. The bone shards were a mess half-buried in the ashes, and the fire burned low with short, half-formed flickers of flame, sparking into nothingness, receding and flaring without cause or reason. It worked against itself, pushing where it ought to pull, stopping up air where it shouldn't. With so little internal consistency in the hearthfire, Kindred was surprised it was even holding *The Errant* up at all.

The captain had been right: without the strong wind, they would have been dead in the grass.

Kindred opened her mind to the hearthfire, feeling its power rush through the well-worn channels in her mind. Its sparking, fragmented flames stilled in her presence, and she began singing quietly, preparing the way. She reached for the bones.

The bandages were smoking, heating too fast before Kindred realized what she'd done. Like a fool, she had reached both hands into the flames – burned and unburned alike. She yanked her bandaged hand back, cradling it to her chest.

The spirit of the fire, always so present and calming in Kindred's mind, her ghost, her kind haunting, pulled back.

'No, no,' she whispered.

To keep the hearthfire was to make covenant with the flames, to trust the fire and be trusted by it. It was a conversation, and one the fire was now frightened of having with her.

Other hearthfire keepers – every other one Kindred had met save the Marchess – treated the fire and its bones like machines to be wrenched and fixed and owned. But Kindred's way was different. She worked by touch, by feel, by the song she heard from the fire. And right now, that song was uncertainty.

Kindred looked around and saw crew and captain desperately trying to not watch her, to appear casual and busy and focused elsewhere.

With a breath, she prepared to try again.

'I wouldn't,' a voice said from above her, and Kindred tried not to look too startled as she turned around. Ragged Sarah hung from the mainmast, her medicker's bag slung from one shoulder, a roll of her black cloth in hand. She dropped the rest of the way to the deck and settled down next to Kindred, like a wall between her and the rest of the crew.

'How long until the numbness goes away?' Kindred asked, keeping her voice low.

'In your hand?' Ragged Sarah asked, cocking her head but matching the quiet of Kindred's voice.

'Yes,' Kindred said, holding out her black-wrapped limb. 'There's not much pain, but I'm having a hard time moving it.' She gestured toward the medicker's bag. 'Do I just have to wait out the salve's effects or do you have something else to bring back movement and feeling?'

Ragged Sarah set down her bag but did not open it. She stared down at her own hands for a long time.

'Kindred, none of the salves I use have any numbing effects.'

'But . . .' she began, looking down at the formlessness of her hand beneath the swaddling cloth.

'The burn,' Ragged Sarah said, 'it went . . . deep. I've never seen anything that bad. Skin charred and tough, like dried sailcloth. I did everything I could, Kindred, but . . .'

Kindred wanted to speak, to clarify or understand, but she could not. Ragged Sarah's voice rolled over her.

'I can't say if you'll ever be able to use your hand again, not with any articulation. It's possible the salves may work to recover some of the feeling or maybe even all of the feeling, but it's also just as likely that they won't. My medicines have been keeping infection away, which is the primary concern right now, but they won't last. We need real medical care, more than I can give on this ship . . .'

Kindred lost her focus on Ragged Sarah, on the ship, on the

crew and captain who depended on her to keep them sailing.

She didn't know if she could keep the fire with just one hand; she'd never seen it done before, didn't even know if it was theoretically possible.

And if she couldn't keep the fire?

Kindred had finally found a communal purpose, fitting herself into the delicate, beautiful machinery of the ship. She had just found her niche aboard this vessel, had learned to love her place in and among the crew. But what if she could no longer fit into that machinery, if she was no longer a part of the whole? Ships did not sail with excess crew members – every sailor had a purpose; every sailor was a resource perfectly suited to her position.

Was she doomed to fail before she had even truly begun?

A rill of fear spiked through her as she realized she would have to tell the captain, she would have to confess that she couldn't keep the fire any longer, could no longer serve the ship, the crew.

She found herself thinking of the Marchess, walking away into the Sea. Trading the many for one, leaving behind her own beautiful machinery and her place in it, seeking out something for herself.

And unsought, unasked, an image rose in Kindred's mind, forming out of the miasma and chaos of the last few days.

She saw herself falling down through the Sea, the green fading into black and then a darkness without color or shape but inhabited nonetheless, first by wyrms and their slumbering vines and ants and roaches and then by larger creatures, some with eyes like the world, glowing, some with fearsome teeth and tails and tusks, some whispering endlessly in languages never written down or heard. She saw the world below and herself, alone, or perhaps not alone, falling through the Forever Sea, through the forever that no one talked about. Below the waves, Kindred found everything.

'Kindred? Hello?' Ragged Sarah snapped her fingers in front of Kindred's face, pulling her up and out of the darkness. 'I said I'll check back later on to change the bandage and give you some more salve.'

Kindred nodded, feeling the dregs of the daydream leaving her. As she got up to go, Ragged Sarah put a hand on her shoulder.

'I know it doesn't mean much, but I'm really sorry.'

Kindred put her own hand – the left one, unwrapped – on Sarah's but didn't say anything.

Alone, Kindred returned to the fire, to her fear.

She sang high, soft songs of entreaty and reached for the fire with her unburned hand.

And pulled back, hissing her pain at the flames.

She sang low, pulsing songs of demand and reached for the fire with her unburned hand.

And pulled back.

She sang quick and pulled back.

She sang dissonance and pulled back.

Again and again she tried, but the fire had taken her seed of fear and sown distrust. It did not see her as a friend and it did not see her as one to be trusted.

Kindred felt tears of anger pushing at her eyes, and suddenly she was a young girl again, ten years old, maybe eleven, and she was sitting on the deck of *Revenger* as the Marchess lectured her.

'You can't be afraid of the fire, child. It's a living thing, this blaze, and it responds to strength and self-possession. Do you have strength? Do you know yourself?'

Kindred had flexed her muscles, eliciting a laugh from the Marchess.

'Not strength of arm. I mean here.' She pointed a finger, poking Kindred in the chest. 'Do you have strength here?'

'I don't know.'

'You don't know?' Her grandmother shook her head. 'You have to know.'

The Marchess stared into her eyes and stuck her hand into the flames.

Kindred gasped, but her grandmother only laughed, opening her mouth wide, letting the mirth escape onto the wind.

'Now you.'

They'd sat on the deck all day, her grandmother pushing her, encouraging her, mocking her, entreating her, and Kindred snaking a single finger toward the fire at first, then a few fluttering fingers, then a hand – flashing into the fire and then back – and then, slowly, beginning to sense the fire in her mind, she had put her hand in and held it.

Her grandmother sang during each attempt, and when Kindred finally left her hand in the fire, feeling the waves of flame caress and flicker around her skin, welcoming her, she'd heard the fire singing back, a ghost voice echoing in the long caverns of her mind.

'Do you hear that?' her grandmother stopped her song and asked, smiling wide.

Through the astonishment, the sting of tears in her eyes, Kindred could only nod, mouth open, hand buried in the hearthfire.

It was a memory she cherished: her first time communing with the hearthfire, her first time feeling purpose aboard a ship.

Sitting in front of the fire now, memories of pain raging through her hand, Kindred felt anew the poke into her chest, the intelligent eyes appraising her. *Do you have strength? Do you know yourself?*

'Yes. Yes,' she said, gritting her teeth. She plunged a hand, unburned, faithful, deep into the fire.

It burned at first. Kindred had heard the crude protestations of other keepers on other ships refer to the process as 'breaking the fire,' as one might break a beast, tame it, conquer its spirit. Disgusting and repugnant.

Instead, Kindred thought of it as a self-statement: she told the fire she was strong, she was confident, she knew herself. She did not ask the fire to be anything other than what it was; instead, she asked the fire to see her in itself, to see her for herself.

And after a moment of fiery panic in which the flames pushed back, exhaling heat and worry, the fire saw her, joying again through her mind, an old friend worried for another only to find out she will be all right. The heat faded and left her hand again in the comforting flick and pulse of the flames.

She considered her other hand, the black wrap still smoking slightly, but she knew it to be folly. The fire had welcomed her anew, but it could not cure her hand. Kindred shuddered a little thinking of it, remembering skin bubbling, blistering, blackening.

A pulse of wind came over the deck and Kindred breathed it in, stilling herself. She let her fears and anxieties be drawn away to disappear among the forever thrash of the Sea.

She focused on the task at hand.

The Errant leaned starboard-way, and Kindred looked through the bones until she found the three thick splinters tangled together in the ash that were causing the tilt. Green deckhands, untried and untrained, often stepped aboard a harvesting ship thinking the hearthfire was good only for keeping a ship up, keeping it away from the vast nothing below the waves of green. They soon understood their ignorance.

Singing a high, lilting song, Kindred broke the connection between the splinters, her movements awkward as she found her way with just one hand, missing the dominance and surety of the other.

A wind sighed out from the fire as the pressure from the awkwardly fused bones released. The hearthfire flickered and flushed a deep, contented purple and *The Errant* groaned as long timbers shifted and stretched against one another.

The ship tipped back toward equilibrium.

Kindred watched the deck swing to true and go past, the weight and speed of it all too much. Grasses and seeds and pollen exploded into the air as *The Errant* rocked itself to a point of stability and crushed the Sea plants to either side of it. The sky was briefly clouded with the eructations of the Sea, and Kindred's ears filled with the cheers of the crew.

She was back. *The Errant* sailed true again, and the Forever Sea stretched ahead. Kindred released a breath she didn't know she'd been holding and stood, quieting her song into silence.

Captain Caraway gave her a nod.

'Best keeper on the Sea!' came a shout from above, and Kindred looked up to see Ragged Sarah, her smile wide, looking down from the crow's nest.

Kindred let out a shaky sigh, relief and joy filling her. This new build was a mess, and it would never do for the long term, but for this moment, it was a victory.

'That is a terrible fucking idea.'

Kindred swallowed a gasp at Little Wing's words. Captain Caraway may have given them permission to speak freely when she invited Kindred, Little Wing, and Ragged Sarah into her quarters, but it was still the kind of statement Kindred would have avoided, even now. That kind of language on deck, if directed at the captain, would have guaranteed chains and probably the green dive.

They were all seated around the table, which dominated the captain's quarters, the map covering it having been reworked and added on to so much that it hung off the edges of the table at some points, thirty or forty sheets thick at others. In one corner of the room Kindred could see the captain's bed, a simple hammock like her own. Other than that, the room was spare. The captain lived her life out on the deck.

Kindred wondered why the captain had invited Ragged Sarah. She wasn't unhappy about it, and she was almost too aware of how close her feet were to Sarah's under the table, but senior crew usually meant only captain, quartermaster, and keeper.

Only a few days earlier, Kindred had been suspended, and now here she was, at this table, bellied up to this map. Somehow, she thought with more than a little disbelief, senior crew now meant *her*, although she didn't feel very senior.

'We have to consider every option, Little Wing,' the captain said, her voice was steady, passionless. She gestured to the map; at the center lay Arcadia like an oversized boil, surrounded by the uneven circle of its flattened grasses. To the west was the enormous mass of the Mainland consuming the entire side of the map. The capital city, which Kindred had not returned to since the death of her parents and her exodus from the Mainland, was a star on the landmass's edge.

To the north, the Mists. To the south, the barren Scrubwastes.

And to the east? The forever that gave the Sea its name. Rough grasses as far as any had ever been able to discover. Sure, boats had left for whatever lay beyond the eastern horizon and not returned, and some speculated that perhaps they'd found the end of forever, but there had never been any evidence of that.

'We can make it to the Mainland,' Little Wing said, sitting forward and drawing an arc from their current position – somewhere northeast of Arcadia, halfway out the line where the flattened grasses would give way to the Roughs. 'Cantrev will have created defenses, sure, but that bastard thinks we're traveling east. If we loop north, toward the Mists, we can pass by Cantrev's ships and bypass Arcadian grasses completely. We'd be in the Roughs most of the way, but we can handle it, captain.'

'And our water stores? Cantrev's men took almost all of it. We have five days of sailing left. Six, maybe.'

'We ration. We ration the rations. We can make up for it by skimming dew each morning. And once we get into the Mists, we can open up the rain catches; I've heard sailors say it rains at least once a span there.'

The captain was staring hard at the map, her eyes tracing Little Wing's arc over and over again.

'Even to get to the Mists from our current position would take two span or longer, and that's if we burn hard,' the captain said. 'And even if we could skim enough dew to keep us watered and put out the fires of mutiny the crew would have if I rationed their rations, there's the eidolons of the Mists to worry about.'

Little Wing grimaced and said, 'That's all nonsense. The eidolons don't exist.'

'Sailors don't come back from the Mists,' Captain Caraway said quietly.

'We could,' Little Wing said, sitting up straighter in her chair, jaw jutting. 'With this crew and this ship? With you leading us? We could.'

The captain turned to Ragged Sarah and Kindred, leaving behind Little Wing's disagreements.

'And the two of you? What do you think? We either sail for the Mainland . . .'

The captain traced the same arc Little Wing had.

'. . . or we sail east, into the Roughs, into uncharted grasses, toward the Once-City.'

Little Wing held up her hand.

'I still think this is a terrible fucking idea.'

'We dock at the Once-City and beg sanctuary,' the captain continued, letting her finger slide into the ambiguously labeled Roughs on the map, never stopping on a single point. 'Barter for water and supplies, and regroup. The Once-City has access to all kinds of plants and magics, the stories say; it may be that we can barter for even more than water. A fixed-up ship? New medical supplies? I don't know, but it seems worth a try. And we don't have the casting plants on board to stave off an assault from Cantrev, and even if we did, a bare handful of the crew can cast.'

Kindred looked to Ragged Sarah, who stared down into her lap, strangely silent and nervous. A smile – mischievous or genuine, playful or serious – never seemed far from Sarah's face, and yet now she had the air of someone staring down into her own grave. Eyes wide, unable to still her hands.

New medical supplies? She glanced down at the nothingness that was her hand, hiding in the dark cloth of Sarah's wrap.

'Well?' Captain Caraway said, looking at Kindred. 'What do you think?'

Under any other circumstances, the captain asking for her opinion would have made Kindred sing with joy, but now, given the choice they were making there, she wished only for an order.

'Pirates live in the Once-City,' she said finally.

The captain nodded but said nothing, so Kindred pushed ahead.

'We'll never reach it; if we don't have enough casting plants to defend ourselves against one of Cantrev's warships – and he's certainly dispatched them by now – we won't be able to fight off the pirates who will almost definitely intercept us on the way to the Once-City.'

She paused, but still the captain sat silent, watching her, waiting.

'And assuming we did manage to get there without being caught by pirates, we have to trust the rumors that safe passage is offered to any who "beg sanctuary,"' she said. 'But what if that's not true? Then we're docked in a city full of pirates and there's nothing to stop them from cutting our throats, stealing the plants and bones aboard, taking you, captain, for your bones, and scuttling or stealing our ship.

'But that's all assuming we can get there, because the Once-City is out in the Roughs, which none of us have sailed in before or are prepared for in the least . . .'

Kindred trailed off.

If you seek me, look below.

The Marchess had sailed out into the Roughs before stepping into the Sea. The Roughs, where the flattening, stultifying magic of Arcadia and the Mainland had not yet reached. The Roughs, where wondrous stories grew from seeds into mighty myths, some perhaps even gilded with an edge of truth.

The wonder of the Roughs, the Marchess had said in her letter. Did she sail all the way to the Once-City, looking for answers to the Greys? Did she parley with pirates, converse with their dangerous captains? It was an insane thought, but if Kindred could imagine anyone sailing up to the mythical Once-City and finding a welcome there that didn't involve swords and death, it was the Marchess.

Kindred's first steps had been on the Mainland. The house she'd grown up in. The holes she'd watched her parents buried in. Every bit of the person Kindred had once been was back there. The prairie wind had scoured her clean, had greened her breath and her imagination. There was no going back.

'Yes? It's out in the Roughs. Keep going,' the captain said after a moment, a small smile on her face.

'What? Oh, right,' Kindred said, pulling herself back to this moment. But her certainty that the plan was a bad one had evaporated, and the fire in her voice had gone, too.

'I was saying the Once-City is out in the Roughs, which none of us have sailed in. Not that we couldn't, but *The Errant* would take damage. And even after we sail through the Roughs – if we do – there's the problem of finding the Once-City, which is apparently only discoverable by someone who has already been there, if you believe the stories.'

She finished with a note of uncertainty, suddenly unsure where she stood. Little Wing was nodding, as if Kindred had only validated her point, but the captain was still smiling, broader now.

'I happen to believe the stories. And we have someone aboard who has been to the Once-City.'

Kindred started at the captain for a moment, trying to understand what she was saying, but Captain Caraway said nothing more, her single eye alive with that same manic energy from before, that same need to push further, that same wild light.

'But only pirates have been to the Once-City,' Kindred said, speaking slowly. 'You're saying we have a pirate aboard?'

Captain Caraway said nothing.

Little Wing shook her head, frowning.

Ragged Sarah held Kindred's eyes with her own for a moment and then, with a sigh, said, 'Me.'

SILENCE commanded the room, weighty and uncertain.

'You're a pirate?' Kindred felt far away from this room, this conversation. She floated, confused but unaffected by it somehow.

'No,' Ragged Sarah said, eyes wide. 'No. Not anymore.'

'Not anymore?'

'I was born in the Once-City, but I left as soon as I could. I hated it there.'

Kindred thought of the pirates who had chased them into port only a few days before, of the pirates who had stolen ships and killed friends of hers, of Little Wing's friend aboard *The Blue Sky*.

'But you were a pirate at one point?' The question came out of her mouth in a dry, emotionless tumble. She floated.

'I . . .' Sarah looked around, eyes small, quick things. She leaned forward toward Kindred and, her voice soft and pleading, said, 'Just when I was younger. But only for a few years, and then I left, Kindred. I moved to Arcadia and lived there, doing small jobs and going on single tours with ships when I could.'

Sarah had created a conversation just for the two of them,

but Kindred listened as if she were on the outside of it. She saw the colored strands of Ragged Sarah's hair anew, the tattoos ranging across her skin, the quick flash of her teeth as she spoke.

'Did you know when you hired her?' Little Wing asked, and Kindred realized another conversation was going on. Little Wing spoke as if Ragged Sarah didn't exist, her body fully turned toward Captain Caraway. One hand, Kindred saw, rested on the hilt of a sword.

'I did,' Captain Caraway said, speaking to everyone in the room, stomping out the smaller conversations.

'You've known this whole time? And never told the crew?' Little Wing's eyes were hard, and she sat dangerously still, a spring curled tight.

This was Captain Little Wing, Kindred thought. This was a woman ready to command her own vessel, to lead a crew, to make decisions.

'Ragged Sarah has my full confidence,' Captain Caraway said, speaking slowly. She stared back until Little Wing looked away. 'And none of you were brought in here to question Sarah's fitness to serve. We have a decision to make, and it's one I don't take lightly, which is why I'm not making it.'

This had been the arrangement as the captain had explained it. She would abstain from voting, and the three of them would decide. A group decision for a group action.

'I vote – ' Little Wing began, but Captain Caraway raised a hand, cutting her off.

'I want you to take the rest of the day to think about this. It's a decision that will change our fates, and I want none of us' – she cut a look toward Little Wing – 'making it without full consideration. We

175

will meet again at sunset, and I expect your answers then.'

A knock at the door pulled Captain Caraway to her feet. Outside, Cora the Wraith stood.

'A quick question, captain, if you have a moment.'

With a calculated look at the three of them, the captain stepped out of her quarters and closed the door.

Little Wing stood up, one hand still on a sword, the other planted on the map as she looked down, shaking her head slowly.

'You're a pirate?'

'No,' Ragged Sarah said. 'I was a pirate. *Was*. I was a teenager, and yes, I did some things I'm ashamed of, things a dumb teenager raised in that place would have done. But I turned my back on all of that. I gave it all up and left when I realized what it meant to be a pirate and what my life would be like.'

'Did you know the pirates who were chasing us into port two days ago?'

'What? No, of course not,' Sarah said.

'*Canticle* was captured by pirates twenty days ago. *The Nettle* just a few days ago. Did you know the pirates who did that?'

'No, I don't know any – '

But Little Wing continued, her voice building like a storm.

'We're not sure, since no one survived, but if that pirate attack is like any of the others actually witnessed, the pirates took the captain for her bones and tossed the keeper overboard. Without her aboard, the hearthfire would eventually die away, so *Canticle's* crew probably watched as their captain sailed away, already getting butchered for her bones, all while they sank into the Sea.'

'It was a lifetime ago, Little Wing – '

'Do you know the pirates who did that?'

Sarah did not respond.

Little Wing's hand slapped the table, the flat of her palm exploding against the wood.

'Do you?'

Ragged Sarah looked ready to break, though whether she would break toward anger or terror, Kindred didn't know. She looked across the table at Kindred, eyes asking what she could not.

'Enough,' Captain Caraway said, her voice low and dangerous. She stood in the doorway. 'We have enough against us without crew turning against crew. Little Wing, do you really think I would let someone on board my ship without making damn sure they were not a danger to my crew and vessel? She has my full confidence, *and so, by extension, does she have yours.*'

The captain stared at them all, one by one.

'Votes by sundown. You all have jobs to do.'

One by one, they stood and left the captain's quarters. Little Wing first, the muscles of her jaw bulging as she walked out. Sarah went next, but not before looking at Kindred and saying, very quietly, 'I'm sorry I didn't tell you. I wanted to leave all of that behind me.'

Kindred walked to the door last but stopped there, wishing she had a less tumultuous opportunity for this conversation.

'Captain? I hope it's all right, but I need to talk with you about the hearthfire.'

Already, the words she had practiced, the easy tone in her voice, the confident, almost casual way she was going to hold her arms – already, all of it was dripping away from her mind, lost as Captain Caraway turned a distracted, harried look upon her.

'What is it? More problems like before? Or with . . .' She looked down at the dark cloth swaddling Kindred's hand.

'Oh, no. No, no,' Kindred said quickly, moving her hand around behind her back. 'All fine there. But if I'm now the senior keeper, we will need to find a junior keeper. To help. Not because I need it. But in case we're chased again, and definitely when we reach the Roughs.'

It was all coming out garbled, little fragments of her logic, and the cracks running between them were glaringly obvious. She should've waited. Or said nothing. Maybe she could scuttle the whole idea and struggle through on her own, find some way to keep the fire with just one hand. Just long enough to reach . . . wherever they were going.

'It's probably too much to think about right now,' Kindred said, filling the space with more words as the captain continued to stare at her, expression unreadable. 'I'll just keep on and we can figure something out once we settle on a course and reach our destination.'

'No, Kindred,' Captain Caraway said, putting a hand on her shoulder, her face clearing suddenly into resolution. 'It's a good idea. Better to be prepared. Shall I pick someone? Or would you like to? We've always put out a call on the Trade board in Arcadia for new crew in the past; I confess, I don't know how best to manage it while we're out at Sea.'

Excitement thrilled through Kindred as she tried to maintain whatever composure she already had.

She nodded, frowning at the problem as if she hadn't already thought this through, as if she didn't already have a plan.

'There's a test my grandmother used to do, one that she gave me when I started keeping the fire. Just a basic aptitude test. I can run it for the crew and pick the best person based on that. If it's all right with you, of course.'

The sounds of struggle filtered in through the partially open door, and the captain cocked her head, listening, her already divided attention split even further.

'That's just fine, keeper. Do you have everything you need?'

Are we done? was what she was really asking.

'Absolutely, captain. I'll let you know once I've finished.'

'Excellent,' the captain said, already moving toward the door. 'Have it done soon, if possible. And don't forget: I need your decision by sundown.'

It had been a lie, in a way. Her grandmother had never given her this test, but she had seen the Marchess give it to others, the few new crew members who came aboard *Revenger* during Kindred's time there.

First up was Long Quixa, her arm still in the sling Sarah had rigged up for her. Long and tall and thin, easily twice Kindred's age, Quixa settled herself in front of the fire as Kindred had instructed, her willowy legs forming tight angles as she sat on the deck. She was always serious, Quixa, her blue eyes always seeming to take in more of the world than anyone Kindred had ever met. She said little and saw much.

'Good,' Kindred said, sitting opposite Quixa, across the fire. 'Do you know the basics of the hearthfire?'

Quixa nodded after a moment of thought but said nothing.

'Can you tell me what you know?' Kindred said after a moment of silence.

'Yes,' Quixa said, and a horrible moment of silence followed that in which Kindred thought she would need to prompt Quixa again. She had worried about it being odd, her one of the youngest sailors aboard, testing the crew, many of whom were old enough to be her mother, and it was turning out exactly that way. But then Quixa spoke.

'The hearthfire is the beating heart of the ship. Its power keeps us afloat over the grasses below, and it gives us forward push as well as stability. Without it, the wind might push us forward thanks to the sails, but it would be no use; we would sink.'

'Yes, good,' Kindred said. 'And a keeper's job is to build structures of bone inside the fire to aid in those things.' She gestured to the arrayed bones in the bone closet; she had propped open the door. 'Certain builds are better suited for certain actions, and a keeper uses her magic – and the magic of the fire – to shape the bones to those purposes.'

'Why do you build them in the fire?' Quixa asked, her eyes moving slowly over to the door of the bone closet, which she would have seen filled with the rows of bones. 'Why not build them ahead of time and simply drop the appropriate build in?'

Kindred nodded and smiled. It was the right kind of question, and maybe, just maybe, it meant Quixa had some natural inclination with the fire.

'The bones need the magic of the flames to be joined together. Without it, there's nothing to hold them. String or cloth would burn away before a keeper could get in to join the bones together in a true way.'

Quixa nodded slowly, chewing over Kindred's response.

'But all of that comes much later. Right now, let's just start with the basics. There are five rules to keeping the fire,' Kindred said. 'One: speed in tenuous length. The longer and leaner the build, and the longer and slimmer the bones, the faster the ship will go. Two: solidity in bolstered support. In rough grasses or high winds or any other situation where you need support, a build that is bolstered on all sides will offer more stability to the ship. The same goes for builds where tight turns are needed.

'Three: arcs in green; spirals in gold. In green grasses, shape bones toward arcs; in golden grasses, shape toward spirals. Four: the fire burns first and hottest at the base.'

The Marchess had never been so clear about such things. It was always demonstration only, forcing Kindred to interpret her movements, her songs, her builds. If Kindred wanted to learn something, she would have to steal it from the casual, worn practices of her grandmother.

Except for the last rule, of course, the one Kindred had been given by the Marchess and not the fire.

'And five,' Kindred said finally. 'Do not circumscribe the fire. Never, under any circumstances, should you ring the fire in bone.'

Quixa had been silent through all of this, her eyes watching Kindred's movements, arms and hands moving to demonstrate what she was saying, but now she said, 'Why not?'

'It would kill the fire,' Kindred said quietly. 'It would be the green dive for everyone on board.'

If you seek me, look below, she thought.

'Well,' Quixa said after a moment, slow and ponderous. 'We don't want that.'

'No,' Kindred said, nodding quickly. 'We don't. But you don't need to worry about any of that now. I just wanted to give you a sense of how these things worked before we begin. Let's begin the test.'

'All right, then,' Quixa said, her nod as careful and measured as her speech.

'I'm going to test you for any natural ability with the hearthfire. First, I'll test your singing and then your listening. For this first part, I want you to mimic me as exactly as possible. This is a simple song for asking the fire to burn through the build faster, which in turn should push us along faster.'

Quixa nodded again.

Kindred sat forward a little and sang, her song simple and insistent, calling to the fire in its language, asking for hunger and heat. The flames, until then a bland orange, shivered and flared into a deep, lush purple. She sang for a few bars before changing the melody and letting the fire sigh back to orange. In her mind, the music of the fire rose and fell as it burned first faster and then slower.

'Okay,' she said, sitting back, hearing the song in her head fade again into the background, always there. 'Try that.'

Kindred kept in a smile as Quixa, her voice normally so low and stately, sang in a high, scratchy register that skittered about, trying and failing to find the simple melody Kindred had demonstrated.

It was no good. Kindred watched the fire, and felt it, but it did not respond to Quixa, even in the few instances when she found the right notes or sang the correct words in the twisting language of the hearthfire.

'Good,' Kindred said as Quixa finished. Her grandmother used to cackle with glee at the awful results of her tests, hooting at the frayed voices and missed notes. Kindred could never tell if there had been any teeth in it, any edge to her laughter, or if it had simply been the wild joy that seemed always to be present in her grandmother.

But she was going to do it differently, and so she smiled encouragingly at Quixa and nodded.

'That was very nicely done. Now I want you to listen carefully – not just with your ears but with . . .' How could she describe what she barely understood, what she had done for so long by intuition and feel alone? '. . . with your whole self, if you can. Try to still your thoughts and let your whole body listen for the fire. I want you to tell me if you can hear its song.'

'It sings?' Quixa said. 'Is it singing right now?'

'Yes,' Kindred nodded. 'But very quietly. Listen, and I'll encourage it to sing louder.'

Singing quietly at a low pitch, Kindred leaned forward and shifted the build – the simplest that she could manage with just one hand. A single bone was moderating the amount of air entering and leaving the build, and Kindred lifted it out of the fire.

In answer, the fire climbed high, flames dancing in different colors, first red, then blue, then a vibrant, powerful orange. The song in her mind, such a constant friend that Kindred often forgot it was there, rose louder and higher, bounding from joyful note to joyful note.

Quixa sat, silent and still, until Kindred reached into the fire, again with just one hand, and replaced the bone. Almost immediately, the fire settled back down.

'Well?'

Quixa shook her head.

'I didn't hear anything but Cora stumbling around with that empty barrel,' she said, looking over across the deck where Cora the Wraith was lugging a half-full barrel of water – skimmed that morning – while cursing to herself. As old as Quixa but half as tall,

Cora was next on Kindred's short list of crew who didn't have any other jobs and could serve as a keeper to be trained.

'Thanks, Quixa. Cora,' Kindred said, loud enough to be heard over the cursing. 'Your turn.'

Kindred's list – Long Quixa, Cora the Wraith, Stone-Gwen, and Scindapse – was not nearly as long as she would've liked it to be, but given that only a portion of the crew had made it back on the boat during the escape there were only a few people who actually had jobs that could be dropped in favor of aiding her with the fire.

Cora the Wraith – short and muscular, with dark hair cut close and a gap-toothed smiled that played constantly across her face – showed some ability in singing but none with listening. Like Rhabdus had been, Cora was a good mimic, parroting the words of the hearthfire's language even though she didn't understand or recognize them as anything more than noise. Cora often entertained the crew with imitations of other people – crew, captains of other ships (never Captain Caraway), well-known personalities from Arcadia. Probably that explained it. It was something, and Kindred could make it work.

Stone-Gwen was next. She had suffered an accident as a child that had left her with only one ear and a permanently distended lower jaw, but she could still hear and sing just fine. Stone-Gwen was the only devoutly religious member of the crew, at least as far as Kindred knew.

She was fat and strong. Kindred had once seen a huge steel-banded cudgel in her room and asked her about it, and, with some prodding, Gwen had told Kindred stories about her days fighting for the crazed king on the Mainland. Afterward, Kindred had tried to lift the cudgel and only barely managed it.

Unlike the others, who sat back from the fire, Stone-Gwen showed a surprising comfort with it, sitting right next to the blaze. Unfortunately, she could barely find even a handful of the notes Kindred sang, and she couldn't hear anything in the hearthfire. Not really a surprise, of course; only a bare handful of keepers could ever hear the music of the flames.

Last was Scindapse, youngest member of the crew and the newest addition to the ship. She had been brought on after one of their harvesters had retired, but *The Errant* was unlikely to be doing any harvesting soon, so Kindred put her name on the list, along with the other harvesters, Quixa and Cora. Stone-Gwen was only a deckhand, and since she seemed to help with everything, it had made sense to try her on the fire, too.

'And five,' Kindred said to Scindapse, watching the young girl, barely seventeen, shift and fidget where she sat on the other side of the fire. 'Never circumscribe the fire.'

'Okay,' Scindapse said, with a quick bob of her head.

Poor girl, Kindred thought. *She has family back on Arcadia, and here we are, sailing anywhere but home.*

Her voice, when she finally sang after some prompting from Kindred, was shaky and weak, but the fire flickered violet for just a moment, and Kindred felt, with some surprise, *The Errant* push forward, gaining speed in some small amount.

'Great,' Kindred said after Scindapse finished, her eyes squeezed shut against her own singing. 'And now I want you to listen –

with your whole body, if you can. Let your mind go quiet. And stop that fidgeting.' She gave the younger girl a smile that, with a self-conscious glance down at her hands, Scindapse returned.

'I want you to tell me if you can hear anything from the fire – words, a melody, anything. Ready?'

Scindapse nodded, and Kindred took away the bone again. The fire climbed high, and once more its song soared.

'Nothing,' Scindapse said after Kindred replaced the bone and the fire had settled back into its steady state.

'That's all right,' Kindred said, smiling again. 'You did a nice job.'

Scindapse nodded, stood, and walked off.

'Wints! Gwen! Check the grommets on the foremast sails! Step to!'

Captain Caraway ordered the ship with calm and ease from the wheel, seeing everything, always in control.

Kindred stood a few steps back, waiting for her to finish directing Wints and Stone-Gwen. Scindapse and Little Wing were working on the aft casting-fire basins, which had been damaged in their flight from Arcadia. As she waited, Kindred listened to Little Wing directing Scindapse, her tone kinder, more generous than usual.

Captain Little Wing, taking care of her crew.

'We only have a bit of sunlight left, sailors; let's use it!' she said before turning to Kindred. The sun hung low in the sky, soon to crash through the horizon.

But first this.

'Cora, captain,' Kindred said, stepping forward. 'It'll have to be Cora.'

'Fine,' Captain Caraway said. 'Begin her training at once.'

'Thank you, captain,' Kindred said. 'I don't expect it to take much of her time, so . . .'

A melody, familiar and frustratingly off, pulled at Kindred's attention, and she forgot what she was saying. For a moment, she looked back toward the hearthfire still blazing happily amidships. But no one was there, and its melody, faint in the back of her mind, had settled back into something slow and staid.

'Keeper?' Captain Caraway stared at her, one eyebrow raised. 'Are you all right?'

Where was that melody coming from? It was painful to hear, almost every note just slightly off, the tone splintering as the melody climbed higher, the voice weak and untrained, and –

'Scindapse!' Kindred said, nearly shouted, as she whirled around to see the young girl working away at one of the basins.

And singing to herself.

'What?' she said, startled, eyes wide as she looked up. Kindred almost tripped as she ran over to her, leaving Captain Caraway looking confused at the wheel.

'Sing that again,' she said, dropping to her knees in front of Scindapse, who, after a moment of silence, did.

'I thought you couldn't hear anything,' Kindred said, unable to keep her voice from rising with excitement. 'You said you couldn't hear the fire!'

'I couldn't,' Scindapse said, leaning back slightly. Next to her, Little Wing was watching with bemused interest.

'But . . .' Kindred started, tilting her head to the side and considering Scindapse. 'But where did you hear that melody you were just singing?'

'I'm not really sure,' Scindapse said after a moment, shaking her head slightly. 'It's just in my head, I guess.'

'*That's the music of the flames,*' Kindred said, leaning forward and putting her hands, one swathed and one not, on Scindapse's shoulders, her grin wide on her face. 'You can hear it, too!'

'You keepers are all nuts,' Little Wing said, smiling and returning to her work.

'Captain,' Kindred said, standing and turning back to Captain Caraway, who was watching, her mouth still open in confusion. 'Scratch what I just said. It'll be Scindapse; she's the new junior keeper.'

'Fine,' Captain Caraway said, looking between her and Scindapse and Little Wing, obviously weighing if this was something she wanted to ask about or not. Her other concerns won out as she turned back to the wheel. 'Start as soon as possible,' she said over her shoulder.

'Aye, captain,' Kindred said, before turning back to Scindapse. She could remember how Rhabdus had treated her right away, scornful of this new keeper, angry at having more responsibilities and angrier at having to share what she saw as her place on the ship.

Kindred would not be a teacher like Rhabdus; that much she was sure of.

'I'll show you the basics now, but we'll really begin after sundown,' Kindred told her, smiling wide.

She had a decision to make, and the dying light meant she had to hurry.

'Sarah,' Kindred called up the mainmast. 'Sarah.'

At first, there was no response, even though Kindred knew Sarah was there. But she couldn't shout for fear of drawing attention, particularly the captain or Little Wing's, and so Kindred continued to whisper-call up toward the crow's nest.

'Sarah. Ragged Sarah.'

She could hear conversation, low and quiet, coming from the wooden confines of the nest, and Kindred felt a twist in her stomach at the thought of someone being up there with Sarah, someone sharing her secrets.

'Sarah,' she called again, louder this time.

A wild-haired shadow extended from the cloud of darkness that was the crow's nest in the gloaming.

'Kindred?'

'Can you come down? Maybe you're busy, I – ' Kindred began, but Ragged Sarah was already moving, her shape blooming from a shadowed head to all of her, plummeting closer as she dropped down the mainmast. As she did, several dark shapes, each the size of a fist and flitting almost faster than Kindred could see, darted out into the sky.

Of course. She had been talking to birds.

'Wanted to talk with you,' Kindred finished as Sarah landed on the deck with surprisingly little sound.

'What is it?' Sarah asked, warily.

She looked miserable. Eyes red and tired, her nails worried away to almost nothing. Even as she stood there, she brought one hand to her mouth. It made her look young. And sad.

'I . . . Are you okay?'

'I'm fine,' Sarah said, not meeting her eyes.

'You know, Little Wing doesn't – ' Kindred began, but Ragged Sarah cut her off.

'I didn't kill anyone, you know.' Her voice was urgent, the words spilling out, as if she'd been letting them build and expand and heat up inside of her all day. 'I sailed on a few trips, and I stole some stuff from ships, but I never killed anyone, and I was never on a boat that did. I wouldn't do that, and I left once I realized that we – *they* – were. I stopped being a pirate a long time ago.'

She paused to take a shaky breath, and it seemed to calm her down. Her chin rose a little, and she looked Kindred in the eyes.

'The captain knows, and it's not anyone else's business, but I want you to know the truth. Because I . . .'

Kindred took one of her hands. Testing for a new hearthfire keeper had made her feel bold, decisive, as if she were really *senior* there, despite still being younger than almost everyone. Even Sarah had at least three or four years on her.

But she took Sarah's hand in her own, feeling the heat of it.

'I'm glad you told me,' she said, quietly.

They stood that way for a moment, feeling the last light of the sun on their cheeks, hand in hand, until a bawdy song from Cora filled the deck, filtering up from below, breaking the moment. Most were down at dinner, and the deck was blessedly empty, if no longer quiet.

'Have you told the captain your decision yet?' Kindred asked.

Kindred knew Sarah hadn't been down from the nest since the meeting, but she wasn't going to confess to having watched Sarah all day.

'No,' she said, looking everywhere but into Kindred's eyes. 'I haven't decided yet.'

'Me neither. And I'm sure Little Wing is really wrestling with the choice, too.'

Sarah quirked a smile, small and tentative, but it disappeared quickly.

'I . . .' Kindred started, teetering on the edge of what she had to say.

If you seek me, look below, she heard in her mind, as she had since reading her grandmother's letter, still snug in her pocket.

'Can we actually claim sanctuary at the Once-City without them killing us?'

'I think so, unless everything has changed in the ten or twelve years since I left. The Once-City is built on the bones of old traditions like that, and most people, especially the ones on the council, stick closely to them.'

'And what about that thing the captain said about new medicines there? Do they have anything that could . . .' She raised her burned hand, holding it between the two of them.

Sarah stared at it, chewing at one lip.

'They could fix it,' she said finally, and Kindred's breath stopped up in her chest. 'But I don't know that you would want that.'

'Why?'

'They have a very *unconventional* way of healing serious wounds in the Once-City. They could fix your hand, but the process, if it's still the same as when I lived there, it would change you, Kindred. You wouldn't be the same after.'

But Kindred was barely hearing her. If she was almost decided before, this gave her the weight of certainty.

'I'm voting for the Once-City,' she said, confident. She sucked in a big breath of prairie air, letting it fill her, before continuing. 'If they can heal my hand, all the better, but you read my grandmother's letter. She's out there, Sarah. And I'm never going to find her by going back to the Mainland. If we go there, we'll never leave. And that's assuming we make it.

'But we're not going to stay at the Once-City. Maybe afterward, we'll cut out toward forever and the mythic dawn coast. Or down toward the southern mountains. All I know is that my grandmother left a note for me to follow her, and this is the first step toward that. It has to be. It has to.'

Did saying it make it true?

Sarah was watching her in the low light, very faint by then, some of that sadness still in her eyes.

'And you want me to vote for that, too?'

Kindred, after a moment, nodded.

'I swore I would never go back, Kindred,' she said finally. 'That place has a way of trapping you in its web. Pulling you in closer, keeping you there. I barely got out the first time, Kindred.'

'We'll get out,' Kindred said, leaning forward, her face close enough to see the bare twist of anxiety in Sarah's lips, the worry tracing thin lines on her forehead. 'We'll have each other, and we'll get out.'

'Mainland,' Little Wing said.

'The Once-City,' Ragged Sarah said.

The captain turned to Kindred, last in the line standing in front of where she sat at her table in her quarters. A plate with half the rationed portion of food sat forgotten on her bed. Instead, the maps on the table showed far more attention – lines and paths and the captain's close, careful scribble filled the mostly undefined green space labeled The Roughs.

'Keeper?'

Kindred felt the weight of the decision, hers alone now.

Cantrev casting a net behind them and a pirate city lost in a swath of forever ahead, both tinged with the promise of death.

Doubt like a sudden cold rain caused her to pause. So many threads of life were pulled together by this ship, every crew member with their own hopes and fears and worries and futures bound together by *The Errant*.

I go to lose myself in it, she heard, her own voice in her head speaking her grandmother's words.

'The Once-City,' she said.

Next to the wall, Little Wing cursed.

'Good,' the captain said, standing. 'That's settled. I'll tell the crew and – '

A knock broke the tension of the room.

'What is it?' Captain Caraway asked, opening the door on Scindapse.

'Sorry, captain,' the young girl – the young *keeper*, Kindred corrected herself – said. 'Kindred, you told me to watch the fire and let you know if anything changed.'

'What is it?' Kindred asked, stepping toward her, already reaching out with her senses for the fire. She had been so focused on the decision that she had let her concentration on the hearthfire fade.

But now, as she listened for it, she heard a snag in the hearthfire's song, a tension in its power.

'I'm not sure,' Scindapse was saying as Kindred stepped toward the door, listening hard to the song. 'The flames were still that same color as before – orange, I guess. But they started changing, just a tiny bit. I thought it was nothing at first, but it kept happening, orange for awhile, and then flicking over to – '

'Black,' Kindred said, the air stolen from her chest, her heartbeat a frantic tattoo in an empty house. She turned to the captain.

'We're caught,' she said, her voice a whisper of fear. She could hear the fire now, its song clear and frantic in her mind. 'Something is pulling at us.'

Kindred didn't have to say what she suspected; apart from Scindapse – her inexperience on the Sea plain on her face – they were all thinking it.

Every sailor learned about forged flowers and the vines that snaked away below them, spiraling down into the darkness where the beast waited. The flowers were lures, pretty yellow things meant to attract bugs and birds and ships. As soon as they were touched, the flowers stuck, and the vines growing from their stems shot up, wrapping around whatever unlucky soul had blundered into them.

But the flowers and vines were only the parasite, bonded to the wyrm below, a creature too large, too light-averse to live and support itself higher up in the thinner grasses of the surface.

No, wyrms lived in darkness below, where the stems of the plants were thicker and stronger, able to support their heft and weight. The forged flowers grew from the wyrms, sending out thick, white roots throughout their skin, drawing sustenance from the prey they trapped and pulled down into the wyrm's hungry maw.

The others followed as Kindred ran for the fire. Ragged Sarah broke from them and became a shape scaling the mainmast, climbing for the crow's nest.

By the time Kindred reached the hearthfire, the flames were spasming between orange and black, and the song in her head was a ragged, jagged thing.

'What's going on?' Scindapse asked. The captain roared out a command as she followed Kindred – 'All crew to arms! Cut away those fucking vines!' – and already the footsteps and shouts crowded the air. 'Should I stay here with you? What's happening?'

Ragged Sarah's call from above sliced through the chaos.

'Forged flowers! We're caught! We're caught!'

Scindapse sucked in a breath and clutched at Kindred's shoulder with one clawed hand.

'A wyrm? A wyrm has us?'

'Get bones from the closet, at least two of each,' Kindred said, settling herself in front of the fire before turning to Scindapse. 'Hey. We're going to be okay. The fire needs our calm right now, okay? So, take some breaths. We'll do this together.'

'Keep us up,' Captain Caraway said, leaning down toward Kindred, her mouth set in a tight grimace. 'And give us whatever light you can. We're going to need it.'

Kindred nodded, already singing words of calm and strength, wrestling the melody in her mind back toward stability.

Scindapse breathed loudly, big gulps of air in and out, as she opened the door of the bone closet with shaking hands.

On the deck, crew moved about quickly, swords and spears and axes hefted to cut at the thick vines mounting the deck, crawling and slithering over the gunwale. Already, *The Errant* had slowed to a crawl.

Already, the vines had begun to pull them down into the Sea.

Stone-Gwen climbed up from belowdecks, her gargantuan steel-banded cudgel held in one hand, the stone-braided robes of her faith rustling and clicking with her movements. The cudgel would do little against the vines, but soon there would be something bigger and hungrier to deal with.

Kindred tried to remember the stories she had heard about wyrm attacks, tales of huge beasts waiting below, sending up their false flowers and waiting to pull sailors to the deeps. It was said wyrms were impervious to magical attacks and too large, too powerful for the thrust of a single blade or the cut of an axe to be anything more than an annoyance. Given enough time, a full crew might drive away or kill a wyrm, but no one ever had enough time.

So few ships survived once they had been caught, and so often it had less to do with clever strategies or the power of those on board and more to do with chance and luck.

Kindred reached one hand into the fire, her song low and steady, a march. She imagined her words to be the plodding steps of a sailor weighed down by much but unwilling to slow or stop. Ever onward. Ever forward.

'Burn them high and bright as you can!' It was Little Wing, crossing the deck at a run, shouting at the crew piling fuel on the casting fires.

'Cut, cut!' Cora the Wraith was shouting, cutting away the vines as fast as they slithered aboard.

'Stow the sails! We're going under!' Captain Caraway shouted, climbing up one mast herself to aid in the endeavor.

The ancient timbers of *The Errant* groaned in protest as the ship came to a full stop, and only then did it become clear how far it had sunk into the Sea, how fast it was still sinking. Plants of all kinds angled over the gunwale, obscuring the gripping vines and flowers, growing over them.

'It's going to be okay. It's going to be okay,' Scindapse whispered as she dropped an armful of bones next to Kindred and squatted across the hearthfire from her.

Kindred spared her a glance and felt something in her break.

Chaos and fear were everywhere on the deck; the sounds of blades slicing through vines and biting into wood permeated the air, what little light the sunset offered growing more and more distant as the ship sank deeper into the Sea.

Scindapse was still a child, really, the relative of some wealthy someone on Arcadia who got her a spot on a ship before she was ready, before it was right.

Not unlike me, Kindred found herself thinking.

'Hey,' she said, breaking her song for a moment and pulling Scindapse's terrified eyes toward her. 'You're a keeper now. Your battle is here. Keep your focus on the fire and let the rest go. *This*' – she gestured at the fire, which she had wrestled back into a state of stability – 'is our fight. Mine and yours. Okay?'

Scindapse nodded and took another shaky breath.

A hush fell over the deck as the night sky disappeared overhead. No one moved or spoke as the open-aired freedom of the Sea and sky were replaced by beautifully striated walls of plants rising all around them. Axes and swords held for a moment, gripped tight in fists or dug deep into wood; voices stilled, and breath stopped. No one moved. No one spoke as *The Errant* dipped below the surface of the Forever Sea.

No one but Kindred.

'Look for me below,' she whispered.

Darkness pressed in on the glow of casting fires, on the wild illumination of the hearthfire. Grasses rasped against the hull of the ship as it sunk lower and lower.

'Blades up! Backs to the deck!' Captain Caraway broke the reverie on board. 'Wyrms hate noise and light, so keep those fires blazing, and when you finally face it, scream. And rage. Let's give this beast the worst it's ever had.'

The cheer in response was veined with fear. Kindred added her own voice to the chorus.

'Cora, Quell, Talent, Grimm,' the captain said. 'You keep cutting at those vines no matter what. We're not seeing the surface again until they're gone.'

The rest of the crew formed a rough line around the main deck, shields and weapons held ready, lashing out at any vines they could reach. Cora, Quell, Talent, and Grimm – Stone-Gwen's partner of many years – rushed back toward the edge to do battle with the waves of vines reaching aboard for a better hold.

'Calm your mind,' Kindred said, finding and holding Scindapse's wide-eyed gaze. 'Just like we practiced. Deep breaths, listen for the fire's song, join it, and then ease your hands in.'

Scindapse squeezed her eyes shut, listening hard for the song.

Kindred wondered what her grandmother would say in this moment, her ship sinking below the waves, pulled down to the deeps by a horrifying monster, an untrained, terrified keeper sitting in front of her.

Knowing the Marchess, she would probably laugh and call it a good day. She was always bending to life, a strand of true-green grass arcing in winds wild and smooth, happy to move.

'Keeper.' Captain Caraway dropped into a squat next to her. 'It might be that we scare this beast back with shouts and blades long enough to get cut free. If it's a young one or if it's already eaten, chances are it won't be interested in this kind of tussle.

'But if not, it might come down to you. You understand?'

Kindred felt the sweat that had broken out across her body cool suddenly, shrinking back against her skin.

She understood.

When all else failed, the last chance fell to the keeper. She could flare the hearthfire, giving the flames fuel and song enough to become a conflagration, an event bright enough and loud enough to scare the wyrm back.

Kindred thought of the fire back at the Trade. It had been so hungry, so uncontrolled. Like a child, mindless and joyful, leaping and destroying all in its path.

And this was what she would need to turn the hearthfire into.

'I understand, captain.'

'Only as a last option,' the captain said, leaning close, cutting Scindapse out of the conversation. She flicked her eye around at the grasses now enclosing them.

Kindred nodded. The wood of the ship was covered every year with a thick coating of fire-resistant lacquer, but the grasses around Arcadia hadn't been burned for years beyond count. They were dry and thinned out by too much harvesting. All that magic keeping them flat prevented fire from lightning or other natural causes, but the hearthfire wasn't natural. If she lost control of it, the whole Sea would be ablaze, from Arcadia all the way out to the Roughs.

And the wyrm would be the least of their worries.

Captain Caraway put a hand on Kindred's shoulder and squeezed, offering a brief smile.

'Best keeper on the Sea,' she said, and then she was gone.

Fire once defined everything in the world: it was the annual cleansing of the Sea. A prairie fire that blackened and charred the grasses, leaving behind a smoking ruin that, after a miraculously short time, gave birth to myriad plants rising in eager shoots. New veins of rich life were said to spring up after those burns.

Kindred shuddered as she looked again into the fire, its build and movement settled for now, the best she could manage while they sank lower in the grips of the vines. Here she was, surrounded by an expanse of dried grasses begging to be cleansed by fire, and it was her job if nothing else worked to build a fire so large, so wild, that it scared even a monster of the deeps, all without letting the blaze go so uncontrolled that it swept into the Sea.

Little Wing moved along the deck, one sword already out, the other in a sheath at her hip.

'Let's send this big fucker back to the deeps!' she shouted, clapping crew members on the back.

A sound like the world breathing cut through the noise of the Sea and the rallying of the crew. The wyrm.

Hungry. Wild. Terrible.

And close.

'Our fight is *here*,' Kindred said again to Scindapse, catching the young keeper's eyes and nodding to the fire. 'This is our work. Stay right here.'

'Starboard! Starboard!'

Heads swiveled toward that side of the ship, but Kindred looked up, to where Ragged Sarah leaned out from the crow's nest, removed from the shred of safety the deck and the crew offered.

'Get ready!' Captain Caraway shouted, drawing her own sword, teeth bared in a fear-twisted grimace.

Next to her, Little Wing loosed a wordless shout, her twin blades jagged splinters caught by the hearthfire light.

All around, the crew of *The Errant* roared their challenge to the wyrm.

I go to lose myself in it, Kindred heard in her mind, and for a breath, there in between the fear and the fact of the attack, she felt herself bend.

The wyrm rose from the darkness, its impossibly long, pale body writhing and wriggling up from the deep, the diminutive, stunted stubs sprouting from its sides gripping the grasses in clawed fingers. It scrabbled up the side of their ship, which sank farther beneath its weight, and curled above them all for a moment, a wedge-shaped head tipped with three bulbous eyes and a great crescent-shaped horn cutting out from one side of its head.

Longer than any mast was tall – and still with more of itself yet to rise from the deeps – and with a width capable of devouring four or five people at a time, the wyrm was the biggest thing Kindred had ever seen.

Its off-white skin was a webbed morass of root systems supporting the flowering vines stringing its body.

The crew shouted in one voice, desperate in their hope, stinking in their fear. Weapons were raised, and even as the wyrm hung in the air, its lower half still below the ship, its nostrils wide and wet – even in that moment of possibility, some crew members hurled knives and axes and spears, burying them in the wyrm's great hide.

Against the added weight of the wyrm, the hearthfire gasped and spasmed. For a terrifying moment, *The Errant* dropped before the fire found its control again.

'Both hip bones here and here,' Kindred shouted over the noise, pointing first at the two bones, like bleached shields on the deck, and then at either side of the overstrained structure in the fire.

Rule number two: solidity in bolstered support.

The bones clattered for a moment against the deck as Scindapse clutched them in shaking hands. When she brought them in, the fire belched and roiled its displeasure, and Kindred nearly retched as *The Errant* dropped farther down.

'Sorry!' Scindapse choked out, recoiling from the flames and dropping the bones in her fright.

'Sing,' Kindred urged. 'You have to make connection with the fire first!' But the ship was dipping too quickly now, and she didn't have time for Scindapse to pull herself together.

Her voice when she sang was lost amid the shouts of the crew, but the fire heard her, and it flared a bright yellow, a tiny, resilient sun burning in the darkness below. With movements rough and quick, Kindred kicked off her boots and pulled one of the dropped bones over to the fire with her bare feet.

She couldn't hold the bone in place and mold it to her build all with one hand, and so this would have to do. Kindred had once seen the Marchess construct a build completely with her feet on a bet from Maggie the Tall; they had been docked over the cradle at Arcadia, so there was no danger in it failing.

It was no joke now as she held her feet in the fire, bone pinched between them, and hunched forward, movements as imprecise and unpracticed as those of a new keeper. The magic of the hearthfire tickled her fingers as she fused the bone to one side of her structure, a wall of stability around the spiderweb grace of the build.

Immediately *The Errant* halted her fall, and Kindred chanced a look up at the battle before she continued with the other bone.

Sinuous, the wyrm scuttled and slithered around the outside of the ship, trying to break through the ranks of crew members lining the deck but thrown back until it simply set about its feasting, the only sounds its hurried eating and the panicky shouts of those aboard. Kindred watched the great maw open, the powerful muscles of its neck propel the head forward, and then Taliesa, a young crew member not thirty years on, was gone, screaming and then silent in the wyrm's jaws.

Little Wing rushed forward, her scream fearsome, her face an ugly mask of anger and fear. She cut deep furrows into the monster with her curved blades.

Cora the Wraith left off cutting vines from the ship for a frantic moment to score great stretches along the beast with lashes from her many-tailed whip.

Captain Caraway plunged a great spear into the wyrm, over and over.

Talent and Quell leapt forward and simply tore off the wyrm's stunted arms and the vines growing from its hide, pulling them up like flowers bursting from the soil, roots and all.

Stone-Gwen and Grimm slammed their steel-banded cudgels into the wyrm, making divots in its skin.

Arrows sprouted from the wyrm's hide, shot from above by Ragged Sarah in the crow's nest.

The crew caused all of this damage and more, but the wyrm was too big, too strong, its thick skin of root systems protecting it from most harm. Against this colossus, weapons were mere distraction and annoyance.

The wyrm continued its path of destruction, lashing out with its tail, which had finally made it aboard, knocking several crew members back onto the deck. It snapped out again and pulled a few crew members toward itself until Little Wing streaked forward, burying an axe and leaving it inside the wyrm's head. Where her crescent blades had gone, Kindred had no idea. Lost, probably, in the madness.

The wyrm released the crew, who stumbled or crawled or were pulled back, but if the wyrm noticed the axe handle rising from its head, giving it a second horn, it didn't show it.

Kindred stared around at the wyrm's enormous body garlanding their ship; it appeared almost lazy as it nearly encircled the deck and rose to slough over the quarterdeck and forecastle. It had them surrounded.

The Errant dipped, listing drunkenly, and Kindred felt the snapping of bones in the hearthfire even before she saw them. The flames bulged with pressure as the ship strained to stay up, as more and more was asked of the bone structure. Jagged ends hung in the writhing flames, severed from the neat lines where Kindred had set them.

Kindred reached for the other bone but it was gone, and she looked up to find Scindapse, her mouth moving in words too quiet to hear above the din of devastation, hands holding the bone in the flame.

She was doing it, and a stab of pride shot through the fear Kindred was feeling.

Quickly as she could, Kindred joined the support to the structure, trying to ignore the wall of flesh circumventing most of the ship.

'Hold these together!' she said, pointing to the ends of bone exploded from the center of the build. 'Hold them! Scindapse!'

But Scindapse's hands were still and frozen, as if the hip bone were still clutched between her fingers. Her wide, dazed eyes followed the mesmeric slither of the wyrm, which continued its rampage, rough skin tearing at the ship as it slithered, a whirlwind of stinking, cratered flesh. Blood poured from its wounds, coating the deck as it oozed and pooled against the gunwale, trapped there by the increasingly sharp tilt of *The Errant*.

The crew had become an ever-tightening ring, moving in imitation of the wyrm. Circles and circles moved around the fire, and Kindred felt suddenly nauseous, the swaying, shifting movement like that of a deck pitching in wild seas.

'Cut the vines! Cut them!' Captain Caraway's voice pulled at Kindred through the screams and shouts, through the sounds of the wyrm's *feasting*.

But Cora, Quixa, and Grimm were blocked from the vines by the wyrm, which was a wall of flesh around the deck, protecting the grasping vines.

And still the ship dropped lower.

'Cut through!' Little Wing shouted, sprinting forward, her twin blades back in her hands. But Kindred could see even as she was forced back by the wyrm's snapping jaws that it would take a full day's work to butcher a path through the body of the wyrm. It was just too big.

They needed another way.

'Hold fast, everyone!' Kindred shouted, moved by a sudden idea. It was barely a plan and hazed over by the memory of waking up on the ship, her hand numb, mouth dry, confused and without any clue how long she had been asleep.

But one thing was clear in her memory: *The Errant* pitched over sideways, wrenched out of true by a hearthfire build a child might have stumbled into making.

'Be here, keeper,' Kindred said, as much to Scindapse as to herself.

She pushed Scindapse's hands out of the fire before she set to her work, singing a child's ditty, simple and misguided and wandering, melodies tripping away from resolution and into other keys.

And she broke the logic of her build.

Instead of fusing the broken bones back together, she scattered them about the fire, careful always to maintain the merest whiff of solidity around the base, but adorned with fragments and fractions of bones pointing here and there, stopping up air or the flow of energy here and letting it breathe too freely there. The fire coughed and wheezed an acrid white smoke into the air.

It was nonsensical, and *The Errant* groaned as the deck pitched portside-down.

With a cry surprisingly high and soft, half of the wyrm slid from the deck, its heft and weight doing the work once enough of it had disappeared off the edge. Its stunted arms clutched and scrabbled for purchase on the deck, tearing anew the wood into splinters, but it was not enough, and the greater part of its body slid away.

Its head and tail, though, had linked together on the starboard side of the ship, and as they trailed the body, the wyrm lashed about, turning head and tail to blunt destruction.

Sailors were lifted from their feet and thrown through the air, crashing into masts or stairs or the gunwale or each other. Stone-Gwen swung her steel-banded cudgel into the beast's head just as it collided with her, and the impact she made after being thrown against the mainmast had the distinctive sound of bones breaking.

The wyrm disappeared over the edge of the ship, ripping most of the ship wall of the gunwale away with it.

The remnants of the crew stared after it for a moment, clinging to whatever they could to avoid sliding down after it.

'Wyrm away!' called a voice above, and Kindred looked up with a start. She had forgotten Ragged Sarah was up there, and she saw her now, hanging from the crow's nest with one foot and one hand, leaning over to look down into the abyss below, her face flushed with a wide, courageous smile.

'Up, Kindred! Bring us up!' Captain Caraway cried, pushing up the hill of the deck with sword in hand, heading for the vines still clutching the ship there.

Rise, Kindred thought, her attention snapping back to the fire.

'I'm here,' Scindapse said, her voice quiet and terrified, but she had returned to the fire, leaning in a squat against the slope of the deck.

'Good,' Kindred said, surveying the mess she had made of the hearthfire, barely able to see through the thick smoke. 'Help me break this down. Just follow my lead.'

She began to sing in a sharp, clear voice, loud and powerful as she could manage without choking on the smoke.

'Courage! So warped, so sunk, once pass'd?
Skies! Alight with feverish cast?
Rise, again, like questions once ask'd.'

The fire, its flames still contorting and bulging, quieted somewhat under Kindred's ministrations, and she reached in, breaking down and spreading out her build with an outstretched hand. Scindapse followed, and bones fell as the magics in their hands and Kindred's song worked on them, breaking bonds.

'A rough circle,' Kindred said, stopping her song to gesture at the build. 'But with breaks at the four directions.' She pointed fore and aft, port and starboard.

It looked a mess, and the flames still coughed and warped, but *The Errant* righted itself and began to lift from the dark below to the dark above.

'Vines away!' Cora the Wraith called, her blade severing the last of them. 'Free and clear!'

The rough cheer of the crew was buoyed by the ascent of the ship, and for the space of a long breath, it looked like they were going to make it.

'Belay! Belay! Wyrm rising!' Sarah's call came a moment before the sounds of the wyrm's own ascent, its soft, high-pitched cry nightmarish in the dark. Kindred opened her mouth to sing, to scream for speed, but it was too late.

The wyrm became a blurred comet rising portside, up and above the ship, and Kindred realized it must have leapt from below; the grasses here were too thin and weak to hold it up, and its claws clutched nothing as it rose and curved above them.

The crash when it landed on the deck, beaching the top half of its body on the slab of *The Errant*, was enough to destroy Kindred's hearing for a moment and hurl her backward, replacing the song of the hearthfire in her head with a high whistling.

Scindapse was gone when she looked up, replaced by the wyrm, its great maw puckered. For a terrified moment, Kindred thought the wyrm had killed Scindapse, eaten or fallen on her. Kindred's heart juddered to a stop at the thought, but then leapt again when she saw

Scindapse thrown to the side, prone on the deck.

The wyrm cocked its head just slightly, neck coiling for a strike.

Three eyes trained on her.

The circle of defense had shattered, and she was revealed at its center.

Up so close, Kindred saw the skin of the beast, which was like a latticework of calcified spiderwebs, weaving through and around one another, exposing great, black holes burrowing in and through, roots and skin and wounds interchangeable.

Kindred launched herself away from the wyrm's horrible, curious gaze. Her back collided with the mainmast, an explosion of pain seething across her body. Lances and axes and swords flashed in a corona around the wyrm, but Kindred could not see who wielded them. Someone was screaming.

The wyrm held her gaze as it moved closer, somehow soft in its movements, unaffected by the violence around it, the violence being done to it.

A voice, so quiet and distant it might have been a horizon away, screamed at Kindred.

'The fire, Kindred! The fire!'

Who was that? Who were they speaking to? Questions bloomed and died rapidly in the expanse of Kindred's mind. Every muscle in her body strained, pushing her back into the mast, as if she could retreat into it, become the ship, but her mind had gone suddenly calm in the immediacy of the wyrm's gaze.

As the wyrm wove closer, it pulled more and more of its body aboard, carving a runnel of splintered, fractured boards.

The wyrm mewled and stretched closer, the bottom of its scaled neck stretching over the hearthfire.

The hearthfire.

Resilience stirred in Kindred, deep down, past the fear and manic stillness that had taken her over. This was not the end. This was not her end.

The wyrm screamed, high and victorious.

Kindred screamed, too, in a language none on deck understood, save for a few words here and there. She screamed in a language meant for flames, for burning.

And reached for the fire.

A melody, first light and sweet and then savage, a panoply of major chords sung in a ragged, rising voice, lit through Kindred, blaring through the echoing corridors of her mind and body, singing along her bones and giving rise to the hairs on her arms and neck. Words in a language like kin sang for Kindred, every line a question.

The hearthfire rose, its voice a triumph in Kindred's mind, its colors blazing a sunset streak as it reached flicking fingers up, stroking the wyrm's fattened gullet and leaving trails of blackened, bubbling flesh.

To speak was to exercise power, and Kindred spoke, calling the fire friend in its own language, giving it leave to devour air and feast wildly, to reach skyward and seaward.

Kindred understood the language of the hearthfire, and every syllable sparked and sang in her mouth. Other keepers perhaps excelled in the bone arts or in designing and classifying builds, in teaching or in constructing hearthfire basins, but *this* was Kindred's gift. The language of the flames had always felt like hers, too.

She scored the air with her defiant shout, and the fire grew.

Long lashes of red and gold and black whipped out from the hearthfire basin, an explosion of color and sound and heat, and the wyrm was blasted back, its head colliding with and snapping the topmast yard with a meaty *thwap.*

The Errant shook from the impact as the wyrm fell, sluggish and slow, to the deck, coiling into itself like a wet rope. Screams of pain and triumph melded together, and someone was calling for her, but Kindred could hear none of it.

Unconscious or dead, the wyrm unspooled from the deck into the dark, limp and heavy.

Kindred saw only the flames.

The hearthfire reached farther, a hungry thing, hungrier than the wyrm. It left trails of black along the deck and burned gaps between crew members who dove aside, shocked from their moment of triumph and victory. Like the fire back on Arcadia Kindred had loosed, the blaze here joyed in the expanse of freedom. It devoured air, leapt in long arcs of light, up and up before plummeting down, splashing against the deck and across the masts.

And moving toward the Sea.

'No,' Kindred whispered, the word a moan of distress. Every muscle in her body felt bruised and exhausted, the energy rushing through her system suddenly drying up, boiled away to nothing. Her hand hurt. Her back hurt. Her whole body hurt.

Above, the mainmast broke the surface of the Forever Sea, and starlight softened the wreckage on the deck.

They were rising, but not fast enough. The fire was racing for the grasses receding around them, like a boat running in a full wind, cutting smooth lines.

A tendril, flashing red and orange, curled through the air, angling to go up and over the gunwale.

Kindred coughed out a halt, begging the fire to slow, but her voice was ragged from the smoke she had inhaled, from the singing she had done, and the fire was mad with its lust for more.

It was done. The Sea would burn.

The arc of the fire was a beautiful thing as it leapt toward the hole in the gunwale the wyrm had left, and it was as if everything else stopped, the Sea suddenly stilled. How long had it been waiting to burn? How long had it been waiting to be reborn?

A shadow detached itself from those too stunned to do anything but watch, and there was Captain Caraway, leaping into the air, a bloodied blade still in her hand.

Without a shield, without protection of any kind, Captain Caraway placed herself between the fire and the Sea.

And the fire burned.

The tendril of flames burst against Captain Caraway's chest, a shock of colors cascading out as she screamed in pain. She became a shooting star, burning as she fell to the deck, sparks and scintillas of fire coruscating across her body as the hearthfire snuffed itself out.

The captain slamming against the deck broke the watchful spell; the crew moved again, some in simple terror, some with purpose, but all moving. Little Wing was shouting for help with the captain, while others cried for medicker's attention or screamed in anguish for those lost.

Kindred found Scindapse where she had been knocked over and gathered her up, saying her name over and over again, rubbing at her cheek until she was awake and looking back into her eyes.

A cough of relief rattled up from Kindred's lungs as Scindapse breathed deeply and sat all the way up.

'Are you okay?' Kindred asked, her hands running over

Scindapse's shoulders and arms, searching for broken bones.

'I'm okay,' Scindapse said, nodding. 'I'm okay.'

'I need you to watch the fire,' Kindred croaked out. 'Can you do that?'

'Yes, I think so.' Scindapse nodded again.

She moved toward the blaze, which had settled into a miserly, satisfied burn low in the basin.

Kindred lurched to her feet and toward the captain.

'Is she breathing?' she cried, dropping down beside Little Wing, who cradled the captain's head. 'Is she alive?'

Little Wing looked up, covered in blood that might have been her own or someone else's.

'I don't know.'

Kindred let her eyes drop to the wound on the captain's chest, and she had to bite back the rush of vomit. Burned masses of greyed and blackened skin, like a map of scorched, dead lands, covered her chest, and beneath all of that Kindred could see no hint of the rise and fall of breath.

Around them, the unburned grasses of the Forever Sea whispered secrets to the prairie wind.

8

I did this.

Kindred lifted Captain Caraway, carrying her shoulders as Little Wing lifted her feet. Kindred did her best to ignore the pain blossoming along her back and arms, seeded by the fight.

'Sarah!' she yelled, just as Little Wing screamed 'Medicker!'

Strung between them, the captain's body sagged.

They shuffled forward between crew members working or weeping or dying. Cuts and what would be bruises festooned Little Wing's body, but she held herself like a woman unhurt.

'Scindapse! Mind the fire!' Kindred shouted.

Sarah examined the captain, and the burned spectacle her chest had become.

'I need supplies. Get her into her quarters,' she said before rushing off belowdecks toward the medicker's closet.

'Quixa! Take the wheel! Get us moving forward again! Everyone able, we need to move.'

A moment of uncertainty followed Little Wing's orders. Was the captain dead? Was she the new captain? What was going on?

But the machinery of ship and Sea, wind and prairie moved onward, and crew, those able to, began making order on the deck again. Long Quixa stepped up and behind the wheel and, in her slow, steady voice, began directing the crew.

Kindred pushed open the captain's door and they moved her inside just as Ragged Sarah arrived, her medicker's bag now plump with bottles clinking together. They lay her on the floor and in the slim light of her lit lanterns the captain looked bad. Worse.

I did this, Kindred thought. *I killed her.*

'She's not,' Ragged Sarah said, her eyes on Kindred for a moment, speaking as if she could hear Kindred's thoughts. She slid into place next to the captain and began her work, flicking open her eyelids, placing careful fingers along her throat. 'Not yet. And I'm not letting her.'

Kindred stripped her thick outer shirt away and pushed it into a pillowed mass beneath the captain's head. A small skin of water hung from one of the chairs, and this she grabbed.

'Kindred,' Little Wing said from behind her.

'She needs water,' Kindred said, keeping her gaze on the captain's face, looking anywhere but back at the wound, at *her work*. 'Right? She needs water.'

'Kindred. The fire.'

'Scindapse can handle it.' She dripped and trickled water into the captain's mouth, running it over her cracked lips and past her teeth.

So near, this person Kindred had feared and adored and maybe even begun to love in some small part became just Jane. Her dark hair clung in sweaty tangles to her forehead and temples. Skin grown accustomed to prairie winds pulled tight to her cheekbones and jaw, and *there*. The bare, short breaths, like steam as they slipped from the back of her throat.

'Kindred!' Little Wing balled a hand in the back of her undershirt and lifted her to her feet. 'You've done enough here. I need you at the fire.'

'I can use her,' Ragged Sarah said before Kindred could respond. 'Kindred knows the hearthfire better than anyone on board; she can help me with this burn. And I need another set of hands anyway.'

After a moment, Little Wing let her go.

'Fine. Do you have everything you need?' she asked, turning to Sarah.

'For now, yes.'

'If she dies, it's your fault. Both of you. Understood?'

She left without a backward glance, without letting them answer, and soon her voice was commanding the remaining crew out on the deck.

The penalty for killing a captain was death. The green dive.

'This is bad,' Sarah said, surveying the captain's chest as she rolled up her sleeves. She splashed something that smelled strongly like alcohol on her hands as she leaned over the captain, getting close enough to the wound to smell it, to taste it if she'd wanted.

'How bad?' Kindred asked, but that wasn't right, not the question she wanted.

'Honestly, I've never seen a burn this severe. Is this grey coloring around here typical of hearthfire burns?' she asked, pointing down at the burn.

A tendril of fire flowing through the darkness, innocent and hopeful, a child's finger reaching for more. Kindred saw it in her memory, watched it blossom into a blaze, a firestorm, a sun on the captain's chest.

'Kindred!' Sarah snapped, her hands moving around the wound. 'Focus. I need to know about hearthfire burns. Do they act like burns from nonmagical fires? How do they affect skin and blood? Hydration? What about infection? Tell me everything.'

Bits and nonsenses, the Marchess used to call all of that, the stuff taught by the bookmavens at the schools, the same schools Kindred had failed out of. The Marchess's philosophy had been a simple one: listen to the flames, pay attention to your surroundings, and blend with the world around you. If you did all of that, you wouldn't need to know things like what effect a hearthfire burn – a serious one like this, not the nips that new keepers would get – might have on the blood or skin.

'I don't know,' Kindred said.

'You can't tell me anything?'

'I've never seen anyone get burned, not in any real way. And I didn't make it long enough in the schools to learn about this.'

'We're both working without a guide, then, I guess.' Sarah shook her head, still working at the wound, which Kindred held her gaze away from.

'Did I kill her?'

The question – the right one, flickering in the tendril of fire reaching again and again in her mind – slipped from her mouth, heavy.

Sarah stilled, just for a breath, before continuing her work.

'You did what you needed to do. And so did the captain. I'm not going to let her die. And neither are you. But I need you present for this. Stop feeling sorry for yourself and help me keep our captain alive.'

The tendril of fire reached again in her mind, but Kindred squeezed her eyes shut and hissed in and out a breath, forcing it away. When she opened them again, she said a quiet 'okay.'

'Good. Now pick up that bottle with the green thread around the neck and drip it on the edges of the wound when I tell you.' Sarah gestured toward her bag, and Kindred saw the one she meant. It was a tall, smudged stretch of glass containing a murky liquid. A strip of green wound around its neck.

'I don't know anything about healing wounds,' Kindred said, reaching for the bottle.

'It doesn't matter,' Sarah said, voice sharp. 'I just need you to be a set of hands.'

Kindred swallowed her instinctive reply: she couldn't be a set of hands anymore, not after her own burn, but this wasn't the time for it. Instead, she waited, the bottle opened. The smooth surface of the glass slipped against her sweaty palm, but Kindred braced the bottle against her knee and bandaged hand, waiting to be called to action.

'Three drips there,' Sarah said, and Kindred extended the bottle over the captain's wound, her hand trembling with the pressure she was exerting to hold the slippery glass still, to not pour too much, to pour just enough.

So close, the wound was a blackened sun: a ragged swirl of charred skin and red flesh coalescing inside a torn corona of burned and singed cloth. Skin and scraps of the captain's robe had fused together, hardening into petrified veins stretching across and through the wound.

'Steady,' Ragged Sarah said, her voice losing some of its edge. She worked carefully, wielding a plain-looking but wickedly sharp knife.

'Count them out,' Sarah said, her eyes still on her work. 'One.'

'One.' Kindred tipped the bottle, watching the murky liquid race for the opening. She held her breath as it neared, neared, and then a single drop fell, huge and glistening through the air, and landed with a pop and a tiny hiss next to Sarah's blade.

'Good. Now.'

'Two,' Kindred whispered, letting another drop fall, following the slow cut of the knife.

'And three.' The last drop fizzed as it connected with a patch of skin and cloth burned together. Where the liquid landed, it spread, lightening to a green that reminded Kindred of the Sea on a cloudy day. The skin it touched disappeared beneath it, but the patches of burned cloth surfaced on the liquid, floating up. Sarah plucked these away with the tip of her knife, working to separate skin from robe.

Kindred was asked four more times to pour liquid onto the captain's wound, each time letting loose a triad of drops just behind or ahead of Sarah's knife. After a short time, it became almost hypnotic, the pouring and the counting, and Kindred forgot about the wound, forgot about Little Wing and the wyrm, and her whole world instead became a bottle gripped in one hand, a few numbers, and a liquid like the Sea.

'Good,' Sarah said. 'Cork that and grab the yellow bag.'

Next to the stand of bottles were several small bags, each a different color. Kindred retrieved a cloth bag smudged a dirty yellow.

'Take one of the heads out,' Sarah said, her eyes on the captain's wound, her hands steady and constant in their movement, cutting and applying pressure, at times stopping to pour foul-smelling liquids onto parts or all of the captain's chest.

Kindred loosened the drawstring holding the bag closed and opened it to find the severed heads of several coneflower plants bundling against one another. Petals of light purple surrounded a central disk of dark red spikes, and in the darkness of the bag, each head was a study in contrast and beauty.

'Coneflowers?' Kindred asked, reaching in and scooping one out, the head of the flower fitting snugly in her palm.

'Narrow-leaf. Stunted in their growth,' Sarah said, her eyes still down, her focus still on the wound, 'but easier to use than Sea-harvested. Take off three of the petals and hand them to me.'

Kindred did, though it took longer than it might have if she could have used both her hands. One by one, she handed them to Ragged Sarah, and one by one, Ragged Sarah stuffed them in her mouth, chewing them into a thick, bulging wad in her cheek, working at the clump.

Captain Caraway shifted, her face creasing in pain, her breath shifting from a shallow stirring to a hissed intake.

'Hold her,' Sarah said out of the corner of her mouth, her jaw still grinding the coneflower petals in her mouth.

Kindred, her own breath held high and tight in her chest, placed her unburned hand on the captain's shoulder and leaned one knee onto the captain's leg, using her own body weight as much as possible.

But it wasn't enough.

Captain Caraway began thrashing about, her body contorting beneath Kindred's weight, displacing her and making it impossible to stay atop the captain.

'Fuck! Hold her!' Sarah held her hands poised above the wound, batting away the captain's arms as they clawed toward her chest.

'I'm trying!' Kindred wrestled with the writhing captain, keenly aware of her own pain, the numbness in her burned hand. Captain Caraway's eyes remained closed, but her mouth was a rictus of pain and effort. Sweat stood out on her face, dimpling her temples. She thrashed nearer the bottles standing nearby.

'Keep her still!' Sarah all but shouted, spittle tinged with purple flecking from her mouth. She moved to sit astride Captain Caraway, abandoning her work on the wound in favor of holding her down. Between the two of them, Kindred and Sarah managed to hold the captain down if not still.

'Black thread,' Sarah said, gesturing to the bottles. Kindred found the bottle – a grey, viscous liquid sliding around in the belly of a squared fistful of glasswork – and gave it to Sarah.

In a fluid motion, Ragged Sarah leaned forward over the captain, faces mirrored. The wad of coneflower distended against her cheek for a breath, and then Sarah spat the pulped mass into the captain's mouth, saliva and juices splattering the captain's lips. The grey liquid was next, straight down her throat, even as Sarah scraped the bits of pulped coneflower around the captain's lips into her mouth.

'Clean cloth,' Sarah said, holding out a hand. Whatever other benefits of the coneflower, it had the immediate effect of calming the captain's unconscious writhing, and Kindred was able to stand and grab one of a few recently washed cloths from the bundle of supplies.

'Will she live?' Kindred asked, feeling numb all over now.

Sarah felt for the captain's pulse, spent a long moment listening to her breath and counting quietly to herself. She checked the wound, even leaning in to sniff around the edges, before washing her hands with more alcohol. She picked up a new knife, this one smaller, with a dull metal handle.

'I don't know. The coneflower paired with the sleeping drought will keep her still and restful while I work. I need to debride the wound and clean it as best I can. If she can make it through the night, I think she might last long enough to get real help. And *she's going to make it through the night.*'

Sarah said this last with such conviction that it took Kindred a moment to realize what she was saying: the green dive. Little Wing's promise. Sarah fought for their lives just as much as she fought to save the captain's.

'What do you mean, "real help"? Can't you heal her?'

Sarah shook her head.

'I can buy us two span, maybe longer. But I don't have the abilities to heal a wound like this, and without any real idea how to treat a hearthfire burn, anything else I might try is just as likely to kill her as save her. We need real help. Real treatment.'

Kindred looked down at her hand, hidden away, and almost laughed as a thought struck her.

'The Once-City! What about their way of healing? Could they help the captain, too?'

Too, she thought, because of course she would get her hand healed.

Sarah nodded, though something troubled her eyes.

'Yes. They might be the only ones who can. Mainland healers have nothing to heal such a wound. But Kindred, the healing back at home – at the Once-City – *if* they can save the captain, and *if* we can reach them soon enough . . .'

She shook her head.

'Their healing changes the patient. Forever. The captain would never be the same.'

'Would she be alive?'

Sarah offered a reluctant nod of her head.

'Then that's enough. We go to the Once-City, claim sanctuary, and they heal the captain.' *And me.* 'I'll get Little Wing,' Kindred said. This would work. It had to.

As she left, Kindred looked once over her shoulder.

Ragged Sarah bent against the captain's still form, diligent and gentle as she worked, keeping the embodiment of their hope alive.

'She needs more help than Ragged Sarah can give her on the ship,' Kindred said in response to Little Wing's questioning eyes.

Kindred felt the prairie wind catch at her face, her hair. The shadows cast over the deck by the lanterns hid some of the wreckage left by the wyrm's attack, but not enough.

The Errant's starboard side was a wreck: the deck, depressed now from the wyrm's imprint, sloped gently toward the Sea. No gunwale rose to separate deck from grass; for most of the starboard side of the ship, it was simply gone.

Rigging had been torn away or left hanging untethered. Blood stained the deck, the masts, the sails in a red so dark, it appeared black in the lantern light.

It was a mess. Even the wheel had suffered damage in the attack; it no longer described a perfect spoked circle but was chipped and broken, spokes torn away or splintered.

Little Wing stood solid, though, one hand on the broken wheel, both eyes on the Sea ahead.

'Just toss them overboard, Cora!' Little Wing roared, and Cora the Wraith tossed the armful of fractured fragments of timber and rigging she'd been collecting.

Little Wing returned her attention to Kindred.

'The pirate can't save her? Is that what you're telling me?'

'No,' Kindred said quickly, and then. 'Yes. The captain's wound needs more than any ship's medicker closet would hold, and more skill than any ship's medicker likely has. Sarah is keeping her alive, but she doesn't have much time.'

'How much time? It's going to take at least a span and a half to reach the Mainland from here.'

Hope died away in Kindred's chest.

'I thought we sailed for the Once-City,' she said after a moment.

'The Mainland is safer, more known. We can make it; I'm sure of it.'

Little Wing paused for a moment, and when she spoke again, her voice was quiet, ruminative.

'We sail under cursed skies. Five dead. Ship torn apart. Captain hurt bad.'

She turned to look Kindred full in the eyes.

'And you think I should sail us out into the Roughs toward a pirate city? Even with a ship in perfect fucking condition, the Roughs are dangerous.' She leaned toward Kindred and dropped her voice even further. 'Even with a keeper fully capable of keeping the fire, the Roughs are dangerous.'

She glanced down at Kindred's hand.

'I'm fine,' Kindred said. 'I can keep the fire just fine.'

'I've pretended at being fine enough in my life to know what it looks like.' She held up a hand as Kindred protested. 'I don't blame you, keeper. I admire it, actually. We *should* break ourselves for this crew, this ship, this captain.'

Something Little Wing had said snagged in Kindred's mind. A span and a half to reach the Mainland. Fifteen days, and well within the two span Ragged Sarah had promised for the captain to stay in her suspended state.

But Little Wing didn't know that.

'Only a span,' Kindred said, cutting her eyes down as she spoke.

'What?'

'We only have a span for the captain. Sarah can only keep her asleep and alive for a span at most.'

'*Shit*,' Little Wing said, her voice a near-whisper. 'Only a span? There's no way we reach the Mainland in ten days. Are you sure that's really right?'

'That's what Sarah said.' Kindred spoke the lie quickly, hoping her face showed none of the nausea prickling her stomach. Would Little Wing see through her lie somehow? Could she tell, just as she could tell that Kindred had been lying about keeping the fire?

'There's some healing that can be done at the Once-City,' Kindred continued, 'something that Sarah says can heal the captain.'

'Kindred.' Little Wing's voice went suddenly hard and she grabbed Kindred's arm.

Caught.

Little Wing pulled her close, her grip on Kindred's arm like stone.

'Are you sure that she's telling the truth? Are you sure we can trust her?'

Ragged Sarah. She was talking about Ragged Sarah.

'Yes,' Kindred said, meeting Little Wing's eyes and saying the only true thing she could think of. 'I trust her. *We* can trust her.'

Little Wing looked toward the deck, where the crew, beaten down and almost broken, labored to bring the ship back into some kind of order.

'All they've been through, and I have to tell them that we're sailing to the Once-City. *Fuck*. I'll be lucky if they don't mutiny.'

She released Kindred's arm and for a moment, she said nothing more, just stared out into the never-ending stretch of Sea dancing in the darkness. 'I'll tell them now, one or two at a time to soften it. Tomorrow, in the afternoon, senior crew will meet. You, me, Quixa, and the pirate. If we're going to the Once-City, we'll need a plan. I'm not going in empty-handed or empty-headed.'

Kindred nodded.

'I'll go check on Scindapse at the fire,' Kindred said into the troubled silence between them, turning to go.

'*Norther*,' Little Wing said. 'That's what I named the ship – my ship – waiting on the Mainland. I saw in some old book when I was studying for the captain's exam that norther was the name for strong winds back when everyone thought it was the breath of the gods. A norther came from Radicle, Best of the Gods, and was stronger and colder than all other winds.'

For a moment, a smile caught at the starlight on Little Wing's face, but then it was gone.

'It's stupid. But it was mine. My whole fucking life was back there on the Mainland. And now it's gone. All of it.'

'Little Wing, we'll get back to – ' Kindred began, but Little Wing spoke over her.

'I would do anything for the captain. And I'll do this. Because fuck Cantrev. And fuck those pirates. And fuck anyone that gets in my way.'

She looked up at their sails, limp in the low wind.

'But I think this might be our last voyage.'

9

'OH, good,' Scindapse said as Kindred settled in across from her. 'I couldn't remember any of the rules you were telling me earlier. Or the builds, either. Except for the simple one. The first one you showed me.'

Child's Build, it was called. The first build Kindred had ever learned, and the only one she had had time to properly show Scindapse.

It was simple: three bones, each of approximately the same length and width, leaning against one another in the fire. It was stable, solid, easy to build and maintain.

And Scindapse had made a mess of it.

Five bones instead of three, leaning in at different and precarious angles. Even as she sat, Kindred saw one of the bones begin to slide away, and she moved to catch it.

But Scindapse was faster. Singing a gentle song of just a few simple notes, Scindapse caught the bone and set it again against the build.

Kindred's first span aboard *The Errant* had been tumultuous and exciting and scary every moment, but she would always remember her first build in the fire and Rhabdus's snide, sarcastic comments, punctuated by slaps or shoves out of the way.

'You're doing great,' Kindred said, smiling through the firelight at Scindapse. 'Nice catch.'

Scindapse's grin sparked with pride, and Kindred felt a sudden drop in her gut. What if she was wrong to push them out to the Once-City? What if Little Wing's fears were right? Had she just lied her way to the death of everyone on board, including Scindapse, whose joy was a bubble of brightness against the dark of the night and wreckage of the wyrm's attack?

You did what you needed to do, Ragged Sarah had said. Somewhere inside her, in the cave where her wind and wishes roared together, Kindred knew she needed to do this, too. Something was killing the Sea, some sickness that moved in it, and she would not find the answer on Arcadia. Her grandmother had told her to follow, and so it would be the Roughs, the wilderness beyond. Nothing would stand in Little Wing's way when it came to what she wanted, and nothing would stand in Kindred's way, either.

In her letter, the Marchess had written of something calling to her, something from below, something that she suspected called to Kindred, too.

If you seek me, look below, she had written. The Once-City was not below, not truly, but it was a step.

Kindred would answer that call, the world be damned.

As dawn caught fire on the edge of the world, and after giving the young keeper a chance at a short nap, Kindred worked with Scindapse, rejecting the style of Rhabdus, offering advice instead of sneering condescension. Like her approach to the fire itself, Rhabdus had believed a keeper had to be broken, subjected to a teacher's will, before any real education could happen.

She had force-fed her ideas to Kindred.

The Marchess had been the opposite, giving Kindred tiny scraps of knowledge, enough to pull her further into the craft. The rest, though, Kindred had stolen in glimpses and interpretation, through watching and mimicking, through failure after failure after failure, until her own success bloomed before her.

'Do it as I do, but as you would do,' Kindred said. The words were the Marchess's, and Kindred almost laughed as Scindapse stared back at her in familiar confusion. The Marchess had never responded, never relented to Kindred's questions – What does that even mean? Can't you just tell me how to do it? Why do I have to steal it from you? Why can't you just give it to me?

But when Scindapse said, 'I still don't understand,' Kindred found that she couldn't offer vague wisdom as the Marchess had always done. It wasn't that she couldn't regurgitate the sayings she had heard from her grandmother most of her life. Instead, she didn't want to. She could offer help to this person, and so why not? Was there a line between Rhabdus's forever-closed fist and the Marchess's forever-open one?

'Try it like this.'

'Two bones are better near dawn.'

'You need to think about *what* you're singing in relation to *how* you're singing it – fast or slow, high or low, smooth or choppy. All of it matters. Here, I'll draw a chart for you.'

On and on she answered questions, trying to give Scindapse room to experiment but enough knowledge to do so with confidence.

With the sun lighting a calm morning on the Forever Sea, Kindred stood and surveyed Scindapse's work.

Everything about it – her technique, her singing, her movements – left room for improvement. Her build, too, still looked like a poor drawing dictated by a person who had seen a hearthfire once or twice.

But she was improving, and she smiled when she worked, which made all the difference.

'You're picking this up far quicker than I did. Soon enough, you're going to put me out of work,' Kindred said, grinning.

Scindapse blushed and shook her head even as a small, bright smile lit her face.

'I'm going to get some sleep,' Kindred said. 'Just until noon, and then you can get some rest. Keep the build simple and let me know if you run into any trouble at all, okay?'

Scindapse nodded at her before singing again, the melody and tone all wrong, but the heart right where it ought to be.

She would be fine.

Kindred caught Little Wing's eye as she walked toward the steps. How she was still standing, still so strong and unflagging, Kindred didn't know. There was no evidence that Little Wing, like everyone else aboard, had fought off a wyrm below the surface of the Sea only the previous night.

The remaining crew had all already taken a turn at rest. Once the majority of the destruction had been cleared away, they had begun dropping away in twos and threes, snatching at slips of sleep. Only Little Wing remained, the cornerstone of the crew.

And Ragged Sarah.

The door of the captain's quarters remained shut, and Kindred had seen no sign of Sarah since leaving. She itched to knock on the door, to peek inside and know what was going on with the captain, if there had been any developments.

But there was nothing more she could do. They sailed east, toward the Roughs and the Once-City beyond. Everyone aboard had been told, and there had been no mutiny, at least not yet.

Her cabin was quiet and calm as she entered, the dream of the ruined reality on the deck above. She sank into sleep immediately and had no dreams of her own.

When she woke to take over from Scindapse, Kindred's body felt ragged, every stretch of muscle and fat and skin and bone and tendon bruised and singing with pain. It took effort to simply stand and endeavor to climb the stairs. Scindapse, when Kindred put a hand on her shoulder, looked just as bad. Exhausted and cramped from sitting too long without stretching. She walked off to get some food and sleep, holding her back like a woman three times her age.

The Errant still sailed on Arcadian grasses, flat and easy, sails filled, running with a cool tailwind. Sailing like this, fast despite the damage aboard, Kindred built for a fire that offered stability and let the wind do the work.

'It's time,' Little Wing said, squatting down next to her. 'We're meeting in the captain's quarters.'

'Have you slept yet?' Kindred asked, squinting up at Little Wing, whose mouth hung slightly open, whose eyes roved restlessly, whose face had become a haggard mess.

'No time,' Little Wing said, shaking her head. 'I made Quixa my second, but she needs sleep more than I do. And there's too many repairs to manage with the Roughs coming up.'

The Roughs.

A shiver of excitement rushed through Kindred at the thought. This was forward. This was onward.

She followed Little Wing into the captain's quarters, giving Cora the Wraith, who held the wheel, a wave before entering.

Inside, the room smelled of death and medicine.

Whatever Sarah had done with the wound was now hidden away, wrapped up beneath layers of the same dark cloth that hugged Kindred's burned hand.

But the evidence of injury littered the room – the stinging stench of medicine, the crumpled, soiled remains of once-clean cloth, knives flecked with blood and skin.

In the light of day lancing in through the windows, the captain looked like a fresh corpse on the ground, her arms too straight, her body too still. The rise of her chest was the barest suggestion beneath the wrap swaddling her chest.

'Good,' Quixa said when she saw the captain, her voice slow and deep as ever. 'She is breathing.'

'For now,' Sarah said from where she sat on the floor next to the captain. If Little Wing looked bad, Sarah looked worse. Eyes hung with bags of exhaustion, hands splayed on her legs, face waxen and slack.

If the captain looked dead, Ragged Sarah looked to be dying.

'We sail for the Once-City,' Little Wing said without preamble. 'It's what the captain wanted, and it's what you two stupid shits voted for. Are you sure they can heal the captain there?'

This last she asked of Ragged Sarah, who only nodded. She looked on the edge of falling asleep where she sat, her clothes run through with sweat and blood and errant splashes of her medicines.

'Good. We'll be to the Roughs in less than a day. How far past the Roughs is the Once-City?'

'I don't know,' Sarah said, eyes down on her hands. 'It moves. I need to do a calling to find it. Probably somewhere between three and six days' sailing, maybe more.'

'It better not be more,' Little Wing said, looking down at the captain, and Kindred felt a shock as she remembered her lie, tiny and passing though it was. A single, tenuous fiber pulling them east.

'It won't be,' Kindred said. 'We can burn harder if need be. We have the bones. We'll make it.'

Little Wing gave her a nod before turning back to Sarah.

'You can beg sanctuary, is that right? And it will protect us for the stay? All those kids' stories about that are true?'

'Yes.'

'Good. Then here's what we'll do. We dock. You beg sanctuary. Me and a few others go with the captain to get her healed. Everyone else stays on board. Once she's healed, we pay whatever we can, barter the rest for water and food, and get the fuck out.'

'Okay. That's fine,' Sarah said, her voice breathy and tired.

'Anything goes wrong with you begging sanctuary, or I get the sense that you're pulling us into some kind of trap, and –'

'You'll kill me, I know.' Sarah's eyelids hung heavy as she looked up at Little Wing looming over her. 'I'm not those pirates who kill and steal. I left that life for this one. I'm part of this crew.'

She stood, or tried to. Her legs slid away beneath her, and Kindred darted forward to slide an arm around her. Sarah offered Kindred a look of sleepy appreciation. Together, they got her upright.

'The captain needs rest now, and there's nothing more I can do for her. I'm going to sleep, and then I'll do the calling. I'll get us to the Once-City and get us inside. I want the captain to live just as much as you all do.'

Sarah pushed off from Kindred and walked out, unsteady.

'I should throw her in chains,' Little Wing said, staring after her.

'She saved the captain,' Kindred said. 'You should give her a medal.'

'Maybe I should throw you in chains,' Little Wing said, rounding on Kindred. 'For nearly killing the captain.'

'Maybe you should give me a medal for saving every person on board from that wyrm,' Kindred retorted. Sarah's exhausted resistance had stirred something in Kindred, and she thought again of Sarah telling her to stop feeling sorry for herself.

Little Wing's face hardened into something murderous and mad. Maybe this had not been the best time, with everyone on edge and Little Wing sleepless and stressed, to speak out.

'She's right,' Quixa said, her wide eyes haunting in the afternoon light filling the cabin. 'Without Kindred doing her magic with the fire, we would all be dead at the bottom of the Sea or in the wyrm's stomach right now.'

Little Wing stared between them, her mouth opening and closing soundlessly.

'She's going to get us there,' Kindred said. 'You can trust her, Little Wing. We're going to save the captain.'

'She's part of the crew, Little Wing,' Quixa said. 'No matter her past, she's part of the crew.'

Little Wing must have told her, Kindred realized.

'*Fine.*' Little Wing spat the word at them both. 'Quixa, take the wheel. True east. Kindred, get the fire in order for the Roughs. I need Scindapse for help with repairs.'

'Aye. I'll tell her.'

As Kindred followed Quixa out, she turned to look once more at the captain.

Little Wing crouched next to her, holding one of the captain's hands in her own, finally letting the mask of captain fall away to reveal the sailor, the friend, the person beneath it.

It was a near-perfect reflection of the scene Kindred had left the last time she had walked out of this room, Ragged Sarah and Little Wing watching over their captain in the only ways they knew how.

Kindred pulled the door closed as she left that moment behind.

The Roughs were coming.

Before sending Scindapse away for repair work, Kindred used her help to create a build of preparation. A strong construction with pockets and alleys that might be easily opened or closed off to deal with immediate changes in Sea level. Kindred used her one unburned hand to guide Scindapse as the younger keeper placed bones of all kinds inside the build, hidden potential that they might unlock when they reached the Roughs.

'That's crazy,' Scindapse said after they'd finished, sitting back and surveying the complicated edifice of bone inside the fire. 'Did you learn to do that from one of the books?'

'The books don't have builds for sailing into the Roughs,' Kindred said, shaking her head. 'The bookmavens have some vague ideas about what a Rough build should do, but they don't really know.'

'Where did you learn it, then?' Scindapse asked.

'From my grandmother,' Kindred said. She had told Scindapse a little of her training but had carefully clipped off the bit about her failing out of the hearthkeeping schools. Scindapse was already anxious about keeping the fire; best she didn't know that her teacher had been taught by a madwoman and knew few of the prescribed builds and theories.

'Did she sail into the Roughs a lot?'

'Only once,' Kindred said, thinking of *Revenger* at port in Arcadia, hull scored with great slashes.

'Will this really work?' Scindapse asked, staring still at the build in the fire.

I hope so.

'Absolutely,' Kindred said, smiling. 'And now you're needed for repairs. Talk to Quixa and she'll tell you what you need to do.'

'Okay. But I can be back here with you when we get to the Roughs, right?'

Kindred could remember exactly this: the feeling of excitement when she discovered her natural connection with the hearthfire, the sense that she had found something she was actually good at, something she could actually do. It had felt like purpose.

'Of course. I need you,' she said, and though Scindapse's grin was enough to show she thought Kindred was just being gracious, it was true. With just one hand, she would need Scindapse there for the Roughs.

She tended the build for some time, as afternoon stretched into evening. A bare meal of dried soldier beetle and rationed water was delivered out to the crew, and Kindred ate hers before the fire, chewing slowly at the dry crumbles to make them last longer.

The Errant was sailing east again and the hearthfire was as prepared as it would get. Kindred stood and moved to the bow. She climbed the wrecked stairs up to the quarterdeck, moving around the wyrm's destruction or leaping over it when possible, until she stood fore.

The Sea before her, Kindred let herself float for a moment, away from the captain, from the Once-City out there beyond the horizon, from her grandmother and the deeps, from Ragged Sarah. She floated and looked out upon the Forever Sea.

The sun sang poetry amid the waves of grass bending and arcing endlessly in the wind. Green and green and green swelled and shushed and slipped, a study in chaos, a lesson in infinities.

Kindred closed her eyes into the prairie wind, feeling its familiar whisper against her cheek, neck, eyelids. The low-slung slant of late-afternoon light might have grown too warm, but the wind tempered it until Kindred's face felt perfectly warmed, perfectly cooled.

In that light, blues and greens and reds flared to life, and the world became as it always might have been. The sun stretched her light between the plants of the Forever Sea, webbing luminous among a rill of big bluestem still too young to harvest, highlighting a splash of purple and white from a small patch of granny's bonnet. Light yawned between blades of grass thinner than Kindred's arm and shouted, brash and reflective, off of blades wide enough to engulf a person, to carry her down to the darks, to the deeps.

The Sea, a shadow-and-light world of its own, wove and sang in its endless expanse, stretching back toward the docks at Arcadia and the Mainland beyond that, stretching away toward the Mists in the north, the Scrubwaste in the south. And before *The Errant*, the Sea went the way of the sunrise, running toward the horizon, toward forever, toward an eternity that maps and stories could only wonder at.

It was all Kindred could see, all she could imagine. And yet. And yet.

A darkness, a less-known, less-knowable forever, stirred beneath the waves of grass and green. Promising a world, many worlds, below. Kindred felt herself falling down through those waves, the silken slide of grass rubbing her arms, cushioning her back as she descended into the unknown, every breath a discovery, every new sensation a wonder.

Listen for me in the grasses and listen for me below.

A shiver having nothing to do with the wind wound up Kindred's back, and she opened her eyes, considering forever, forevers.

'Keeper.' Ragged Sarah appeared next to Kindred. The miracle of sleep had restored Sarah to herself, eyes once more sharp with that mischievous glint, mouth tipping perpetually toward a smile.

'Caller,' Kindred said, turning toward Sarah with a smile of her own.

'I need you,' Sarah said.

'You . . . what.' Kindred felt her face glow with heat as Sarah's mouth finally found a grin to match the glee in her eyes.

'I need to do the calling now, and I was hoping you could help me. I need your help.'

'Oh, of course. Sure. What do you need?'

She followed Sarah down to the mainmast, where Sarah grabbed a rope and began tying a complicated knot in a thick rope hanging from above.

'I'm going to be doing a greater call,' Sarah said, returning to her work with the knot. 'Huge amount of energy, lots of plants burned, but if it goes well, we'll get a good picture of what's up ahead and where the Once-City is. Normally, any one of those things would require two or three separate calls, but there's no time.'

Sarah finished the knot and turned to Kindred.

'And that's why I need you. Normally, I would just light the fire in the nest basin myself, but a calling like this needs a splinter of the hearthfire.'

A *splinter*. Kindred remembered her grandmother using that same word to talk about hearthfire that moved. Others on board talked about 'some of the fire' or 'part of the fire,' as though it could be simply cut up or halved.

Sarah was asking for Kindred to do exactly what she had done when they fled Arcadia, the action that had left her hand burned beyond feeling.

Kindred nodded, trying to keep her mind from fixating on the feeling of fire eating away at flesh, the feeling of the hearthfire cupped in her hand, blistering and blackening and burning.

She took a breath and moved to the hearthfire. As she sang to the flames and selected a slender length of charred bone, one unnecessary to the preparatory build, gripping it awkwardly in her left hand, Kindred saw Little Wing back at the wheel, watching her.

Kindred let the air leave her lungs, exhaling everything, forgetting what she could and briefly ignoring the rest. She lifted the splinter, singing a beseeching melody, one to calm the fire and herself. The flame flickering from the bone in her hand burned a deep, almost-black blue, contrary to the rich, golden flames burning in the hearthfire. Already, it had become a new entity.

And already, it tired her.

She cast a skeptical eye over the hearthfire, making sure it would burn all right while she helped Sarah. Once satisfied, she walked back over to where Ragged Sarah was waiting for her.

'A trip to the great blue, love?' she asked, holding out her hand, pitching her voice like one of the merchants calling out to the shills in Arcadia's bazaars.

'I . . .' Kindred traced the mainmast up and up with her eyes. It seemed to lance up into the clouds. 'I don't know if I can make it up there with my hand.'

'I figured. I'm going to help you up.'

Ragged Sarah slipped a hand holding a rope around Kindred's waist, slowing there for only a moment, pulled together, sharing the same air, the same breath. Kindred felt swept up in Sarah's surprising closeness, the light filtering through the wave of her colorful hair in the wind.

Everything out there had become confusing and strange, and Kindred felt pulled in every direction – forward for the captain, back for Little Wing, below for herself. Something important was happening inside of her, and though she couldn't yet articulate it, Kindred knew in that moment that somehow, Sarah was part of it, this woman who seemed to be one thing but held a secret, softer side away from the world.

'There. Lean back on that,' Ragged Sarah said, tying off the rope, making a looping chair for Kindred. From the forest of ropes hanging and slung and tied off from the mast, Sarah took one and pulled, and Kindred ascended, the new hearthfire cradled in one hand.

The mast was a spike of reality in front of her, cut through with the gold and silver and blue lettering of ancient spellwork – a relic of an age when the Silent Men of Arcadia still carved the masts from Trees of the Valley, a single mast offered by a single tree, carved and enchanted all in a single night.

Kindred had never met the Silent Men before they shut their abbey doors forever, great locks on the outside filled and sealed with clay, doors on top of which huge wooden crossbeams were angled, nailed, and secured. The story went that, after the last beam was put in place, the abbey forever sealed away at the edges of Arcadia, a bag of coin – the final payment for the builders – was launched out of one of the high windows along with a note. It read only, Forget about us, for we have forgotten about you.

It had taken several years for anyone to become familiar with mast-making, with the delicate spellwork necessary to hold a prairie ship together. Finally, after a period of intense despair among the shipping world, a man from the Mainland, the Border Baron, had found the answer and begun production of functioning masts again, each one carved with the necessary magical runes that could pull the hearthfire's magic into the rest of the ship and keep it afloat.

Still, with the shipping delays from the mast-making families, Arcadian sailors had out of necessity taken chances on the inexperienced work of the guild mages in those in-between years. Kindred shuddered at the memories of stories told over drink in taverns: ships ripped apart in the Forever Sea's fickle winds, masts enchanted wrong and unable to sing in tune with the hearthfire, spontaneously catching fire or fracturing with great, doomed *cracks*.

Kindred stared at the etchings as she rose; below, Ragged Sarah's arms moved in a steady, slow rhythm.

At the top, Kindred placed one careful foot onto the crow's nest and then the other, pulling herself under the guardrail with the crook of her arm, not trusting her burned hand beneath its many layers of cloth. She sat down on the small wooden platform, cradling the splinter of hearthfire in her hand.

From here, the Sea was an impossible beauty, a world of green describing the wind's dance. Kindred peered through the space in the guardrail, feeling every dip and rise of *The Errant*, every pitch a hundred times over, understanding the ship's movements in drastic ways.

'Spectacular, isn't it?' Ragged Sarah said as she appeared, scaling a single rope with ease. She climbed into the crow's nest and slumped back against the guardrail.

'It's amazing,' Kindred said, hushed and reverent, letting her eyes rake over the endless green of the Sea. She felt as though she were seeing anew a person she'd known forever. Here was her Sea, seen and loved as if for the first time. 'I can't believe I've never been up here to see it before.'

Ragged Sarah laughed, sitting easily in the cramped space, her legs folded in front of her and yet somehow still splayed, the bend of her knees and fall of her arms at once constrained and luxurious.

'I've yet to sail on a ship where the nest wasn't the best place to be.' Sarah looked out toward the Sea, and Kindred let herself imagine for just a moment that they saw the waves in the same way. Not as a field from which to harvest plants, coin to be snatched. Not as a space to be traversed, an obstacle between a sailor and her destination, her next payday. Not as the flat, featureless thing so many believed it to be.

It lived wildly. It moved and danced. It breathed and offered breath.

A prairie Sea, sky-deep and stretching past the horizon. In the sliding fingers of wind, grasses flipped and angled, darkening away from the sun's direct light. From so high up, it looked like great shadows skimming over the surface of the Sea, driven by the wind, searching endlessly.

'Let's get started,' Ragged Sarah said, gesturing to the metal bowl set into the floor of the crow's nest.

Kindred set the splinter carefully inside.

Ragged Sarah nodded, dropping in a few stray plants pulled from her pockets, curious curling leaves, a deep red flecked through with bits of green and gold.

'What are those?' Kindred leaned close, forgetting about the hearthfire for a moment, which stretched high and flicked a gentle warmth on her jaw and face.

Sarah pulled back, eyes wide.

'Careful,' she said, panic in her voice.

Kindred looked up, confused, still wondering after the strange, beautiful plants now burning bright.

'What?'

Sarah's eyes were wide as she reached out one, two fingers to touch Kindred's jaw where the fire had caressed her. Kindred felt her face flush as Ragged Sarah's callused fingers slid over her jaw and cheek, which were both probably smeared with day-old coal dust.

'No burn? I know you can hold the fire and work it with your hands.' *Hand*, Kindred thought involuntarily. 'But your whole body is safe from it?'

'I have given myself over to the fire,' Kindred said, slow and confused. Had Sarah never spoken with the keepers on her previous ships? Was it different on pirate vessels? 'As long as I'm careful' – she held up her still-bandaged hand – 'and don't ask too much of myself or the fire, it won't burn me.'

Ragged Sarah shook her head, flashing her teeth in a grin.

'Amazing. I didn't know you had such control over it.'

Kindred grinned, too, shaking her head.

'It's not control. It's trust and partnership.'

Sarah cocked her head but didn't say anything.

'I'm sure it was the same on your . . . previous ships, wasn't it?' Kindred asked, nearly saying *pirate ships* instead.

'The keepers from the Once-City I sailed with treated the fire like an enemy to be watched warily and, when the time called for it, beaten into submission. They were nothing like you,' Ragged Sarah said, shrugging. 'I've never met a hearthfire keeper – even one on Arcadia – who moved with the fire like you do, Kindred. You're different.'

Kindred felt warm blood fill her cheeks, and she was grateful for the shout from below.

'Get a move on!' came Little Wing's voice from below.

'Right,' Ragged Sarah said, winking at Kindred. 'We're not up here to talk, sadly.'

Kindred laughed a little and nodded.

'Can you make the fire burn hotter and higher?' Sarah asked, pulling more plants from her pockets.

'Sure,' Kindred said, smiling. She sang then, a song of entreaty, and the fire answered, blooming higher, flames reaching up, shifting colors until they settled on a bright red.

'What language is that?' Sarah asked as she rummaged through her pockets, pulling out more plants. 'It sounds like what Rhabdus used to sing in, but not quite.'

Kindred tipped her head from side to side.

'It's close to that, yes. We all sing in the language of the hearthfire. Some have memorized the songs with little or no understanding of what they actually mean. Like how most sailors know that bones in the hearthfire means a ship goes, but they don't know why or how. Most hearthfire keepers sing words that are not their own in a language they don't understand, and they sing them *at* the hearthfire.'

'And you?'

Kindred smiled.

'My words are all my own, known and understood. And I sing *with* the hearthfire, not *at* it.'

Ragged Sarah shook her head and laughed as she dropped more plants onto the fire, some of which Kindred knew and many which she didn't. Some burned but most only smoked upon contact, coughing out great gouts of writhing smoke, thick and thin tendrils, each one a brilliant, bright, shifting set of colors – one moment reflecting the shine of the sun like a coin or blade might, the next a spark of silver shooting through a storm of grey, a bolt of lightning echoing through clouds.

The smoke snaked sinuous in the air, reaching out and doubling back but always expanding its circumference, pushing out a little farther.

'Good. Move back.' Ragged Sarah put a gentle hand on Kindred's shoulder and pushed. In that moment, Kindred wanted nothing more than to enjoin her own hand there, but she allowed herself to go back, sliding across the platform until she felt the rough wood of the guardrail behind her.

'Stay back there,' Ragged Sarah said before stepping to the fire, to the smoky nebula it had become, allowing herself to be consumed by it. Kindred could barely make her out in the flashing and changing colors of the smoke, which swirled and cut around her with increasing speed.

Ragged Sarah began chanting in a high, ululating voice, singing without melody or music, like poetry. Words ran together into a slip-slide fall, eliding and colliding, a murmuration that threatened to entrance Kindred. Staring into that well of shifting, sliding smoke, staring into those kaleidoscopic colors, listening to Sarah's strange litany, Kindred felt herself drifting away.

Ragged Sarah's voice dropped away for a moment and then she spoke a single word, low and heavy, in a language Kindred did not know.

The storm of thick smoke exploded.

Tendrils raced in every direction, some leaping high, high into the sky, nearly disappearing in the cloud, their tails describing shifting, calamitous colors. Others dipped low, skimming the surface of the Sea and slurring the grasses there, while some spiraled corkscrews through the air before disappearing, only to blur into existence farther away, grey and black and silver punctuation marks dipping in and out of perceivable space, traveling forth in their skipping, stuttering jaunt.

Smoke streamed from the tendrils, as though *The Errant* were the epicenter of a great, sorcerous explosion, one that continued to affect the world, the edge racing forever on. Soon, many of the tendrils had disappeared over the horizon, blinking out of existence, leaving Kindred staring at Ragged Sarah, naked of her smoky cover, her breath labored, her face running with sweat.

'Now,' Ragged Sarah said, slumping to the platform, exhaustion plain on her face, 'we wait.'

'What's it like?' Kindred asked into the slow-sky of the crow's nest. She had never realized how quiet the nest was, how unaffected by the work on deck it was. Apart from the steady song of the hearthfire in her mind, playing behind her thoughts and assuring her the fire still burned steadily in her absence, Kindred felt totally distant from the ship below.

'What's what like?' Sarah asked, looking up from the small bundles of plants she'd been organizing and placing into her various pockets.

'The Once-City.'

Ragged Sarah shrugged and looked out into the sky.

'Most of the stories aren't true, at least as far as I can remember it. Pirates aren't cannibals; they don't drink prairie air and feed on the darkness of night. They weren't created from the chaos beneath the Sea.' Sarah said all of this in a low, mock-serious voice, arching her eyebrows at the conspiracies.

Kindred laughed, but then a thought struck her.

'How does begging sanctuary work? I'm guessing it's more than just running up a white flag.'

'Slightly more than that, yeah,' Sarah said, chuckling. 'It's not flying a white flag or walking up to the first pirate you see and saying "Sanctuary!" You have to ask in the ancient prairie languages, the ones that are carved into the central column of the Once-City.'

Sarah leaned back, smiling, her eyes far away.

'I hated just about everything in that place, but I loved looking at that enormous wooden column and seeing languages older than anyone could remember.'

Kindred tried to imagine it, but she couldn't, and so she settled for watching Sarah's remembering.

Without warning, Sarah's voice shifted, and she spoke words in a language Kindred didn't know, a language like no other Kindred had ever heard. The syllables made Sarah sit upright as they rolled from her tongue, as if demanding respect, and Kindred found herself sitting up straighter, too. Sounds like power, old as paths underfoot, thrumming with meaning. The crow's nest filled with the sound of Sarah speaking, and Kindred realized it was the same phrase or sentence or verb or *something* said over and over.

Finally, Sarah stopped, and Kindred felt breathless. She was smiling, wider than before, without realizing it.

'That's begging sanctuary,' Sarah said. 'If you can't do it correctly, there's some test you have to pass. I never knew any to take it, though I left the Once-City quite young and didn't have much to do with that side of things. I taught the captain how to beg sanctuary correctly, but I can just do it when we arrive.'

Kindred leaned in close and said, 'Teach me.'

Sarah laughed, and so she did, sounding out bits of the whole and encouraging Kindred.

'Does everyone there speak this language?' Kindred asked when the syllables began to congeal together on her tongue and she had called it quits. She would try again later.

'No, no. Apart from a few phrases like that one, it's mostly forgotten. And it's only one of the old prairie languages – there are others that have even fewer remembered bits. It's all carved into that central column, the languages mixed together. I used to think the letters and symbols up on the central column were like grave markers. Only a few people in the Once-City can actually translate and understand it – we'll need to have one of them come out and verify that we've correctly begged sanctuary.'

'How big is the Once-City?' Kindred asked, trying to picture it in her mind.

'Much bigger than most think. It's a city, but really, it's more like several cities, each a different level, stacked on top of one another like wheels. Most of it is below the Sea, you know.'

Kindred shook her head. The only thing she'd known about the Once-City was that it floated in the Forever Sea, always moving.

But a whole city mostly below the Sea? Kindred thought of the Marchess and saw her own steps toward the deeps.

'If it's below the surface, how will we find it?' Kindred asked.

Ragged Sarah smiled into the wind.

'You know those insane stories about the Once-City being carved into the trunk of an enormous tree?'

'Yeah, of course,' Kindred said, remembering the drawings she had seen, done mostly by children, of people living inside a vast tree.

'They're not just stories,' Ragged Sarah said, grinning.

It began with birds like stars in the sky.

Kindred saw them in the distance, tiny tinklings of white, an entire flock of birds, angling to catch the sun's light on their back one moment – a brilliant white constellation – and then disappearing the next.

Ragged Sarah had been saying something about ointment, when to put more on her hand or how much to put on or something like that, but Kindred felt herself pulled away.

She could remember every time she'd ever seen a bird on the Sea.

A wilting loon, her third year aboard *Revenger*, seen from afar.

A great condor, her fourth year aboard *Revenger*, its body tangled in the grasses of the Sea, magnificent and terrible and so, so sad in its death.

A rainbird, only a few spans past, though it had been so far off that no one aboard had gotten a good look at it. The captain had demanded they turn and give chase, hoping to sail beneath it and fill their water stores with the mythical rain the stories promised surrounded the rainbird, but even *The Errant* racing with full sail, hearthfire raging, couldn't catch it.

But this, to see a flock, a family, a coterie of birds in flight. Kindred felt her heart race at the discovery of it, the sheer impossibility of seeing so much amid the endless forever of the Sea.

'Gods,' she whispered, pulling herself upright and grasping for Ragged Sarah's longsight. Ragged Sarah chuckled and handed Kindred the instrument.

Through the circumscribed magnification of the longsight, Kindred could see them, and she began to describe what she was seeing aloud, because wonder, true wonder, must be shared, must live on the breath.

'Eight, nine gembills. At least, I think they're gembills. Long wings, white and brown feathers, bills sparkling even from here, like they're crusted with precious stones.'

Kindred remembered Messit's *Birds and Dragons of the Forever Sea*, a book she'd spent many long afternoons poring over, studying the pictures and memorizing the names, the minutiae and ephemera of the creatures Messit had spent his life seeking. Another life spent reaching into the unending world of the Sea.

'Only nine? I must be losing my touch,' Ragged Sarah said, and Kindred barely registered the wry humor in her voice, the smile apparent in her tone. Kindred cared only for the patch of sky shown in the longsight.

'They're flying in a strange pattern, almost as if they're circling something. Messit's book said they flew only in long, elegant lines, but this, it's – oh.'

The flock of birds flickered in and out of existence – not the play of light on their backs giving them form and then reducing them to faint shadowed lines. They disappeared entirely, gone from sight, no more – wait. There. A single bird remained, one of the larger gembills, its color darker, its bill etched with thick veins of vermilion-colored gems and smaller glittering tributaries of dark, rich blue and black.

The bird flapped for *The Errant* with speed and purpose.

A raucous cacophony sounded behind Kindred, a rich coughing of wry laughter and chortling. She turned quickly enough to stumble, hungry to see what she hoped, what she thought – and then a hand on her hip, steadying her, Ragged Sarah's voice in her ear.

'Easy. They're not going anywhere anytime soon. You've got time enough.'

In her amazement, Kindred sank back against Sarah.

A rowdy tangle of crows sported in the air just off *The Errant*'s bow, chuckling against one another like clever children, their play one of just-misses and daring dives. Too, too close: leaves of the same branch. The awed exclamations of the crew below filtered up to where Kindred and Ragged Sarah stood.

The birds were near enough to see with her naked eyes, but

Kindred hungered for specifics, so she brought the longsight up again, joying in the waxy glisten of black, the adolescent amusement in curving beak and talon.

But there – distant as the crows were close, a pair of birds, just visible as they flew in front of a low-slung cloud. As if meant for the sky, the birds flapped their wide, white wings only occasionally, their movement stately and graceful, easy even as they cut through the air. Long, perfect, with speared grey heads splashed with a vivid, bloody red, they neared, and Kindred felt everything in her go unbearably still.

'Sandhill cranes,' Kindred said, voice hushed into reverence.

'What?' Ragged Sarah stiffened suddenly, shifting around and taking the longsight from Kindred's hands. 'It can't be.'

Kindred barely heard her, not needing the longsight to see the approach of the cranes – and, approaching from what seemed every direction, the wonder of birds streaking through the sky toward *The Errant*, many of them close enough now to make out specifics: the way a pair of feet were held up under the body in flight, the teeter-totter tip of wings catching updrafts. She saw great larks and lesser larks, edgewings, Potter's loons, prairie geese, white pelicans – birds that brought to life memorized pictures in her mind and birds that she'd never seen before.

'This is bad,' Sarah muttered, her voice dark with despair.

'What do you mean?' Kindred asked.

'Different birds offer different information. Some speak to the character of the Sea. Some weather patterns approaching. Some what lies before, others what lies behind. They're signs to be read, interpreted.'

'What do sandhill cranes speak to?' Kindred asked.

'Enemy vessels.'

Kindred sucked in a breath.

'You need to get low,' Ragged Sarah said, the longsight still pressed to her eye. 'Very low.'

'What?' Kindred said, staring wide-eyed at a still-far-off lone bird headed their way, one she'd never seen a likeness of before. Two sets of wings, grey and green, preceding a tail that twisted and swirled behind, caught in the sun and articulating colors Kindred had no names for, colors she –

Ragged Sarah pushed her to the platform a breath before huge explosions of sound ripped the air apart.

The birds were landing, huge talons longer than Kindred's hand wrapping around the guardrail surrounding the crow's nest. Shushing wings and clicking beaks suddenly existed in too little space, and Kindred could only watch, breath held captive in her chest.

Where there was only one bird – as was the case with the lone remaining gembill – it arrived in a rush of speed and, head cocked to the side, intelligent eye glaring at Ragged Sarah, offered a series of clicks or chirps or caws or warbles, all of which Sarah took down on a scrap of cloth she produced from her pocket, scribbling frantically with a chip of charcoal.

Where there were multiple birds – as was the case with the party of crows – one was sent, emissary-like, the other members of its flock holding their place in the air, no longer laughing or diving about. The entire process had an air of formality about it, as though the trip to *The Errant* had been an opportunity to exorcise any jittery anxiety or playful exuberance, and now it was time for business.

One by one the birds arrived, filling the guardrail, a congress of wings and beaks, the air heavy and oppressive with their intent.

And in the middle stood Ragged Sarah, listening and writing, her face showing focus. And fear.

When a bird finished its recitations, it took off again, buffeting Kindred with a cyclonic rush of air, stirring up any dust left on the crow's nest.

The last to arrive were the four-winged beauty and one of the Birds of the Dawn, which nearly brought Kindred to tears as it arrived, alighting on a patch recently vacated by a blacklark. The Bird of the Dawn puffed wide its sky-blue wings as it landed, its talons curving around the railing without a sound. It was grace made manifest, and it held itself high and proud.

The four-winged bird landed opposite, its size and weight making a silent landing impossible. It landed with a crack and a creak that promised repairs later on. Its body was bigger, more powerful than any of the other birds Kindred had seen – there or in Messit's book – and its beak gave way to a ridge of wicked teeth when it vocalized, releasing a long, low croak, like a toad. Horns curled back and away from its head, emphasizing the slit of its pupil, a black sliver in a sea of white.

When the birds were finished, they, too, took off, angling for the sky, disappearing like the others had apparently, for the skies were suddenly empty again, save for the quick-moving shadows of a very few messengers racing for the horizon. The last to disappear was the four-winged bird, which Kindred watched until her eyes hurt and it was only the shape of her imagination against the blue of the sky.

'I've never seen anything like that,' Kindred said, slumped back against the guardrail – now gouged and clawed from playing host to so many talons.

'Dammit,' Ragged Sarah said, frantic, looking over the paper in her hand once more before moving quickly, grabbing for ropes, fashioning again the seat for Kindred. If the greater calling had tired her out, she didn't show it now. 'You need to get down to the hearthfire.'

Kindred heard the panic in her voice, the self-assured cockiness gone. A wave of cold ran down Kindred's arms.

'What did the birds tell you?'

Ragged Sarah offered the rope seat and helped Kindred into it, pushing her off the edge into space and lowering her in short, jaunty drops.

'We're being followed.'

10

KINDRED dropped to the deck in a clatter of boots on wood. She had only really begun to disentangle herself from the rope around her when Ragged Sarah crashed to the deck nearby, her fall too fast.

'Shit,' Sarah muttered, wobbling a little as she picked herself up, favoring one knee but moving quickly away anyway. Kindred dropped the last of the rope around her and hurried to follow through the collections of joyous crew, all of them talking and laughing and grinning about the calling. Many of them plied her with questions and entreaties, but Kindred ignored them and caught up with Ragged Sarah on the quarterdeck, where Little Wing stood at the wheel.

We're being followed.

Kindred looked behind the ship, into their wake and up to the horizon, but she could see nothing.

'What is it?' Little Wing asked, her face hardening as she looked from Sarah to Kindred.

'Five ships follow us at a distance, captain, each flying Cantrev's banner. They may not reach us before the Roughs, but they will catch us before we reach the Once-City. They burn bones with abandon and do not have to deal with the damage aboard we do.'

'Fucking Cantrev. What else?'

Kindred frowned. What else? Five Arcadian warships following them with abandon wasn't enough?

'There's a thistle reef stretching before us just past the beginning of the Roughs,' Ragged Sarah swept her arm in front of the ship, indicating a swath that covered half the horizon toward which *The Errant* sailed.

'How long to sail around it? Maybe Cantrev's idiot soldiers will try to cut us off and run aground the thistles.'

'At least two span,' Sarah said.

'Fuck. And you're sure the captain won't make it past a span?'

'*Two* span,' Sarah said, frowning in confusion. 'The captain will be out for two span. Beyond that, it gets unsafe to keep her unconscious.'

Blood roared in Kindred's ears. Her unburned hand stiffened at her side, and her teeth snapped together with a decisive *click*.

Slow, like day rolling into night, Little Wing turned her head to stare at Kindred. Her eyes were pits, dead and dangerous.

'I was told we had only a single span for the captain.'

Sarah was looking back along their wake, searching perhaps for Cantrev's pursuing vessels, oblivious to Little Wing's stare.

'No. Two. A day fewer now, I guess. Either way, we can't go around the reef. But there is a way through,' Ragged Sarah said, 'though, from what the birds could tell me, it's dangerous and narrow, like a mountain pass but bounded by steep banks of thistle. If any of Cantrev's ships manage to follow, they would gain quite quickly just by simply sailing in our wake.'

With an effort of will that pulled veins from her neck like swollen rivers, Little Wing turned back to Ragged Sarah.

'So, we burn hard,' Little Wing said. '*The Errant* can outrun any ship if we push her, even with the damage. We reach the pass through the reef before Cantrev catches up and then – '

'No.' Ragged Sarah's voice was pained and sharp as she interrupted. Kindred realized she was holding her breath.

'Sorry, it's worse than that. Even if we could make it through the reef without being caught or damaged enough to sink us – even then, we won't be safe. Cantrev's ships aren't the only ones with an interest in our path.' Sarah took a breath and then said, 'Our position has been noted by a group of pirates, and I'm told they have three cutters converging on us now from the Roughs this side of the reef and a dreadnought waiting for us where the pass through the reef terminates.'

'The birds told you all that?' Kindred asked. It was her turn to be amazed at Sarah's abilities.

Ragged Sarah nodded, her eyes far away, one hand pulling at the edge of her jacket.

'Cantrev's ships burning hard behind, three cutters closing from the side, a needle-thin pass through an enormous thistle reef, and a dreadnought waiting for us on the other side if we make it through. No time or space to turn around. Herded into the pass and that cursed city beyond. Is that the truth of it?' Little Wing spoke in a monotone as she glared at Ragged Sarah.

Ragged Sarah nodded.

'Pushed where we should never have been in the first place,' Little Wing said, flicking her eyes to Kindred before making her decision. 'We make for the pass. Keeper, ready for the Roughs. Sarah, back in the nest. Now.'

They scattered, each to their own place.

Except Kindred, who was pulled backward by Little Wing as she tried to move back to the fire.

'If I didn't need you for the Roughs,' Little Wing said through mostly gritted teeth, 'I would kill you here and now. I don't know why you lied, but it's clear you've put yourself and whatever childish ideas you have about the Once-City ahead of crew and captain. Any injuries, any deaths – they're on your hands. You understand? This is your doing.'

Little Wing shoved her back, hard enough that Kindred spilled onto the deck hard.

'Get back to the fucking fire and do your job.'

Little Wing was off before Kindred could get to her feet, shouting orders to the crew, directing action to prepare for the Roughs, to ready aft and fore defenses.

Kindred joined in the chaos of the ship, feeling the residue of Little Wing's anger, of her own betrayal. She thought of the Marchess leaving her crew to the tangled terror of the Roughs because she stayed true to her own desires. Could she follow her own path without betraying someone? Could she follow her own dreams without burning someone else's?

Head spinning with these thoughts, Kindred moved through those running about the deck until she reached the hearthfire. Scindapse was already there waiting for her.

Before settling down, she pulled an armful of bones from the closet, enough for an extended run, and dropped them between where she and Scindapse sat.

'Don't let those go anywhere,' she said.

'Speed, keepers! Get us up to speed!' came Little Wing's voice through the tumult and movement aboard.

'Aye' was the only appropriate response, though Kindred felt some of the familiar annoyance. The hearthfire could not, would not respond immediately to the whims of its keeper. Little Wing knew this, Kindred imagined, and just chose to push for the impossible.

Kindred thought of stories she'd heard from other keepers of captains demanding a dead halt from a speeding run or an exact map of the Sea – 'draw it using the coals of the fire; maybe that will work,' one keeper had said, laughing and imitating her captain, though quietly and with looks about before and after.

'What should I do?' Scindapse asked, eyes wide, hands restless.

'Sit still and pray this works,' Kindred said.

Bones arrayed beside her like the fragments of a forgotten language, Kindred leaned toward the fire, whispering a soft song of beginnings.

'*Arise, begin, reach sky with flame,*
We race for Sea, the endless line,
We go, we go, arise, arise.'

With her one unburned hand, Kindred reached into the flames and pulled one long rib bone from her build of preparation. If she and Scindapse had done their work well, the removal of the rib bone, which had been stopping up the flow of air and heat in the build and forcing the fire to burn only around the outside, would awaken the structure. No longer a closed mansion of bone, the build would light with heat and air and power, channeling the magic of the hearthfire through its various caverns and hallways, a wonder of Kindred's own making.

Instead, when she removed the rib bone, the entire structure slouched and crumpled, like a child's tower built too high with unsteady hands.

It tipped.

It fell.

And with it, the speed of *The Errant* fell away too.

Scindapse let out a guttural groan as the whole of the structure collapsed into an ugly pile of bones at the base of the now-roiling fire.

'Dammit, Kindred! Speed!' Little Wing's roar sparked the crew back to action, and Kindred returned her attention to the fire.

'Let me think, let me think,' Kindred said, holding up her hand to forestall Scindapse's questions.

Kindred conjured in her mind the structure she wanted to create as she cleared away the mess of her failed attempt: a design of her own she'd named *Centicipitous*, after the children's stories of X'Niar, the hundred-headed beast guarding the caverns below the Forever Sea. The structure was a simple one: a central stalk of bone buried into the coals and several – perhaps ten or twelve, an approximation of X'Niar's many more heads – extensions reaching up and out from the central stalk, extensions either pulled from the stalk itself or flicks of other bones grafted on. One by one, the extensions would burn away, hard and hot, building the speed of the ship with a steady increase. When it was finished, the structure looked more like a bouquet of flowers than any of the drawings she'd seen done of X'Niar, but Kindred preferred her imaginative name still.

But she'd never created *Centicipitous* with only a single hand before, and she didn't have time to explain it to Scindapse. It was worlds beyond what the young keeper was currently capable of.

Kindred ground her teeth together, feeling more than ever the inability to use both her hands. She breathed – in through her nose, out through her mouth. This would not beat her.

She abandoned *Centicipitous*.

She flicked through the builds in her memory, searching and searching. *Tesu's Wreck* could be done one-handed, she thought, but was focused on solidity in huge winds, and so provided little speed. *Three-Fold*, too, could be built with a single hand but it was designed for accentuating speed while beating windward.

'Back to the five, Kindred,' she told herself, just as she used to as a younger girl, angry at the Marchess for keeping so much knowledge from her.

She whispered the litany to herself, remembering the rough deck of her grandmother's ship, the close quarters there, the sound of its single sail pulling and straining in a fierce wind, the life she had aboard *Revenger*.

'*Speed in tenuous length*.

Solidity in bolstered support.

Arcs in green, spirals in gold.

Fire burns first and hottest at the base.

Do not circumscribe the fire.'

Crew continued to run across the deck around her, and shouts became ubiquitous in the air.

'Speed with a transition to stability,' Kindred muttered to herself, trying to work out their situation. With the reef still some distance ahead, the Roughs coming close, and ships pursuing from behind at speed, she would need something that began tenuous, that offered speed over stability, and there was no way she could create a build like that with only one hand. She could picture a rudimentary version of what it should be: a single stalk rising from the coals with a hellishly complex and intricate bony bolus perched atop it. To graft and twist all of that together would be too difficult for Scindapse, certainly, but for Kindred and her one usable hand? No, it was not possible, not in the fire.

She needed some way to build the structure outside of the fire first, but without the hearthfire's magic and heat, she couldn't graft and mold and pull the bones.

'Ships sighted! Aft!' Ragged Sarah's call stilled the crew for a moment, and Kindred suddenly became aware of Little Wing standing over her.

'What the fuck is going on, Kindred?' Little Wing demanded, surveying the wreckage of Kindred's attempts, bones like so much detritus littered around the fire. 'Can you do this or not?'

'Yes, I can,' she said, unable to focus on Little Wing as she fought to come up with some plan, some build that would work for them.

And there, so close to the heat of Little Wing's anger, trapped and ready to dissolve, Kindred had an idea.

An insane, terrible, mad idea.

But an idea.

'*Child's Build* until I get back,' she said to Scindapse as she pushed herself roughly to her feet and ran for the edge of the ship. On the way, she shouted over her shoulder for help, a pair of strong hands to hold her. A voice shouted 'aye' behind her, though Kindred did not know who said it. Her focus lay ahead, on the Sea. As she ran, Kindred picked up one of the harvesting harnesses – a webwork of rope meant to hold a harvester while she was lowered into the Sea to cut precious plants. At the gunwale, she began to step into the harness, hoping her instinct was right about this.

'Be ready to pull me back,' Kindred said, handing the line trailing from the harness back to Little Wing, who had followed her. Her mind was chaos, racing through the danger and possibilities of this build, this plan, this madness.

She clambered over the gunwale and set her feet into the ladder, the Sea before her, racing by, though how much longer the scattered build she'd left in the hearthfire would last, Kindred didn't know. She needed to work fast.

As she put one foot below the other, Kindred felt a shot of joy and excitement move through her chest, buoyed by the whisper-shout of the grasses below her as *The Errant* cut through them.

At the ladder's end, Kindred pulled once on the line to make sure someone had her. After she felt the tension on the line, she shouted up, 'Let me down slowly.'

'Aye.'

But Little Wing was already lowering her down into the moving chaos of the Sea, a whiplash riot of green.

Kindred took a deep breath in – the scents of dry grass and life pulling by her and burning in her nose.

'Good there!' she shouted up, hoping her voice didn't betray the fear she suddenly felt. Would Little Wing drop her? How easy it might be, Kindred realized, to make it seem an accident. A bad rope. A broken harness. A current too strong, a ship speed too high. Any of it could justify Little Wing turning back to the deck, her hands empty, Kindred falling below into the black.

Still, she dropped lower.

Panicked now, Kindred grabbed the rope and tugged on it twice, and shouted louder.

'Hold there! Hold!'

Finally, after another drop down, she stopped, the rope above bending toward the ship as Kindred was pulled a little behind the course, dragging.

Despite the constant press of green parting around her and the intense feeling of closeness, Kindred let out a sigh of relief.

Listen for me in the grasses and listen for me below.

Her grandmother's words moved through her, unbidden, and Kindred thought of the promise of a wide and impossible world waiting beneath the green. A shiver of anticipation ran along her spine.

Quickly and with as much force as she could manage, Kindred grasped at the passing grasses, swiping forward and pulling her fingers together into a fist. Her reward was a bouquet of green blades, each half as wide as her hand and as long as her arm, a few with their ends still trailing in the Sea. It would do.

Kindred pulled again on the rope with her bandaged hand and was quickly pulled up. At the top, Little Wing hauled her aboard, the might of her muscles making Kindred feel like a slim sack of dried plants.

'Thank you,' Kindred said, looking up to meet Little Wing's eyes, but she was gone already, moving back into the work aboard without so much as a backward glance.

Dropping the harness, Kindred rushed back to the hearthfire, frantic and eager to test this new idea and just as fearful of its huge potential for failure.

At the fire, she placed her green bounty next to the bones and pictured again the structure she would need to make. It would be a crude thing with so little time to plan and no time at all to experiment.

'I need you to tie these bones together with this grass fast as you can. I'll hold them two at a time where they need to meet, and then I need you to fasten them together. Understand?' She spoke quickly to Scindapse, who had constructed the *Child's Build*. Wrong again, though less wrong this time.

'We're building it out of the fire?' Scindapse said. She had already pulled out a strand of grass and was holding it ready.

'Yes,' Kindred snapped, frantically sorting through the bones they had out and pairing them with the bones she was imagining for the build in her head. 'It's a terrible idea, and you should never do it, and there's no reason any good hearthkeeper would ever try it, and I'm out of fucking ideas, so we're doing it, now tie several knots *here*.'

She held out a long, straight bone and jabbed at a point on its length where a small notch had been created, either during life or after. Scindapse began tying without asking a single question.

And they set about building the structure *out of the fire*.

The heat and flames of the hearthfire enchanted bones, allowing them to stretch and pull, to find purchase in and among one another. In the hearthfire, bones became malleable spirits eager to bend to the experienced keeper's will and imagination.

Working on a structure out of the hearthfire was like trying to sail a ship on land, the keel buried deep in rock and mud, rags up, shouting at the crew to gain more speed.

But Kindred pushed past all of this, hoping cleverness might win the day when magic would not, could not.

A manic desperation moved Kindred as she found and held up bone after bone for Scindapse to tie, examining and piecing together the build in her mind as she and Scindapse did it there on the deck.

As it came into being, Kindred smiled, realizing that what they were building looked uncannily like a sail, caught full in the wind, blossoming in it, supported by the strong thrust of a mast.

A delicate wristbone, tied tight to the mast.

Strong arm bones to serve as the yards, radiating out in as many directions as possible.

Fingers looped by grass hung from the yard and tied to a boom below, a sturdy sternum.

Thick section of spine tangled in the growing net of the sail.

Arc of white strung through the now-choked tangle of bones in the sail.

'Keeper! Get us moving!' Little Wing's shout pulsed with an undercurrent of fear, and Kindred remembered the ships behind and ahead of them, Cantrev and the pirates closing on them like jaws.

Kindred dropped back to her work, trying to focus on the bones, the grass, the hearthfire still blazing before her, though she thought of Little Wing's litany of horrifying acts done by pirates, and she thought of being caught, boarded, the pirates stealing their bones, stealing the captain for her bones, and forcing the crew to take the green dive, down into the deeps.

A shiver of something that was not totally fear ran through Kindred.

She shook her head, blowing a quick spurt of air out of her mouth, releasing those imaginings for the time being.

'I think it's ready,' she said, nodding to Scindapse as she finished tying the last bit of grass and bone into the structure, which tinkled and chattered in the wind, strangely musical.

Scindapse took the whole of it from her while Kindred reached into the fire and began to sing. She let her voice lurk beneath the chaos on deck like a secret, a song only for the hearthfire, a covenant between her and the flames.

With her free hand, she patted down the coals and embers into a firm foundation, a rich pasture of glowing reds and oranges, letting the magic of her song seep into the spent bones, asking them to welcome this new structure, to fuse the grass instead of burning it away, to aid it in joining the bones together, at least until Kindred and Scindapse could magically firm up the connections.

The whisper of the hearthfire, a counterpoint to her song, was encouragement enough. With a nod to Scindapse, she took the structure – *Mast and Sail*, she'd decided to call it – and placed it in the flames, burying the mast deep in the coals and feeling a pull as the hearthfire took the bones as its own.

Kindred continued singing, fighting to keep the anxiety and tension out of her voice. The flames began to burn in earnest at the base of *Mast and Sail*, and Kindred felt the familiar push of speed as *The Errant* rushed forward, the tenuous length of the mast offering up its bounty.

But the fire reached higher, not yet burning through the bones but making itself known to them. Kindred moved as quickly as she could with just one hand, and Scindapse worked at the easier joints, the two of them twisting and pinching bones together, magic flowing into and through their fingers, grafting the lengths and clusters of white onto one another in the arcane heat of the fire.

And though the grass began to smoke and wail, adding a third voice to the melody Kindred and the fire and now Scindapse had created, it held, just, as Kindred had hoped it would, at least long enough for her to knit the bones of the sail together.

Scindapse leapt in the air and whooped her joy to the sky as their build channeled heat and air into power and speed. A few of the crew noticed, too, and added their own calls of joy.

A whistle from above pulled Kindred's attention up, and she saw Sarah leaning out over the crow's nest, extending out as far as the rope she held would let her, grinning down.

And for a moment, Kindred floated in that grin, her eyes on Sarah's as *The Errant* raced east.

THE calls came on the heels of one another, three shouts from Ragged Sarah above, barely a breath's space between them.

'Pursuit! In sight! In sight!'

Breath.

'Roughs ahead! Reef ahead!'

Breath.

'Pirates! Starboard fore and heeling hard toward! And warships aft! Aft! Aft!'

A moment of tranquility filled the deck – brief, so brief – and then movement and voices shouting and ropes coiled and uncoiled, sails shifted to better catch the wind, to better aid the push of the hearthfire.

Kindred leaned in closer to the fire and was surprised to see the grasses still wound through *Mast and Sail*, their twisting, winding, knotting lengths no longer a brilliant green but a covetous, singed black.

The grasses should have fallen apart by now, burned away, ash on the wind. And yet they remained, looking as though they might even still have held the structure together if Kindred hadn't pinched and pulled the bones together in the magic of the flames.

'Push, Kindred!' came Little Wing's shout from where she stood at the wheel, hands wrapped around the handles, eyes alight. This was her element, the wilderness of the Sea, the danger of pursuit, and it was easy enough to see Captain Little Wing there, commanding her own ship.

'Sing a melody low and fast, but don't touch the fire or the build,' Kindred said to Scindapse before leaping to her feet, scuttling up the mainmast, and wrenching herself up along the shroud until she could see clear of the forecastle.

She could sense the Roughs ahead, could probably calculate the distance well enough to burn hard and then pull back for stability, but she needed to see it.

Kindred gasped. The curated, carefully maintained level of the Sea exploded in front of them, grasses reaching high in multilayered bunches, their rise tangled through with other plants – creeping, rhizomatic vines and dramatically colored flowers and the burnished bronze of clipweed and the bunched orange of butterfly weed and a thousand thousand others, rising and falling in hills of color and texture. This was the Forever Sea as it should be, untamed and unchallenged.

Just beyond the start of the Roughs, Kindred saw the thistle reef like a mountain range, huge and foreboding, holding up the sky, its impossibly broad shoulders stretching off farther than Kindred could see in either direction. Its slopes and peaks twinkled like stars in the sunlight, the promise of countless thorns and thistles.

Before this, all of it known and unknown, a world neither built nor cultivated for her, Kindred grew large: her roots sank deep, her leaves and petals drank in the same sunlight as the reef, the Roughs, her heart the Sea's, the Sea's heart forever hers.

Kindred shouted with joy and dropped back to the deck.

The fire was burning hot and hard by the time she returned, the flames responding to Scindapse's song. Kindred joined her voice with Scindapse's, nodding at the younger keeper as she changed the melody into something like a chant, a plea for speed, for a fire that burned through the remnant of the mast still rising from the coals.

Her voice sparked through laterals and trills, sharp sounds like explosions against her teeth and tongue. The language of the fire was often a gossamer thing, diaphanous and ghostly, a south wind haunting, but now Kindred dug deep into the language's harder, sharper side, running through every fricative phoneme she knew and then pushing past those, inventing verbs and names and sounds to push the fire on. Scindapse fell away, unable to do anything more than hum quietly.

And like a faithful friend, the hearthfire grew – hotter and bigger and wilder. It had been a burning grey, steady as a wall of rainclouds, but now it reinvented itself in a flash of vivid viridian flames, a swirl circling the mast and flaring out at the sail.

Kindred reached her unburned hand into the flames, pinching off part of the remaining mast, slimming it down just enough to allow the fire to chew through it faster and with more added speed. She worked entirely by instinct and feel, holding the distance to the Roughs and the reef in her mind, sensing how much length they would still need on the mast before the safety and stability of the sail was needed.

The Errant rushed forward as the hearthfire burned. Kindred laughed at the sudden push of speed, her heart light in this new world.

'Aft casting fire!' Little Wing called.

'Aye,' shouted Kindred in response before turning to Scindapse. 'Stay with the fire and keep encouraging its speed. You're doing great.'

Kindred reached into the fire and scooped a coal up in her hand, singing quietly, smiling at the pulses of energy the coal sent up her arm.

She moved between crew rushing about, feeling purposeful, and at the aft casting fire, she found Little Wing waiting, a bundle of blackroot in one hand, a bundle of trimmed wisteria in the other.

Of course. With only a few on board who could cast, and with Little Wing strongest among those few, she would be there, where strength was most needed. Quixa held the wheel.

The joyful beat of Kindred's heart in this new world faltered a little at the hard look on Little Wing's face.

Kindred bent to light the casting fire, accepting a few strands of blackroot from Little Wing, who knelt down and said only, 'We're fucked.'

'Little Wing – ' Kindred began, but Little Wing cut her off.

'Save it. Do your job.'

She turned from Kindred, focused on the fire, which had taken in the basin and was burning well now. But Kindred could hear Little Wing still talking, whispering furiously to herself, words snatched away by the wind before they resolved into anything other than anger, rage.

Kindred backed away slowly, leaving Little Wing to her dark mutterings.

The sounds of impending battle grew from whispers to shouts to screams punctuated by Little Wing's terse orders, shouted from wherever she happened to be at that moment: the wheel, the casting fires, the rigging. She was everywhere, trying to be everything for this ship, this crew.

Ships pursued – pirates or Cantrev, it didn't matter at this point.

At the hearthfire, Kindred prepared for the Roughs, for her own battle, while the songs of violence and fear flooded the deck. One of the songs, a battle hymn Kindred had composed, rang out like a silversmith's hammer joying against an anvil.

'We need something steady to keep everyone casting in time,' the captain had told Rhabdus, who had passed the job off to Kindred. 'The words don't matter. Just the heartbeat. We all need the same heartbeat.'

Listening now to the hymn pulsing through the chaos, Kindred heard one heartbeat in the music, and it was this she focused on while making her own preparations, setting the bones she would need in front of her like a woman setting a table.

'Yo ho, we go, a song to fight,
Cast bright, scream loud, a fight, a fight!'

Spell light flashed across the deck for a moment, doubling Kindred's shadow – one for the sun, one for the spell, though whether it was friendly magic or enemy magic, she didn't know.

A lower-back bone, a chipped vertebra, round and cupped, old and yellowing in age. Kindred spoke her thanks, to bone and fire, and handed it to Scindapse.

'Keep hold of this and be ready with it.'

Orders rang out on deck, blending with the battle song giving form to the fight.

'Quixa, the wall! There the wall!'

'Hooks! Starboard!'

'For sail and Sea, for crew and sky,
For these we fight, for these we die!'

Next was a fingerbone, delicate and small, made for intricacy, perhaps one that had sewn sails or threaded the clothing of sailors now dead. Kindred spoke her thanks, to bone and fire, and gripped it tight in her hand.

Shouts strangled in strange, new voices began to filter into the chaos on deck, signaling the proximity of enemies. They closed.

Kindred could see glimpses of the Roughs ahead, the pass through the reef twinkling in silver and promise. There was nothing for it. *The Errant* would hold until the pass or they would all perish. The time for speed was gone.

Their hopes lay in the possibility that Cantrev's ships were not prepared for the Roughs and would peel away as soon as they entered, but of course, that left the pirates for whom the Roughs were familiar grasses.

Explosions in triplicate rocked the ship, pushing *The Errant* off course for a moment, throwing Kindred to her side. As she righted herself, she looked back and up, thinking for a mad moment that it was Captain Caraway back at the wheel, her wild smile a balm for the mounting panic in Kindred's chest.

Instead, it was Quixa who held the wheel, her eyes locked ahead, turning desperately to get them back on course, teeth showing in a grimace of fear and effort. If Little Wing had joined the casting – were they boarded? Was that the shout about hooks? – the battle could not be going well.

Or worse: had Little Wing fallen? Did they sail without an acting captain of any kind?

Kindred pulled herself back to true. She was the ship's heart, and if she was not beating, its mighty arms could not work. Her job was here. Her battle was here.

She settled the bones she'd already placed back into their spots before continuing with her quiet struggle.

'*So cast, so sing, so shout, YO HO!*

One blade, one arm, one crew, we go,

The sky is clear, the Sea runs on,

Spit flame, strike true, one arm, one crew.'

Kindred pulled from her pocket a handful of teeth that devoured sunlight with their black-and-grey depths. She had never burned these before. Rhabdus had kept them around as a theoretical necessity should *The Errant* ever find herself in grasses unkept and untamed by the mage guilds.

'Teeth?' Scindapse asked, staring down at the collection in Kindred's hand.

'In rough grasses, burn teeth,' Kindred shouted back. It was all she had ever heard or read on the topic. No strategies or builds, no plans or schema. She wondered for a moment how the Marchess had sailed *Revenger* into the Roughs. Had she used teeth? Some other method? Or had she, even then, been thinking so completely of the deeps that she had done nothing special? Certainly, the scars that decorated *Revenger*'s hull suggested something like that.

Kindred spilled her rotted bounty on the deck before her, hemming in their escaping rolls with her arms, cupping them together into a small mound. It wasn't much but it would have to last; she didn't have any more.

The grasses began to chop and chuff against *The Errant*'s hull, sounding a warning call to any who were listening. Kindred ignored as best she could the sounds of battle and focused; this was her battle, and it was one she intended to win.

'Roughs! Roughs!' came Ragged Sarah's shout from above, signaling to the crew what Kindred sensed in every part of her body, heard in the hum and sway of the hearthfire, felt in the shiver of the grasses beneath them. She leaned forward, eager for the unknown.

The Errant pulled hard portside as it cut into the Roughs, sloughing along a bank – a bank! – of rising prairie grasses populated by flowers and plants and vines and stems Kindred felt through her connection with the fire but could only guess at identifying.

It occurred to her as she pinched off the remaining stem of the mast still burning in the fire that she was lost – happily, joyfully, terrifyingly lost – in this situation. She had no idea what song to sing, no guide or book or lesson to inform her build in the flames. Kindred sailed off the known map.

This was intuition. This was art. This was Kindred giving herself over to the world, a sail caught and pushed by a true wind.

Kindred hummed a light, airy melody as she dropped teeth like beads into the flames, feeling them bounce and ping off the nest of bones making up the mast. She used only a few, wanting to hoard the teeth for whatever was coming.

The effect on *The Errant* was immediate. The ship sank low, deep into the Sea, into the Roughs, no longer sailing atop it but carving a swath through it, the ship's wake like a thick scar. Kindred felt the pull of the fire as it devoured the teeth, heard the groan of *The Errant* as it pulled itself upright, no longer heeling precariously against the rise of the bank.

The ship should have lost its speed – the grasp of the Sea, especially with the hull sunk so far down, should have brought them near enough to a complete stop – but *The Errant* pushed through. Somehow.

The fire in front of Kindred blazed with a ragged, perverse light, flaring with bilious greens and yellows, slapping her face with flashes of heat, warning her away, reacting strangely to this new Sea, these new bones, Kindred's song.

'Get away!' she shouted to Scindapse as the fire raged.

Kindred flinched back, bringing a hand to the rising sun she felt her face had become. Tentatively, she began to sing again – the light, quick melody hadn't worked, so she reached out for something different. A dirge, slow and low, like heavy bags of sand swung back and forth, back and forth, low, slow, low, heavy, heavy –

Heat struck Kindred like a slap, hard across her face, deflating her lungs and pulling sweat from her skin all in an instant. She pushed herself back from the reach of the flames, which had turned chaotic. On the other side of the fire, Scindapse had moved as far back as she could manage, and she sat with wide eyes, the vertebra still clutched tightly in her hands.

Normally, Kindred could see the pattern in the fire, like a rhythm guiding the flourish of a melody. But this fire, its flames shifting and paling in colors that burned Kindred's eyes, flared in no pattern she could see. If there was a rhythm to its music, it was beyond her.

She tried every song she could think of as *The Errant* continued to carve its trench through the Sea, still somehow raging along at enormous speeds. Nothing would match the fire – none of the songs she'd stolen from her grandmother, none of the songs Kindred had composed herself, nothing worked. It was as if the fire rejected melody, twisted away from the rigid confines of rhythm.

'I don't know what you want!' she shouted at the fire, which shifted and shook, a friend suddenly unrecognizable.

Scindapse sang from where she sat, her voice frayed and dissonant, as always. She had already started to improve in the short time Kindred had worked with her, but still she strove and failed to find notes and melodies.

Kindred sucked in a breath, shocked.

The fire, which had simply tolerated Scindapse's singing before, now joyed in it, flaring in unison with her missed notes and failed melodies, straightening itself into uniformity when Scindapse slowed or sped up unintentionally, arrhythmic and lopsided.

Nonsense, Kindred realized. *The fire wants nonsense for this nonsense build.*

Kindred enjoined her voice with Scindapse's, wincing at the dissonance, the just-missed harmonies, the uncoupled rhythms.

If it was poetry, it shifted from villanelle to free verse with abandon, from couplets to quatrains with no thought. But it was not poetry.

If it was music, it married major and minor keys without concern for time or meter. But it was not music.

If it was story, characters lived without dying and died without living; worlds without purpose became metaphors that devoured themselves. But it was not story.

Kindred and Scindapse mumbled and hummed and shouted and cackled and sang and spoke and whispered nonsense to the fire in an oft-broken, pitched stream. And the fire, like a lock finally greeted by the right key, opened.

She saw into its madness, saw the chaotic influence each

burning tooth had in the flames. There were six of them in the fire, and each one burned like its own sun, floating aloft in the tangled morass of bone, loosing light and power into the fire, into the ship, into the world.

The teeth burned hotter and wilder than anything Kindred had ever put into the hearthfire, and it was their force that pushed *The Errant* down into the Sea and propelled her so quickly forward.

They cared nothing for the delicate balance of a keel slicing cleanly through prairie grasses. In their heat and power, they demanded the world fall around them, and so it did.

Kindred marveled at the sheer power, brute and monolithic, from things so small, so ubiquitous in the world. Though even in her wonderment at the possibilities – how would the fire change with an odd or even number of teeth? With teeth of a larger or smaller size? With teeth the ghost-grey of a long-serving captain or the pristine yellow of a sailor recently tested and turned captain? – Kindred felt a deep, dissonant disgust.

The teeth burned bright and hot, and *The Errant*, if anything, had gained speed since falling down into the grass. And yet the whole thing, the colors and heat and whiplash crack of the fire, felt wrong to Kindred. Obvious and brutish. To keep the fire was to court delicacy, to articulate a plea both poetic and selfless. It was poetry and prayer together, melodic as the wind.

But this was muscle without articulation, noise where there ought to be music. This fought the Sea, fought the wind, pushed when it needed to and when it didn't.

Above, the sails told a story of listless, light winds – the kind of winds a hearthfire might supplement but not overcome. This was a fire that cared none for wind – it would rage in calm and storm alike, scream through grasses in becalmed seas. It rebelled against the natural world, and the longer Kindred considered it, the longer she spoke and sang with it, the more her stomach turned.

A great explosion behind *The Errant* cracked the air.

'Keep this going,' Kindred said, gesturing to the fire, as she rose and moved back to the mainmast. It took effort, but by twining a rope around one arm and using her unburned hand, she was able to climb high enough on the mast to look back over the aftcastle, tracing her gaze along the trough *The Errant* carved in the Roughs, down, down, down the hill they climbed to see the calamity ensuing at the bottom.

Cantrev's warships sailed without the stability of burned teeth, their hulls raked by the Roughs, their movement wobbly and dangerous. They sparred with the black-sailed pirate cutters at the base of the hill, their mages trading volleys, spells arcing off of and slamming into and smashing through defensive magic on both ships. One of the pirate ships, a cutter, slim and wicked, wobbled dangerously, one of its masts reduced to a ragged digit rising from its forecastle, flaming holes spotting its hull like a sickness, spreading aggressively. A volley of violet magics, buzzing through the air loud enough for Kindred to hear, arced from one of Cantrev's ships and exploded onto the deck of the pirate ship, lighting it ablaze and sending it spinning down into the depths of the Forever Sea.

'Kindred! Get down from there! The reef!' Little Wing's voice cut through the air, picking Kindred out where she clung to the shroud.

Little Wing had returned to the wheel and clung to it, and the blood spattering her clothes and skin described injuries that Kindred couldn't see but knew were there.

Kindred swung around to look ahead.

And stopped breathing.

The Errant crested the hill and the world broke before it: huge shards of reef shattered the surface of the Sea, impossibly tall, like monuments to gods forgotten, queens and kings of ages lost to time. The reef, for it was all of a single piece even if it jutted and rose in myriad heights and forms, dominated Kindred's vision and mind, and she lost the nonsense song the fire sang in the back of her mind, letting it flare into unmitigated chaos once again. She no longer cared – the reef was all, and she felt herself grow to impossible heights in the face of it.

She dropped back to the deck, her knees crying out, though distantly, a cry barely heard through a gale. In her mind, the reef. In her eyes, the reef.

'Hold on!' Kindred shouted to Scindapse as she fell into place before the fire again. 'The reef is coming!'

The Errant pitched forward, rushing over and now down the hill, spilling into it, hurtling toward the reef and the pass cutting through it.

'Reef! Reef!' Ragged Sarah called out, as though there was anything else, had ever been anything else.

'Aye!' shouted Little Wing.

'Aye!' shouted Kindred.

'Two ships still in pursuit!' Ragged Sarah shouted.

She did not know what would become of the battle behind them or who continued to follow, but Kindred could not dwell on it for long.

The Errant fell into shadow.

Darkness at night or a heavily clouded day – these were phenomena Kindred knew and understood. On the eternal flatness of the Forever Sea, these were the only interruptions to the eternal sunlight feeding the grasses.

The reef appeared on either side of *The Errant*, interceding in the sun's rays, inviting the ship deeper into its shadowed pass. Kindred could feel the reaching thorns of the mountainous reef, sharp and wicked, rising from either side of the ship, strong enough to tear the hull asunder with little effort.

More than anything, Kindred was shocked by the quiet in the pass – the thistle mountains seemed to absorb sound, to devour it whole, and so, after the battle before entry, *The Errant* was calmed by a sudden quiet that reached aboard the ship and stilled song and shout. The deck became silence, holy and reverential somehow in the darkness of the reef.

This might have gone on, but a whisper-slap broke the stillness: the green hands of grass, the myriad-colored fingers of flowering plants and vines reached over the rail, onto *The Errant*'s deck, pulling at bundled equipment and spooking those few crew members not keeping the sails or engaged in defense. The burning teeth had brought them too low and now the Sea was coming aboard. The grasping plants eagerly reached for *The Errant*, some with the dangerous cut of razor edges, others with the blustering blow of fortified stems.

The Errant would not be able to handle this.

Hemmed in by mountainous reefs on either side, followed by enemy ships, sailing straight for an enormous pirate dreadnought, *The Errant* cut forward. Kindred watched as plants – many the familiar species she had long sought and harvested, now grown wild and unruly – left long, elegant slices in the deck and pulled bundles of rope or equipment roughly to the gunwale before tearing themselves asunder as the ship raced forward and out of their reach.

'Kindred, pull us up!' Little Wing shouted, racing across the deck. She was no longer engaged in battle – the teeth burning in the hearthfire had pulled *The Errant* far ahead of where Cantrev's warships battled the pirate cutters, minus the two that still burned hard in pursuit.

'What do we do?' Scindapse asked, looking through the fire at her.

Kindred felt exhaustion sweep over her, and pain, too, in her knees, her back, neck, shoulders. Aches and bone-deep exhaustion, and all she wanted was to stop, to give in to the silence of the reef, the pull of the Sea, to step to the gunwale and dive headlong into the darkness. It occurred to her then that her grandmother had been sailing the Roughs when she had walked away into the Sea.

And yet there was Long Quixa, taking the wheel again.

There was Little Wing, her face still clouded with fear and suspicion but her purpose pure as she climbed the mast without hesitation, slung herself up to the sail, and put out the fires still smoldering there from the prairie mages' attacks, began patching despite wind and danger, despite Roughs and reef.

There Stone-Gwen, recoiling rope, restacking casting plants, keeping *The Errant*'s little world in order.

There Castor Twin-Made, executing the more dangerous bugs and creatures finding their way aboard the ship. The crew would eat well that night if they survived the pass.

There Wints, helping.

There Syl Shieldqueen, helping.

There Grimm and Cora the Wraith, helping.

Here, Scindapse, young and untrained and terrified and ready to do whatever she could to help.

Everywhere Kindred looked, her crew helped one another, bolstered the endeavor they all shared: the ship, their purpose, their lives, like a network of roots wrapped completely in one another, tied so tightly as to give no sense of an end or beginning.

The Errant screamed through the valley pass, shadowed and sunk deep, plants and bugs, the life of the prairie, spilling onto the deck.

'Kindred! Get us up!'

'Ship ahead!' Ragged Sarah shouted, nearly speaking over the captain's order. 'Pirate dreadnought! We need to get up!'

Caught, Kindred thought, a chill running echoes through her body, remembering Ragged Sarah's report of the calling.

She rose unsteadily and ran forward, ignoring Scindapse's cries behind her, feet unsure beneath her, her progress slowed by trips and falls at times. But yes, there before them, a great pirate ship, masts rising from it in multitudes like weapons, its hull a huge, imposing shield, blocking their way. The ship took up much of the pass with its enormous girth, and even from this far away Kindred could see the casting fires burning all across the deck, pirate mages ready to fling forth their violent magics.

'Warships behind and closing still!' Sarah shouted from above.

A pirate dreadnought ahead; Arcadian warships behind.

And between them, like a rodent caught in the closing jaws of a predator, *The Errant*.

'Kindred! Pull us up!' Little Wing shouted as she ran past toward the front of the ship, making ready the defenses there, paltry and few as they were.

The steep, thorned slope of the reef pass gave them no

chance of escape, and they would have no chance at any kind of defensive magic aft or fore if the Roughs continued to claw aboard the ship the way they were now.

Kindred returned to the hearthfire and stared into it, frightened and unsure what to do.

'What do we do?' Scindapse asked, voice quiet and frightened.

'Bring us up, Kindred! And give us speed! We might be able to skirt around them,' Little Wing shouted, though with a look of desperate doubt.

'Warships closing!' Ragged Sarah called. 'Dreadnought ahead!'

Kindred reached into the fire to pull out the teeth, to bring them up, but she stopped, stilled by the silence of the reef and a sudden image of the Sea below, the stillness of the deeps, unperturbed by the quarrels and quibbles of the surface world.

When they had gone under before, it was the wyrm pulling them down. They were unwilling victims to it.

But now?

Enemies before and behind and nowhere to go.

Up, Little Wing ordered.

Up, the crew screamed.

Up, Ragged Sarah cried.

Down, Kindred's heart told her.

As the crew shouted at the appearance of the dreadnought, as Little Wing bellowed again, as Cantrev's ships pursued.

Kindred reached for the hearthfire and sang.

12

'KINDRED, dear, bring those bones over here.'

Kindred lifted the armful of bones and brought them to her grandmother, who squatted next to the hearthfire.

'Would you like to help me keep the fire?'

Kindred shrugged, silent. She knew her grandmother was worried about her, that she'd gone beyond the required period of mourning-silence, but she simply felt no urge to speak.

Silence, she'd found, was addictive.

This was the Marchess's most recent attempt to bring Kindred out of her mourning. *Revenger* had been in at port for a few days, and the Marchess had pulled Kindred out of their room at the inn to sail around the harbor. Red Alay had even volunteered to take the wheel while the Marchess taught Kindred, and so the three of them toddled around Arcadia's harbor.

'Or we could cast out for dinner? We might get lucky and catch a fire ant or two. I think there may even be *tcaz qoilti* in these grasses.'

Not even the possibility of her favorite meal could tempt Kindred. She frowned, shrugged, and looked back toward her book, which she had borrowed from her grandmother's shelf and which lay on the deck near the closet of bones. It was one she'd read before – the story of Laris Thrice-Born, the mythic hero born once in the sky, once on the land, and once in the Sea. Kindred found herself reading the final chapters over and over, the pages filled with descriptions of Laris's birth deep in the Sea, the wyrms and leviathans singing the hero's mythic arrival. For some reason, reading of the dread deeps offered her something – not comfort exactly, but a calming, numbing quiet that complemented her silence. She imagined herself wrapped in the dark nothing found at the bottom of the Sea. For so many, stories of the deeps had become nothing more than children's tales, myths meant to entertain and frighten, but hollow of substance. What good were stories of bottom-dwelling beasts with glowing skins like fire and whole civilizations living and speaking and warring in the dark deeps when the real world, filled with sun and ships, offered gold to be earned, homes to buy, drinks to be had? For Kindred, though, they offered relief and a sense that somewhere else, somewhere deeper, a different world lay waiting to be discovered.

'Come on, little ghost,' Red Alay called from the helm, smiling. 'It's about time this old ship got a new keeper, I'd say. Go on and learn a thing or two.'

The Marchess flicked her eyebrows up and down and smiled at Kindred, who sighed and sat by the hearthfire, near enough to watch her grandmother but far enough away to be safe.

'For you, my dear,' the Marchess said, sitting down next to Kindred, 'I will break with tradition and offer you a piece of knowledge, free of guilt or grift. The old ways dictate that a new hearthfire keeper must steal the techniques and knowledge of those who have come before her. And the old ways are best. She must work to understand for herself, by herself. But for you – '

The Marchess reached out one long finger and tapped Kindred's nose.

'For you I will break tradition and offer a truth. Now lean in, away from prying ears.'

The Marchess nodded her head toward Red Alay, who chuckled and looked pointedly away. Kindred leaned in.

'Never, under any circumstances, circumscribe the fire,' the Marchess whispered, her voice rough and hot against Kindred's ear.

Kindred frowned and looked at the hearthfire, which burned a bright blue. An intricate structure of bone curled and swooped inside the flames, beautiful to Kindred even then. She knew the word – circumscribe – had read it in a book, just as she experienced most words for the first time.

But what it had to do with the hearthfire or the Sea or the ship, she didn't know.

She turned back to the Marchess, who still leaned in and had fixed her with an expectant look. Kindred huffed out a sigh.

'Why?' she whispered, and the Marchess smiled, radiant and enormous. When she'd first met her grandmother, Kindred had thought she had the smile of a madwoman. She thought the same still, only now she loved it.

'Ah-ah. You have been reading of Laris Thrice-Born recently, yes? Of his third and final birth deep in the Sea. Would you like to see him down there? Down in the darkness where secrets and whispers live? Would you like to visit the peoples of the deeps? Drop like a stone into their world? The quickest way down, my darling girl, is to circumscribe the fire. Put it out and the heat will keep the ship afloat for some time, days perhaps.'

Her grandmother leaned in close to Kindred, smiling and mad and wonderful.

'But ring the fire in bone, and it's the deeps for you, my dear.'

Kindred reached into the fire and made of it a ring of bone.

It took a moment – her single hand fumbling with bones, breaking apart the remnants of the sail still holding in the flames, scattering to the edges the fiery comets the teeth had become.

'Oh, no!' Scindapse shouted, watching Kindred's actions with dawning understanding. So quick to learn. She would be a good keeper someday.

The chaotic song of the hearthfire gasped for breath, strangled, as Kindred pushed the last section of the circle into place, a collar for the wild beast the teeth had made the fire. Rebellious heat pushed at the ring of bones, and Kindred felt them flex, straining at the power of the flames, but the circle held.

Silence and stillness enveloped the world for the space of a single breath. Kindred heard the remnants of shouts hanging in the air, begging and demanding and pleading for the ship to rise, to again skim grass and cut sky. Bugs paused in their scrambling to get aboard or off. A plague beetle, as big around as Kindred's head and the purple of plums, clung to the gunwale with one furred, clawed leg; its myriad eyes gazed shock.

The world stopped and held, and for that instant, Kindred felt the Sea, not just the grasses near the ship.

No. Her hand in the fire, the circle closing and closed, Kindred felt the song of the deep, heard the shush-hush of subsea winds pressing through endless stalks of grass, tasted the bitterness and sweetness and earthiness of plants that had never known sunlight.

In that single breath, Kindred fell spirit-deep into the Sea and knew the reach of tentacles longer and wider than a ship. Creatures like cities, populated and hungry, meted their impossible widths through the widening arches between pale stalks, throwing the world around them into garish, distorting light.

Plants with flowers that drank in darkness and extruded glowing red sludge. Vines with bulbous, bulging pockets of pus that whispered possible futures into the eternal night. Rocks bigger than houses, hollow, filled with the twisting ridges of labyrinths, holding dead languages at their centers like prizes or punishments. Soil that flashed with heat and then extreme cold.

Kindred saw all of this, all and more.

And then *The Errant* dipped down. Kindred knew what was coming, and the sudden drop still pulled at the base of her stomach and forced her to cling hard to the mast at her back.

Other crew members were not so prepared.

Ragged Sarah shouted in alarm. Long Quixa yelped and dropped her spear in favor of grabbing on to a pair of taut lines. Syl Shieldqueen, who had just finished scooping a plague beetle off the ship with her great shield, actually rose into the air before dropping back roughly to the deck. Scindapse was ready for it, being so near to the source, and she stayed in place.

Kindred tried to shut out their cries of distress and anger – Little Wing's voice cutting through clearest of all. If they were going to survive this, the fire would need the whole of her concentration.

Quickly, as though it had never existed at all, the sky above disappeared from view, eaten by the rough surface of the Sea, though not before Kindred saw flares of magic fly by overhead. The dreadnought.

And then *The Errant* sailed through a cathedral of grass and darkness, the last hints of light filtering down from above disappearing, disappearing, disappeared. The world became only the walls of this cathedral, holy and pure, like the folds of thick cloth cinched tight high above, plants climbing for daylight bowing around the heft of the ship to create a shifting pocket in the Sea's close press, lit by the aft casting fire and the flickering, feeble light of Kindred's gasping hearthfire – now a weak, pale blue.

How different it was to sail below of her own choice, not dragged down but *diving*. Choosing it. Her own path, taken by her own choice.

Silence there was a near ubiquity, the only sounds the constant whisper of *The Errant* as it pushed through thick grasses, parting them like a veil, endlessly.

No one spoke, no one shouted. Orders were useless in this world, logic and hierarchy figments from a bizarre imagination. Here were only the cathedral of the Sea and the prayers of the penitent.

Around Kindred's outstretched hand, the hearthfire began to die. The ring of bones continued to drive the ship down, and as the flames shrank, whispering their pitiful dirge, the descent of *The Errant* sharpened, the nose of the ship pulling down and down and down.

Kindred tried and failed to calculate whether they were past the dreadnought by now, but she couldn't know, and whether or not they were, it was time to act. The hearthfire was down to a few flickering flames, and if it died completely, *The Errant* would be halfway to the bottom of the Sea by the time she got it started again.

A part of her thought that sounded like a very good idea.

Kindred shook her head and, focusing, sang a song of breaking, of destruction, though quiet and low, observing the holiness of this place. And she pushed at the circle of bone, which broke.

The hearthfire burst into song, filling the green cathedral with music – loud and visible, manifesting in colors like the lights Kindred had seen in the sky on those cold, clear nights on the Sea. Like phantoms, ghosts dancing in and out of existence, the lights moved with the music of the flames, no longer just in Kindred's mind but ringing out over the deck, striking off wood and writhing around lines, confronting and infusing the crew.

Some stood, soft-jawed and silent, eyes wide.

Some collapsed, unable to bear the weight of the hearthfire's music.

Some wept, for its beauty.

Kindred often forgot that she alone could hear the canticle of the hearthfire. Why it sang for all now, she didn't know, but as those around her fell into amazed silence at its song, Kindred felt a spike of fear.

Something was wrong with the fire. Within its song, she heard decay, and in its flame, beneath the riot of shifting, rippling colors, she saw a broken ending. Though it flared and roared with life, Kindred saw an absence at its heart, growing.

The teeth still burned and were holding *The Errant* down, and so Kindred, trying to ignore the sadness inside the fire, moved forward and grabbed one of the few unused bones nearby. She stabbed it deep into the hearthfire's heart, burying it in the soft loam of the coals, speaking her simple message: *Rise.*

Kindred's simple build overwhelmed the drag of the teeth, and the hearthfire roared, the music swelling over the deck, the colors flashing bright for a moment – reds and golds and purples – before they disappeared, swallowed by the ambient fading daylight creeping through the grasses.

To Kindred, it was a goodbye.

The Errant rose, gaining speed and altitude, climbing, rising, rising.

'Hold on!' Kindred shouted, the speed of their rise pushing her back against the mast, flattening her against its solidity.

The surface broke before them, and *The Errant* cut high into the air, its speed carrying it wholly out the Sea, leaving a zephyr of cut leaves and petals trailing behind the ship, connecting it back to the Sea, describing its arc.

Above her, Kindred heard a shout, and she watched as Ragged Sarah, who had been climbing down from the crow's nest, fell to the deck, her descent checked and hindered by tangled ropes and shrouds, lines and sails. Still, Kindred heard the snapping of bones – a sound she knew well, very well – as Ragged Sarah hit the deck and was silent, still. Kindred tried to push herself forward, but *The Errant* angled up and had become a shifting hillside, impossible to traverse.

Frustrated and anxious, Kindred held her breath as the ship rose, and clung with all her strength to the mast as it crested, slowing to a near halt there in the sky, touching its apex and stopping for a bare moment before completing the arc, diving back to the Sea.

The bare bits of food she'd eaten in the last day – boiled ant stew, red leaf salad – shifted ominously in her belly as the descent sharpened.

With a world-shaking crash, *The Errant* rejoined the Sea, and next to Kindred, the hearthfire pulsed and groaned, reasserting its upward hold on the ship, checking its rapid descent.

Kindred's teeth slammed together upon impact just as her body collided with the deck. Her shoulder exploded in pain, and her knees knocked at the wood of the deck hard enough for her to think for a moment that she had shattered them, though she could still move and flex her legs, so maybe not.

And then *The Errant* was sailing again, rocking back and forth in the Sea as it moved forward still, crew bathed in sunlight and cheering, shouting their joy into the sky.

Kindred heard betrayal in those shouts, felt the dissonance between the crew's joy and her own longing to dive back under, to experience again that cathedral of shadowed green and the promise of a fuller darkness below.

But she couldn't think of that now. Kindred pushed herself up, her whole body feeling like a muscle overextended and seizing, but she was up, lurching and lunging forward to where Ragged Sarah lay, a huddled mass, unmoving. Kindred knelt and felt for Ragged Sarah's pulse, leaned in and listened for her breath.

And listened.

And felt.

And listened.

Finally, there, a quickening under Kindred's fingers and a soft breeze, slow and thin, moving in and out of Sarah's mouth.

Kindred leaned in, paying back her debt to Ragged Sarah, placing a kiss on her forehead. She found the broken bone – her leg, twisted at an awkward angle. It would be painful, but she could move Sarah without worry.

And then she was up, pulling Sarah toward the mainmast,

tying her there, securing her against whatever was coming next. Kindred checked once more, assuring herself of breath, of pulse, and then she was moving back to the hearthfire.

It gasped and coughed, spasming to great heights and then sullen coals. Kindred listened for its song and could barely make it out, the notes no longer powerful, no longer victorious. Instead, it wheezed a minor melody, and it slowed, careening toward an end, a finality. Its last song.

Smoke coughed from the flames in ragged clots; sickly reds and whites shot through the flickering fire.

'What do I do, Kindred?' Scindapse asked, sprawled before the fire. 'The song is fading. I can barely hear it.'

The Errant continued to list and rock, sloughing back and forth, and Kindred realized it had nothing to do with the aftereffects of their dive back to the Sea.

The hearthfire was giving up.

'No, no, no,' Kindred whispered, leaning in to the fire, singing, flicking aside the remnants of the burning teeth still caught in the coals, sweeping out ash, calling to the flames and encouraging them.

But it was no good. The hearthfire's song continued to slur and fade, like a fresh painting left out in the rain, first losing articulation, definition, and then fading and mixing together into a mess before finally, finally washing away into nothing, emptiness.

But ring the fire in bone? And it's the deeps for you, my dear.

'The dreadnought comes about!' came the call from Quixa, who had climbed foremast, filling in for Ragged Sarah. She paused, and then shouted, her voice different, awed somehow. 'Ahead! The Once-City ahead!'

Kindred didn't know how much longer the hearthfire had. Already, *The Errant* had begun to lose speed and power. They needed to dock and soon.

Kindred pushed through the cries of protest from her body and climbed the mainmast again, looking back and seeing the dreadnought coming about; it would catch them soon if they didn't sink first.

And then she turned around and looked forward.

The tree gave lie to the Sea, challenged *forever*, contested *infinity*. In the shattered thrust of its branches, in the round resilience of its enormous trunk, in the ghost-grey of its furrowed, livid bark, the tree anchored the present.

Vines rose from the deeps and covered the tree in an autumnal funeral gown, bursting flowers of orange and red, goldenrod and brown. They snaked and wormed in and through the tree, coloring it with life. As Kindred stared, flowers opened and closed demurely, like eyes. A warning and invitation alike.

Dotting the field before it were more trees, smaller and boasting branches full of green leaves.

But below, a rash of desolation in the beauty of the Once-City, were the Greys. Stretches of the dead and dying grasses striped the Roughs around the tree, trapping it in, banding its many-colored beauty in iron blight. Avenues of clean, clear grasses wove through the patches of Greys, but it was clear to see: the problem was there as well. The Marchess had been right; the Sea was dying.

And then Little Wing was shouting for her, shouting as *The Errant* dipped into the Sea and then resolutely rose again, listing starboard and then sailing true.

Kindred fell-climbed down to the deck, narrowly missing

Ragged Sarah, and then she was at the hearthfire again.

'Kindred! I've got no control!' Little Wing shouted from the helm, her whole figure set against the wheel, which jerked and wrenched in her hands.

'The fire can't hold!' Kindred called back. 'It's giving up the ghost.'

Kindred looked at Little Wing, expecting anger or confusion or an impossible order.

Little Wing only nodded, her jaw set.

'Make ready emergency port! All crew make ready! Make ready!'

Kindred returned to the hearthfire, which, in its death throes, had grown greedy, devouring much of the bone Kindred had placed in it. She rushed to the bone closet and took out several more, more or less dumping them into the fire. It needed fuel without articulation or elegance, and though it pained her to do it, Kindred knew it was the only way. There was no time for a proper build, and no need.

The Errant slowed and sped in great lurches as it caught on and broke through morasses of the Greys, each one threatening to halt the ship entirely, kill its momentum, and pull them all down.

'Port ahead! Port ahead!'

'Slow, keeper! Slow us down!' Little Wing called. She hauled hard on the wheel, every bit of strength she had, it seemed, to pull even the slightest bit, to steer them away from the trenches of Greys.

'Aye,' Kindred called, flattening the bones in the fire, giving them as much stability as she could, and as little speed, though still enough to push through any remaining Greys. It was shoddy, speculative work, and Kindred did it quickly. She could cut the fire off, she knew, end its suffering totally, but she needed to see what she was doing; she needed to see the dock, the port, whatever it was.

Once more, she pushed herself up, and as the rest of the crew rushed about the deck, grabbing emergency supplies, stuffing bits of this and that in their pockets, making ready to leap from the ship, Kindred climbed the mainmast and looked.

The great tree was larger now, a monolith of impossible proportions in front of them, and she could see great docks extended. For a moment, she wondered how they were held up, but then she realized.

They weren't docks. They were roots, great winding roots that had been mostly straightened somehow and that reached across the surface of the Sea. Some had ships already docked along them, and Kindred imagined there must be a cradle of some sort strung below and between the roots. They were close enough now – and growing ever closer – to see people standing out on the roots, watching their staggering, rough approach, pointing and shouting and staring.

The Errant was curving into the space between two extending roots, neither of which had any ships docked, and Kindred saw where Little Wing meant for them to disembark. She was going to run them alongside one of the roots, and if Kindred could slow the ship enough to let the crew leap from the side, then maybe they could all get off safely, and maybe the cradle – or whatever they used here – would stop *The Errant* just as it had in Arcadia days earlier.

It was thin, Kindred knew, but it was something.

'Slow!' Little Wing shouted, and Kindred dropped back down to the deck, lunged for the hearthfire, and, as she had done only a few days earlier – a few days in which everything had changed, in which her world had grown, had *deepened* – Kindred threw her cloak over the fire and fell upon it.

The fire coughed a last breath, a last flare of power and control and song and life, and Kindred flashed to her first time stepping aboard *The Errant*, her first time singing to the fire, *with* the fire. It had been her best friend aboard the ship since she joined – her only friend for so long – and she bid it farewell now, singing her thanks into the muffled folds of her cloak, whispering her gratitude to the flames.

The hearthfire sighed and gave in, its work done.

The Errant tipped forward.

'Off! Off!'

Kindred pushed herself up, feeling the great vibrations running through the ship, vibrating the hull and deck, and she began untying Ragged Sarah, and lifting, straining to lift, straining and pulling and she didn't have the strength. Like the hearthfire, her muscles were ready to give up.

'Help me!' she called to Scindapse, who rushed over to lift Ragged Sarah with her. Together, they started toward the edge of the deck.

'Move,' Little Wing shouted, racing past her. She had abandoned the wheel, tied it off, and had darted into the captain's quarters. She ran now with Captain Caraway held in her arms like a child, cradled there.

In that moment, Kindred recognized Little Wing as a captain, who wouldn't let any of her crew go, who was loyal to her ship and her people until the very end.

And they moved, running for the edge of the ship. Prairie grasses and vining plants and flowers and thorns and a hundred other species Kindred didn't know had begun to reach aboard as *The Errant* sank, and Kindred realized it wasn't any sort of cradle grinding against the hull – it was the root, the dock. Little Wing had turned *The Errant* into the extending root, perhaps to slow them down.

The Errant was sinking.

She was sinking.

The Sea reached for the ship, devouring it.

Kindred ran.

Little Wing ran.

The Sea reached.

Kindred leapt to the gunwale, taking all of Ragged Sarah's weight from Scindapse, knowing the jump would be easier with just one of them carrying her, and then she was in the air, Sarah hanging over her shoulder. Ahead, Little Wing arced from the ship, the captain still held safe in her arms, the ship disappearing into the Sea beneath, behind her. Kindred hit the worn wood of the root dock and tumbled, losing her grip on Sarah, who rolled to a halt nearby.

Kindred came to her own stop and turned in time to see the spike of the mainmast fall beneath the waves, extended like a single finger reaching for the sky.

As the sickened Forever Sea took *The Errant* for its own, Kindred felt tears in her eyes, and she whispered her farewell in the lilting, shifting language of the flames.

'But the pirates of the Once-City will have to wait,' the storyteller says, breaking off from the tale to a chorus of disappointed gasps and sighs. 'I suspect we could all use a rest.'

He is eyeing the smaller of the two fires, which, unlike the other, has not been fed throughout the tale and is fueled by a single tangle of thorns and vines. Every community has their own way of tracking time and what might pass for days, but Twist is the only one that burns row vines, which take somewhere near a whole day – what would once have been the length of the sun's race across the sky – to burn down. The storyteller can feel the sun still lighting the world, and he knows it is actually midmorning there in Twist, but he says nothing.

If it is night in their minds, then it is night.

The fire has burned down to only a tiny flicker of amber flames.

'Rye and I will take first turn at watch,' the First announces as the crowd begins to disperse, each to their own carefully hidden burrow or warren. The First and Rye – a tall youth of no more than fourteen or fifteen – bid the storyteller a good rest and move off in opposite directions, each one carrying two large bells. No weapons or shields.

In an attack from those things that live in the dark, a single sentry's last remaining moments are best spent warning the others. Against such power, a single life cannot be expected to accomplish much.

'I can't tell you how overjoyed I am that you've taken my offer,' Praise says, the lone person to stay behind. Everyone else has lit torches from the fire and walked off into the dark. 'We're all so thrilled that you've come, and it's a mark of honor to host you in my humble home.'

He wasn't so poetic last time, the storyteller notes. Perhaps he is more anxious this time. Or maybe it is just that he is older, closer to death, more afraid of the darkness and what it promises an old man like him. Whatever it is, the storyteller does not mind this new layer of dissembling. The world is made new and anew in every place he goes, and it is enough to keep the dust from settling entirely on his mind.

'Lead on,' he says, leaving behind the empty makeshift dais and his half-full glass of water. It will still be there in the morning, he knows.

He follows Praise along the ruin-filled path that, in a previous life, had been a street, shaded for much of the day by buildings on either side. The buildings are mostly rubble now, covered by vining growths or wiped away clean, replaced by the world-breaking reach of grey-green obelisks rising into the darkness, like columns holding the roof of the sky high, high overhead. The street is always in shadow now, but still the storyteller can see its past.

'We are doomed to live in the remains of a past we cannot get back,' he says, breaking the silence. He can feel Praise's anxiety; the quiet has that bitter quality that grows in held breaths and racing hearts.

'I suppose,' Praise says, cutting left between the empty shells of two buildings. One is almost totally stripped down to the frame, but the other still has most of a thick wooden door intact, half-filling the black of a doorway, and as he passes by, the storyteller can see the bare flecks of paint that once made up a flower.

'How many days do you expect your tale to take?' Praise asks as they emerge from the alley and cut toward a series of low, squat homes. Praise's is the third one in.

'Two, I imagine,' the storyteller lies. 'Just this day and tomorrow should do it.'

'Hmm,' Praise grunts, his poetic flair gone.

They walk in through the empty space that once held the door. The torch Praise carries combines with the luster of the storyteller's skin to light this first room, which is just as clean and spare as the last time. A table. Two chairs.

Three doorways lead off, though only one of them has an actual door filling the space.

'Toilet,' Praise says, pointing to the first empty doorway on the left before moving on to the next. 'Through there is where I sleep. And this last room is your bedroom.'

It's the room with the door, which is thick wood, strangely sturdy in this place where everything made or constructed seem to fade with each moment.

But, of course, some things are never allowed to fade, and some things are never given space to change.

Inside the room is a hammock – woven together out of a mixture of cloth and twine and grass, strung from rusting bolts driven long ago into the stone of the walls. Other bolts, unused as of yet but rusted with time all the same, dot the walls like eyes.

The hammock is new, but the peaceful rot in the room is not, nor is the almost perfectly concealed place along one wall where a window once was.

'It's a lovely room,' the storyteller says, stepping inside and putting one hand on the hammock, which begins a slow sway. 'This will do me just fine for my stay.'

'It was my sister's,' Praise says. It was his brother's the last time.

'Oh? And where is she?'

'Gone,' Praise says, after a heavy silence. 'She was on watch, and no one heard her bells . . . or her screams . . . until it was too late. The roaches left her in pieces.'

The storyteller takes a step toward Praise and puts a hand on his shoulder. Emotion blanches Praise's voice, and the storyteller sees the beginning of tears in the old man's eyes.

'She raised me,' Praise continues. 'Taught me everything I know. Our parents died when we were only kids, and so she was my whole world, my everything, ever since I was a little boy. And then she was gone, just like that. No sense to it, no reason. Just gone.

'And I couldn't even bury her, of course – the smell of what they had left behind was likely to attract something else that might not be so likely to get scared off by the ten or so of us who showed up with torches and weapons.'

Tears fill the aged cracks and ravines of Praise's face as he talks.

'I couldn't even say a real goodbye. Instead, I had to drop my only family, the only person in the world I loved, off the edge. The darkness took her just like it takes everything.'

Praise drops his head in grief, and the storyteller pulls him into a rough hug.

It's all a lie, of course. Praise never had a sibling, not really, and his parents died well into his adulthood. The storyteller met them two visits ago.

But lies are flowers that grow from a seed of truth, and the storyteller doesn't doubt the emotion in Praise's voice or the truth of the tears still wetting his face. He has almost definitely seen someone he cares about ripped from life too soon by some monster in the darkness. He and every person in Twist have seen horrors that would bend the mind and warp the soul.

And the storyteller grips the man hard for these truths hiding behind the lies.

Praise sniffs and takes a step back.

'I'm sorry. It's a tough life. I suppose it's the reason we're all so grateful to have you here. For just a little while, we can live without being in constant fear for ourselves and those we love.'

The storyteller nods. Finally, the first step.

'I don't suppose you'd consider staying on here in Twist a bit longer than tomorrow, would you?' Praise asks after a moment in which he must gather his courage. 'Three of our people just had babies, and the whole community could really benefit from moving and building and gathering freely. One of the mothers – Four Wish – still doesn't have a decent home, and it would mean the world if we could all help her and the little one out without having to post guards and always be watching the dark.'

The storyteller thinks of asking why Four Wish and her child have not been given this room, but he holds back. He has asked, and will ask again, the people of Twist to be a believing audience, to live in his story, and so he is happy to give the same to Praise.

'I am sorry for these hardships,' the storyteller says. 'And sorry, too, for what this community faces each day. Give me this night to think on what you have said, and I will give you an answer in the morning.'

Praise releases a sigh that he has been holding since the outer scouts first reported back that the storyteller was approaching and the First told him of her plan. Before Praise, the storyteller remembers, it was a large, quiet person named Tulloch. And before Tulloch it was someone called Lim.

But there has always been this room, always this plea, always the grasping for what is just out of reach.

'I'll thank you for that,' Praise says finally. 'Let me know if there's anything you need tonight. I don't sleep well. None of us do, really. What with all the . . . Well, I'll most likely be awake should you need anything.'

'It's okay. I understand.' And he does. To exist in a world that might devour you at any moment, it's enough to drive a person to the kind of desperation that asks for the impossible and demands it anyway.

'Rest well, storyteller,' Praise says, leaving the room and closing the door behind him. It clicks shut.

For a long time, he stands still and silent in the room, eyes open but seeing nothing, the slowly dying sounds of Praise settling in for the night flittering through the walls. He is lost, his mind wandering paths that were and that might have been. Near him, the hammock still sways slightly, a whisper-creak in the bare light of his skin.

Long after those who can sleep have dropped away, the storyteller moves to the hammock and sits down. The walls seem to lean in close, holding him in. He slides his pack from his shoulder and cradles it for a moment in his lap.

Twist is silent in the manner of a person practiced at playing dead, and it is into this silence that the storyteller speaks as he opens his bag and peers into the darkness inside.

'Where are you, keeper?'

'Good day, storyteller. I have some breakfast here if you'd like.'

Praise is waiting for him when the storyteller emerges. On the table, Praise has set what is, for the people of Twist, a feast. Charred vegetables of various kinds surround three separate cuts of meat. A large cup of water sits next to the plate.

'Is this wyrm meat?' The storyteller leans forward, eyeing the plate.

'It is,' Praise says, proud. 'We can't do much about the big ones, of course, same as that lady from your story, but every once in a while, we find a young one we can all take down. Feeds us for thirty, forty days.'

'This is kind of you, but I'm not hungry, thank you,' the storyteller says after a moment. Drinking water he can manage, but the thought of chewing through meat and fibers that once thrilled with life is enough to stir something like rage in him. He steps out the door and onto the street outside Praise's home.

'That's no problem at all,' Praise says, catching up to him. They begin walking back toward the fires. 'Did you sleep well?'

The storyteller can hear the crowd gathering around the fires even from this far away. How quickly they grow comfortable with him and his protections, he thinks.

'I'm afraid I cannot extend my stay in Twist,' he says as the two of them begin walking toward the fire. 'I must continue spreading my stories, however much I might like to stay in one place.'

This last is true – though there is of course only the one story. Were he to stop moving, the slow fade of his body and mind – along with the last bits of himself he still clutches – would go, the transformation finally completed.

And it's best, too, he has found, to deliver the rejection with confidence after the appearance of having thought on it.

Let us get where we're going, he thinks.

'Please, storyteller,' Praise says, walking beside him. 'Please. Just a few days.'

The wheedling, begging tone in his voice is like a bug crawling across the storyteller's neck.

'I'm sorry, but no. I cannot. I will stay through today and then move on. I expect to finish by the end of the day and can take my leave as Twist goes to sleep.'

Silence falls between them for a moment, and the storyteller can almost hear the pleas turning hard and bitter between Praise's teeth.

'I understand, of course,' Praise says, finally.

They walk the rest of the way without speaking.

'Sing, memory,' the storyteller says as he steps back on the dais, looking out again at the people of Twist. 'Sing of that which the Sea takes and of that which the Sea can never touch. Sing of a crew stranded among enemies and of a city floating beyond the ken of any map.'

He pauses, drawing them in, letting them feast on the anticipation.

'Sing,' he says, offering a wide smile, 'of *pirates*.'

A healthy laugh burbles up from the crowd. This is what they went to sleep thinking of, and it was their first thought upon waking.

'Sing of the hanged, of the Gone Ways, of a city once bent to a green law, a city that has lost its way.'

He lets his eyes roam to where the First is in close, quiet conversation with Praise.

'Sing of betrayal. And sing of redemption.'

He reaches down for the cup of water, still where he had left it, where he knew it would be. He holds it up and slowly pours the remaining liquid onto the ground.

'Sing of thirst, and the dread ambition of those who would quench it.'

A pause, during which he shifts the pack on his shoulder and looks down at his feet for a moment.

'Sing of a sailor, a seeker, a light searching for darkness. Sing of the fire, and sing of its keeper.'

13

BOOTS struck the dock in eerie unison as pirates erupted from the Once-City like maddened ants spilling from a disturbed hill. Kindred looked up to see her crewmates mobbed by more and more pirates. Some fought, creating tiny, skirmishing circles among the masses, but they all fell.

Little Wing stood from where she crouched protectively over the captain. She roared at the oncoming attackers, lashing out.

Long Quixa and Cora the Wraith rose with fists and teeth, elbows and knees.

Stone-Gwen battled. Scindapse shouted.

Kindred crawled to Ragged Sarah and checked her pulse before cradling her body away from the violence. Nearby, the captain lay on the dock, breath husking out, shallow and dry. Her eye opened blearily, rolling about, as if drunk, uncomprehending.

The pirates took her, too.

A man struck Little Wing once in the head with a simple club, its weight cutting through the air and eliciting a sickening crunch as it collided with her head. She fell, her body limp.

'Sanctuary!' Kindred heard someone cry, a terrified voice in the storm. 'We beg sanctuary!'

But that would not do; Sarah had made that much clear to Kindred.

Languages carved like gravestones into a central column. Words old as paths underfoot.

Kindred cast her mind back to that pocket of joy she'd found with Sarah up in the crow's nest. Through the haze of her exhaustion and fear, pain and worry, the sounds of that language were distant, garbled in her memory.

A prairie wind filled her lungs as Kindred sucked in a breath before speaking, trying desperately to remember the feeling of sounds that could pull the curve from a spine, words that built a house of power from tongue and teeth, lips and lungs.

She raised her eyes above the fray as she spoke and was struck by the sudden realization that there were people *living* in the branches. Rounded, curved constructions of wood and cloth bumped out from the larger branches, like growths on an arm or leg, and from these more people were emerging. They carried weapons and climbed quickly down.

But the moment Kindred began speaking, the pirates stopped and the storm of violence stilled. Heads snapped toward her, eyes widening. She heard a hiss of breath nearby, but Kindred could not stop. Where was the end of the phrase? Had she spoken it already? Where had she started?

Still the language spilled from her; she spoke without understanding.

Two men stepped from the crowd, one with a long face and long nose, black hair tied behind his head. The other was shorter, grubbier, with tangled hair and a look of shock and something else – surprise? Excitement? – playing across his face. A frown creased his brow, his eyes wide as he stepped close to Kindred, the larger man just behind him.

They listened to her.

Breathless, her voice cracking, Kindred stopped. As she drew in another breath to continue, the men looked at one another, and the grubby one, his mouth set in a disappointed slant, said, 'So very close. But not quite. It'll have to be the test for them.'

'Please, some of our crew need medical help. Please,' she said.

The larger man nodded and stepped close to Kindred, his hand rising and falling in a strike.

Stars and darkness slashed across Kindred's vision.

After that, she watched as if from a distance as her hands and those of her crewmates were tied, and each one of them was carried back down the dock and into the Once-City, through an enormous archway carved into the trunk of the tree.

Behind her, Kindred could just hear the sound of the Forever Sea still rustling from the descent of *The Errant*, from Kindred's choice.

Inside the archway, they descended a grand stairway cut into the wood of the tree, circling around and down a central column.

And the whole of it glowed, emitting a light like sun and honey and fresh-gathered goldenrod nestled into the crook of an elbow.

The pillar around which the stairs descended was carved with all manner of pictures and runes and languages, all of which Kindred longed to rake her eyes over but could not conjure the energy to. Here were the languages Sarah had talked of with such awe, made of deep cuts from ages before.

Down and down they went, and Kindred let her head loll

against her captor, giving in to the pain in her head and letting her eyes unfocus and follow nothing, the carvings in the central column passing before her over and over and over. Nausea swirled in her stomach and she wondered somewhat idly if she would throw up on this person carrying her.

It wasn't sleep that took her finally, nor was it unconsciousness. She simply floated away on the long waves of pain rocking her head, still aware of her body, still aware of being carried by this pirate deeper and deeper into the Once-City. Questions moved through her mind without weight or importance: How deep did this go? What would the pirates do with the crew? Was she about to die? About to live? Was this the end?

Finally, she was set down in a place darker than the central staircase, and she rested for the first time in days, sleeping finally, dreaming not at all.

Kindred woke to screaming and the dying song of the hearthfire running through her mind.

The screams came from far off in the darkness, muffled and distant, but they jerked her upright nonetheless. Groggy, sore, and thirsty, Kindred looked around, trying to piece together where she was and how she'd gotten there. Slowly the memories came tumbling to her through the darkness, bits that she stitched together into something like sense. The pirates. The staircase. The great tree.

The Errant.

She listened to the melody picking out notes in her mind, like her hearthfire but not. She looked around but found no fires.

Maybe it was the songs of pirate vessels nearby, burning bones with abandon. Or maybe the hearthfire of *The Errant* – her hearthfire – still burned below, wrecked on the Sea floor but still alive, calling out for her.

Kindred swallowed the pain that thought conjured and focused on her surroundings. She looked around, still feeling disoriented. She was in a cell, the space big enough perhaps for ten paces from wall to wall, the floor a wood so hard, it felt like stone. Above, the ceiling hung close, low enough that Kindred thought she could probably touch it while standing.

The cell was dark, but not so dark she couldn't see.

Forming a third wall before her were bars made of what looked like plaited Sea grass, and as she grabbed one, Kindred was surprised to find it didn't give with her weight. It felt like metal, like stone, solid and unbreakable. Kindred stared hard at the bars for a moment before looking past them.

Breath hissed from her as she sat back, pushing away from the bars.

A person squatted there, a mass of shadows in the low light of what looked like a hallway. A man, she thought. Barely visible, he did not react to Kindred. He did not move.

He watched.

'Water,' Kindred mumbled, her voice cracked and dry. 'Can I have some water, please?'

No response.

'Can you hear me? Hello?'

No response. As if he didn't exist. Or she didn't.

Kindred slumped back, eyeing the man and trying to figure out what to do next.

A soft whisper sounded behind her, a sound like coming home, and Kindred turned to find the Sea.

Where a fourth wall should have been was instead empty, a vast swath of nothing standing between Kindred where she sat on the too-hard wooden floor and the shifting, shadowed happening of the Sea.

Like something out of a dream, the Sea moved before Kindred, great lengths of plants of every kind rising just past the edge of the floor, each one catching edges on the diffuse light from the hallway, looking like shadow dancers moving on the edge of seeing. Behind and beyond and beside them was the darkness of the deeps, like an invitation.

Another scream sounded in the distance, not fearful but defiant, and Kindred knew without question to whom that voice belonged: Little Wing.

Voices rose in response, and soon Kindred heard the whole crew – at least those still alive after the flight from Arcadia, the wyrm attack, the journey to the Once-City. They, too, were in cells, much like Kindred's if their shouted descriptions were to be believed. Two solid walls. One with bars. Each had a watcher seated just outside their cell.

And each cell had a missing wall, and beyond it, the Sea.

Another similarity that Kindred had not noticed at first: a line of white, chipped and faded, painted on the floor parallel to the missing wall, with width between it and the Sea of no more than the length of a person. Once she noticed the line, Kindred couldn't stop looking at it. The unevenness with which it separated the cell into two spaces – one larger nearer the bars, one slimmer hugging tight to the Sea – gnawed at Kindred, a puzzle she did not have the pieces to solve.

Most of her crewmates sounded far away, and she imagined them all in a row, cells spread out from one another, separated perhaps by blank walls or empty cells. No one seemed to know what had happened to Ragged Sarah or Captain Caraway. Some guessed they were in their own cells but still unconscious, as Kindred had been only a few moments earlier. Others speculated that they had been taken away.

And a few thought them dead.

They were nine strong. Only nine left from *The Errant*'s mighty crew.

At first, Kindred thought these shouted conversations between the crew would draw the ire of the man outside her cell or the ones outside any of the others, people Kindred assumed to be guards.

But her quick glances over her shoulder showed no change in Kindred's guard. When the crew made halfhearted attempts at planning an escape – impossible, they all soon realized – the man sat silently, watching. As Cora the Wraith sang a bawdy song insulting pirates in every way she could think of, the man sat silently. And so, apparently, did the watcher outside Cora's cell, because she went on for some time.

Kindred even heard Little Wing shouting directly at her watcher. Snatches of her anger floated through Kindred's cell.

'. . . cowardly monsters. I will be blight and ruin upon your world. I will be sickness and fever. I will curse your fucking skies. I will . . .'

Kindred even tried begging sanctuary again in that old prairie language, directing the torrent of sounds at her watcher.

But no matter what they did, individually or as a group, the watchers did not move.

Finally, they fell into a kind of stupor, silently tending their own thoughts – except for Little Wing, who continued to curse her watcher and the pirates who employed him.

Hunger had begun scraping the inside of Kindred's belly, and her head had begun to swim with dehydration. She searched her mind for any clue, anything at all. The pirates didn't want them dead; that much was clear. But why the cells, then? And why the watchers?

Kindred thought back to what Ragged Sarah had told her of the city, her mind working slowly, picking over the memories with clumsiness. Something about a column with words. And wheels stacked atop one another. And begging sanctuary. And Sarah leaving at a young age.

And a *test*.

It had been an offhand remark, Sarah mentioning a test – something she knew little about – for those who couldn't beg sanctuary.

A test.

Had someone else said that? Kindred let her mind move slowly back to the moment she'd been hit – her head throbbed at the memory – and yes, she heard that man, his hair matted and grubby, say something about a test.

A *test*.

Kindred looked back at her watcher, seeing not a phantom meant to inspire fear but a man evaluating her. She looked around her cell, her gaze catching in the movement of the Sea for a moment before settling on that unsettling line of white.

A test.

Of what?

'Hey!' she shouted. At first, Kindred had shouted toward the wall through which she thought more of the crew were located, but she had since realized she had no real idea which side was better. And shouting while staring at her watcher seemed monstrous, so Kindred faced the Sea as she hailed the ragged remnants of the once mighty crew of The Errant.

'Hey! Everyone quiet!'

It took a few moments for Kindred's call to reach everyone. A few had to shout down others who had fallen to their own madnesses. But finally they were quiet.

'This is going to sound insane, and it probably is, but I think this whole thing – the cells, the line, the watcher' – she peeked over her shoulder, and despite scratching at his temple, the man in the hallway was unchanged – 'all of it is a test.'

A flurry of confused responses returned to Kindred.

'For what?'

'To stay?'

'So they don't cut our throats?'

'To drive us mad?'

'Who is that? Is that Kindred?'

Though distant, she recognized Little Wing's voice as the last one, and chilled at the anger in it, directed at her now.

'We're here because of Kindred,' Little Wing shouted. 'She lied to me – to all of us – so she could come here. Her and that pirate Sarah.'

'Little Wing – ' But the once-acting captain of The Errant, the future captain of Norther, would not be interrupted. She told it all: Sarah's past, Kindred's betrayal, her own plan to take them to the Mainland, to safety.

'Our ship is gone because of Kindred. She and that pirate plotted to bring us here. I'm not listening to a damn thing she says.'

Silence troubled only by the movement of the Sea followed

Little Wing's shouts. Kindred opened and closed her mouth, trying to find something to say.

How could she make them understand the tiny fire that burned inside her, fed by the words of her grandmother's letter and the imaginings of *something* truer than this surface world? How could she translate her dreams to them when they made so little sense to her?

Why the Once-City? Because it was a step in her grandmother's wake. And because it was a step to a world wilder than what she had known. The Marchess had gone to find forever below the waves, and she had held a hand back for Kindred.

If you seek me, look below, she had written.

I'm chasing after my grandmother, and I'm chasing after the magic of a place I think exists below, she wanted to say. *I'm seeking questions in the dark while you all are grasping for answers in the light.*

'Is that all true, Kindred?'

It was Scindapse asking, her voice quiet and broken. Kindred imagined her sitting alone in her cell, the excitement that had burned in her eyes while keeping the fire gone now, replaced by the soul-gnawing terror that she would die there, that they would all die there, that she would never see family or friends or sunlight again.

Pain stabbed through Kindred's stomach at this, nearly doubling her over. The rest of them were hardened crew, veterans of more voyages out than most people had years alive. But not Scindapse.

'Yes. I wanted to find my grandmother, and it was the best chance I had to come this way. When the captain proposed the idea of sailing out here, I voted for it. And when there was a chance we would turn around and head back, I lied to make sure we sailed east. I thought it would work out. I thought we would be okay. We're *going* to be okay,' Kindred said. 'We're going to make it out of this. We just have to pass this test.'

'What's the test, Kindred?' Quixa's low, sonorous voice came next, turning hard when she said Kindred's name.

She explained the little Ragged Sarah had told her, and as she spoke, she realized how little she could offer. There was a test for those who couldn't beg sanctuary. Or there had been once. Maybe.

'Why should any of us trust you on anything?' Little Wing shouted from her distant cell.

'Because I want to get out of this cell, too,' she shouted back. 'And because we don't have anything else.'

Yet after what felt like too long examining their cells, even some approaching the line and the abyss of the Sea beyond, nothing had changed. The watchers watched. The Sea moved. And they were, all of them, fading. If it was a test, they were failing.

Kindred found her voice had begun fraying with thirst, so she was happy to rest. She lay down in the middle of her cell, listening to their yelled discussion and deliberation. After a time, Little Wing declared it all another of Kindred's lies and went back to cursing pirates and raging at her imprisonment.

She thought of the buildings on Arcadia – small and big, blocky and angular, finite and contained, as if they were a bulwark against the maddening forever of the prairie Sea just outside the island. Buildings for huddling together, spaces created to cultivate human dimensions, to cut off the sight of a horizon impossibly far away.

The cell, though, was exposed to the Sea; grasses frayed against its edges at all times. There, a prisoner was forced to confront the Sea's sights and songs, its horrors and beauties. Staring into a space too big for imagining, a space not built for human comfort – a space not built at all – a prisoner could lose their mind.

Infinity was the air there; forever a noun, not just an adjective.

There was the true fear all sailors faced every day on the Sea: that beneath them lay an unknown world, one they ignored at every opportunity. The Sea was for traversing; it was a great plane stretching in only two directions.

This, Kindred realized, was the Marchess's great crime; this was the cause of Cantrev's sneer, of the confusion and bewilderment among *Revenger*'s crew, of the guard on the dock who had so callously delivered the news to Kindred: the Marchess had allowed the Forever Sea, the prairie, to become a place of depth and complexity, a place of the unknowable, and that seeing – that way of knowing differently – was a threat none of them could abide.

Kindred felt her gaze pulled back again and again to the Sea, and she wondered if that same sickness had not already begun to work on her. While the rest of her crew shouted and screamed and cried, Kindred watched the Sea.

And still she heard that melody, fractured and broken and lagging, like a hearthfire singing out of tune, set edgewise, off.

A shape – something furry and long, brown flashing to red – slid by the Sea wall, there for just a moment and then gone. Kindred could not summon the energy to feel fear. Bare hints of light threaded down through the Sea from the sky above like ghosts from a previous life, stripped of anything like the warmth of an afternoon sun or the cool austerity of the moon. The movement of the grasses left room only for light, bereft of time.

A ghost wind riding a deep-Sea current pushed through the grasses, curving lines of green and animating shadows, and Kindred let her lungs fill with its susurrating sway.

In the prairie wind, out the prairie wind. It was a phrase her grandmother used to whisper, in moments of panic and moments of fear. The natural world always held the answer to her grandmother's problems, and Kindred gave herself over to that same sentiment now. The litany ran circles in her mind as she breathed and watched, wondering if the man behind her stared at her still or if he, too, found rapture in the Sea.

'Fail!'

The shout disturbed Kindred from her examination of the white line. She'd been entertaining the possibility that whatever the test was had something to do with whatever lay buried *under* the line, but there was nothing but more wooden floor underneath it. She'd bloodied the fingers of her unburned hand picking at the paint, and all for nothing.

'What was that?!' came Little Wing's voice. 'What's going on?'

Confused responses quickly settled into crew members sounding off. They had been nine only a few moments before: Little Wing, Kindred, Stone-Gwen, Grimm, Scindapse, Long Quixa, Cora the Wraith, Talent, and Quell.

But Grimm was not responding.

'Grimm! Grimm!' Stone-Gwen's voice rang out, louder than Kindred had ever heard it, calling for her partner over and over, breaking each time.

They all called her name. They called for her watcher. Over and over they called.

Grimm did not answer. Whatever the test was, it seemed she had failed.

At some point, the movement of the Sea rubbing against her cell walls had the happy effect of dropping a few leaves of a plant Kindred recognized into the cell. The sheaves of green cut down through the air, shifting and slipping back and forth, to land near the white line.

She scampered forward, bringing her body right up to the line and then shooting a hand over it, quick as could be, snatching the leaves and scrambling back.

The rest of the crew had stopped talking with her by that point. Some too tired to talk at all; some flinging curses back at her questions and ideas.

'Leave her be, traitor,' Cora the Wraith had said when Kindred tried to join in the comforting of Stone-Gwen. 'You've done enough.'

'Look, we need to come up with a plan,' Kindred said back. 'I don't want anyone else to fail. If we can just work together, we can –'

'We're not working with you. You turned your back on all of us, Kindred,' Cora shouted, and a low chorus of agreement sounded from most of the other cells.

'I'm sorry.'

'Not good enough.' It was Little Wing answering. 'You put your own interests above the safety of everyone else here. Choke on your apologies; they're not bringing back the crew we lost.'

'Bloody dock,' Kindred said to herself now, recalling the plant's name even as she began chewing the leaves, savoring the rich flavors that seemed to capture the heaviness of dirt, the levity of sky.

She couldn't say how long it had been since anyone had last spoken. The numbing silence made the others feel impossibly far away.

Kindred hummed along to a fragmented melody in her mind as she chewed.

But the name gave her pause, and she followed her thinking, letting it wander before her.

What was *bloody dock*? Some attempt to chain and corral the wildness of the world into a handful of letters, a bare mouthful of sounds?

She thought again of *Arcadia*, the name itself both prison and bulwark against the madness of the prairie. A defense of language rather than wood and stone. A name to pen in forever, to sap the Sea of its infinity and grant it human purpose, human use.

And yet a name could be a tribute. Without *bloody dock*, would there be space between it and a strand of bluestem? Space between it and a sheaf of flat leaf? Would it exist outside of lettuce or prairie pate or any of the other thousand thousand plants insinuating themselves into the motion of the Sea, so many dancers moving in unison and yet worlds unto themselves? Without names, was the Sea only a roiling mass of *much* but not *many*? Without names, would it be easier to forget a thing after it was gone? Or did names make the burying easier?

Kindred chewed and stared out into the Sea, grateful for its gift to her, wondering if she was the problem or if it was.

'Fail!'

'Fail!'

'Fail!'

In the cell, listening to the chorus of the Sea, Kindred began to lose her grasp of time. When each call came, she couldn't tell if they were on the heels of one another or spread out, breaths or sleeps apart. But she could follow Little Wing's frantic shouts for her crew, her friends, who would not answer.

Talent.

Quell.

Stone-Gwen.

In the prairie wind, out the prairie wind.

Kindred drifted. The Sea, the cell, pulled at the seams of her mind.

Kindred woke closer to the white line, unsure when she'd fallen asleep or when she'd moved. Her extended arm reached for the Sea, her fingers dangling dangerously close to the white line.

She did not move it back.

Still that melody – broken and off-kilter – played through her mind, echoing and loud, painful.

Her throat clicked as she swallowed, and a powerful ache stormed in her head. Her gift of bloody dock had been the only one the Sea had offered, and its effects were long gone. Sitting up proved too dangerous and nauseating a task. She didn't know how much longer she could make it without water.

No shouts disturbed the Sea's song; her crewmates had fallen silent. Kindred felt her cell holding its breath, uncanny in its quiet. Behind her, the man watched.

Her eyes felt like rocks in her head as she slowly focused on the Sea, seeing it not just as a haze of green, beginning to pick out individual plants again. An errant voice sounding in the back of her mind wondered if these plants would be the only real audience to her slow death there. Them and the watcher in the hallway.

Her gaze slowly, painfully rose, following the stems upward to the ceiling of the cell. Something was important there, something she couldn't grasp. It was like seeing the face of someone from her past, someone she should know but couldn't yet place. Tiny, tumorous growths beaded along the length of the plants, growths she couldn't remember seeing before. Did she recognize them? From one of her books? Could they be harvested?

Increasingly stupid and impossible questions proliferated in Kindred's mind as she stared at the grasses before her, her vision swaying sickeningly.

'Pass!' a voice Kindred didn't recognize shouted from a distance, and then just a moment later, Little Wing's voice.

'They're coming for me!'

Kindred's circular thinking stopped as she listened.

'The watcher and two more are coming in,' Little Wing continued, her voice somehow still strong. Kindred could almost hear the snarling smile in her voice. 'They're not going to like what they find. Come on, already!'

Distant sounds of fighting barely broke the sound of the Sea. The shouts were silenced too quickly for it to have been much of a fight. Little Wing let loose one final yell, more frustration than battle rage, and then she too was quiet. Cora the Wraith called for her, but no return came.

Kindred let loose a shaking sigh, too numb and sick to mourn properly.

Understanding like a lightning strike lit up her mind. Her confusion dissipated as Kindred dragged her eyes back to the plants before her. Back to the pebbled bits of *something* jeweling the stems before her.

The pebbled bits of *dew*.

Dew.

A harsh, dry laugh slithered out of Kindred's mouth. Maybe they were coming for her next, to kill her as they'd killed Little Wing, but for this moment, she would live.

It took her three tries to sit up, the nausea threatening to pull her back under each time. But finally she rose, to one knee and then to a squat. Slowly, slowly she moved forward, one step, another, until she stood at the white line.

Beyond it, the Sea, its movement too unpredictable for this to be at all safe. Kindred thought again of that shape moving through the Sea just outside her cell. Was it a beast that hungered for meat? Did it wait even now just out of sight, watching her through the shadows of the Sea?

And if it didn't grab her as she neared, the Sea itself might. Kindred watched the chaotic movement of plants, stems and leaves and vines like so many clutching hands.

Behind her, the safety of the cell. As she looked back, Kindred saw the watcher shift. He leaned forward slightly, as if this whole thing had just gotten more entertaining.

'Fuck. You.' Kindred whispered the words, suddenly hating the man. He'd shown no interest when she'd been forced to piss in one corner of the cell, hadn't cared when she begged for water. But now that she wobbled toward what was almost certainly a sure death, he was interested.

In the prairie wind.

Kindred stepped.

Out the prairie wind.

Kindred stepped, fully beyond the line now, her vision a swimming mess.

'I go to lose myself in it,' she whispered.

She stepped toward the Sea. Her feet neared the edge, and she peeled her boots away, letting her toes flatten on the cool precipice, letting them curl just so, curling and holding. The multitudinous grasses of the Sea filled her vision, and she opened herself to them, enraptured.

She loosed her hands into the Sea, holding her arms up and out like a worshipper, feeling a part of the prairie as it chafed and stroked her skin. That same fragmented music in her mind became her hymn, swelling and fading behind her eyes as she leaned forward into the Sea.

Dew coated her arms, an embarrassment of water running down to her shoulders, and Kindred drank, slurping and sucking at her sleeves.

Her weight shifted dangerously, and she swayed like the grasses in a storm, and still she drank. Perhaps she would fall forward, but in that moment, Kindred found she didn't care. The water tasted sweet on her tongue, and the Sea was a gentle instrument she played with her hands. All was as it should be.

'Pass!' came a shout from behind her, and Kindred looked over her shoulder to see her watcher, a wide smile stretching his face, standing and working the lock on her cell door. Two others flanked him, their smiles directed at Kindred.

The Sea pulled at her, jealous of the watchers entering her cell, and Kindred felt herself falling forward.

'I go to lose myself in it,' she said, drunk on the Sea's gift, delirious. The Marchess had followed the Sea's invitation down, and so Kindred would, too. It all sounded so simple, so easy. Why hadn't she done this before? Why had she led captain and crew so far off course when she could have done this all along? What nonsense to dream of a safe, measured descent, one step to the Roughs, another to the Once-City, and a third to what? A staircase she would discover leading below? A ship capable of diving to the bottom of the Forever Sea? Some magic powerful enough to transport her to the Sea floor, so many thousands of lengths below?

Why should she wait when she could leap, and before the end, she would see what lay below, would fall through a world long ignored.

In the prairie wind, out the prairie wind.

Arms wormed around her waist, yanking her back, stealing her weightlessness. Kindred's feet slapped hard against the floor, and her breath, so steady and even, tripped to a near halt.

'Welcome to the Once-City, citizen,' came the watcher's voice in her ear.

14

KINDRED was drag-carried out into the hallway, the tiny remnants of her strength fading even as her confusion grew. She'd passed? How?

Citizen?

The watcher had wild hair and a weak jaw accentuated by a thin, curling beard. Dirt and grime streaked along his face and neck in uneven bands. He was the same man from the docks, the one who had listened to her beg sanctuary. He was grinning.

'So sorry about this. All of this nonsense is nearly done. I wish I could've just allowed you in on the dock, but rules, you know. With so many words mixed up, I just couldn't . . . although your pronunciation was quite good! Well, it's all past now. Sorry about this,' he said again as he pulled a strip of cloth from his pocket and gagged Kindred with it. He looked genuinely sorry. 'We can't have you giving away how to pass!'

Kindred could only stare at the man. She wouldn't have been able to give anything away even if she'd been ungagged, even if she had any clue where her crewmates were located.

With an effort that felt heroic, she turned her head first to the left and then the right. Punctuating the length of the hallway were a few more watchers, more than a stone's throw away from where Kindred stood. She felt her brain sloshing through confusion and exhaustion as she counted them.

Three.

Which meant only three of her crew remained in the cells.

Long Quixa. Cora the Wraith. Scindapse.

'It should be over soon,' the watcher said, patting Kindred on the shoulder. 'It's been quite some time since we've had a group so big take the test all at once. Normally, it's just a few, so we don't have to follow these brutish rules about keeping you quiet.'

The man gestured to the other two who had helped pull Kindred out of the cell.

'You both can go. I'm sure the others will need you soon.'

They went, one in either direction, leaving Kindred alone with the man.

'Your friend, the big one, she did not take her welcome well.' He shook his head and frowned, though his eyes widened as he saw Kindred's look of concern. 'Oh, we didn't kill her! She's fine. Took four guards to subdue her, but she's fine! But a gag wouldn't quite do it for that one. Far too big. And far too . . .' He cast about for the word a moment and then, as if disgusted by what he'd found, said, '. . . *angry.*'

He shook his head and then smiled again at Kindred. He smiled like someone with practice.

'And so, I'm pleased that you're taking it better! Once this is all over and that gag becomes unnecessary, you will have to tell me all about your controlled dive at the end of the passage through the reef! I don't normally sit in on these tests, but I simply had to know how you would do it. The hearthkeeper who dove her ship below the waves!' He clapped his hands with delight, eyes alive. 'I was looking through a longsight, but I'm sure it was much more dramatic aboard your vessel.'

'What about the crew who failed?' Kindred asked, not even trying to follow what the man was talking about.

Or she tried to say that. The words grew together into a sopping mess as they hit her saliva-soaked gag. It took three more attempts and a host of sluggish gestures for him to understand.

'Ah. Right.' The excitement was gone now, disappeared faster than it had appeared. 'That, I'm afraid, is the unfortunate part of this test.'

Kindred peered at him, bleary. The dew she'd slurped was sitting uncomfortably in her stomach, and her head had begun to hurt again. She shook her head, suddenly understanding the worst.

Dead? Killed?

'Oh, no! No, no, no!' the man exclaimed, reading her sudden revulsion. 'Gods, no. They're fine. Everyone is allowed to stay, of course, but some are given . . . other tasks.' He picked his words carefully at the end, speaking lightly and with meaningful glances at the ceiling. 'You won't be seeing them around as much – except occasionally when they're back from voyages. Those who can't pass the test are given tasks on long-range vessels: the mappers and harvesters who sail far, far afield. They're usually happier with that sort of task anyway, but it does mean you won't see them as regularly. I'm sorry about that.'

He ran a dirty hand through his frazzled hair, looking at

Kindred as if he desperately wanted to say more but didn't know how to, or couldn't.

'It's tradition, you understand, and practical besides. Those who fail demonstrate a fundamental inability to thrive in the Once-City. But I shouldn't say more at the moment. All will be made clear soon, once you meet the council.'

Too tired for shock or surprise, Kindred could only nod.

'Pass!'

'Pass!'

The two watchers to her left loosed their shouts at nearly the same time, and then they were standing and opening the cells, smiling as Kindred's watcher had, rushing in to congratulate.

'Yes!' the man beside Kindred said, clapping his hands again before turning to Kindred and wrapping her in an embrace.

What is happening? The thought dribbled through Kindred's mind.

'Two more citizens!' he said, pulling back. 'And let me guess – both harvesters? They're both harvesters, right? They have that half-mad look.'

Kindred watched as Scindapse and Cora the Wraith were carried from their cells, both looking like Kindred felt: exhausted, powerless, bewildered. Their watchers, too, gagged them and began excitedly whispering with each. Kindred longed to wrap Scindapse in a hug. The girl looked even younger in her misery.

Cora the Wraith looked past her watcher to Kindred before looking pointedly away. Scindapse looked at Kindred with glazed, unseeing eyes and did not turn away.

Kindred didn't know which was worse.

'Just one more to go,' the man said, turning toward the last watcher perched outside the last holdout, the last test taker: Long Quixa.

'I'm Seraph, by the way.' He grasped her hand as he introduced himself. 'Hey,' he said, looking around, secretive, 'if I take your gag off and give you some food, will you be able to keep quiet? I'm sure you're hungry.'

Seraph reached into a pocket of his grubby robes and pulled out a few crisped stalks of a plant Kindred had never seen before.

She nodded, her eyes fixed on the food in his hand. She could smell it, and the gag crossing her mouth pulsed with saliva. She was so hungry.

Seraph pulled the gag away and held it away from himself as it dripped.

'I'll just leave this,' he muttered, dropping it on the floor nearby.

Before the food, before anything else, Kindred spoke, the words like dried wood splintering in her throat.

'Where is Sarah?'

'Who?' Seraph frowned and shook his head.

'My . . . Our,' Kindred said, pausing to cough once. '. . . crow-caller.'

'Oh! She's receiving medical care – but she's fine! No need for her to take the test, of course. But she's fine. And your captain, too, of course! They'll both be fine.' Seraph smiled, real kindness in his eyes, and it was enough – knowing that Sarah was okay, that the captain was okay, knowing that neither of them were in a cell somewhere, dead or dying – to loosen every bit of strength holding Kindred back.

Tears in her eyes, she scooped the food from Seraph's hand. Her jaw hurt, and her throat still clicked painfully, but she didn't care. She shoved the stalks into her mouth. One, two, all of them, chewing with desperation, too fast to taste the food. Soon, they were gone, leaving behind a few stray fibers in her teeth and a half-remembered sting of something savory and smoky.

It was enough to remind her how empty her stomach was. She needed more.

Seraph laughed and rooted around in his pockets, coming up with a few more scraps of food: some she recognized, most she didn't. Kindred ate it all: a rolling handful of whitish berries, sweeter and more refreshing than any she'd ever eaten, a crumpled leaf veined with red, two short roots still ticked with dirt but delicious all the same.

She ate.

'I didn't know pirates ate so well,' she said through a mouthful.

Seraph's face twisted in disgust.

'Oh, no, those branch-dwelling fanatics don't eat anything like this. It's all bird meat and dried stalks with them.'

'You're not a pirate?' Kindred asked, chewing more slowly as her stomach rumbled with discomfort.

'Gods, no! You don't think everyone in the Once-City is a pirate, do you?'

Kindred couldn't even bring herself to nod at him.

'The pirates are only one of the factions, and while I won't deny they've gained in numbers recently – enough to gain a majority on the council – they certainly aren't everyone here! The pirates live above, up in the branches of the tree. Zealots one and all – downright fanatical in their pursuits. But some of us still keep the old ways and don't resort to plundering innocents.' He gave a little shiver.

The old ways. Kindred blinked at that, just as the last watcher shouted out the verdict.

'Pass!'

The four of them – Kindred, Cora the Wraith, Long Quixa, and Scindapse – met in the hallway. The other three exchanged nods, hugs. Scindapse looked the worst off. Her eyes, normally alight with excitement and interest, roamed the hallway with hollow apathy, glazed over. Loose, mottled skin cuffed her neck, and her hands skittered against her legs like bugs.

'I'm sorry,' Kindred said, trying and failing to meet their eyes.

Cora the Wraith put her arm around Scindapse and held her there, protective.

'You're not part of this crew,' Cora the Wraith said, her voice bereft of every bit of the wry humor Kindred had come to expect of it. Her eyes were bright with betrayal and anger. 'You got what you want; now leave us alone.'

Behind her, Long Quixa stared at Kindred, her face morose and unmoving. Scindapse would not meet her eyes.

'I can still hear it,' Scindapse muttered, her eyes, wet with tears, rising briefly to Kindred's before dropping away.

Seraph, who seemed oblivious, patted Kindred once on the shoulder before leaving. 'I'll be seeing you!' he said as he rushed off in the other direction.

Their watchers moved them forward, down the hallway. The other three walked ahead, and Kindred lagged behind, together but not.

'Berries,' Cora said to Quixa, nodding down at Scindapse, who she kept a supportive arm around as they walked. 'We both had berries growing right outside our cells. We ate them at the same time.'

'It was dew for me,' Quixa said.

'Me, too,' Kindred said to their backs.

'Maybe you had to eat or drink from the Sea?' Cora said, ignoring Kindred.

They walked out of the low hallway and into a vast, open space. Kindred stumbled as she tried to take it all in.

Low, rounded buildings made of some sort of stone or clay huddled near to one another like gently arcing hills, somehow accentuating the stretch of this space instead of filling it. It was Arcadia's opposite in every way: although a huge wall ringed the level, blocking out the Sea, this was a space that imitated the prairie's openness. It didn't shy away from the maddening wide smile of the Sea; it embraced it.

Light, too, filled the space, emanating from the stairway that rose through the center of the level. The wood itself was suffused with it, glowing like a gentle sun. Her memories of being carried down those stairs began returning to her. She didn't know how long it had been since they arrived – days or half-days or whole spans – but it felt a lifetime before. Before descending those stairs, the Sea had been an imagining, the darkness below only something she'd kissed for a moment.

But now.

Kindred looked with new eyes, breathed with new lungs. She had seen the shape of the Sea, loosed her hands in its shadowed dance. If some madness had gripped the Marchess before her fall, before her leap, then it now gripped Kindred, too.

Something had changed within her.

She felt wild.

The glow of the staircase was a soft gold, as if it held within it the slow beauty and reinvigorating laziness of a cloud-free evening, sun dipping but not yet gone, light the color of sweet honey. Though they were far below the surface of the Sea, the light suffused the very air there, picking out the buildings in soft curves.

In the prairie wind, out the prairie wind, Kindred breathed as she followed the watchers and the others along a path cutting between two rows of the hilly buildings. There were no windows that she could see, and no doors either. As they passed within an arm's reach of one, Kindred thought she heard a whispered conversation coming through the wall, spoken too quickly for her to understand, and in a language she couldn't grasp. It mingled uncomfortably with the music still twisting through her mind, and suddenly Scindapse's words – 'I can still hear it' – echoed in her head, and Kindred realized what that melody she had been hearing really was.

A hearthfire. Broken, fragmented, *wrong* – but it was the music of a hearthfire nonetheless. Scindapse must have thought it was *The Errant* still sounding its melody from the deeps.

Maybe it was from one of the ships above, but that seemed wrong, too, somehow.

A burst of whispers emanated from one of the hilly buildings nearby, startling Kindred.

'What is that?' she asked one of the watchers, the woman who had been crouching outside of Scindapse's cell.

She shook her head, stopping to listen along with Kindred.

'No one really knows,' she finally said, smiling at the mystery of it. 'Sometimes, they whisper. We've cracked open a few, but they're always empty.'

'You didn't build these?' Kindred asked, cocking her head to the side.

'Oh, no. The first citizens carved the stairs and the levels from the tree,' the watcher said as they walked, gesturing around herself at the vast open space of this level, 'but these are more recent, within the last few hundred years or so. They're not even buildings, so far as we can tell. They're growing. Plants from the prairie, we think.'

Kindred slowed, seeing anew the low shapes, hearing anew the strange whispers.

'There will be time for exploring later,' the watcher said, grinning at Kindred and continuing on. 'And these aren't even the best mysteries.'

They walked up and through the second level without stopping. As they rose, the music of the hearthfire Kindred had been hearing faded from her mind, first to a whisper, then a suggestion, then gone.

After trying and failing to talk to the others, Kindred gave up and simply followed, letting her eyes wander. She had to keep reminding herself that now – right now, with this step and that one – she was below the Forever Sea, closer than ever to her grandmother and the great unknown that lay below.

Now that her stomach no longer wracked by hunger and her thirst was dulled for the time being, Kindred let herself open to this wondrous, weird place. As they climbed the stairs past the second level, Kindred thought she spied trees – *trees!* But it was too dark, the glow of the staircase dimmed there from its glorious gold to a sedated green, and they were moving too fast to stop and see.

Instead, Kindred examined the central column of the staircase, picking out the shapes of characters and letters etched into the wood. Scenes, too, were carved there: boats cutting through waves of grass, cloud-crowded skies roaring with once-in-a-year storms; people, taller and strangely shaped, striding across the Sea as if floating, hands afire with magic, smiles wicked; the Once-City itself, etched deeply into its own bones, shining like a torch. Languages and scenes and figures took up every bit of space on the central column, the carvings perfect and sometimes layered over one another, tiny scenes cut into the space between letters, words tumbling around the outline of a ship.

On reaching the first level, they emerged into a chaotic city. It was as if the Sea itself had been transplanted and brought inside, unbroken and alive unlike the flats around Arcadia. Here, plants of all kinds bloomed and interlocked with one another, a slow wrestle of greens and golds, reds and blues, silvers and whites and browns.

And just as wild were the people moving through the space, running and laughing and playing and working and living. Kindred saw a nearby clutch of bush morning glory – so rare in the flattened grasses around Arcadia that she couldn't even begin to calculate how much a single flower might sell for. The plants rustled precipitously and then exploded as a young girl came running through, followed closely by an older man, his laughter the same melody as hers, only weathered. Father and child.

The bush bounced back from their quick egress, though Kindred watched in horror and amazement as two flowers, lavender-pink petals funneling down to dark purpled throats, fell slowly to the rich soil.

Soil, Kindred thought, wriggling to look back down the steps. She'd thought nothing of the black bands between levels, dismissing them as simply the floor of one level, the ceiling of another. But now she saw it differently: the thickness of the separation, the dirt and soil spilling through slats of wood ringing the staircase, containing the great amounts of dark earth.

The watchers stepped off the staircase and entered the wilderness, moving among and laughing with those already there.

'New citizens!' one of the watchers shouted, gesturing toward Kindred and the others, who moved close to one another, unsure of themselves in this space, forgetting for the moment the fracture between them.

'Hooray!' came a chorused shout, from some Kindred could see and some obscured by the storm of plants around them. 'Welcome!'

What was this place? Were these people, smiling and joyous and welcoming, the same who cut into Arcadian grasses and destroyed ships and lives in their reaving? Did these smiles curdle into cruelty? Or were they the ones Seraph had talked about, the ones who still kept to the old ways, and the pirates were entirely separate, living above in the branches of the tree?

She couldn't reconcile the stories of pirates, the *fact* of them, with this, and so Kindred walked with that dissonance, picking at it like a scab.

'This is compass plant!' Cora said, gesturing toward a stalk boasting beautiful yellow flowers rising next to the path they followed. 'I thought it was extinct. A handful of those flowers could buy you a mansion on Arcadia! Two, maybe!'

A watcher walking beside her laughed and plucked off a few of the flower heads. She handed them to Cora.

'There you go. I don't know about a mansion here, but they make a wonderful soup if prepared correctly.'

So it went.

Plants only rumored, flowers only ever described in wistful tones late into the night, vines mentioned in increasingly esoteric texts: Kindred saw more and more pieces of the world they had always just assumed to be gone. Their responses moved quickly from loud exclamations to silent wonder.

Soon enough, the plants began to give way to settlement, though not as Kindred would have expected. Instead of plants cut back to make room for houses and streets and market stalls, all those things had simply been integrated into the wilderness itself.

Walls were braided together out of living grasses and plants; roads and paths were simply the places where the wilderness had been parted and pulled away to form structures. Entire homes were built from the still-living growth of thick plants braided and plaited together.

Children stuck their heads out of windows framed by wreathed blue grama, and Kindred saw a man walking into his house through a doorway made of living switchgrass and covered in tendrils of prairie smoke dropping down from above, making a door of sorts. The people of this city lived in this wilderness – *in* and *with* it.

Kindred thought back to Arcadia and the layout of the island, every building and road and structure created to keep the Sea at bay, to keep the natural world either out or contained in tiny squares.

Cantrev had always talked about how the pirates living in the

Once-City were different from Arcadians, how they were cruel and dangerous and evil. But Kindred saw now a truer difference.

Arcadians fought against the prairie wilderness, bending it to their wills whenever possible.

The people of the Once-City lived within the prairie, had in fact bent themselves to its will.

Where that left the tree-dwellers who lived above, Kindred didn't yet know.

A memory at once painful and sweet rose in Kindred: her grandmother standing aboard *Revenger*, gesturing up to the sails as the ship pulled out from port. The Marchess was always happiest when leaving the city.

'Let us bend in the wind as the grasses of the Sea and only then be ourselves,' she had said, smiling at Kindred, who thought it a quote from one of the scribes until Red Alay corrected her later that day.

'Ah, no, little ghost. Them's your grandmother's words, through and through.'

Maybe the Marchess had never set foot there, but Kindred felt her presence all the same. In the respect given to green growth, in the grin of a child crawling through creeping vines, Kindred saw her grandmother. As she walked behind the remains of *The Errant*'s crew through and out of the wilderness at the center of the first level of the Once-City, Kindred thought about wind, about wildness, about the world.

The chaos slowly coalesced into more familiar scenes: streets and paths made of stone and untangled by prairie plants growing over and around them; houses and buildings made of wood and brick and stone, though these were still rare in comparison to the structures built of grasses – cut from wherever they had once grown but grasses nonetheless.

Soon, Kindred found herself in front of a tall building backed against the outer shell of this level. The building appeared to be made entirely of prairie grasses woven together in increasingly intricate braids and loops. It towered over her, a feat of craft three stories tall. She found herself looking up and up, to the top of the building and beyond, wondering how the wilderness dominating so much of the center of this level was sustained and fed.

Above she found her answer.

Great apertures had been cut into the uppermost part of the shell all around this level. Sunlight reached long-fingered hands in through these cuts, and that alone might have been enough light for the plants, but then there were the shields.

Like coins or eyes or drops of rain, metal shields covered the ceiling of this level, their surfaces buffed and scrubbed until they shone, their placement angled to reflect the incoming sunlight down into the air, nourishing plant and person alike. The staircase offered its golden glow, but these shields caught and angled in the naturally occurring sunlight from outside the city.

Kindred longed to keep looking, but the rest – watchers and crew members alike – were walking into the building.

Inside, there were no rooms, not in any sense Kindred was used to. There were no interior walls, and the exterior walls, Kindred realized, had been plaited and set in such a way as to create all curves inside. There were no safe angles and straight lines there, no small boxes to cultivate human domination. This was a world of slow curves and luxurious arcs, of spaces that seemed to continue, always continue.

It was the Once-City itself but in miniature. This first floor was a single, large room and had a few people working at simple desks made of grass and arranged with no particular pattern or method. A winding staircase rose up from the center of the floor.

Kindred was escorted up this staircase to the next floor, which took up the remainder of the building, the ceiling vaulting up and up, pulling her eyes with it, demanding she see it.

Figures danced in the grasses braided together to form the ceiling, animals and plants and humans all articulated through the twists of green, the interplay of light radiated from torches stationed around the room and the shifting shadows they created. Kindred felt her breath pull a little as her eyes caught on one figure amid the huge braided tapestry, a woman with wings curving away from her back and with a halo of what looked like bird feathers. While other figures like her were shown flying high above what Kindred took to be the Forever Sea, this figure appeared to be flying down into it, diving deep with a knowing smile, flickering with joy in the torchlight.

It was the Queen Who Laughed, one of those mythic figures from children's stories, a story every person on Arcadia knew, even if only the children believed it – but here she was enshrined, braided into the fabric of this building, celebrated in a way that could only mean she was more than a playful tale peddled to kids. Kindred shivered.

She walked forward and found Little Wing already there.

Little Wing looked terrible. Her face was nearly unrecognizable amid the blood and swelling. Only one of her eyes was visible, and it was a bare slit of rage between pummeled flesh.

She greeted the other three with handshakes and careful hugs.

When she reached Kindred, her jaw worked for a moment before she spit, blood and saliva mingling, onto Kindred's feet.

'You were the curse,' she said before turning her back on Kindred.

She spoke in a mutter, though whether it was from exhaustion or the pain and obstruction of her purpled jaw – most likely broken – Kindred didn't know. Little Wing stood hunched over, favoring one leg, her arms held in close to her body, a portrait of defeat and brokenness.

Two people – guards, by the look of them – stood near Little Wing.

'. . . so much excitement,' a man sitting at a long table with several other people was saying with a frown. Dark hair fell in gentle waves to either side of his face, and he brushed it aside as he spoke, a gesture he seemed to not even notice.

'My apologies for what certainly must seem to you a barbaric and outdated test,' he said to the group standing before him. 'But you've passed! And we're delighted to welcome you as citiz – '

'Fuck. You,' Little Wing said, drawing everyone's attention. The guards behind her tensed and moved a hair closer.

The man frowned again, as one might at a particularly naughty child. 'Little Wing, quartermaster? Acting leader in your captain's absence? Is that right?'

Little Wing spit once, red-flecked, but said nothing.

'I am trying to congratulate you. There's no need for this continued anger. You've passed the test!'

'Fuck your test. And fuck your congratulations.'

Little Wing jerked forward, lunging for the man, but her captors restrained her, slamming her back and looking at those sitting at the table with panicked eyes.

The man who had spoken turned to the others along the table, eyebrows raised. Kindred noticed a placard in front of him that read, Ebb-La-Kem. A few nodded back at him, though none spoke. There were eight seated at the table, eight members of whatever council or ruling body this was.

After a moment of deliberation in which Kindred didn't know what was being deliberated, he nodded to the outside of the room, where a man in a robe stood next to one of the torches.

No, not a torch, Kindred realized. It looked more like a brazier, like a portable fire pit.

Like a casting fire.

The robed man took a few leaves of a plant Kindred had never seen before and dropped them into the fire. Slowly and then in a rush, the flames turned from a gentle orange to a bellicose violet, the sway of the fire constricting into a staggering, stuttering ripple.

The mage – for surely he was a mage – spoke a series of low words over the flame and flung a hand out toward Little Wing, who took a step back, wary, though there was nothing she could do. The spell took hold of her and then she was floating, dreamlike, rising a short distance into the air, her limbs loose as if she were floating in a pool of water.

Kindred watched Little Wing's mouth move, first to speak and then to scream, but no sound emerged. The spell, whatever magic the mages worked with their array of strange plants, held Little Wing there adrift.

'Stop!' Kindred demanded, stepping toward the table, palms out and open.

'I'm sorry for it,' the man said, shaking his head. 'We do not, as a rule, restrain or oppress our citizens. But disrespect and violence are not tolerated here, not in any way. One who threatens the safety of another citizen must be stopped.'

Kindred cast a look to the others, but there was nothing to be done.

'Get to the business,' another said – a man long of leg and face sitting at the end of the table. He looked unhappy to be there, his thin face pulled down at the eyebrows and corners of his lips. He was familiar, and it took Kindred only a moment to realize why: he was the one who had struck her on the docks, halting her attempts to beg sanctuary after Seraph had found her efforts lacking. His placard read Morrow Laze.

'*Proceed, proceed, this talk grows stale and dull,*' two people at the other end of the table said, a man and a woman both speaking at once. They were nearly identical: long, green, ropy hair falling well past their shoulders, discomfiting green eyes, uniform yellow teeth. They spoke in unison, their voices harmonizing in a way Kindred found at once entrancing and horrifying. A single placard sat in front of them: The Word.

And down at one end of the table, sat Seraph. He smiled at Kindred and waved.

The man – Ebb-La-Kem – began to talk again, moved forward by his colleagues.

'You have been brought before the Hanged Council,' he gestured to those sitting at the table, eight people, 'so that we might decide how best to respond to the appearance of you and your crew. Your willingness to cooperate with the council will signal a gesture of goodwill for the rest of the crew.'

Kindred nodded, following the intrinsic threat in the man's words:

your mistake is the crew's mistake. Kindred eyed Little Wing, still floating idly, though she had stopped screaming and was listening.

Ebb-La-Kem began speaking as he read their names from a document in front of him.

'Little Wing, quartermaster. Kindred Greyreach, keeper of the hearthfire. Long Quixa and Cora the Wraith, honored harvesters. Scindapse, young deckhand.' He looked up, gesturing at those before him. 'It's a pity your captain and crow-caller aren't in better condition, else we might have them here, too. But welcome, all of you, now citizens of the Once-City!'

A polite susurrus of applause sounded from those seated at the table.

'Who will speak for you in your acting captain's absence?' Ebb-La-Kem let his eyes drift over them, a polite smile on his face.

'I will,' Long Quixa said in her slow, measured way.

'Very well. As I was saying just a moment ago: you have all passed what must seem to be a terribly onerous test. But it is an important one! Arcadians fear the Sea – this is why your island is surrounded by flatness. You cannot deal with a wild world around you, and the thought of darkness and wilderness below . . . True terror for an Arcadian.

'But here, we live in the Sea! It is not only a surface to be harvested and skimmed across. Before the test, anyone could come here and live, but this place drove some mad, and many lives were lost because of this. And so we built the cells, with their openness to the Sea and their white lines. Those who can move past the white line and do so with purpose – whether it be to drink from the Sea's bounty' – Ebb-La-Kem nodded at Kindred – 'or to fashion a weapon' – he nodded, begrudging, at Little Wing.

'Any purposeful movement beyond the line, not motivated by the madness of fear, shows a person might live here without being a danger to themselves or our community.'

He smiled at the line of people before him.

'And so, congratulations. And welcome.'

'What about the rest of the crew?' Long Quixa asked, ignoring the praise.

Ebb-La-Kem frowned – he seemed to do that a lot. 'All in time. For now, be glad of what your crew here have earned!'

Morrow Laze sighed heavily. 'Get on with it, Ebb. I haven't time for this.'

'Fine!' Ebb-La-Kem said. 'Your other crew, the ones who failed, will be taken care of, given the same food and clothing and amenities to which all Once-City citizens are entitled. They have either been assigned to long-range vessels or given a spot on the crews of our dew-skimming ships. To fail the test suggests a person cannot or will not thrive in the Once-City. You Arcadians fear the Sea, and we have seen – too often – those who fear the Sea go mad while living here. But even despite that, we will take care of your crew by giving them the life on the Sea they desire, only working for a different flag now. They will live on the Sea – either aboard a vessel sailing for the horizon or living in the quarters on the dew-skimming ships, riding out each morning to resupply our water stores. The Once-City will use their labor, just as it will use yours.'

'What do you mean?' Long Quixa asked.

'This situation is complicated,' Ebb-La-Kem said. 'Though true citizens of this place, your arrival has also brought danger to our great city. Danger and the threat of great violence.'

'What danger and violence have we brought?' Kindred asked.

She thought of the pirates who had chased them into port so many days before and the pirates who had threatened to destroy them as they neared the Once-City, who might have done so had Kindred not plunged *The Errant* into the Sea.

Silence, rife with unspoken meaning, filled the room as the members of the council exchanged pointed looks. Finally Ebb-La-Kem spoke again, ticking the items off on his fingers.

'A shipful of Arcadians, long a group antagonistic toward our people' – Ebb-La-Kem nodded at Little Wing – 'and several of whom could not pass our simple test. A captain with a record even we have heard of. A chaotic train of enemy ships moving through the thorny pass. A ship crashing into our dock and causing damage to the exterior of our home as it sinks.'

Ebb-La-Kem finished with his voice raised, all semblance of the courteous lord gone now. The other council members were nodding along with him – all except Morrow Laze, Kindred saw. He stared up at the ceiling, as if bored.

'So, you can see that not all is as simple as it might be. What is it to be done about the damage to our city? How to make up for this? And what – '

Too long being trapped in her cell, of listening to her crewmates wail and scream and go silent, all of it had made Kindred bold.

'That's all nonsense,' she said, aware that Long Quixa was looking at her, trying to get her attention, but Kindred looked straight at Ebb-La-Kem. 'We *Arcadians* were running from Arcadia. One ship couldn't damage this place, not in any serious way. And Cantrev's warships never docked here – we led them near the Once-City, but if they didn't dock, they won't be able to find it again, not once it moves. There's no way Cantrev's ships will be able to restock, gather more ships, and make it back before the Once-City is away. They'll be looking without any help in all of the Forever Sea.'

Most of the councillors were exchanging looks of annoyance. But The Word, their strange green eyes unblinking, watched Kindred with interest, and Morrow Laze had dropped his gaze from the ceiling to consider her as well. At the other end of the table, Seraph was openly grinning at Kindred.

'Ridiculous!' Ebb-La-Kem said, though he had lost some of his righteous anger, and he ran a hand through his hair, disturbing the careful waves of it. 'You have brought danger to this place, and that's simply all there is to it!'

Something odd was going on.

'What our hearthfire keeper is trying to say . . .' Long Quixa began, already trudging into an apology, damage control.

But Kindred wasn't listening. Memories that seemed a lifetime away but were only days old moved through her mind: *The Errant* rising from the deeps, hearthfire already beginning to sputter, warships making contact behind and the Once-City ahead, her first look at that fabled place. A tree rising from the Sea, prairie antithesis, its bark and bulk home to a patchwork panoply of vibrant flowers, their vines reaching from the Sea like fingers, reaching –

Reaching.

Kindred's breath stopped up in her throat.

The Greys, a rash spreading over the Sea, circling the Once-City, poisoning its grasses save for a few carefully maintained paths through.

She made eye contact with Seraph, who nodded at Kindred, watching her figure it out.

Vines with impossible colors winding their way around the tree, vines growing up from the Sea. The Greys, circling like a cage.

'You're stuck here,' Kindred said, her voice cutting into Quixa's attempts at apology. Ebb-La-Kem flinched as Kindred spoke, and she saw a ripple of eyes widening as the other councillors turned to stare at her. 'We're all stuck here.'

Seraph laughed.

'The Once-City doesn't sail anymore, does it? All those stories about the dreaded Once-City cutting through unknown swaths of Sea beyond the horizon – they're not true anymore, are they? It doesn't matter at all if Cantrev hasn't actually docked here – they don't need the special magic you get from that to find the Once-City, because it's not moving anymore. You're here, waiting to be found.'

Ebb-La-Kem opened his mouth to speak, but no words came out.

'Clever,' Morrow Laze said after a sigh. 'How did you know?'

'The vines. The Greys.'

Morrow Laze nodded, his eyes going up to the ceiling again.

'I told you she was good! Didn't I tell you?' Seraph said, turning to the councillors around him, all of whom seemed too shocked by Kindred's deduction to engage with him.

'*The City floats adrift with anchor down,*' The Word said, their voices sending chills up and down Kindred's skin.

Kindred felt the blood stop up in her veins as she thought of the ramifications. Cantrev and the other warmongers on Arcadia had always been reluctant to attack the pirates, because they believed the Once-City was always on the move. In addition to navigating the Roughs, they would be sailing out into a Sea that, as far as any mapmaker in history was concerned, went on forever. It was impossible if a person trusted the stories about the Once-City – stories that had apparently been true for some time.

But now Kindred and everyone else aboard *The Errant* had given Cantrev enough information to call the Once-City's bluff. They knew where the Once-City was, and even if they only came back in an effort to track the Once-City, they would find it again.

'Now you see,' Morrow Laze said, leaning forward, angry eyes the color of storm clouds. 'It will only be a few span before they return.'

Kindred did see, and silence filled the room as she imagined the violence to come.

The violence and death and destruction she and everyone else aboard *The Errant* had accidentally brought.

'I want to hear about the controlled dive you performed to make it past our dreadnought!' Seraph said, interrupting the conversation and leaning forward, eyes bright.

'I've only heard about that sort of thing in a theoretical sense, but here you are!' He clapped his hands together and smiled, excited and eager. 'How did you do it? Beachroot? Or no, skull shavings mixed with crushed bluestem? No, no that wouldn't work, I suppose. What ab – '

'Thank you, Councillor Seraph. That's enough,' Ebb-La-Kem said, his voice stern, reclaiming the conversation. The two of them exchanged a long look: Ebb-La-Kem frowned at the disheveled man, and Seraph looked bewildered.

'Looks like you already found your people here,' Cora the Wraith whispered to Kindred, her sneer ugly and mean.

With a sigh, Ebb-La-Kem turned back to them.

'Now you see our predicament.'

'I care only for the safety of the crew,' Long Quixa said, her voice quiet, steady. 'We have no allegiance to Cantrev or his warmongering. Our escape from him is what brought us to this place. It was never our intent to bring danger to the Once-City.'

Ebb-La-Kem nodded through Quixa's speech, his brow furrowed, eyes almost theatrically sympathetic.

Kindred suspected she might grow to hate this man.

'I appreciate the sentiment, truly,' he said. 'Though I'm sure you can understand the predicament you have placed us in. Some on this council have called for your deaths and an end to the whole affair.' A few of the other councillors nodded. Kindred saw that Morrow Laze and Seraph did not.

'But we do not kill our citizens. This is a place of safety for those who seek it.' He paused. 'And there is use for you, perhaps. Cantrev's forces will arrive soon; of this we are reasonably certain. Though we have some experience with his warships, there is always more we might learn if we are to successfully defend the Once-City. Your captain and your quartermaster will provide any information they possess regarding the Arcadian fleet, the magics they may employ, their tactics when attacking, and any other details our defensive leaders may require. Your other crew members will be assigned tasks as befit their abilities and our needs.

'Councillors Laze and Uz will supervise your aid in this matter,' Ebb-La-Kem said, nodding to Morrow Laze and a bulky woman sitting next to him. 'For this, we will begin the process of forgiving and mitigating the danger you have brought on your new home.'

Begin the process of forgiving? Kindred thought on the strangeness of that phrase, wondering what else they might be required to do to be forgiven. But given their lack of other options – *The Errant* sunk, their crew split up, fractured, Sarah still injured – the beginnings of forgiveness would have to do.

Long Quixa thought for a long moment before responding.

'I cannot speak for the captain, but I will do all I can to convince her, and the crew will perform their responsibilities as well, but I want something in return.'

'The safety of this place is not enough?' Morrow Laze asked, not angry anymore. Just curious. 'Safety even for your crew who failed the test? The pirate majority on this council would gladly see all of you, failed and passed alike, killed, and you ask for more than safety?'

Kindred remembered Seraph talking of the pirate majority on the council. As Morrow Laze spoke, The Word, Ebb-La-Kem, Uz, and a broad, fat person sitting behind a placard reading GladWill nodded. The pirate majority, apparently. Four of the seven places.

'A life stuck on land in a place unfamiliar to us is not much of a life,' Quixa said, speaking with conviction and confidence. 'If we are to help you in this way, give us a chance at life again. A ship, nothing special, equipped with stores enough to make it to the Mainland. We work here for forty days, offer whatever knowledge and insight we might have. In return, we get our lives back.'

'You barter with little to give,' Ebb-La-Kem said, though he did not dismiss it immediately.

'The captain has sailed out of Arcadia for more years than many of you have been alive,' Quixa said, eyeing each member of the council with slow deliberation. 'The knowledge she has seems more than enough to barter with.'

A hurried discussion ensued among the councillors. Kindred heard almost nothing of what they said, though she was sure the word water was spoken several times, and then Ebb-La-Kem reached below the table and produced a calculating wheel, one Kindred had seen the Number-Children using as they grappled with huge numbers. Ebb-La-Kem spun the wheel with deft mastery, muttering numbers and sums to himself, shaking his head at the offer of coal and leaf to write on. After a moment of intense silence in which the only sound was the whir of the calculating wheel spinning and stopping, spinning and stopping, Ebb-La-Kem finished, apparently satisfied, and the talks resumed.

Little Wing began to silently scream again, catching the attention of Long Quixa.

'It's the only way,' Quixa said. 'If we're ever going to leave, we need a ship.'

'You really think the captain will do it?' Cora asked.

'I don't know.' Quixa shook her head slowly. 'But I don't know what else to barter with.'

Sarah had said the sailors from the Once-City didn't understand the hearthfire any better than the typical Arcadian keeper; they burned bones and built structures without any true understanding.

'I can help,' Kindred said, and though she was looking at Long Quixa, she spoke loud enough for everyone to hear.

'Yes? What?' Ebb-La-Kem said, that same condescendingly pleasant smile resurfacing on his face.

'I'm the best hearthfire keeper sailing out of Arcadia, maybe the best alive,' Kindred said. No time for modesty. She heard scoffs from those at the table, and even from Cora the Wraith, but she continued. 'I know your ships sail without any clear knowledge of how the hearthfire works, and I'm sure you burn through bones far more quickly than you should. I could teach your keepers how to do their jobs and perform the kind of basic maintenance of your hearthfires and basins that I'm sure no one here has ever known how to do.'

In the silence that followed, Kindred took a leap.

'If you grant this crew a ship,' she said, careful to speak of *this* crew and not *my* crew, 'and supplies enough to journey to the Mainland, I will do everything I can to fix the hearthfire of the Once-City.'

The music she had been hearing below, the music Scindapse had said she could hear, too, confusing it for *The Errant's* hearthfire – this was her hope, her leap. It was not the melody of a hearthfire from some boat in the harbor; it couldn't be. If the Once-City had once sailed, and if it still floated above the black below, it had to find lift somewhere.

The song had been a bent and broken thing, uncanny, *almost* right.

Maybe, just maybe, the vines and the Greys were only symptoms of the real problem in the Once-City. A ship with enough power, willing to burn enough bones, could push through the soupy morass of the Greys.

Maybe the real problem was with the hearthfire at the heart of this place, though how massive it would need to be to power a whole city, Kindred couldn't imagine.

'Brilliant!' Seraph cried, slapping a hand down on the table in front of him. 'I told you all, didn't I? That dive was no accident! She can help me with the hearthfires of the ships and in dealing with our *other* issues.' He winked at Kindred conspiratorially.

Ebb-La-Kem opened his mouth to speak, but Seraph continued. He had the clever tendency, Kindred realized, to take a breath two or three words before the end of a sentence, which allowed him to continue into the next without a pause.

'We have some problems, of course; typical things: bone efficiency, fibrous constraint, heat and breath regulation, all things I'm sure you've worked with before on your ships. How many builds would you use on an average voyage? Average time for a single hearthfire to burn? Any familiarity with – '

Ebb-La-Kem cleared his throat and gave Seraph a pointed look. Kindred got the distinct impression that Ebb-La-Kem's role on the council was mostly dedicated to keeping Seraph in check.

'We can discuss it later,' Seraph said. 'I'm just excited that you'll bring your expertise and help me work with the hearthfires.' He beamed at Kindred.

The council returned to its deliberations, and Kindred tried to ignore the looks of the other crew. Finally, Ebb-La-Kem cleared his throat and spoke.

'Do your ships not normally sail with two hearthfire keepers? Your expertise promises much, Kindred, but is there another who might help with this? Our hearthfires can be particularly unpredictable here; should you suffer an accident, might there be another who could step in for you?'

Kindred cast a glance sideways at the crew next to her, at Scindapse, whose eyes had widened in fear as she stared at the ground.

'We lost our other keeper on the journey here. It is just me,' Kindred said, turning back to the council, before adding, 'but I will be more than enough.'

Seraph laughed and slapped the table again.

'Very well,' Ebb-La-Kem said. 'Conditioned on each member of your crew helping in the ways previously specified, and assuming your keeper can deliver on her promises, the council is will to offer a required time of fifty days of labor followed by the delivery of a ship. Are we agreed?'

Quixa looked among the crew, including Kindred for a long moment, before nodding.

'Agreed.'

Somehow, despite everything, Kindred felt excitement. What would pirate hearthfires look like? What did those ships find out in the fields of forever? And did they know something of what lay below?

'Wonderful,' Ebb-La-Kem said. 'Most agreeable. Well, then, that wraps things up. One of The Word's city guards will lead you to the housing we have set up for you, and instructions will be provided for each of you to follow your tasks.'

Ebb-La-Kem paused for a moment, sitting up straighter in his chair and making eye contact with each one of them before continuing.

'Your old lives are done. You are no longer Arcadians. Welcome to the Once-City. Welcome, new citizens.'

15

'**WE'VE** assigned you to Cruel House.'

Finally, pausing his nonstop narration, Seraph gestured with a grand smile at the house behind him. Kindred looked up at the towering three-story building, one of the few made entirely of wood and stone. Farther up, the sunlight lanced through the apertures cut into the outside walls and redirected down by the many reflective shields hung from the ceiling, had over time bleached the building until it had become a pale brown, like dirt sapped of all moisture. Windows dotted the front of the house, and the door was only a hollow frame.

'This place has a long history in the Once-City! There are several speculations, each stranger than the last, about when exactly Cruel House was built. Some argue that . . .'

Since leaving the Hanged Council's chambers, and seeing Little Wing taken off to the house of healing, Seraph had talked about everything from history to the Sea, of his time on the Hanged Council, of life in the Once-City. He had spoken of everything, it seemed, walking beside Kindred and occasionally asking her questions. When did she begin sailing? How long had she been keeping the hearthfire? Did she regularly perform controlled dives? Was it her captain's orders or her own?

A ripple of discomfort moved around the faces of the others at these questions, the loss of their ship – the only real home the older women had known for some time – still too near. Seraph spoke as if they were all friends, citizens together for longer than half a day, and even as Kindred was pulled nearer to him by his questions and her answers, she felt the distance grow between her and the crew.

'We've dealt with ships below Sea level, of course,' Seraph said, grinning at Kindred, oblivious to the pain around him. 'The Once-City, is after all, perpetually below the Sea. But the way you managed it! Elegant and precise and amazing! Once we're through getting you settled, you can talk me through the theory.'

This was their walk to Cruel House, a hundred questions and a thousand answers, and though she felt some of the stabs of sadness in thinking of *The Errant*, shattered at the bottom of the Forever Sea, she couldn't help but also feel a growing sense of possibility. Here she was, walking the streets of a fabled city floating farther out in the Forever Sea than she had ever been, in a place that seemed on a fundamental level different than Arcadia.

Below the Sea. Among the Sea. In spaces that opened themselves to the world outside.

And so she listened to Seraph speak, interested in this place and finding, to her surprise, she was interested in him, too. Had she ever tried compass plant in build? No, she hadn't; she'd only just today realized it still existed. Would she like to join him as he experimented with it in the next few days?

She found she did.

None of this was the linear path of progress espoused in Arcadia. This was not serving her time, gaining experience, building her credentials to get her own ship, to grow her riches, to buy bigger and better. Kindred felt herself pulled by some inchoate thing inside, something that felt impossible to separate from the world just outside, closer than it had ever been. She breathed *in the prairie wind, out the prairie wind* and listened to the heartbeat of this new world.

Soon enough, they stood before Cruel House, which sat at the edge of the first level, backed nearly all the way to the outside wall. So close, in fact, that standing there, Kindred could hear the sway of the Sea as it brushed against the Once-City, could see its dance just through one of the apertures cut high above.

A man emerged from the open doorway, filling it with his bulk for a moment before stepping out and walking toward them.

'Ah, yes, right,' Seraph said, his eyes catching on the man before he turned back to them, speaking lower than he had been. 'That is your warden, Barque. Each neighborhood in the Once-City is watched over by a warden, each in The Word's employ. They're here to make sure you get your ration of food and water each day, to take into account any concerns you may have, and to serve as a liaison between you and the council. Barque is . . .' Seraph trailed off, looking quickly back at Barque and waving. He turned back. '. . . a completely odious man. A brutish bully; I can't understand why The Word keeps him in their employ. Watch yourself around him.'

All of this was spoken in a quick whisper, and Seraph broke off as Barque neared, inventing a smile on his face so as to seem cheery and chipper again.

Barque was large, broad of shoulder and with a size that seemed to fill his robes in strange ways. As he approached, Kindred recognized what she thought were tattoos like Ragged Sarah's – swirling lines tracing across his skin in unbroken patterns, disappearing beneath his robes and appearing later.

But then he stepped within their circle, and Kindred saw them for what they were.

Not tattoos.

Not ink and raised skin.

Plants.

Barque's skin was covered in the close cluster of stretching plants: vines and stems and roots, rhizomatic in their reach and weave, diving in and out of the top layer of his skin. Green and gold shoots stretched and moved with him, as if part of his body, as natural as the flex of an arm, the flash of a smile.

Closed buds punctuated the run of the plants like gems, curled tightly into themselves.

'You're the Arcadians.' It was not a question. His voice was deep and slung through with the same loose accent Kindred had heard from other citizens of the Once-City.

'New citizens, Barque!' Seraph clapped his hands, looking around at the group of them, his clandestine whispering gone now. 'I'll leave you all in your warden's capable hands; he'll have job assignments for each of you. I have council business to attend to, of course. And Kindred, I'll stop back tomorrow sometime, once you're rested up, and we can get to work! I can't wait to hear all about your dive!'

He giggled to himself, the sound childlike and strange coming from this unkempt, grey-haired man. Kindred wasn't sure she had ever met someone so unabashed, so unaware, so purely himself. Anyone other than her grandmother, of course.

'Food and water inside,' Barque said as Seraph disappeared back down the road, into the tangle of grass buildings rising up into the vast empty space of this level, huge and encompassing somehow even as it was bounded by walls and trapped by a shield-studded ceiling. 'I'll deliver them each day. I have your new tasks as well; fifty days is what I was told.'

Kindred nodded along with everyone else. Fifty days of work – fifty days of offering whatever each crew member could – the muscle in their arms or the knowledge in their heads, and then a ship, their lives back, a chance to leave.

But where would they go? Back to Arcadia? Around the island and all the way back to the Mainland?

Or would they sail farther out, toward the unknown and the uncharted horizon?

And perhaps most important: did Kindred think of herself as part of that they anymore? She looked around at sailors she had only truly begun to know, at stories she had only just started.

'Outside of your assigned tasks, you're allowed to move among this first level freely.' He spoke with the recitative quality that Kindred had heard from news-shouters on Arcadia, standing at the juncture of two roads and speaking the news of the day, over and over.

'This is Breach,' he continued, gesturing to the entire level around them. 'The second level is the Forest; if you have permission, the guards at the Forest entrance will help you through the paths. The third level is Wisdom, which you all have some experience with.'

A hint of a smile played across Barque's face, and Kindred

realized he was making a jab at their time spent in the cells, taking the citizenship test. But instead, she thought of all those sloped buildings growing up from the floor on that third level and shivered. The cells they'd been kept in down there were probably on the others' minds, but Kindred couldn't push the thought of those whispering growths away.

What had that watcher said? *We've cracked open a few, but they're always empty.*

This was a place of mystery, sure as can be, but unlike everywhere else, the Once-City seemed to exist in harmony with its mysteries, to move with them. It reminded Kindred of sailing, of bending to the wind. It reminded Kindred of keeping the hearthfire, of not berating the mystery at the heart of the flames.

It reminded her of her grandmother.

'Where do we go to see the captain and Little Wing?' Cora the Wraith asked, eyeing the big man before them.

Barque turned his head slowly, regarding Cora for a moment before saying, 'She will be down with the healers in the Forest. You're not allowed back there.'

'Sarah, too?' Kindred asked. 'Is Ragged Sarah, the crow-caller, back there?'

Barque was just as slow, just as imperious as he considered her for a long moment before answering.

'She is.'

'I'd like to see her,' Kindred said, before adding, 'and the captain and Little Wing.'

'Official requests to visit the Forest can be passed to your neighborhood warden for consideration.' Again, that tone of speech one hears in oft-spoken words.

'Isn't that you?' Kindred asked.

'It is,' Barque said, nodding. 'Your request has been considered and denied.'

Cora coughed out a laugh, sarcasm and a snide smile on her face. 'What an ass you are.'

'Welcome to Cruel House, new citizens,' Barque said, ignoring the barb and walking back toward the doorway. 'Follow me and I will show you your new home.'

'Fifty days only,' Long Quixa said, looking around at Cora, Scind-apse, and even Kindred. 'Then we leave him and the rest behind.'

They followed Barque in.

Unlike the council's building, Cruel House had interior walls of old brick. Every so often, a brick or two had broken away or been pushed out, like a child's lost tooth, a break in the pattern, offering little passages from room to room for an eye to look through, a hand to pass through.

Kindred found a table in one of the rooms on the first floor, a three-legged thing that looked as if it might slip into splits at any time. Atop it was a sack containing food: strips of burnt jackal grub. Next to it was a small barrel half-full of water.

They all drank and ate, sighing at the relief of water coating their throats, of food filling their stomachs. Afterward, Barque showed them the rest of the house. Some of the rooms had beds in them, mattresses made of twice-woven grass snugged into the corners. Some held nothing but stories of time and disuse. Up and up they moved; Barque said little to nothing about the house, and Kindred found herself missing the kind chatter of Seraph, who, even if some found him annoying, had at least provided information.

Scindapse and Cora split off to explore a hallway that sloped down slightly and ended in three rooms, and Long Quixa stopped in a small, two-windowed room that contained a mattress.

'I'm going to sleep,' she announced to no one in particular. She was down and still before Kindred had time to leave.

In the end, Kindred settled in a room on the top floor, the roof partially eroded and giving her a view of the shields affixed to the ceiling of Breach, winking and shining down at her, escorting in the fading sunlight. A wind played through the air in this room, and Kindred let it move over and through her.

It was not her cabin aboard *The Errant*, which had probably shattered into nothing at the bottom of the Sea by now. There were no neat bookshelves, no hammock strung inside a wooden cocoon. Though the Sea was nearby and all around, she could not hear the shush of grass against hull that she had so loved while sailing. She swallowed back the rush of pain as she thought of *The Errant*, their home, sinking into the depths.

When she had sailed aboard *Revenger*, Kindred had been the little ghost, trailing after her grandmother and sneaking quietly around conversations. Aboard *The Errant*, she had become her own woman, capable and one of the crew. The young girl from the Mainland that had moved with deliberate, careful steps as she climbed aboard her first vessel was well and truly gone.

But was the Kindred who had longed for a place aboard her own vessel gone as well? Had that woman who suffered under Rhabdus's instruction sunk with *The Errant*?

And if she was gone, who might Kindred become in this new place, so close to the darkness below?

I go to lose myself in it. The words from her grandmother's letter mingled with the sound of the wind in her mind, and Kindred found herself laughing suddenly. Barque entered the room, alarmed, but Kindred didn't care.

After a moment, a look of confusion and disgust on his face, he left Kindred alone to her madness.

'If this isn't being lost,' she said, to this new room, to this new place, to no one in particular, 'then nothing is.'

They all met up again downstairs after taking time alone. Quixa looked somewhat refreshed from her nap, and Cora the Wraith had regained some of her levity, but Scindapse appeared little recovered. Her eyes were clouded, dead pools. She said nothing, drank little, and ate not at all.

Kindred, though, felt a new energy, a light ghosting through her, stirring memories of being lowered to the Sea with the Marchess, breathing in the prairie's air, and giving thanks for a stalk of bluestem that connected sky and ground.

They sat in silence mostly, punctuating their thoughts with occasional wonderings about the captain's health, or Little Wing's or Sarah's. Free in a storied city, they did not know what to do.

Barque returned after a short time, a list of their assignments in his hand.

'When can we go visit our sick?' Kindred asked as soon as he walked in the door. She had been thinking of Ragged Sarah, of her fall from the crow's nest.

'Kwee-ex-sa,' Barque said, ignoring her question and looking around. Kindred could tell he had mangled Quixa's name on purpose. Mischief glinted in his eye, and the plants webbing his skin shifted slightly.

'It's pronounced Quick-sa,' Quixa said, though without any real venom.

'You've been assigned to sail repair.' He handed her a leaf of green with charcoaled writing on it. 'That's got your new overseer to report to and a map to get there. The sail weavers can be found on this level, over in the Crook'd neighborhood, not far from here. Cora.'

'At your service, warden,' Cora said, sarcasm untarnished.

Barque grinned at her.

'You've been assigned bilge cleanup. You'll join the other bilge crew above on the docks each morning.' He passed her a leaf, instructions scrawled there. 'I'm sure you had water to help you clean your ships back on Arcadia. We dry-clean them here.' Barque's grin widened.

'You'd be wrong there,' Cora said, shaking her head and sneering at Barque. 'Waste water on cleaning a ship? Not likely.'

Barque's smile soured for a moment as he stared at Cora, clearly trying to figure out if she was making fun of him or telling the truth. He moved on.

'You must be Scindapse,' Barque said, regarding the young crew member's still form. When it became clear she would give him no satisfaction, he dropped the leaf with her assignment on her lap. 'Cooks. Up here on Breach. Other side of the level.'

'And the hearthfire keeper. Performer of miracles.' Barque turned to Kindred, upper lip curling slightly. 'You're Councillor Seraph's new pet. He'll be by tomorrow to collect you.'

Barque dropped Kindred's leaf to the floor as she reached to take it from him.

'What's wrong with you?' Cora asked, shaking her head and staring hard at Barque.

'The councillor wouldn't stop talking about your dive,' Barque continued, ignoring Cora, eyes on Kindred. 'How amazing it was. How incredible. But I was on the dreadnought, and all I saw was a scared boatful of Arcadian filth running from a fight.'

Not even Cora had a retort to that.

'And what about visiting our sick?' Kindred asked, as she bent to the floor to retrieve her leaf. It held only a single line of instructions in loopy, wide handwriting: *I'll come by in the morning!* S

Kindred brought her eyes up to Barque's and flinched back from the anger there.

'You don't want to visit them, trust me,' he said, rubbing at a vine curling behind his ear.

'Don't tell me what I want,' Kindred said, feeling her own anger rising. 'When can we go visit them?'

'You can go visit your sick when I say you can and not before. This is my territory, my rules.'

Kindred looked down from the window of her room at the top of Cruel House. The crew had all drifted apart, some to meditations, some to sleep. They all waited for what was next, it seemed. But not Kindred.

Barque, promising that he merely wanted to be helpful, had stationed himself just outside the front door of Cruel House. He sat on a chair he'd taken from inside the house, his gaze drifting away. Kindred could see the anger still working through the tense line of his shoulders, the clench-unclench pull of his jaw.

Perfect.

She walked downstairs, looking for a back door or window, but found none. She looked on the sides of the house and found none there either – just more brick and wood, stacked and neat in its unevenness, another kind of prison.

Even on the second level the only windows were on the front of the house. Every opening in the building faced the middle of Breach and the staircase. Kindred guessed it was because no one wanted a view of the outer wall rising behind the house, stark and blank.

Kindred looked again at the central staircase, imagining herself scampering down the stairs. The only thing between here and there, though, was Barque, who knew the house well enough to know the only way out, by window or door, was through the front.

She returned to the third-floor room and slumped onto the mattress, eyes drifting up to the place where a ceiling had once been.

Kindred supposed she could wait until Barque got bored, or some other warden responsibility called him away. Or she could wait for the captain or Little Wing to return with the hope that they had news of Ragged Sarah.

Waiting and hoping.

Waiting and hoping for things to be different.

No, she thought, holding the word like a small, hard rock in her mouth. She twined the fingers of her left hand in and out of the grass mattress as an idea knitted together in her mind. She would not wait anymore. Her hopes would be her own.

She stood and watched Barque for the space of thirty slow breaths – *In the prairie wind, out the prairie wind* – but he did nothing more than shift in his chair and let loose heavy sighs.

Scanning the nearby houses, she saw other structures similar to Cruel House: old buildings, beautiful and dilapidated, clearly fallen into disrepair and disuse. A few stood off on their own, distanced from the small path running before them, but one stood quite close by, two of its walls remained standing, the others crumbled away into hills of broken, tumbled brick. If she could just sneak over to it, she might be able to get away.

It would have to do.

She returned to the mattress and began working at it with her hands, the process slow and made slower because of her burned hand, though eventually she loosened the weave enough to begin sliding the great length of grass loose. At first, she imagined the mattress must have been made using several blades of grass all tied and strung together, and Kindred figured she would have to retie them once she'd managed to undo the weave, but no. The mattress was made from a single artfully worked blade of grass, wound around and through itself over and over until it took on form and depth, structure and volume. It was the work of an artist, and Kindred undid it.

The strand of green crinkled and curled around the room several times, like a wyrm skin recently shed, a memory of what it once was. Kindred took one end and tested its strength, and though it creaked, the grass held together, and Kindred marveled for a moment at the strength of the Sea. This blade of grass had probably been cut from the Sea at least ten years earlier – maybe more – and still it held power in itself.

Kindred tied off the end through one of the holes in the wall between this room and the next, looping it around twice before setting it in an under-under knot. For just a moment, she remembered pulling at the fire in the Trade as if it had been a fool's knot, unleashing the flames and helping to save the captain. How long ago that time seemed; how at once strange and intimate those concerns felt now.

The knot secured, Kindred tugged on her makeshift rope, tentatively satisfied that it would hold her weight and hoping that she was not wrong. Bundling up the rest in her arms, she tossed it up and over the wall, out through the patch of missing ceiling. It took her a few tries, but finally she got it, and the grass cascaded out and down the back wall of Cruel House, opposite Barque, the grass chittering down the side like a rush of insects moving over skin. It was an eerie sound, one that tickled at Kindred's spine and made her think of grasses shuttling about in the deeps.

And it was not quiet.

Kindred hissed in a breath as she leapt back to the window, looking down to see Barque turned back toward the house, his eyes no longer glazing over, squinting in through the doorway. She fell back as his gaze moved higher, dropping to the floor to avoid being seen.

'Just go,' she whispered. Her chance, if it existed at all, was quickly vanishing. She had to move.

Voices below filtered up to her, and, alarmed, Kindred recognized Barque's voice.

'—going on? What was that noise?' she heard him say before Quixa's low, steady voice responded with words Kindred couldn't make out.

'Just *go*, Kindred,' she whispered to herself.

To reach the top of the wall, she had to pull in two more

mattresses, rushing to other rooms on the third floor and dragging them through the doorway. Kindred stacked them up on one another, trying to be quiet at first and then, when that seemed impossible, simply focusing on speed.

The voices below raised in volume as Cora entered the conversation.

'We don't want to be here just as much as you don't want us here, warden-man,' Cora was saying as Kindred scrambled atop the mattresses. She leapt one, two, three, four times at the top of the wall, grasping at the edge with her unburned hand and failing each time. But on the fifth leap, she managed to hold on long enough to wrench herself up, resting one and then two forearms on the top of the wall, which harbored enough dust and grime in the cracks to make her sneeze several times.

And then it was the rest of her body up, pulled slowly, until she could swing one leg over, as if she were riding the top spar aboard *The Errant*, repairing a sail or untangling ropes, looking out over the Sea.

There were huge rips in the wall, each one an ingress for the Forever Sea. Plants of all kinds grew in through these tears: flowering vines and grasses and herbs and a thousand others, all glad to bask in the reflected sunshine. Some had clearly been trimmed or trained to grow back out into the Sea, but at least five tears gushed greens and reds and golds and blues into Breach; the plants ran along streets and swirled around structures, occupying much otherwise habitable space.

Kindred saw a rare fruiting vine that had woven itself into a tall, grass-built structure and bloomed violently bright yellow flowers at the building's apex along with huge, bulbous fruits the color of blood, which hung out the windows of the building, weighty and strangely enticing.

In all of these ingresses, Kindred saw similar stories of the Sea's reclamation: roads turned into rivers of green, open spaces choked and devoured by grey, drooping blossoms, structures housing families of bluestem and coneflowers and a hundred others.

Had the Once-City been moving still, had it not been anchored in one place for so long, these tears might not have been a problem. Bugs and some of the smaller furred creatures might have come in from time to time, but a steadily sailing Once-City would have meant none of the plants had time or opportunity to establish themselves.

But with the Once-City stopped – as it had been for years, apparently – the great gaping wounds in the wall had become a problem.

And Kindred suddenly understood why this level was called Breach.

An argument, closer than before and frighteningly clear, brought Kindred back to her situation.

'Kindred! Hey, Kindred!' Cora's voice echoed off the walls of the building and through the holes in the ceiling. Kindred could hear Barque's grumbles along with Cora's calls, and they were both close, on the stairs, she thought.

Kindred began moving again, gripping the strand – rope, she decided; it had become a rope now – and lowered herself, her left hand and arm exhausted from doing double duty. She wrapped her legs around the rope and tried to make use of her right arm by crooking her elbow and pinching the rope against her ribs.

Slowly at first and then a little faster, Kindred slipped and slid down the rope, careful not to cut herself on the rough grain of the grass.

She heard Cora shouting for her. Quixa, too, had begun to lend her voice, low and soft and concerned now.

Kindred dropped as quickly as she could.

Barque's voice joined the other two, a voice of authority and irritation, and she could hear footsteps now, their sounds describing the last few stairs being climbed. Quickly.

Kindred let herself slide faster, feeling the fast heat against her palm each time she let the rope slide.

Somewhere around the second level, a horrible thought struck her: she had never checked to make sure the rope made it to the ground. The sight of the breaches had distracted her, and then the voices from below, and she was moving.

Kindred looked below and saw the end of the rope twisting and flicking with her movements, entirely too close to where she was now and not touching the ground.

She would have to jump.

She would have to fall.

As she slid the last bit down to the end of the rope, losing the comforting feel of the grass locked between her knees, Kindred heard a familiar voice from above, and she looked up to see Long Quixa's face, cocked to the side in confusion, eyes looking down at her.

Kindred's legs swung free of the rope, the muscles in her arm and chest tensed, holding tight to the rope even as her body swayed freely in the air. Untethered to the world, Kindred flew.

She stared up at Quixa.

And Long Quixa nodded once, eyes crinkling just slightly, before turning around and speaking. The even tones of her voice were too quiet to hear, but Kindred understood all the same: Quixa was buying her time.

Kindred kicked out at the wall of Cruel House so she wouldn't be dropping straight down.

And fell.

Her legs collapsed beneath her as she landed, and Kindred rolled forward onto her shoulder, every muscle in her body surging into action, trying to protect her burned hand. She managed it, but barely, and as she stood up, she felt the strain in her legs and hips and feet. One ankle twisted painfully beneath her as she put weight on it.

A frustrated shout from above her drove all thoughts of pain and strain from Kindred's mind, though, and she looked up to see Barque staring down at her, teeth bared in a grimace, one of the buds jeweling his skin opening just a little, a spike of color just under his jaw.

Kindred ran, ignoring the pain singing up through her body, and instead felt the freedom of no longer waiting, no longer hoping.

16

KINDRED became the vines coughed in through the breaches; she remade herself into the Sea recapturing the City. Instead of running along the main road to the staircase, she veered off between buildings, her footsteps rhizomatic, unseen and unknown, angling and lancing randomly. Like the plants occupying spaces meant and not meant to be occupied, Kindred went everywhere: on another road for a little bit, walking when she saw people, running when she didn't; sliding between the wide and slim spaces between grass-woven houses; mingling in and around what seemed to be a small market, walking along and existing there for a few breaths before moving on. She became intensely aware of her dun-colored clothing amidst the brightly woven attire of the Once-City citizens she passed by.

But though she drew some attention, it was nothing more than a few curious looks and whispered conversations. Some Kindred passed on the streets had clothes like hers, and these she knew to be other sailors. Their faces bore the script only the prairie wind could write: lines and creases telling of days sailing the Sea and nights adoring the stars.

As she neared the staircase, she entered again the rampant growth that surrounded it, feeling her breath returning amidst the green. Somehow, in that chaos of plants and people, Kindred felt calm.

She emerged out of the tangle, having followed a thin footpath that wound about before depositing her at the staircase, and was happy to find the stairway host to several people – none of them Barque – about their own business, coming and going.

Kindred tried to look as though she belonged as she stepped onto the staircase and went down.

The Forest.

Kindred stared, unmoving, as citizens of the Once-City moved around her in the never-ending up and down of their lives.

She stared, forgetting for a moment the man chasing her.

She stared, not forgetting the Sea or her grandmother or her new place in this world but feeling them all the more powerfully.

She stared into a dark, dense wood.

The second level hugged the staircase, allowing only a small space to exit before huge trees standing shoulder to shoulder stopped any further movement.

The blue-green light from the staircase faded as it reached the trees, their leaves like shields, their trunks like sentinels arrayed in some formation that looked at once chaotic and purposeful.

A ghost wind, like the one she had heard coming through the Sea wall into her prison cell, spun secrets through the leaves as

Kindred stood on the staircase, and she wondered if the first was the only level with breaches.

Kindred stepped from the stairs onto the soft loam of the Forest and approached the single path winding quiet through the trees.

'Not another step,' a voice said, and for a moment Kindred thought the trees had begun speaking to her, warding her off, as though they knew she had escaped from her guard, had become a disease running unchecked through the veins of the Once-City.

But it was a woman, short, muscled, mean. Instead of the cudgel carried by Barque, this woman carried two narrow-bladed swords, one on each hip. Tattoos covered most of her visible skin, reminding Kindred of Ragged Sarah. This woman walked out from where she had been leaning against one of the trees, blanketed in shadow. Another woman dressed and armed exactly like her, though taller and broader of shoulder, also emerged.

These were the pirates Kindred had heard of from bookmavens and council leaders, from men and women too far in their cups to bother holding back their thoughts anymore. These were the pirates Little Wing spoke of. Their every move was power, violence, hostility.

Kindred fought the urge to flee back up the stairs. Did they know? She could still run: she might somehow avoid Barque, might make it back to Cruel House. She could plead ignorance, take whatever punishment the man drummed up.

She stayed, feet firm.

'Who are you here to see?' the first guard asked, putting her body and blades between Kindred and the entrance to the Forest.

'Ragged Sarah, Captain Jane Caraway, and Little Wing,' Kindred said, keeping her eyes ahead but listening for the sound of feet stepping off the stairs behind her, for the sound of panting breath and Barque's cudgel whistling through the air.

The taller woman consulted a list written out on a curling length of Sea grass while the first continued to eye Kindred.

Moments passed, and Kindred tried to keep breathing, to not look as though she had run there, to remember herself as a person who belonged in this place. That ghost wind rattled the leaves of the trees again, the sound dry and old, like sickly breathing.

Did she hear something behind her? The sound of a humiliated man cursing under his breath? Kindred couldn't tell if it was the wind speaking in little voices, playing to her imaginings and fears. She longed to look, and it must have shown in her face, because the first guard stepped nearer still, one hand going to her blade, as if she knew something was wrong and was prepared to cut her way to the solution.

'Yep,' the second woman said, breaking the tension with the mundanity of her response, the mundanity of her job taking over again. 'Here it is. All three cleared for guests.'

Cleared for guests. Barque must have known and still kept Kindred and the others away out of spite.

'And what's your name?'

'Kindred.'

Writing this down, the woman said, 'Yllstra will take you.'

Yllstra, the first sentry who had called out, looked Kindred over once more, squinting, before saying, 'Follow me and do exactly as I say. If you don't, you will likely die.'

She offered this statement without bluster, and the other guard gave no sign of mockery or humor.

Yllstra set off along the discreet path burrowing its way through the thick press of trees. As she rounded a curve into the Forest, Kindred looked back down the path, but there was no sign of her pursuer. She followed Yllstra.

The ambient light from the central column was soon crowded out by more and more trees, and, as the path grew narrower, Kindred and Yllstra had to walk in single file in almost-total dark. Yllstra stopped beside a small wooden sign sticking up from the side of the path at a slight angle. The sign read only, Pursuant.

'The Forest does not allow fire along the paths,' Yllstra said. 'You will have enough light to see by, if only just, so let that be enough. It is some distance to reach the Healing Glade and once we begin moving, it is unsafe to stop. Follow me no matter what you see in the woods around you.

'And most importantly, do not stray from the path. Many things live in this Forest, all of them hungry.'

As they continued along the path, Kindred had the discomfiting realization that Yllstra had taken her blades out, one in each hand. She followed.

Darkness pressed close, and Kindred was wondering what Yllstra considered 'enough light' when the guard's form began to mingle with the shadows. The path was an afterimage before and below her, and the trees around her were barely visible.

It was some time into the walk – the only sounds Kindred's breathing, Yllstra's breathing, and the sound of the path beneath their feet – when lights like stars began appearing deep in the forest.

'What are those?' Kindred asked, the trees suffocated her words with their density, their depth.

'Lantern bearers,' Yllstra said.

'How come they can have lights?' Kindred felt cheated. 'I thought you didn't allow fire on the paths.'

Yllstra slowed but did not stop. 'I didn't say I don't allow fire on the path. I said the Forest doesn't allow it. Those are not people on other paths. Do not look at them. Pay no attention if they approach.'

She picked up her pace again, and Kindred struggled to follow.

But despite Yllstra's warning, Kindred couldn't help but look off into the darkness. She was entranced by the strange lights floating and bobbing about in the black. And after a time, they did seem to be approaching, though Kindred couldn't tell if their path brought her nearer the lights or if the lantern bearers moved through the trees somehow.

As the lights neared, they resolved into the shape of lanterns: old, boxy things dangling, she thought, from short chains. The bearers themselves remained subsumed in darkness; their forms described the absence of light. Nearest was a tall bearer carrying a lantern floating higher than the rest, a lantern swinging in long, measured arcs articulating the slow, rhythmic steps of its bearer.

Myriad lantern bearers swam through the darkness toward Kindred, approaching from both sides now.

'Eyes on me,' Yllstra said, her voice percussive and jarring amid the lights' hypnotic approach.

But Kindred had seen something behind one of the lanterns, something that couldn't be, and though she continued to follow behind Yllstra, her attention lay with the darkness and the mysteries moving through it.

'Ouch. Fuck!' came Yllstra's exasperated shout as Kindred stepped on her heel.

'Sorry,' Kindred muttered. 'Sorry, I'm not trying to . . .' But she trailed off. She'd seen it again.

'Ignore them and keep moving,' Yllstra said, casting a quick glance to the lantern bearers before striding forward.

The lantern bearers were close now, very close, close enough for even the meager light of the lanterns to do their work and reveal some of the bearers. Though, Kindred realized, looking at the nearest one, the lantern itself – this one and all the rest – gave off very little light, and the illumination it did provide was soft and cold, a ghost light for a ghost wood and a ghost wind. Even this close – close enough that a leap would have brought her to the being behind the lantern – Kindred caught only shifting glimpses, a short person, a man, no, a woman, dark robes falling around her, ratty hair nesting around her shoulders, her face still in shadow until – *there*.

Kindred stopped walking, and though Yllstra might have continued ahead, Kindred didn't care, couldn't.

The lantern bearer smiled in the ghost light.

It was Kindred. She stared at herself holding a lantern and smiling from the darkness.

A song, one of the creation stories she'd heard first from her grandmother aboard *Revenger*, whispered out from the darkness, and though the lantern bearer did nothing other than smile – her teeth lit from behind as though she held a fire deep inside, her own hearthfire – Kindred was sure the song came from the bearer.

The words and music caressed Kindred, warming away the chill she had experienced upon seeing herself. The song told the story of the gods and goddesses who created the Forever Sea, of their triumphs and falls; it was an epic of great sadness and even greater joy, loves lost and found across time.

The bearer had begun walking beside Kindred, little more than an arm's length away, and though the lantern showed nothing of the inky ground between them, Kindred saw the way to herself clearly.

She wondered, not so idly, if this smiling Kindred standing in the wood, lighting her own way in the darkness, might know the path she might take in her own life. She thought of her grandmother, also lost somewhere in the dark, and wondered if this bearer might know where she was, might give Kindred the secret of the Sea, of walking out into the green and black, of walking away into the Sea.

And as if the bearer could hear Kindred's thoughts, she smiled and nodded, gesturing with her lantern, inviting Kindred to follow, to follow and to know. In her smile, Kindred saw self-knowledge, a lantern in the dark.

Kindred reached a hand toward the darkness, and the lantern bearer reached, too, her backlit, fiery smile growing, consuming her face, still Kindred's smile but now predatory, and Kindred grew cold as she reached, grew unsure, grew afraid.

'No!' came a shout from farther down the path, and then a body collided with Kindred's, knocking her down to the path hard enough to dizzy and shock her, hard enough to slam her teeth together with a definitive *click*.

In the near-total darkness, Yllstra lay on Kindred, her face kissing-distance away, her eyes furious, her breath heavy.

'What did I say? I said don't stray from the path. I said eyes on me. I said pay no attention to the lantern bearers.'

Yllstra pushed herself up and then pulled Kindred to her feet. Yllstra's profile was cut from the darkness by the lantern bearer's light, though the bearer no longer bore the easy smile and inviting eyes Kindred had seen before.

It had transformed, its smile stretched beyond its face, pulling past cheeks, blurring into darkness at the edges, lips framing teeth that snagged and curled against and around one another, teeth for biting and ripping. The bearer's eyes slid down her face, one oozing down and over her now-scarred, now-torn nose, the other dripping off her face and out into the blackness.

'You walk off the path, and that's it for the rest of us,' Yllstra said, pulling her blades out again. They had begun to glow a sullen red in the darkness, as if on fire themselves, and the lantern bearer shied away from their light. 'The path is safe so long as its sanctity isn't broken. Imagine a barrier separating the path from the Forest – every arm or leg or body that goes through it weakens the barrier.'

In the darkness of the Forest, Yllstra peered more closely at Kindred, calming enough to really see her.

'You're a new citizen, right?'

'Yes.'

'And this is your first time in the Forest?'

Kindred couldn't focus on Yllstra – her lantern bearer continued to shift and change in the darkness, a wraith of weird light.

'Yes.'

Yllstra moved to stand in front of Kindred, blocking her sightline to the bearer.

'You're not scared at all, are you?'

'What?' The lantern bearer was a nebulous outline of light behind Yllstra.

'These lantern bearers call at us. They offer sweet words and promises to trick us into stepping off the path. But once you refuse, they reveal themselves to be the monsters they really are.' Yllstra stepped closer. 'And most people are so damn terrified when they witness it that they run back screaming. Even citizens who were born here. Even citizens who have walked these paths before.

'But you're not scared at all.'

Kindred frowned. That couldn't be right. It was almost completely dark, and she stood on a narrow path carved through a ghost forest below the surface of the Forever Sea – a forest that swam with the lights of . . . something. Of course she was scared.

Wasn't she?

'I'm just surprised,' Kindred said, not making eye contact with Yllstra.

But the other woman was shaking her head, half-smiling.

'No, you're not. Some people aren't like the rest. Some people don't see dark and feel terror. Some people – some of *us* – see dark and feel curious. Some of us see dark and feel *free*.'

I go to lose myself in it, a voice whispered in Kindred's head, and that was exactly it: a feeling that had moved through her for so long, instilled perhaps by the Marchess. Or, more truthfully, called forth by her. The joy in looking out over the prairie – that same expanse so many around her saw as a plane to be crossed or a field to be harvested – and seeing a wilderness that held and hid wonders beyond the simple-angled grasp of people.

The prairie was a mystery, and unlike those who refused to truly see it, or who through might or magic wished to break its mystery to their will, Kindred found she longed only to feel the wonder, the sameness of whatever moved in her also moving among and below the Sea.

Free, Yllstra had said.

And yes, she was free.

'Let's go, citizen. It's time to move,' Yllstra said, though without the same gruffness as before.

Kindred moved.

'What are they?' Kindred asked as they walked, lights approaching from all sides now, even dimpling the darkness above and below.

'Ghosts,' Yllstra said. 'The ones we carry with us, the memories that hold sway over our hearts. Not as they truly were or are in life but as you remember them, as you imagine them. Don't ask me how a bunch of trees know what's in your heart, because I don't know. No one even really knows how these trees are here in the first place. This level used to just be the Healing Glade. And then the trees started appearing, pushing further and further in. And then lights began moving in the darkness.'

As they walked, other lantern bearers came to Kindred, to invite and plead and entice her. They appeared as her crew: Stone-Gwen, her body rippling with flames, her lantern a pit of blackness even darker than the shadows of the forest, her smile plain and quiet, her song only the sounds of her easy breathing. Captain Caraway, smiling that same backlit grin, her hair sparking and crackling over with energy, lightning building and roaming in the clouds of her wild mane, her eye unveiled and pale, bulbous, *hungry*.

'My own suspicion,' Yllstra continued, ignoring the lantern bearers, 'is that it's the Sea itself, like the siren stories of old, trying to conjure beautiful and terrifying bits from inside your own head to pull you down to the deeps.'

Kindred nearly laughed at that – she knew those 'siren stories of old,' had heard them as a child. But this was not a place for laughter, and so she kept quiet.

Cora the Wraith appeared as three distinct lantern bearers, each identical, the look of betrayal on their faces exactly the same. Their lanterns were only pieces of a whole, each one a few floating fragments of metal holding a nebulous, shifting light. Kindred felt herself becoming nauseous as her eyes moved between these lantern bearers, each a not-quite-complete piece of a whole.

The lost crew – those gone in the wyrm attack, those who had failed the test – flickered into being from the darkness of the trees, glaring their anger, their confusion, their heartbreak at her. Stone-Gwen, her lantern caught on the end of her great banded cudgel, her face mournful, walked next to Grimm, their ghostly hands reaching for one another but never meeting.

You did this, they shouted, and Kindred could only nod and continue along, unable to meet their eyes.

Even Ragged Sarah was there, perfect and whole, her body unbroken and unharmed. She smiled and whispered to Kindred, secret things to make her heart break and sing, whisperings of things Kindred desired and things she did not yet know she desired, and the darkness was a blanket around her, one which might warm Kindred, too. This Ragged Sarah called to her, and Kindred felt a hitching in her chest as she turned away.

'If you go with them, you will not come back,' Yllstra said, ignoring her own lantern bearer, who stood deeper in the woods and bore no smile at all. This lantern bearer bore no resemblance to Yllstra. Its lantern was a free-floating flame like the firebugs Kindred had seen floating over the Sea during the last few hot days of a year. Arms like tentacles curved through shadows around it, mere suggestions of themselves, promises of something bigger lurking in the dark. Its face was cruel and bitter, composed of hard angles and lines. This lantern bearer's invitation was vengeance, and Kindred shivered as it stared.

Kindred left Ragged Sarah behind even as the bearer mourned, weeping and speaking of what might have been, what could no longer be.

'This path was once wide enough for five, six people to walk down, shoulder to shoulder, but each time some idiot gave in to the bearers' calls, the Forest pushed in closer.' Yllstra spoke as she continued to walk, casting glances over her shoulders at Kindred to make sure she followed. 'We can perform some spells each span to push back against the Forest's expansion, but they only accomplish so much. The architects in our order have designs for new paths, more efficient ways to move through the Forest, but it takes all of our efforts to keep this one open, and we're losing. It slims a tiny bit every year despite our work. The trees are closing in.'

Kindred considered the path, how narrow and close it felt. She walked closer to Yllstra.

Lantern bearers began appearing more frequently now, coming in twos and threes, in tens and twenties, people Kindred had seen for much of her life walking arm in arm with people Kindred had seen twice, once, never. It was as if the Forest were an artist attempting to paint what it had only ever heard of: lantern bearers appeared that were nearly exact copies of people Kindred had known – *nearly* perfect but always missing something, and Kindred found the missing bits lined up with her memory. There, a man who Kindred could not remember if he was tall or short was both. And there, a pair of girls that Kindred thought might have died aboard a ship, but had it been Antilles roaches that had swept over their ship or a storm that had suddenly come upon them? One of the girls looked waterlogged, her skin drenched and drowned, her mouth and nostrils sluicing out a steady stream of water. The other smiled through the scratches and bites that ranged over her skin, despite the chunks of flesh seized and ripped from her body, a missing ear, her bone-white jaw exposed, an arm half-gone, half-there.

What Kindred remembered appeared in the lantern bearers, and what she forgot blurred them into madness.

'Eyes on me,' Yllstra kept saying, and Kindred mostly did, the task growing easier as the Forest became more and more desperate, flinging lantern bearers at her that were more absent than they were present, people Kindred had seen only once or only heard about.

'Nearly there,' Yllstra said as they followed a sharp curve in the path, and Kindred meant to follow her around it, meant to reach the end of this path.

But there was the Marchess.

It was her, Kindred thought, Kindred *knew*. It was her grandmother, the woman with whom she had spent most of her life, who had trained her to keep the fire, to sail the Forever Sea, to live in and with and from the world.

It was her.

She bore no fantastical lantern. What use did she have for that? She walked on the Sea, in the Sea, and the ways of the world had opened themselves to her.

'Hello, child,' the Marchess said, her voice an undercurrent in the darkness, whispering through it. Kindred found she was crying.

'Hello, Grandmother,' she said, keeping her own voice low. Tears touched her cheeks and fell to the path.

The Marchess looked down at Kindred, eyes kind and warm, smile a little sad.

'I'm sorry to have left without telling you,' she said, looking down for a moment. Her hair was plaited down her back as it had been aboard *Revenger* when Kindred had sailed with her, a long rope of grey hair proudly displayed to the world.

'I miss you,' Kindred whispered, stepping forward a little. 'I feel so lost now.'

The Marchess looked up and nodded, sad.

'You have only begun to lose yourself, child. It gets easier.'

'Are you okay?' Kindred asked, looking her grandmother over.

The Marchess laughed, and Kindred smiled through her tears. She thought she'd never hear that laugh again, and yet there it was, as if it had never left the world. The Marchess held out her arms for inspection.

'I've never been better.'

'Are you . . . you?'

The Marchess thought for a moment, her eyes on Kindred.

'In a way. I am an imagining, close enough to be true.'

Kindred's breath stopped.

'Why did she – why did *you* go?'

The Marchess leaned forward now, smiling that old smile Kindred knew so well, kind and wise and calm and safe and true, a smile that served a good heart.

'To see,' she said.

Kindred stepped forward, the space between them conspiratorial now.

'Can I go with you?'

The Marchess considered her for a moment, eyes pitying, her

head cocked to the side in a look Kindred remembered so well. Her grandmother had once told her, 'I want to give you the world, child. If only I could, if only I knew how.'

And here was that same expression, that same desire to help Kindred, and she felt like a child again, hopes and dreams and sadnesses and great energies crashing through her body, confused and joyous and riotous all at once.

The Marchess extended a hand, and Kindred reached for it.

'I go to lose myself,' Kindred whispered to the Marchess, who reached and reached, nodding to Kindred, ready to take her out into the Sea, out into wonders and worlds unknown.

Yllstra's blades cut the air, flaring an even brighter red, flinging back the darkness, revealing a Forest floor that wasn't, that fell away to nothing, an abyss of starless black that dropped far below, tree trunks reaching down like bones, trees that were not trees at all but the splintering fingers of a beast beyond the world, beyond time, a beast that the world had become. Kindred stood on the path, a bridge suspended over the abyss, and before her, floating on nothing, was the Marchess.

The blades bit into the Marchess's arm, leaving two long, fiery slashes that leapt and roared with devouring flame.

The Marchess pulled her arm back, but she did not scream and she did not transform. She merely looked at Kindred, eyes sad, so sad, cradling her arm, now burning, to herself, and amid Yllstra's cursing and raging, Kindred heard her grandmother's voice once more.

'It gets easier,' she said, and then she was gone, devoured by the darkness, which was only the darkness of a Forest again, and the trees were only trees again, sprouting from the forest floor.

'I'm sorry, I'm sorry,' Kindred muttered, letting herself be pulled forward by Yllstra, who continued to curse Kindred's stupidity as the two of them walked forward, Yllstra moving quickly and keeping her hold on Kindred, her blade free in the other hand.

The glade appeared before them in an instant. Kindred did not see the lighted space, the openness, until she arrived. She dropped to the ground, exhausted, rolling over thick grass.

She lay there, breathing slowly and letting her body calm down even as her mind continued to run.

'The first time is the hardest,' Yllstra said finally, her voice no longer hard. 'Most don't even come to visit when they have friends or family getting healed; they know the perils of the path. Usually, it's just us guiding the healers or carting the sick along the pathway.'

She gazed back at the Forest, where her own lantern bearer dominated much of the darkness. It was a man, bigger than any man ought to be, and though he rose and fell in the darkness, tentacles and flames surrounding him, his eyes were human, distinctly so, and they never left Yllstra's face. Kindred could see an entire history between Yllstra and this lantern bearer, all in those eyes that seemed to contain the world. Yllstra stared back, her expression unreadable.

Next to Yllstra's lantern bearer stood the first one Kindred had seen – the vision of herself, though the bearer's face had begun to split apart, halves of skull and flesh and hair falling away from one another and giving way to the unholy light still burning inside her.

Her song, too, had changed. Dissonant melodies collided together percussively, words in a thousand languages running into and across one another, shreds and frames of songs – now The Crow Prince's Lament, now Once A La, Two A Lee, now a song

Kindred had never heard but that spoke of giants crawling over the night sky. It was enough to drive her mad.

But Yllstra was standing up and her voice was in Kindred's ear telling her to move further in, and it was enough to get her up and walking again, each step away from the Forest's edge another toward silence and sanity.

After the suffocating closeness of the path, the grove was a cool wind on a hot day. The trees receded as they walked across the lush, thick grass, and Kindred, in a fit of joy at the openness of it, removed her boots and let her feet sink into the grass, which webbed between her toes and tickled her heels and rejuvenated her more than any amount of sleep or food ever had.

'Your friends are just ahead,' Yllstra said. 'Once you're done with your visit, one of the healers will find you an escort to return.'

Yllstra began to walk back toward the path.

'Is this what you do, day in and out?' Kindred asked, seeing the woman in a new light. To be forced to walk that Forest path every day, to deal with the ghosts of your past and present and future, to defend the path and the City against whatever stalked that blackness – it was a cruelty.

But Yllstra only nodded, shouldering her burden without fanfare or self-pity.

Kindred watched Yllstra walk back into the Forest, her blades out, her lantern bearer smiling as the darkness took her.

17

COOL grass beneath her feet and the shadow of the Forest gone for the moment, Kindred turned toward the center of the grove and walked toward the enormous structure there.

At first, she thought it to be a building, strangely shaped like a squat vase, rounded, wide at the bottom and curving up to a point at the top. But the nearer she walked, the more she realized it was not a building at all.

It was a great thornbush, its branches angling out and then up, curving high toward the ceiling, which, like that of Breach, was covered in shields reflecting light down into the grove. Kindred noticed that the shields were arranged in a loose circle only above the grove – out where the Forest reigned, the ceiling was dark and unadorned.

As Kindred approached, she began to recognize this bush – smooth, rust-brown branches playing host to leaves, thin and long like fingers, and bright red berries dotted with yellow, clustered along the branches. It was a shepherd shrub. She had seen them hundreds of times on Arcadia, plants that the Sea seeded inland

and that had to be cut back by Arcadians, who had no use for them.

But none of the shepherd shrubs she had seen on Arcadia were anything like this – they grew up to a person's knees, not high above their head. This bush could fit twenty, thirty Cruel Houses in it, Kindred thought, and still have room to spare.

She walked forward to where an archway led through the rising wall of branches.

Inside, the world became a calming sway of thorns and leaves, light filtering through the skyward branches curling up and up, cut back and thinned out to serve as walls. The inside resembled a great sphere, comfortable and comforting.

Rows of beds littered the sheltered grove, although many of them were empty. People Kindred assumed to be healers moved up and down the rows, consulting one another or leaning down to aid the sick and unwell.

A low hum filled the great space, echoing around and redoubling on itself, and it took Kindred a few moments to realize where it was coming from.

The base of the shepherd scrub's trunk, itself nearly as wide around as the great central column and staircase, had a tunnel cored through it; natural or not, Kindred couldn't tell.

But in that empty space at the very center of this enormous plant sat a boy who was humming without cease. Kindred watched him draw in deep breaths through his nose, nostrils flaring, so as not to break his chant. Cut into the grass before him was a fire pit filled with flicking flames from which he drew power. Though he was some distance away, the steady buzz of his humming filled the space, and Kindred felt as though she were standing next to him, her ear pressed to his chest, his voice inside her heart, calming and slowing.

She walked forward and saw that the vibrations of his voice actually flowed up through the trunk, somehow moving from sound to light and energy, dancing across the bark in little twinkling flashes of brightness. The vibrations spread and rippled along the branches, echoing around and through the globe of this place and offering Kindred's mind rest and peace, though she accepted neither.

The entrance to the Forest, still visible back through the archway, continued to promise violence and danger. Had Barque, her warden, followed her along the path? Did he move through his own nightmare world in the Forest even now, chasing her with anger in his heart?

Kindred let her eyes drift again to the ceiling visible through the canopy of the bush, empty of shields over the Forest, dark and drab except for spots of light, weak and diffused, drifting along. At first, she thought them to be stray rays of light cast off by the shields above the grove, but no, they were too soft for that, too ghostly.

A shiver rolled through her, washing away the calm of the grove. They were the light of the lantern bearers, tracking their movements as they themselves tracked those who walked on the path.

And by the look of the lights, someone was moving closer and closer to the grove.

Kindred turned and began threading her way through the beds, not sure if she had judged the lights correctly, not sure if it was Barque coming for her but unwilling to leave her fate to chance. On the far side of the grove, off to her right, she saw Little Wing standing next to a bed containing Captain Caraway. A man who looked to be a guard stood nearby.

Captain Caraway was covered in strange vines and plants, and though she was awake, her eye stared up and away, her gaze catching on nothing, leaving the world behind.

But strangest was the flower, pale pink, and shot through with streaks and jags of black. It sat on her chest or grew from it, Kindred couldn't tell. Like a breastplate, the flower splayed open across the captain's chest, bigger than any blossom Kindred had ever seen.

Little Wing was crouched next to her, clutching the captain's hand, her face a deadened slack.

Kindred turned away.

She found Ragged Sarah near one of the branched walls, sitting up and staring out through a break in the branches, her eyes far away, her hands folded on her lap, serenity embodied. Covering her were vines and branches, some twisting up from the thick grass below the bed, others descending from an overhanging limb, gnarled whorls of brown and gold and black and green, the colors of life and death.

At first, Kindred thought the branches and vines were surrounding her, some kind of strange pirate healing blanket, but as she neared Ragged Sarah, she saw they actually wove *into her skin*, which had begun to take on the colors of the vines and branches at the points of insertion. An arm gone gold all over to mimic several slender shoots of gold curled around and into it; her neck and jaw going from their usual light brown to a shining, verdant green.

'Well. Hello, you,' Sarah said, pulling Kindred's eyes up from the plants. Her voice was a croak rattling around a dry throat, quieter than Kindred was used to, yet a fire that burned low still burned.

Kindred felt the sudden and overwhelming urge to just move, to throw away everything, the man chasing her or waiting for her back at Cruel House, the pirates and this city and the Sea and her grandmother and all of it, to throw it away for the tiny forever there, the existence she saw in Ragged Sarah's dried lips, the collapsing space between where she stood now and where Ragged Sarah lay.

After everything, Kindred found comfort and safety and life here, kindling between the two of them, a fire sheltered in the curving hollow between their two bodies, growing in the pause between one word and the next, feeding on meaning and desire and something deeper and bigger, a force that braided circlets of grass and made mattresses into escape ropes.

'Hello,' Kindred said, standing on the precipice of something.

I go.

'I was hoping you would stop by.'

'I'm sorry it took me so long.'

I go to lose myself.

'I heard about the prisons. The test. You shouldn't have had to go through that.'

Kindred nodded.

'I was worried . . .'

Kindred remembered the feeling of loosing her hands in the Sea, in the chaos of it, her breath containing the world. The feeling of dew coating her arms, fresh and sweet.

The feeling that she could leap out into the green and watch it become *more*.

The space between them collapsed as Kindred stepped forward, her unburned hand reaching out and tangling in the mess of Ragged Sarah's hair, her breath becoming Sarah's and Sarah's breath becoming her own as their lips met, parted just so, cracked and desperate for water and moving against one another. Kindred fell into that kiss, lost herself in it, the weariness of the past days gone in that tiny forever.

'Oh,' Sarah said as they broke apart, her eyes wide.

'Yeah,' Kindred said, her heartbeat thrumming in her chest, her neck, the palm of her hand. 'Sorry, I – '

'Oh, no,' Sarah said, her face breaking into a smile. 'Don't be sorry. We should have been doing that a long time ago.'

A cleared throat brought an end to the moment, and Kindred pulled back to see a healer glaring at her. He was a younger man, balding and bearded, arms folded.

'Visitors are not allowed to walk – or act – freely among the sick,' he said, his voice low and annoyed. Whatever calming effects the grove had, they didn't seem to have any impact on this man. 'You must be accompanied by a healer.'

'Sorry, Sunu,' Ragged Sarah said. While they kissed, she had threaded her fingers through Kindred's, and though Kindred had stood up and taken a step back from the bed, Ragged Sarah still held her hand. 'She didn't know.'

Sunu huffed his displeasure and arched an eyebrow at Kindred.

'I have work to do here. Could you take a step back?'

Ragged Sarah winked at Kindred and squeezed her hand at the same time before letting go. Kindred stepped back, feeling the echoes of Sarah's hand in hers.

Sunu fussed about Ragged Sarah and mumbled almost continuously about 'inconsiderate guests' and 'ignorant buffoons,' but Kindred saw how seriously he took his work and how he cared for his patient. His hands were careful and soft as they checked the vines and branches connected to Sarah's body, applying pressure here or cutting away smaller growths there with a small, bright knife. In one case, he even removed a vine growing into Sarah's leg, offering her a root to chew on before pulling the vine out, his words no longer bitter or angry, his voice suddenly soothing, harmonizing with the hummed chant reverberating throughout the Shepherd Scrub.

He gave Ragged Sarah a drink of water from a skin and told her to take it easy before leaving, eyeing Kindred with plain dislike.

'He's all right despite being so prickly on the outside,' Ragged Sarah said, watching Sunu move along the rows to his next patient. 'He said earlier today that he thought I would be out soon.'

Kindred wanted to reach out for Sarah's hand again, to kneel beside her, to close the space between them again, but this was all new to her.

She had been with men and women before, sneaking into their beds during stays between *Revenger*'s voyages, but this felt different: a relationship beyond simply skin and want. It was a new love, a new language; it shared something with other tongues even as it spoke words only it could speak.

And so, Kindred spoke of simpler things, more immediate things.

'What's going on with these?' she asked, gesturing to the plants connected to Ragged Sarah.

Sarah laughed, and Kindred remembered how much she loved that laugh, so full of ease and comfort.

'Apparently, I broke several bones in my legs and hips, but the grove can heal almost anything. That's why they call this place the Healing Glade – it actually does the healing.' She held up one arm, vines trailing from it, blossoming with tiny, pebbly flowers of grey and black. 'The bush senses where injuries occur and sends out these little shoots to heal the damage.'

'Does it hurt?' Kindred asked.

'Not even a bit. Feels strange, but good strange, you know?' She reached out for Kindred's hand, and Kindred thought she did know.

'I wonder if it could heal my burn,' she said, holding up her other hand, still swaddled in the same grubby cloth wrap. She unwrapped it and offered it to the branch above from which so many of the vines going into Sarah came, and she was surprised when the branch extended a vine, a thin green thing reaching down toward her.

'Wait,' Sarah said, pushing Kindred away from the vine. The gentle smile on her face had gone.

'What?'

'The healing here,' Sarah said, gesturing to the vines threading through her body, 'it doesn't just fix you like a medicker on Arcadia would. It changes you, Kindred. A cut is not given a salve to encourage skin to knit together; roots thread through your skin and fill in the space with bark or leaf. Broken tissue becomes vegetal, broken bones become wood. Look at my leg.'

Sarah pulled away the blanket that had been obscuring her legs, one of which was mottled with bruises and puffed where the vines worked into her skin.

But growths sprung from the skin, too: tiny, gemlike flowers dotted the length of her leg, like dew on a strand of grass, stars in the sky.

'This place will heal you, but it will change you, too.'

The blossoms on Barque's face suddenly made sense. The great flower on Captain Caraway's chest, too.

'I'm okay with change,' Kindred said after a moment, meeting Sarah's eyes.

She pulled off the cloth, baring her puckered skin of her hand to the air, grimacing at the damage, at the curled, defeated thing her hand had become.

The vine continued to drop down from the branch, and when it landed on her hand, Kindred felt a sudden coolness move through her. The vine moved across her fingers and slithered over her palm, as if exploring a new land, as if searching for something lost.

Kindred felt no pain when the vine cut under her skin, branching out along her veins and across her hand, forming a new network of paths below her skin. The original vine broke off from the branch above, rooting itself deep in Kindred's hand, well below her skin, down to the bone, it seemed. The plant shot up through her fingers, discoloring her skin even further and then, strangest of all, it broke through at several places, sending up curious little shoots of dark, dark gold. Each one of these curled in on itself, forming tight spirals across Kindred's hand.

She tried to move it.

Her fingers quivered.

Sarah put a hand on Kindred's arm.

'How does it feel?'

Kindred shook her head and opened her mouth to respond.

But a voice, breathless and hitched, spoke before she could.

'When I say no, I mean it.'

Kindred turned to find Barque, and she had a moment to wonder why she hadn't heard him approach and then realized the same cool, thick grass below her feet had silenced his steps.

Beautiful, she thought as he neared. The buds had opened all across his skin, becoming delicate blue flowers rimed in white tracery, each one moving and swaying in a breeze Kindred could not see or feel. A single flower opened and swayed just below his left eye, a bloom on a venous vine winding up from his neck that Kindred hadn't seen before.

A few healers were moving toward them, clearly aware that something was going on, but they were not close enough. Kindred even caught sight of Little Wing, her eyes raised toward them now, rushing forward.

From a distance, it might have looked silly or strange, this broad-shouldered, surly man playing host to a swaying barony of flowers, but up close, his anger seething through and filtered by the blue-white blooms, Kindred saw beauty and purpose.

This was her last thought before his cudgel caught her first in the shoulder and then upside the head.

Darkness came then, dreamless and empty.

Kindred woke to a head full of clouds and angry voices. She looked around, moving slowly, all of her joints thick and unwieldy.

She lay in her third-floor room in Cruel House on the roughly bundled, grassy mass that had once been a mattress and then a rope. It had been formed into a loose bed, and someone had even taken the time to pile up an extra few loops of grass to serve as a pillow beneath Kindred's head. It was oddly comfortable.

She rolled over, slow as the moon's crawl through the sky, until she was on hands and knees. And then up, kneeling now and then hunched over and then standing, leaning hard against a wall.

The room had changed since the last time she had been inside it. Apart from the grass rope, which had become a loose mattress again, there was another mattress in the room, this one whole and tidy. It had been pulled near Kindred's, the only thing between them a waterskin and, set atop the waterskin, a note that read: Drink when you wake up. – Sarah

She did, and though it was warm, sour water inside the skin, Kindred found relief in it.

Her shoulder ached and she ran a hand over its swollen, bruised mass. It was the same side as her burned hand, which, now that she looked at it, had sprouted even more of those tiny, spiraled shoots of gold.

Something else was different, too – her fingers moved in strange, erratic jumps, like the spasms of a person sleeping through a nightmare.

But they moved, which gave Kindred a shock of joy.

She couldn't focus on that long, though – her head throbbed along with her heartbeat, sending waves of pain down her body.

The stairs were a challenge, which she navigated in short bursts of energy and movement – a few steps all in a rush and then a pause to breathe, to let the world stop spinning around her still-thick head.

All the while, the voices rose and fell below her, growing clearer as she descended, until she could begin to make out what they were saying.

'. . . need her! This is complete nonsense! I don't give a three-throated whisper if your brute here found her flinging shit against the side of the council's building; she is *my charge, my responsibility!* That's just all there is to it.'

'A *beast to break must find no quarter here.*'

Kindred felt nausea ripple through her abdomen at that voice, those *voices*. While she hadn't yet recognized the first speaker – an older man, she thought, maybe – she knew without a doubt who spoke second, those singsong voices threading through one another. If harmony could achieve discord, it was in the music of those voices.

The Word.

The older man spoke again.

'A beast? What a ridiculous idea. They're just people – she's just a person, and a citizen now, too! And this nonsense business of keeping her here for ten days just won't do. It won't do.'

'A *tool, her purpose writ by your own hand.*'

'What are you even saying? You sound like the riddle-speakers back home.' A new voice, one Kindred recognized as Cora the Wraith's, joyful even in her criticism.

'Riddles is right,' came the older voice. 'There's simply no talking with you. Riddles and nonsense. I'm taking Kindred as soon as she's well, and that's all there is to it. I won't let her be locked up here just because Barque swings first and speaks later. And the only way we get this city moving again is if we unlock those hearthfires, and I can't look after the ships and work down there.'

Kindred stepped down the rest of the stairs until she stood in the main room of the first floor. She slowly took in the scene there.

The Word, their ropy hair tied artfully around their heads in matching swirls and loops, stood next to the front door, a thin staff in his hand, a blade of tarnished metal in hers. They smirked at exactly the same time as Kindred came into the room, their mouths quirking into identical slants. Beside them was Barque, his eyes downcast, the buds dotting his skin once again closed, returned to being tightly curled grey promises.

Seraph stood on the other side of the room, his wispy beard sticking out at odd angles, grey hairs converging into tangles and snarls. He still wore messed, dirty robes, and Kindred wondered if unwashed, unkempt existence was the norm for him.

Between the two parties, reclining on the floor with her back against the wall, was Cora the Wraith. She sipped from a small cup of water and waved at Kindred.

'*We speak and she arrives, a beast so tam'd,*' The Word said. Kindred felt her dizziness returning as she watched their mouths move in concert. They offered a nod to Seraph before turning and leaving.

'I have other business in this ward. I will return later. Councillor,' Barque said, nodding to Seraph.

'Yes, yes,' Seraph said, flapping his hands at Barque and turning toward Kindred.

Barque offered Kindred a glare before following The Word. Kindred noticed that the bloom and its vine she had seen below his eye had receded and curved now around the swell of his neck.

'Sorry if we woke you,' Seraph said, taking a few steps toward Kindred. 'How are you feeling?'

'Like someone hit me in the head with a cudgel,' Kindred said, feeling a sweep of nausea as she spoke.

'That big idiot,' Seraph said, shaking his head and scowling out the door. 'I tried and tried to get you all assigned to a different ward, but The Word was insistent. I'm sorry. I feel completely responsible.'

Kindred sat down next to Cora, letting the floor do the work of holding her up. She felt some surprise when Cora shifted away slightly but did not get up. She didn't want to sit next to Kindred but was willing to sit near her. It was a start.

Seraph dropped down next to them.

'I blame those green-haired piss-poets,' Cora said, sipping her water again. Kindred suppressed as best she could the chuckle that rose in her chest, sensing the pain it would cause. But still, she smiled – she'd missed Cora's sarcasm and wit. 'They must have something out for us, huh?'

Seraph nodded, looking glum. Despite being an older man, Kindred realized, he had the spirit of someone much younger.

'He is no great lover of Arcadians,' he said. 'Many here are not. They say the Arcadians began this slow-war we've long been in.'

'That's not true,' Cora said, sitting up straighter.

Seraph held up his hands, palms out.

'I'm not saying it is – just explaining that there are those here who believe it. Long ago, they say, before Arcadians grew fearful of the wilder grasses – the Roughs, I think you call it – sailors from your island ventured further out and came upon the Once-City. The stories go that these Arcadians saw resources for the taking – ships, food, knowledge, culture. And so they stole from us, from the Once-City, which up to then had only moved occasionally.'

Seraph looked between Cora and Kindred, the lines of his face composing kindness.

'The Word, Barque, all of them – they believe Arcadians are why the Once-City first began to hide in the endlessness of the Forever Sea, and they believe, too, Arcadians are to blame for us eventually ending up here, stuck, hiding right where anyone could find us.'

Kindred let that sink in. Was it different from Cantrev and his hatred for anyone other, his commitment to any history that justified his hate?

'That's insane,' Cora said, though even she sounded slightly unsure.

Seraph shrugged and looked down at his dirty, dusty hands.

'Probably,' he said, the dark cloud falling away from his face as he looked back up, smiling now. 'But there's no need to worry ourselves about that right now!' He turned to Kindred.

'We have some exciting work to do. Have you ever dealt with morning's breath petals in a hearthfire? I have a few to show you that I think you're truly going to find fascinating.'

It was as if his disagreement with The Word had never happened. Kindred listened in amazement as Seraph transitioned from a morose recitation of a generations-long war to hearthfire theories and speculations. This was a man unwilling to let his skies be darkened for long.

'Hold on, hold on,' Kindred said, interrupting him and holding up her hands as if they were shields.

'Right, sorry, too much,' he said, nodding and taking a deep breath. His eyes settled on her hand. 'Oh, my. What happened to your hand?'

Kindred looked down at her burned hand, the golden shoots dotting it.

'Hearthfire burn.'

'Can you move it?'

'I'm . . . not sure.' Kindred flexed, and her fingers responded, although delayed and only a little. 'Some, I guess.'

Seraph was quiet for a moment, and then he said, 'You burned your hand before you got here?'

Kindred nodded, and a smile spread across Seraph's face, astonishment mingled with sheer joy.

'With a burned hand, you outran war vessels from your own city, navigated the Roughs, cut through the thistle pass, performed a perfect dive below one of our ships, and managed to keep your vessel afloat long enough for everyone to get off safely?'

Seraph leaned forward, his hands upon Kindred's shoulders, his eyes wild with happiness.

'Kindred! I've never heard anything so incredible in my whole life!'

A giddy giggle bubbled up from Seraph, and Kindred couldn't help but smile. No one on *The Errant* knew enough about hearthfires to understand what had happened as Seraph did. In fact, Kindred had long since become used to and accepting of a world that cared little for the work of hearthfire keepers beyond whether they could execute orders, like a dependable tool.

It was strange to be recognized, to be seen.

'Where is everyone?' Kindred asked.

'The ones from the Healing Glade are back. Captain Caraway went with a few of the councillors, something about a defense meeting. Little Wing, too, though she wasn't too happy about it. Ragged Sarah, Quixa, and Scindapse are all at their tasks – Quixa with the sail weavers, Scindapse the cooks, and Sarah above with the crow-callers.'

Cora stood and set her cup on a table nearby.

'And I actually ought to move along, too. Bilge cleanup for me.' Cora shook her head, disgusted, before growing serious again. She cut her eyes to Seraph for a moment, but whatever message Cora was trying to send, he wasn't receiving.

'Look,' Cora said, with a sigh, kneeling before Kindred. 'I still don't trust you. None of us do. I don't know if we can. But what you agreed to do for the council to get us a ship, all that stuff you figured out – I think that must have been a big part of why they agreed at all. And so . . . thanks.'

She didn't offer a hand, but she did give Kindred a nod, her eyes open and honest, before she left.

'I suppose we also ought to get to work,' Seraph said, standing and offering Kindred a hand up. She took it and immediately regretted it. As she rose, she could feel her heartbeat slamming in her temples, and the sway and sweep of nausea threatened to pull her under.

She sank back down, allowing her head to fall into the crook of her arm.

'Oh, of course, your head,' Seraph said. 'I'm so sorry! I'll get you some water.'

She heard him shuffling around, moving into the kitchen area.

'Oh,' he said, voice quiet. 'Your water stores for the day are gone. Nothing more until tomorrow morning, a half-day away.'

Kindred hadn't even realized it was evening. How long had she been out after taking a cudgel to the head?

'We're not supposed to give out water from our personal stores,' Seraph said, dropping down next to her again. 'But . . .'

Kindred looked up, head pounding, to see him reach into a bag slumped by the entrance and pull out a small waterskin.

He smiled.

'Just don't tell anyone, okay?'

Kindred nodded. She drank, thinking she wouldn't drink the whole thing and then drinking it anyway. She might have felt bad any other time, but she was too exhausted, too hurt to feel anything but complete relief in the cool slide of the water down her throat.

'Thanks,' she said.

'Of course, sure,' he said, taking the empty skin back. 'I tell you what: let's take today off – the day is nearly over, anyway. You can rest, and we'll try in the morning.'

Kindred nodded, and Seraph stood, helping her up and letting her lean on him, all the way back up to her room without a roof, her room with its tangled, undone mattress piled next to the other, still-woven one.

Up there, the light was dusky and thin, and it was clear how late in the day it was. Above, the shields crowding the ceiling were misers, holding the slim, fading light to themselves. This, paired with the constant song of the Sea against the outside wall and the vision of grasses shifting just outside the aperture – all of it said clearly: you are below the waves.

Kindred breathed easy.

'Thanks,' Kindred said as Seraph helped her with the last few steps to her bed and then let her go to drop onto the soft curls of the grass. 'And thanks,' she mumbled, already feeling the pull of sleep, 'for saying that stuff about the hearthfire and my hand.'

Seraph shook his head, smiling.

'No need to thank me. Just get some rest. I'll see you in the morning.'

Kindred was asleep before he was out of the room.

DREAMLESS, Kindred slept until morning, when the shields above became hot, bright pebbles, hurling down sunlight with abandon.

She woke to Ragged Sarah sleeping on the mattress beside hers. One mystery solved, she thought with a small smile.

Sarah's mattress lay beneath part of the roof that was still intact, and so she slept in the shade, completely at peace, breath slow and deep. Kindred lay for what seemed an endless moment, listening to that breathing, remembering how thin and weak Sarah's breath had been after her fall.

The sounds of activity filtered in, a calamitous waking from Breach. Children shouting and sellers selling. Idly, Kindred wondered what currency they used there – coin? She thought she might still have a few in one of her pockets.

And what did they sell there? Food was rationed; was it clothes? Books? Weapons? What was extra in this place?

Kindred floated on these questions for some time, drifting in her curiosity, until Ragged Sarah's breathing shifted and changed.

Her eyes opened, and as she saw Kindred, a slow smile spread over her face, lazy and wide.

'Hello.'

'Hello.'

The mattresses were both positioned roughly in the middle of the room, a few arms' lengths apart. Sarah shifted and scooted to the edge of hers, bundling the cloak she'd been using as a blanket under her head and facing Kindred.

Kindred did the same.

'How are you feeling?' Kindred asked.

'Better. You?'

'Better.'

And it was true. The nausea and pounding headache were both gone, and the muscle aches had even lessened. Kindred wondered if it was the mattress, or the sleep, or this place. She breathed more freely than she had in a long time.

'What did they give you for work?' Sarah asked, scooting closer, though it nearly caused her to slide off her mattress.

'I have to work with Seraph – the councillor – on the hearthfires. I'm not sure. Today will be my first day.'

Sarah nodded.

'I remember Seraph from before when I lived here. He always seemed all right. A little crazy but all right.'

Kindred laughed and nodded.

'Crazy is right. And they've put you up with the crow-callers?' Kindred shifted back a bit, giving some room on her mattress, an open invitation.

Sarah smiled and slipped over, dropping down next to Kindred, their faces suddenly close, their knees brushing against one another, bodies forming two sides of a circle.

'Yeah. Monitoring the skies, sending messages through the birds to scouting ships out on voyages or patrols. Simple stuff – easy enough to do for the time we have to be here.'

'Is it strange, being back?' Kindred suddenly realized that, for all the wonder and weirdness of this place for her, none of it would be new for Sarah. She had grown up running along those streets; she'd probably been one of those children playing in the ingress of the Breaches. What a childhood she must have had, so close to the Forever Sea, living in and among and *with* it.

'Strange is one word for it,' Sarah said, frowning. 'I never thought I'd come back. And even after the captain's plan, I didn't think we'd be staying for any amount of time. Just a little bartering to refill our stores, haggling maybe for better maps, and then on our way, either further out or on a wider arc toward the Mainland.'

Sarah stared off, no longer looking at Kindred but over her shoulder, past and beyond.

'My parents are still here, I guess. Friends I grew up with. Sailors I knew and sailed next to.'

'Have you found them yet? Told them you're back?'

Sarah shook her head and said, 'No. I ended those relationships when I left; most of them were *the reason* I left. I didn't think I'd ever be coming back.'

'But is it so bad to come back? There's no Cantrev here, no one burning down storehouses, no fights over water rights or resource allocation.' Kindred didn't know why she was pushing this – she'd been thrown into a prison, forced to take a test, given to the care of an absolute piss-weed warden, and then knocked out cold when she disobeyed – but she couldn't push away the feeling of being in the right place, of somehow, in some way, moving toward where she was meant to be, of following in her grandmother's footsteps.

I go to lose myself in it, she heard in the beat of her heart and the whisper of the Sea outside.

Sarah focused on her, and she wasn't smiling anymore. When she spoke, it was not unkind, but the warm laziness of sleep had gone from her voice.

'You don't know these people like I do, Kindred. There are Cantrevs here, even if they don't seem like it. You can't trust this place. I don't know why the council gave us this deal – fifty days and they give us a boat? I've never known them to be so giving. But this is the first time I've ever known there to be a pirate majority on the council, too. Nothing makes sense to me here anymore.'

'How does the council work?' Kindred asked, trying to think through the people who'd been sitting at that table in the council's building.

'There are always seven positions on the council, and each position represents a part of the great responsibilities of the Once-City. The head councillor is always in charge of water, and then there is the fleet commander, the wardens, the harvester guild, the trade guild, the hearthfire keepers, and the healers. When I lived here, the pirates – the ones who believe in raiding and pillaging, stealing ships and killing any in their way – only had three of those positions, but it was clear they were growing in power.

'And now it seems they have four.' Sarah ticked them off on her fingers. 'Ebb-La-Kem, water. The Word, wardens. Uz, harvesting guild. And GladWill, trade guild.'

Kindred felt relief in not hearing Seraph's name on the list, though the whole thing was too abstract for her to really comprehend.

And more immediately, she felt distance growing between her and Sarah. They no longer angled their bodies toward one another, and whatever tiny stillness they had found seemed to have gone.

'You can't trust them, Kindred,' Sarah said, eyes hard, voice steady and forceful. 'The Once-City cares only for its own, and no matter how many times they call us citizens, they don't really believe it – not the ones in power, anyway.'

Voices from below signaled that the others had woken up, and Kindred felt the spell in their little room fading.

'Okay,' she said, nodding, concerned by Sarah's sudden intensity. 'I won't.'

Sarah reached out for Kindred's unburned hand and covered it in her own, holding it tight to her chest.

'We just need to do our time, pay attention, and outsmart them before they fuck us over first.'

Kindred nodded again, trying to say something, anything that wouldn't betray what she had begun to build with Sarah.

But she stayed silent.

They came downstairs together a short time later, and Kindred was surprised to find Seraph chatting amiably with Scindapse, the two of them sharing some food together. The others – Cora, Quixa, Captain Caraway, and Little Wing – sat together in a different room, saying little, eating little.

'Ah, fantastic!' Seraph said when he saw Kindred. He shared a few more words with Scindapse, who, in his presence, seemed to have brightened somewhat. She even smiled a little as Seraph patted her on the shoulder and said, 'Just give it some time.'

'Feeling better?' Seraph asked, handing Kindred a few strands of whatever rationed food they'd been given. 'Breakfast,' he said as he passed it over.

'Yeah, I am,' she said, feeling Sarah's proximity and thinking of their conversation. *You can't trust them, Kindred.*

'Excellent. Let's get to it!' Seraph was up and already moving toward the door, his excitement palpable.

'Wait.'

Captain Caraway stood in the doorway of the other room, her face haggard. The flower on her chest was almost completely covered by the robes she wore, though an arc of pink showed just above her collar.

'I'll meet you outside,' Kindred said, nodding to Seraph, before turning back to the captain. It had only been a few days – a span maybe – since she'd spoken with the captain, but so much had changed since then. They were impossibly far from the captain's quarters, staring at the map, wondering which way to go, toward the known or toward the unknown.

'Keeper,' Captain Caraway said, stepping forward.

'Captain.'

'When we made the plan to come to the Once-City, I can't say this was what I wanted.'

Kindred nodded.

'My ship is gone. So are some of my crew.'

Kindred didn't speak. There was nothing to say.

'Instead of bartering for supplies and moving on, we're laboring for pirates with the hope that they'll give us a ship. And to add to that deal, you've offered your services to fix up their hearthfires and teach their sailors how to move more efficiently and quickly. Is that about right?'

'Betrayal,' Little Wing said from where she still sat at the table. She stared down at her hands.

'She betrayed you, Little Wing, not me,' Captain Caraway said before focusing back on Kindred.

'I was serious back on Arcadia, before we lost Rhabdus, when I said I liked that you were wild. The grasses around Arcadia have felt too small and too contained to me for some time now. I see that same sense about you that I feel in myself: the need for more, the need to see and know.'

Kindred nodded.

'But know this: to want more is to leave something behind. You cannot live in two worlds at once, and a step toward one is a step away from another.'

She leaned forward, and when she spoke, her voice grew hard.

'You cannot be truly part of this place and remain a member of this crew. Do you understand?'

'Yes,' Kindred said, simply. To have the growing divide inside her spoken so plainly felt at once painful and freeing.

'Barring disaster, you have fifty days to decide which world you want to inhabit,' Captain Caraway said, turning away, back to her crew.

Outside, Kindred found Seraph, and they began walking. Seraph talked, of course, and as he did, Kindred found herself oddly looking forward to what lay ahead.

How did they build their fires there? From what Seraph had implied, the Once-City keepers had been using grasses and plants for a long time, which meant that Kindred's bit of experimentation to get around being able to use only one hand was perhaps common practice there. What else had they thought of that she hadn't?

A sudden image filled her mind: a build that allowed for a controlled and *stable* dive – a combination of bones and plants so rare as to have been considered extinct burning together to pull ship down and down, not falling but flying – *sailing* – below.

Her heart beat faster as they left Cruel House behind.

Kindred followed Seraph out to the central staircase, up to the surface, out onto the root docks, out to where the unleveled, wild prairie Sea rolled and writhed in endless waves toward the horizon. Plants she had never seen before opened and cut into the sunlight, growing wild, without any human logic governing them.

Just as shocking were the trees growing up through the prairie, far more than she had ever seen before on the Sea. The same magic that flattened Arcadia's grasses also killed off any Sea trees before they could grow, but here they pushed through the surface of the Sea in sun-stealing masses of green. It was a miracle *The Errant* hadn't slammed into one on their approach.

Kindred had spent enough time harvesting to know what she should see in the plants coloring the grasses around the trees: the riches that lay before her, the need to organize and rework such chaotic growth, the need to impose lines, edges, sense.

But there, with a warm wind on her face and the world open before her, Kindred relaxed into the chaos. She had seen the world below this one and did not give herself to worrying overmuch about madness above. She sought a darker logic, a deeper story.

Among the waves of color – green cut with red, blue, gold, white, and all the rest – were veins of grey, dead plants, the same that Kindred had seen beginning to appear around Arcadia. The Greys, not just plaguing the grasses around Arcadia.

'It's here, too,' Kindred said, mostly to herself.

'It's everywhere,' Seraph said, following her gaze to the coiled masses of sickly ash-grey. 'Our long-haul sailors have reported finding swaths of it in every direction, hundreds of days sailing away.'

'I thought it was just Arcadia – some symptom of flattening the Sea.'

Seraph shook his head.

'Sadly, no. Something is wrong with the Sea itself. We've been noticing it for several years, but no one here can figure it out. The damaged grasses – if that's what they still are – are technically sailable, but they do very odd things to the ships that pass through them, as I'm sure the Arcadians have realized. And they are resistant to fire, too, the patches of grey – no restorative burning, which is strange.'

Kindred nodded, staring at the patches, thinking of how much they looked like sick marks on a great body. The Greys, Arcadians called it. What had once been a patch of twenty, maybe thirty different individual species, each with their own name, their own classification and description and colors and identity – now gone, all those identities, all those *names*, devoured by *the Greys*.

Names, Kindred thought, might be ways of owning the world, bending it to a will or breaking it under a tongue, but they were also memorials, built and protected, for those parts of the world that might be forgotten, that might disappear completely. With a name, a sailor could call back into the world the spirit of a conversation, of an adventure, of a lost friend. What were the words she used, Kindred wondered, if not tiny gravestones, neatly arrayed, for that which had come before and that which might come again? What did she speak if not the language of ghosts?

'Do you know what's causing it?' she asked, squinting to see into the mass of ashen grasses but failing.

'No idea,' Seraph said. 'Though if I were to guess, I would place my bets on the Running Ones below. But that's just speculation, of course.'

Kindred turned to look at Seraph, sure that he was playing a joke on her, but his face was the same as it always was: honest, open, curious.

'The Running Ones? From the stories?'

She knew about the Running Ones – every child born or raised on Arcadia or the Mainland knew about them. Kindred had loved hearing the stories as a child, sitting cross-legged on the deck of *Revenger* and hearing her grandmother tell stories of the mages living on the bottom of the Sea whose weapons were not fire and bone but strange books bursting with magical powers waiting to be unleashed. The Running Ones sprinted through the darkness of the Sea's floor, their books held before them like torches, overflowing with light and power.

The Marchess would stand over the light of the hearthfire late in the night, a canopy of stars overhead, and tell great tales of the Running Ones, the monsters they fought, and the wonders they saw.

But those were only little fictions meant to inspire and frighten children. No one older than ten or twelve years actually believed them.

'You know them, too?' Seraph said, turning to her, excited. 'Our histories are probably different here, I imagine, but there are older texts that mention the Running Ones using spells that affect the roots of Sea plants. The descriptions are unclear, of course, but it's too similar to not look into, don't you think?'

Kindred blinked at this, trying to understand what it was that Seraph was saying. Explaining this Sea disease with bedtime stories of monsters and magic populating the floor of the Forever Sea?

Some small part of her – one she'd been unconsciously nurturing ever since the Marchess's disappearance – bloomed at Seraph's words, impossible hope suddenly becoming possible. What if there *were* worlds below? What had seemed to Kindred a chance to recover her grandmother's body, or at least retrace her dying steps, became more. Stories that played at the outskirts of imagination and hope grew into a chance for another life – a real, tangible chance.

'I guess it is,' she said to Seraph, floating on the flare of hope and excitement in her chest. 'Has anyone from the Once-City ever gone below the Sea, ever made it to the Sea floor?'

The brightness inside her dimmed as Seraph shook his head, though he didn't laugh like those on Arcadia would have.

'No, though it hasn't stopped many from trying! Different hearthfire builds, rope ladders, ships built for sailing below, harnessing wyrms or other beasts from below: it's all been attempted. We still have a few of those below-boats down by the hearthfire supplies. But no, sadly we have no real communication with the peoples below.'

'Peoples below?' Kindred felt the world still for a moment around her.

'Well, they have to be there, don't they? We've seen evidence of some kind of civilization below when some of the nomadic plant species rise to the surface to flower and seed. Little things, you know? Scraps of cloth caught among seedpods or scratches on stems that look strangely like language.'

'How do you know it's not just bits that have fallen down from the surface? Arcadia dumps its trash into the Sea, and every vessel sailing out of there that I know of does the same,' Kindred said.

'Oh, no,' Seraph said. 'What we've seen shares little resemblance to anything from Arcadia, the Once-City, or the Mainland – and if it does, it's ages old and shows signs of having been repurposed. Sailcloth remade into clothing and covered in strange markings; bits of structures older than any here can guess, and without any precedent in books or histories that I know of. Just trash from the surface? Oh, no, I don't think so!'

Seraph grinned, and Kindred found herself grinning, too.

People below. Peoples. Somehow, it felt like the clearest, strongest assurance yet that the Marchess was alive below.

Kindred looked back at the plague of withered grey to the ridges of the thorn reef rising in the direction of Arcadia, and she found herself squinting toward the gap between them, looking for any sign of a sail, any hint of Cantrev's ships coming back. She felt such a conflict there between the freedom of this place and the tensions around it – something wrong with the Sea, Cantrev's looming presence.

'Any signs of Cantrev's ships returning?' she asked.

'We have scouts out watching for him,' Seraph said, looking where she looked. 'We'll know if he's coming, though I doubt his ships made it back. The thorn reef takes a toll on a hull if the crew hasn't any experience with it. I think his ships probably sank on their return journey – too damaged from the fight and the reef.'

But Kindred was shaking her head, thinking of Cantrev and his strange ability to persist, his ability to always find an escape, always.

'No. He's coming back.'

She looked around the root docks at the full retinue of ships, some docked, some floating just a little away. It was more ships than she'd ever seen in one place.

'Gods,' she said. 'That's a fleet.'

Seraph shrugged, as though this wasn't something he had ever really thought about.

'I suppose. It's all theirs.' He hooked a finger above, to the clusters of dwellings above, bulging from the myriad branches climbing into the sky. So close, Kindred could see the spiderwork of ladders and bridges and ropes connecting branch to branch and dropping to the dock below, each one made of braided prairie grasses.

She followed Seraph around to the other side of the great tree, to a quieter group of docks reaching out toward the expanse of the Forever Sea, only a few vessels docked on this side.

'Why aren't they on the other side?' Kindred asked, looking around at these ships, crews tying up or letting sheets down, the penitent sound of hammering ubiquitous in the late morning heat. 'Cantrev won't come from this side.'

Over there, she could look out at the true Forever Sea, the expanse that no one, not even the High Mapmakers, had ever fully explored or reached the end of. It was too wide, too eternal to take in, she thought, moving her head side to side, never able to capture the whole of it in one glance.

Kindred had never seen such a thing as this, the Forever Sea unbroken and untamed, writhing and bursting in every color, reaching with the branched arms of myriad plants unknown to her and perhaps to anyone. It was a wild, ecstatic thing, and somehow, Kindred found herself longing for it.

She thought of the leveled, nearly homogenous grasses around Arcadia, a patch of the Sea that had once looked just like this. Before prairie mages came along and ordered it with their magics, it had been just as free, just as true as this.

Can a person long for a wild home they've never known? Can a person love only what a place once was?

'They can get around quickly if they're needed,' Seraph said, walking out on the dock toward one of the ships. 'And there's far worse that can come from out there than anything Cantrev could ever bring. Those on Arcadia are shielded from the true wilds of the Forever Sea with that carefully maintained and leveled circle of prairie. Have you ever dealt with fast-creeping father's hair? Or coughing grubs climbing up spurleaf? Last year, we had a wave of Antilles roaches – bad enough, right? Just after, maybe four days or so, an entire family of mid-grass badgers came from the east. Huge beasts!' Seraph waved his hands around to indicate their size, though Kindred was frowning. Apart from the roaches, she had never heard of any of it.

'Destroyed five of our best ships,' Seraph continued. 'It took the mages ten days to drive them off – terribly hard to kill of course, mid-grass badgers.

'They make wyrms look weak and slow in comparison,' he added, seeing Kindred's confusion. 'Seem to have taken a liking to the greying patches of Sea, too. Very odd.'

Perhaps she should have felt fear at such things – a whole world of monstrous creatures capable of chaos and horror lived out there in the Roughs, creatures Kindred had never learned about from the bookmavens on Arcadia.

But instead, Kindred felt a spark of wonder. If this was just a taste of the unknown, then what else awaited discovery out there, toward the horizon or deep below the waves?

'And, of course, there's always the danger of the return of the Supplicant Few!' Seraph grinned, pointing out toward the horizon. 'A band of seven sailed toward the sun in the east, leaving behind their humanity – '

'To worship nature without cease,' Kindred finished, a surprised smile on her face. It was an old rhyme, one that was common in songs and stories on Arcadia. Everyone knew of the Supplicant Few – the mad band of sailors who had gone east to find the end of the Forever Sea. After a journey of horrors, the stories said, the Supplicant Few found a land of shadow and darkness beyond the horizon, and once there, they traded in their humanity for power, for immortality, for the burden of protecting and praising the natural world above all else. They were men and women turned monsters in every story Kindred had ever heard, and their return was an ominous promise. They would bring death and decay, rampant rot and a sky choked with reaching vines. They would bring doom. They would bring the end.

But they were fictions.

'Another shared story!' Seraph said, grinning.

'You keep ships over here because of a story?' Kindred said, looking at the mass of vessels prepared to stop a children's cautionary tale.

'The Supplicant Few are much more than a story,' Seraph said, solemn suddenly. 'We have artifacts of theirs here in the Once-City, little bits of history from when they docked here on their voyage east. Some day, they will return, and we should all hope to be long gone when they do.'

Kindred could think of nothing to say. She felt a continued

unraveling in her mind, as if these long-held truths that had propped up and structured her world were coming apart, revealing something wilder, something stranger, something more magical that had been lurking beneath all along.

'But none of that is our immediate concern!' Seraph said, clapping his hands and brightening up. 'Have you ever dealt with grey weed in a hearthfire? I've been experimenting recently and have had mixed results. Here, come up on deck; I'll show you what I mean.'

Kindred looked out again toward forever and imagined a world of unending wilds, above and below. A storybook world cut through with magic.

Seraph walked up a plank onto a scarcely populated ship – a smallish cutter, by the looks of it.

The deck of the ship was littered with tools and ropes, and Kindred saw a few sailors, men and women, working up near the prow, fastening on a huge, painted beam, sharpened to a point.

Or no, not a beam, she realized after a moment. It was one of the thorns, from the reef. These sailors were attaching it like a ramming spur. Kindred remembered the damage those thorns had done to *The Errant*, the destruction they had inflicted on the hull. She could still hear the sound they made as *The Errant* sloughed too close to the reef, as those thorns tore and ripped wood strong as time, older than Kindred.

'Over here, over here,' Seraph said, waving her back toward the center of the deck, where the hearthfire burned, low and quiet. She approached and hunkered down next to him, opening herself to the fire by instinct, listening to its song, studying its rhythms and colors.

In the flames was a confused and confusing build, overly

complex and fighting against itself. Bone shards littered the coals, some sticking straight up from the grey bed, others lying flat. Twists of plants Kindred had never seen before moved through the fire, tying together bone shards and whorling away on their own, seemingly without purpose or pattern.

Kindred saw the places where the fire worked against itself: arrangements of bone best used to give a ship stability during a high wind nullifying a slender arc of finger bone – shaved down for reasons Kindred couldn't figure – that gave the ship lift and adaptability for quick maneuvering. She saw a spur of a rib bone burning away that should have propelled the ship forward into the dock, but then spied a twisting net of grasses woven around a pair of wristbones that, though crude and uneven, would pull a ship backward for a time; the two forces battled one another in the scope of the flames, neither winning out.

'As you can see, we've been experimenting with some new builds,' Seraph said, excitement and anxiety in his voice. Although he was an older man, he spoke like a nervous child, worried about showing his secret project to a new friend.

'I don't know how this ship is even afloat,' Kindred said, shaking her head in disbelief and laughing, watching the flames ricocheting between greys and greens, the forces within the hearthfire vying for control. 'By my count, you have at least nine distinct builds in there, and that's not even counting whatever those plants are doing.'

Seraph chuckled, rocking back and forth on the balls of his feet.

'It's a tenuous thing, I'll grant you that! I was aiming for something like balance with this one, though I may have overcorrected on a few. Take a look at the whorlweeds I've used here . . .'

It had been a long, long time since Kindred had talked with a hearthfire keeper like this. Rhabdus and the other keepers on Arcadia – those who learned their craft at one of the schools on the island – always seemed like heavy-headed hammers, beating the hearthfire into submission as if it were an animal to be broken and subjugated. They drew standardized schema and chanted hard rules to themselves, boxed up the hearthfire into neat, logical problems with easy, obvious solutions. Mastered it; stomped on every bit of mystery in the flames.

But here was Seraph, asking wild questions, swaying with the fire, listening to it, chaotic and weird. He reminded Kindred a little of the Marchess.

With a childlike laugh of her own, Kindred leaned in and worked.

'What do you think?' Seraph asked, kneeling next to the sixth hearthfire of the afternoon. Apart from one – so clustered and crammed with bones, some of which Kindred wasn't sure were actually captain's bones – they had managed to fix all of them.

Each was a new challenge, a complicated, twisting problem, and Kindred found a strange, new joy in tromping from deck to deck with Seraph, discussing the theory and art in each hearthfire, the possibilities of each new twist of bone or unidentified plant. The keepers, Seraph confessed, were mostly outside of his control. They took initial classes from him, but with so many ships sailing out and in all the time, it was too much for Seraph to keep up with completely. And so, he and Kindred moved from ship to ship, seeing the strange, experimental, wild builds each new keeper had come up with. It was their job to undo the mess, understand the possibility, and return the hearthfire to as near a fresh palette as possible.

'What are these plants doing?' Kindred asked, pointing to a twisting bunch of red-gold stalks curling around a clutch of bone shards. She could hear a strange note in the fire's song and see the plants' influence on the sway of the flames, but she couldn't tell what it was doing to the ship.

'Can't you tell?' Seraph asked, excited now, giggling a bit. 'You've been so focused on other things that you didn't even notice when you stepped aboard, did you?'

He stood and walked over to the gunwale, waving her over. He shifted his weight from foot to foot, nearly exploding with excitement as he waited for her to figure it out.

She saw what she had missed almost immediately.

The boat sat low in the grass, far lower than any she had ever seen, as if it were moments away from sinking, as if it had been frozen in the very act of going under. A thrill of fear shone in her then, and a sense of wonder. She pushed down the urge to leap from the deck onto the safety of the root dock.

Kindred thought of *The Errant*, first pulled down by teeth burning viciously in the flames and then by her own hand, a circumscribed hearthfire.

But this was nothing like the teeth – the boat wasn't fighting the Sea, and she could hear nothing of antagonism in the fire's song.

And the fire had not been circumscribed, else Kindred and Seraph would have been plummeting down into the depths right then.

'How does it sit so low?' she asked, turning back to Seraph, who looked as if he might burst.

'Isn't it wonderful? Several of our keepers have been experimenting with it. Personally, I've only managed to get it to sit a few lengths below the grass line, but I've started to achieve more or less regular results. It's something to do with the inclusion of certain plants, I'm thinking, though I need to do more tests. Given your controlled dive, I thought you might be interested in seeing some of our own *modest* attempts at a similar effect.' Seraph held his hands up, playing at humility but clearly proud of his keepers' work.

'And what did you do here?' Kindred asked, kneeling before the hearthfire again.

'Oh! Yes, right. These are stems of feverfew I trimmed down, but I've managed to achieve the same effect with other plants, too. But how did I do it? Well . . . I have no idea!'

Seraph threw his hands up and laughed.

'I was hoping you could tell me! Certainly, the effect is something I've started to standardize, but I'm still not entirely sure how or why these specific plants interact in this way with the hearthfire. Did you do much plant work when you were learning to keep the fire on Arcadia? I don't know much about the educational programs there for hearthfire keepers, but I imagine it's a tad more rigorous than our own ramshackle pedagogy!' He laughed and shook his head. 'Oh, I love a good mystery. I bet – '

But Seraph was cut off by the sound of a deep tolling, like a bell but deeper, louder, as if the whole of the world itself boomed in regular, powerful tolls.

She saw Seraph stiffen, his body going taut as he listened to the rhythm ringing out from the tree, vibrating along its dead branches, thickening the air with its warning.

'Oh, my,' Seraph said after the rhythm had repeated twice

over. 'That's the alarm. Ships coming through the reef pass. We need to move.'

He stood and walked quickly off the ship, and Kindred followed. A few sailors who had been up in the rigging fiddling with one of the sails dropped to the deck, their boots explosive on the old wood.

Already, people were streaming around the trunk of the tree, spewing out of the entrance to the Once-City and racing for their ships. Sailors moved with purpose and speed, calling out orders and shouting for crew even as they slung themselves up onto the masts and across the spurs.

Kindred watched as a girl – a child who looked only half Kindred's age – strode aboard the ship they had just been on, waving briefly at Seraph. She began working on the hearthfire, her voice ragged and beautiful as she sang to the flames, her movements practiced and smooth even if her technique was crude. Kindred watched as the girl maneuvered bones in and out of the flames, never changing the basic structure of the build but shifting it enough to give the ship mobility even if it continued to sit low in the grasses.

It was a way of keeping the fire that was totally new to Kindred, nothing like the way Arcadian keepers did it. This was messy and unruled, and yet the ship sailed, and the girl's hands moved carefully and with practice. Was it truly messy? Or did Kindred simply not understand it?

More sailors hopped aboard as the ship pulled out and headed for open grasses, and just before it turned away, pulled into the growing tide of ships heading for the pass, the young girl looked up at Kindred and smiled, toothy and wide and full of joy, a warrior going to battle to defend her home, doing what she knew and loving what she did.

And then she was gone and Kindred was watching ship after ship angle away, around the reaches of the root docks and out to defend. Up this close, she could see that there were distinct flags flying on each of the ships, perhaps denoting ship type or crew affinity; she wasn't sure. She counted four unique flags as the vessels moved by: blue with a grinning black skull, white with a roaring fire, red with a broken spear, and black with two eyes, one green and the other blue.

Kindred moved with Seraph around the trunk to watch as the fleet sailed to defend and intercept, and along the way she saw Little Wing and Captain Caraway, walking with a few guards and councilman Ebb-La-Kem, who moved with a retinue of followers, each carrying a bundle of flags.

'Keeper,' Captain Caraway said, nodding at her and then at Seraph. Little Wing walked beside the captain and kept her eyes on the ships heading to battle.

'With me, captain,' Ebb-La-Kem said, gesturing as one might to a child. He nodded once at Kindred and moved on toward a great wooden structure that workers were assembling on the dock. It rose into the air, a series of platforms from which they might observe the battle from a safe distance.

Little Wing stayed behind with Kindred and Seraph, and they watched Ebb-La-Kem begin scaling the structure, the captain and his flag bearers behind him.

'What's the captain doing?' Kindred asked.

'Giving away Arcadian battle strategy,' Little Wing said, spitting on the ground, a look of disgust on her face.

Right, Kindred thought, remembering the captain's part of the bargain with the council. While the rest of the crew offered what they could to the Once-City, Captain Caraway offered perhaps the greatest gift of all: knowledge of Arcadia's fleet and strategies.

'Why aren't you going, too?'

Little Wing turned to look at Kindred and smiled, showing off a few new bruises adding color over the older ones already ranging over much of her face and skin.

'I have proven to be a less-than-dependable resource, apparently.'

Kindred nodded, noticing that a few guards had remained to accompany Little Wing.

'Kindred! Hey!' Kindred turned around and looked up into the branches of the great tree and saw Ragged Sarah there along with Long Quixa, Cora the Wraith, Scindapse, and several of the guards meant to keep them in line, waving down at her. 'Up here!'

Kindred frowned up at them, unsure of how Sarah had managed it, but then she saw – a sort of ladder had been created with wooden beams stretching the great gaps between the thick ridges of bark on the tree, each gap wider than a person.

Other people populated the branches, far more than stood on the docks. Kindred began to climb the ladder, Little Wing, her guards, and Seraph following her.

Kindred moved up the ladder slowly. The bark ridges extended out beyond the ladder rungs, and so Kindred felt as if she climbed through an arboreal tunnel, as if the tree were reaching out to embrace her. Or devour her.

There, the smell of dry death was strong, and Kindred wondered how long before the tree had given itself up to the world, how many years past it had stopped growing. The flowering vines that covered so much of the trunk and branches had closed for the day and now lay like a rumpled, misused coat over much of the bark, ill-fitting and uncomfortable.

At the top, Kindred stepped off onto a branch wider than most ships she'd ever been on. The branch underfoot was sturdy and well worn, flattened by the impacts of many feet traversing it. Kindred walked down to where it split three ways, choosing the left path and sitting down next to Ragged Sarah where the branch ended in a jagged spur, the rest having broken off at some point. Sarah pushed aside a twist of vines, making room.

Kindred wondered what kind of storm or magic could sever a beam of wood this thick, but the question was gone from her mind as she settled next to Sarah and her other crewmates.

'How are you feeling?' Ragged Sarah asked.

'I'm okay,' Kindred said, glancing in Ragged Sarah's eyes, remembering the tension between them that morning. 'How are you?'

'Better now,' Ragged Sarah said.

Little Wing stood aloof from them, a little way away, her eyes flicking over Kindred and Ragged Sarah and then gazing out at the Sea, where the Once-City fleet had arranged itself and was waiting.

Seraph sat down next to Ragged Sarah, smiling at her as if he belonged. Cora raised her eyebrows at Seraph but said nothing.

'Hey!' Sarah said suddenly. 'I didn't tell you – I saw Stone-Gwen and Grimm this morning! They're sailing together on one of the long-range harvesters.'

'That's a good assignment,' Seraph said, nodding. 'Morrow Laze has control of the long-haul harvesters; he gave some of the ships from his fleet for it. The voyages can be hundreds of days long, but Morrow is fair and honest. Your friends will be okay.'

Together. They were sailing together.

That was something, Kindred thought.

'What about the others?' Kindred asked. Talent and Quell had been in those cells with them, and Kindred could still hear their cries, the shouts of 'Fail' before they disappeared.

'Dew-skimmers,' Seraph said, and Kindred and the others turned to him in surprise.

'How do you know that?' Long Quixa asked, a hint of suspicion in her voice.

'I had a hand in putting them on those ships,' Seraph said, almost shyly. 'The pirates on the council demanded half of the failed citizens for their uses, and so once the other two had been assigned to the harvesters, I argued for these two – what were their names?'

'Talent and Quell,' Kindred said.

'Right. I argued for Talent and Quell to be stationed on the dew-skimmers. It's safer than the other option, which was deckhand on one of their reaping vessels.'

'Reaping vessels?' Cora asked, confused.

'That's what they call themselves,' Seraph said with a distasteful shake of his head. 'Reapers. Sowing death where they go and all that nonsense. It's lucky your friends aren't on those boats. Nasty, terrible stuff they do.'

She had never known Talent or Quell like she had some of the others, but Kindred had always gotten along well with both, and she was relieved to know they were safe, away from the monstrous side of this place.

It must have shown on her face, because Seraph said, 'Oh, no. Don't misunderstand; it's incredibly hard work, what they do on those dew-skimmers, and they're not likely to get more than a half-morning's break from the constant skimming and repair and hauling.'

'They're tougher than anyone you have here,' Little Wing

said. She had been listening and she leaned toward them now. 'An *Errant* crew member counts for ten of the shit-sailors walking around this place.'

'You're probably right,' Seraph said, nodding, his eyes and attention drifting away from the conversation.

Little Wing, unsure what to do in the face of someone like Seraph, who seemed so uninterested in a fight, turned away, too.

'What's that?' Cora asked, pointing back and up into the tree, where the bulk of the trunk split into branches. Right at the split, there was a raised platform, with something on it, something Kindred couldn't quite see.

'That's the old wheel!' Seraph said, eyes wide, grinning at Cora. 'When this place used to move, that's where the leader of the council would stand and control the direction of the Once-City. Really, this place is just one enormous ship.'

'One ship with a few city-sized decks,' Cora said, shaking her head.

'Okay, one *really* enormous ship,' Seraph said, nodding. 'But it's the same principle, really – hearthfire offers lift and power; wheel channels that power. They even used to have sails up in the branches, but that was ages ago, of course.'

He trailed off, lost in memory.

After a moment of quiet, Kindred turned to Scindapse, who sat nearby, hugging her knees tight to her chest.

'Hey,' Kindred said, tentative.

'Hi.'

'How is it with the cooks?' Kindred asked, remembering the assignment Barque had given her.

'It's okay. They're mostly old and nice. It's quiet and boring.

Safe,' she said, and then after a moment: 'Thanks for not telling them about . . .'

She trailed off, but Kindred knew what she meant. The council's proposition, Ebb's question about other hearthfire keepers. In this place, with pirates living in the branches above and dangers all around, quiet and boring sounded perfect for Scindapse.

Kindred nodded and reached an arm around Scindapse's shoulders, squeezing her into a quick hug, before turning back out to the Sea.

She noticed something now that she hadn't on their hurtling arrival: trees. Though much smaller than the one in which she now sat, trees dotted the seascape before her, rising equal to or above most of the masts on the ships that moved around them.

She had spent so long on the leveled surface of the Sea around Arcadia that the sight of trees growing up through the prairie Sea like this was strange and thrilling to her.

Sails could be seen in the pass now – still too far away for Kindred to get a good count but certainly more than a few, and certainly Cantrev's ships.

The flag bearers standing atop the structure with Ebb-La-Kem and Captain Caraway had begun to move now, waving flags of different colors and shapes. Ebb-La-Kem was speaking quickly, furiously to Captain Caraway, who stared away from the battlefield, out toward the open Sea. She spoke little, but whatever it was she said must have satisfied Ebb-La-Kem, because he smiled and then turned to his flag bearers, who raised different flags, sent new messages, offered new tactics. Kindred saw sailors on ships out in the harbor raise flags in response.

The signals were passed between the Once-City fleet, and several of the ships broke away from the main mass: two of the larger dreadnoughts angled forward to block the way and take the brunt of the attack, and six smaller ships sailed farther ahead.

The ships moved slowly around trees growing up through the Sea, though Kindred couldn't tell what they were doing. Harvesting plants to bolster their arsenals? Tying ropes between the trunks? She remembered suddenly the thorn being affixed to the front of that ship and wondered if these pirates were attaching more of them to the trees, perhaps laying a field of traps for their enemies.

'What are they doing?' Kindred asked, pointing to the smaller ships – schooners or something like it, by the look of them. They all sailed under the same flag: a blue field on which a skull was painted. Without them, the main fleet of the Once-City was severely diminished.

'Maybe they want to scout out for other enemy forces coming from either direction?' Seraph volunteered, raising his shoulders. 'Those are all The Word's ships. They have the blue ensign.'

Of course, Kindred realized, looking at the flags anew. Councillors' ships.

'I thought there were seven on the council,' Cora said, speaking the same thought Kindred had. 'There are only four flags out there.'

Seraph nodded.

'Of course. Not all of the councillors are sailors with fleets. Only Morrow Laze, The Word, Uz, and Ebb-La-Kem have fleets. Morrow has the red flags, The Word have the blue ones, Uz and Ebb-La-Kem both have silver flags, but Ebb-La-Kem's have a golden fist embroidered into the middle, and Uz's have a tree.

'But there's no way any other forces would have had time to get around the thistle reef. I don't know what they're doing. It's a little late for maneuvering practice around the trees, I would think.'

Their work apparently done, the ships retreated back to where the dreadnoughts had placed themselves, angled like the tip of a spear, as if to force enemies to either side. The remainder of the fleet waited behind them.

All counted, the Once-City fleet numbered twenty-four ships, which Kindred realized was not perhaps that many on the open Sea, but here, on the Roughs, penned in by the thistle ridge on one side and the great tree on the other, a fleet of twenty-four dominated the field.

Beyond the shield of the fleet, the sails of Cantrev's ships choked the pass, more sheets than Kindred could count, warships and scouts and supply vessels, many with metal-studded ramming prows lancing out into the sunlight.

'Cantrev brought a damn war flotilla,' Cora the Wraith said, pointing a finger out to the pass. Each of the ships, regardless of what purpose they had once served, were now outfitted for war and flying the Collective's flag. Unity against the many mixings of the Once-City's people and fleet.

'I guess we're going home sooner than planned,' Little Wing said from where she stood, grinning around at them, favoring Seraph with a particularly long, nasty look. Cora smiled, too, and even Ragged Sarah was nodding. Twenty-four ships no longer looked so large, especially when some of them were the thin, short cutters and schooners of The Word's fleet. Cantrev had put the best of his vessels out.

Kindred looked out at the battlefield and felt a strange ambivalence. Cantrev had been the man to drive them from Arcadia, the man who would have them under his regime or have them killed.

And here were pirates, the specters of every scary story told to children growing up on Arcadia or the Mainland, some of them the very monsters who had killed Kindred's friends, Little Wing's friends, any number of relatives or loves or friends of those who had crewed *The Errant*.

And who did she hope would win the day? To be taken back in by Cantrev, imprisoned and disempowered just as they had been here? Or to see Cantrev's forces, probably crewed by people she had known for most of her life, sunk and dispatched?

You cannot be truly part of this place and remain a member of this crew, the captain had said.

Kindred shook her head and leaned in close to Ragged Sarah, feeling unmoored, unanchored, lost.

The Once-City fleet had flattened themselves out, forming a rough arc now, the dreadnoughts in the center, the rest of the fleet extending in either direction, arcing toward the Arcadian ships, like a sail curving with the wind, accepting and being moved by it. The pirates looked like a vessel ready to receive the Arcadian fleet.

A rough cry rose from the Once-City ships, a war shout that shook the air, echoed by the quieter, more distant cry of the sailors aboard Cantrev's ships.

The Arcadians spilled from the thistle reef, racing forward to break through the pirate line, and Kindred could almost make out the figures on those ships now as they threaded through the trees, their hulls outfitted with metal, now scratched and dented from the Roughs.

Forward and forward and forward they came, a spear thrown at the heart of the Once-City, the center of the pirate line.

Kindred saw Ebb-La-Kem snap out an order to his flag bearers, and then two of them were up, waving one blue flag each.

19

IT began with the trees.

Shadows fell through the air.

As Cantrev's fleet wormed through the trees, people began dropping from the branches, three or four per tree, leaping from where they had hidden among the foliage.

For a moment, they were smudges of black and green against the backdrop of sails before quickly resolving into the hurtling forms of pirates, blades in hand, dropping through the sky, plummeting into the battle from above.

Kindred had been waiting for the battle to begin, watching the shrinking distance between Cantrev's leading ships and the dreadnoughts sitting at the caved-in center of the pirate line.

Meanwhile, there was the battle, already begun.

'What are they doing?' Kindred asked, shielding her eyes.

'Attacking,' Little Wing said. The pirates dropped from the trees onto Cantrev's ships as they sailed deeper into Once-City grasses, landing among the unsuspecting crew and lashing out with their blades.

'They're all going to die, though,' Ragged Sarah said, shaking her head. 'There are more than sixty sailors on some of those boats. They're on a suicide mission.'

'They're martyrs,' Seraph said, his voice quiet. Kindred thought back to how Seraph had talked about the pirates: fanatics who lived in the trees above, zealots absolutely dedicated to their purposes and goals.

'They're monsters,' Long Quixa said, her eyes wide.

Even Cora the Wraith no longer wore a smile.

Kindred was thinking back to stories told about pirates boarding ships, locking the crews away belowdecks or keeping them at bay while the pirates stole the captain, killed the keeper, and snuffed the hearthfire, striking at the critical points of a ship without needing to shed any more blood than needed. The ship would sink into the Sea, the crew helpless, and the pirates could sail away, their attack perfectly cruel and perfectly efficient.

And here it was, that same story played out.

Arcadian sailors rallied to kill these intruders, hurling spears and leaping forward with swords, but it was too late.

'No . . .' Kindred whispered, rising to her feet, horror rustling through her like a cold wind.

Pirates rushed for hearthfires, one or two executing the oblivious keepers kneeling before the flames, one or two emptying bags of sand onto the hearthfires, snuffing them.

Perfectly cruel.

Perfectly efficient.

The Arcadian fleet fractured, ships listing and sinking, sinking themselves into prairie plants not seen around Arcadia for hundreds of years. Sailors familiar and unfamiliar to Kindred leapt over the bodies of fallen hearthkeepers and pirates alike – heroes and martyrs and warriors and just people – leaping to throw anything into the hearthfire, anything to begin the blaze again.

'Gods . . .' Cora the Wraith said, shaking her head.

Long Quixa had closed her eyes and bowed her head, her lips moving, and Kindred could just hear her voice intoning a prayer to her god or gods. Kindred didn't know Quixa was religious in any way, and she felt some surprise at learning that information now, after having sailed for over a year together. It was as if the Once-City continued to reveal the true selves of any who walked its floors.

More and more of Cantrev's vessels were getting slowed just at the edge of the pass, unable to wind their way into the fight, stoppered up by those who had gone first and now were paying the price. The trees, what had at first seemed a paltry defense between the onslaught of Cantrev's forces sailing two by two down the pass and the Once-City vessels, all twenty-four of them, had now grown into a field of destruction to be entered only with extreme caution. A few foundering vessels had crashed into trees and somehow managed to stay afloat, their decks pitched dangerously, masts angling away.

But most simply sank, whispering their way beneath the green Sea, leaving behind a memory of what they were. As in everything, the Sea was always all that was left, the Sea and the memory of what had once sailed atop it.

Listen for me in the grasses, Kindred heard as she watched sailors flailing against the inevitable, angling blades at pirates who smiled at a job well done.

Listen for me below, Kindred heard as she watched sailors giving in to the Sea, Arcadians standing next to Once-City pirates, silent as the Sea took them.

'Get down!' Little Wing shouted, and Sarah wrenched Kindred to the ground.

Heat like a rash flared in the air where Kindred had been standing, and she looked up in time to see a red bolt cut through the air, arcane energy singing. The spell ripped into a huge tree branch back and up from where Kindred and the others huddled together, cutting into it, leaving a fuming runnel in a branch that must have existed for hundreds, maybe thousands of years.

It tilted sickeningly, cracking with a sound like the bones of the world breaking.

The tree exploded with activity: people running along the branches to get down, the ladders suddenly choked with all of those who had wanted a better seat for the slaughter.

'What are they doing?' Ragged Sarah shouted into the tumult, and Kindred followed her gaze down to where a few Arcadian ships that had managed to avoid the pirates in the trees now cut toward the Once-City line, though as they did, they slung magical attacks not at the enemies before them – the dreadnoughts and other Once-City war vessels – but at the Once-City itself.

Flashes of purple and gold, red and green, flashes of unnatural war magic meant to rend and wreck flared garish against the sunned sky. It was destruction writ polychromatic.

'Being heroes,' Kindred said as she pushed herself up. 'We need to get down from here.'

Even as she said it, more ships from the Arcadian fleet began hurling magical attacks at the Once-City. Even a few of the already-sinking vessels loosed last-breath assaults, bolts of gold and purple that skewed wildly through the air, only a few finding their mark.

People crowded in close, and Kindred found herself trapped,

pushed from behind by Long Quixa and Ragged Sarah and a crowd behind them, blocked in front by Little Wing and her guards and the crowd trying to do exactly what she herself was trying to do.

The tolling of the central column had changed. A new rhythm vibrated the air, and as she looked back toward the battlefield, Kindred saw its effect.

Ebb-La-Kem and the others atop the scaffolding had scampered down, leaving a lone flagbearer above, a young boy waving a single black flag. Already the Once-City fleet had begun to collapse on the suicidal Arcadian forces, slinging their own vicious magical attacks. Kindred squinted and thought she could see Morrow Laze himself, tall and haggard, standing at the prow of one of his ships, huge black lashes of arcane energy extending from his hands, a whip of pure power pulled from strange plants burning in his casting fires, striking again and again at the Arcadian vessels destroying his home.

And there was one of The Word's vessels, flying a blue banner, racing about, foolhardy and brash, a big galleon. It might have once been a storage or transport ship, but now it glowed with the casting fires littering its deck, mages crowding the sides and casting their magics, some holding defensive spells up around the ship, some hurling angry bolts of power, garish greens and golds. The Word's ship was a battalion unto itself, leaving Arcadian vessels foundering in its wake.

'There!' someone shouted, and Kindred followed a pointed finger toward an Arcadian vessel cutting through the morass of foundering ships, angling hard for the City.

'Come on, come on,' Little Wing said, her voice carrying over the sounds of battle and alarm. The press and surge of bodies had momentarily halted, all of them breathing in and out together, watching to see if this ship would make it to the City, if the battle would be brought in from the Sea.

The ship – one of Cantrev's patrollers, Kindred realized – closed on the City, close enough for Kindred to see faces aboard, faces that pulled at memories of nights in bars, faces passed on the street, faces smiling and shouting while boats docked at port – cut close, close, close.

'Come on, you bastards,' Little Wing whispered.

An explosive burst of magic from one of Ebb-La-Kem's vessels hewing close pushed the Arcadian ship back, forcing its trajectory to arc away, its hull smoking from the attack. Ebb-La-Kem's vessel approached, harrying the Arcadians with more attacks, only a few of which managed to find purchase around the magical defenses flickering into being now around the Arcadian vessel.

'Oh, gods. They're going to board,' Ragged Sarah said from behind Kindred, her body pressed up to Kindred's back.

Ebb-La-Kem's ship, flag flapping in the wind, edged in closer and closer to the Arcadian vessel until their hulls grated against one another, the sound somehow cutting through the anarchy of the battle.

Boarding bridges reached from the pirate vessel, extending like long, gnarled digits. Men and women streamed across as the ships slowed to a near halt.

The pirates boarded.

Lances and blades emerged into sunlight, leaping between and among bodies, sowing stillness among the chaos. Sailors fought and fell, death blooming among pirate and Arcadian alike, uncaring for loyalty or purpose or Sea-right.

Kindred jerked back, surprised, as she saw Barque, along with a few other pirates, boarding the Arcadian vessel with rush pits – little more than flattened metal cones that opened just over the shoulder and crossed the back to a point just above the hip. Down in those depths, a casting fire burned, a splinter of a central blaze still roaring aboard the pirate vessel. Like moveable casting fires, rush pits allowed mages to board another ship without losing their connection to the source of their magic.

Barque was one of four or five leaping across the boarding bridges, but he stood out.

His skin had again become a Sea of those eerie blue flowers, each traced in white. They opened and swayed with his movements, covering his skin in patches of their color. From where she stood, pressed in on all sides, Kindred could just make out a wild smile on Barque's face as he moved across the bridge and onto the Arcadian vessel.

'No,' Little Wing said, defeat in her voice.

Kindred watched Barque, his hands shuttling between his pockets and the opening of his rush pit, dumping bundles of plants into the hungry maw. In he dumped the plants and out came magic, raw and unshaped, chaotic, reaching out for someone to shape it, someone who understood the songs to be sung, the plants to be known and loved and remembered.

Other pirates nearby answered the call, their mouths moving in song that Kindred could see but not hear, and then they were wading into the battle, their hands alight with crackling power. Their addition to the fight ended it, and soon enough, not an Arcadian was left alive.

'No,' Little Wing said again.

Ships she recognized, filled with people she might have known, were taken, sometimes kept afloat, sometimes sunk, and Kindred could only stare in horror as it all happened. Lives lost, homes destroyed, all of it for what? Power? Control?

Though more Arcadian vessels were boarded, though Morrow Laze sank two vessels himself and drove five or six more into the attacks of another pirate ship, and though The Word fractured the remaining Arcadian assault, it was too late.

The crowd around her surged again and Kindred looked back along the branch, toward the enormous rise of the trunk.

The tree was on fire.

Flames had begun to peek out from rips and tears in the tree's ancient bark, the magical slashes like smiles flaring with a hungry light. Those still in their homes above were screaming and leaping along grass bridges, seeking any way down.

The Once-City was *on fire*.

Kindred felt herself crushed by the pressure from those around her as branches above popped and cracked, flickering with hungry flames.

She understood suddenly. This hadn't been a mission to capture the Once-City, not a mission to save the Arcadian captives there.

It was a mission to sink the Once-City and all of its peoples – and Kindred realized, with a shock, that was her now – for good. For good and all.

Ahead of her, Little Wing was laughing, her defeat suddenly given wind and light, given hope.

'Bring it down!' she shouted.

Was this war? Kindred wondered. Simply an excuse to give your life in order to end several others? She looked around and saw two sides enacting the same story: My life for more of yours.

My life to bring down your ship. My ship, my crew to bring down your city.

And here was Little Wing, happily adding her own voice to the narrative.

From below, shouts cut through the noise of those struggling to get to the ladders.

'Make way! Make way!'

Guards had emerged from the entrance to the City, bustling toward the ladder and carrying what looked like bundled sails, seven or eight huge lengths of them, each one dripping water.

'Move, dammit! Move out of the way!'

The guards were forcing their way up the ladders now, coming to put out the fires, to save the City.

'No, you don't,' Little Wing said, and then she was off, slithering between and pushing through the crowd, moving with abandon, elbowing people out of the way, some of whom teetered on the edge of the branch, some of whom fell, clawing at the vines hanging down.

In the madness of that moment, errant spells still cutting and singing through the air overhead, no one thought anything of another person pushing forward, seemingly scared for her own life.

But Little Wing was just another person turning herself into a weapon that might extinguish life. She reached the top of the ladder, the guards below her beginning to climb, sheets still dripping. Kindred surged forward, not knowing whether she moved to help or hinder but knowing she could not stand by and watch.

As she edged around a man quietly crying and staring up at the burning branches, Kindred saw Little Wing pull one of her own guards off his feet and toss him down the ladder, his body colliding with those climbing and sending them back down. She had begun to sing, and with horror, Kindred found she recognized the song as the battle hymn she had written for Little Wing.

It had been one of her primary tasks to compose battle songs for the crew when Kindred had come aboard *The Errant*. Both the captain and Rhabdus had thought it would help her get to know each of the crew. Kindred's first few span of days aboard the ship had consisted of composing madly, songs for all occasions: tunes for when the entire crew was working together in concert, battle hymns for defense and attack, for harvesting and sailing in high winds, low winds, rain and sun.

And even more difficult had been the songs for individual crew members, melodies by which they might set the beat of their racing hearts, the rise and fall of their arms, their individual work. The poetry to speak their violence if they fought alone.

Little Wing's had been the most difficult.

Everyone else had taken the melody Kindred had written for them at once. Cora the Wraith had walked about the ship for several days, humming hers as she tied off ropes and bundled harvests; Scindapse was known to whistle hers on particularly windy days. Kindred had even heard the captain tapping out the distinctive rhythm of her own battle hymn on the wheel during long voyages.

All of those compositions had been accepted and loved and given life immediately.

Little Wing's took fourteen attempts to get right. First it was too long, then too slow, then not 'angry enough,' and then 'too angry.' Whatever Kindred tried, Little Wing would listen carefully and then firmly shake her head. Sometimes, she would pantomime battle, her crescent-shaped blades whistling in tune and rhythm to the composition, but it was always wrong, always 'too even.'

Now, standing on the branch of a burning tree, Kindred watched the quartermaster singing herself into battle, praising violence with her own hymn. A medley of consonants and vowels scraped against one another as Little Wing slid into the fight, her arms a blur, her whole body somehow moving with strength and speed and grace after so long with little food and water, after burning with steady hatred for so long.

'Percuss this heart
Bless fight with fire
Ha!
A husk to make
Of you! Of you!
Seeds of sweet assailing song
Burst up and out
Crack sky
Cry oh!'

Little Wing sang the words of her jumbled, arrhythmic song, the melody tripping and stumbling. 'It's better for battle,' she had said after Kindred finally got it right. 'Less predictable, more free.'

And she was right. Kindred watched as Little Wing moved and struck in time to her timeless hymn, her fighting style not a dance so much as a scrap, and yet graceful despite that. She moved unpredictably, leaping and circling and retreating and attacking, all in a blur, strikes and feints fading into one another as Little Wing fought.

But Kindred found no surge of hope in hearing that familiar song this time, no prickle of power and solidarity.

Fear cut through her now, every syllable jarring.

A breath of prairie wind ghosted through the throng of people on the branch then, quieting and calming them all for just a moment, and Kindred felt resolve like a stone harden in her stomach.

She would follow her grandmother, she would fall into the deeps, she would give up these surface games in favor of a darker, truer forever.

But not yet.

And she was not done with the Once-City yet. She thought of the children playing with their parents in the wild ingresses of prairie below; she thought of Seraph, his wild laughter ringing out as he rocked forward, awed by the mysteries of the world; she thought of Scindapse and her pocket of quiet, waiting as patiently as she could for their chance to leave.

She thought of a city that had given itself over to the prairie, that had bent and moved in accordance with the world instead of the other way around.

Kindred would not let all of that be destroyed, not for Little Wing, not for Arcadia, not for anything.

She exhaled – *out the prairie wind* – and pushed forward again.

The guards below were climbing again, unaware or uncaring about the threat from above. In the chaos, bodies falling had become ubiquitous.

Little Wing had managed to grab one of the cudgels from a guard, a man who slumped unconscious on the branch at her feet. As the people below began to climb, Little Wing swung the cudgel in a wide circle, brushing back those who had begun to understand her purpose, and she nudged the unconscious man toward the edge.

Kindred moved, nearly crying out as a stray elbow caught her in the chest, her whole body exhausted and exhilarated at once.

She heard Little Wing's song, listened for the tripping rhythm, finding a pocket of emptiness. She was its creator, after all, and she saw the rhythm of its inner workings laid out before her, its structure like a home whose rooms she knew well, a forest whose paths she had walked many times.

Kindred felt a surge in the bodies behind her, and she used it as Little Wing's song tripped through pauses and syllables. Kindred's shoulder collided with Little Wing's body, and though she was nothing next to Little Wing's stature and strength, surprise could be a mighty thing.

Little Wing let out a surprised oof as Kindred hit her, their bodies tangling, Kindred's arms encircling her former friend, former enemy in a hug as they both fell away from the top of the ladder and the guard lying unconscious there.

They dropped, the curving edge of the branch – flattened from so many years of use – holding them for a moment, but Kindred's momentum was too much, and they rolled, both grasping for the myriad vines rustling beneath them.

Little Wing caught at a few strands but slipped through them, her song stuck on a single, angry note.

Kindred fell.

She reached and grabbed for the empty air between the clots of vines and flowers, her shoulders rising in anticipation of the ground, her eyes squinting nearly closed, her teeth bared in a grin of discomfort.

The fall persisted, time seeming to slow and swirl around Kindred.

Little Wing fell or flew beside her, staring at Kindred with eyes burning and singing fury.

The split between the two of them yawned, and Kindred understood then that her choice had been made, that she had been making her choice over and over in recent days.

Diving below with *The Errant* and sentencing it to the deeps.

Crossing the line in her cell.

Escaping Cruel House to see Ragged Sarah.

Talking to the Marchess in the Forest.

And now.

Kindred saw it all tracing back to the Marchess's letter, every action leading there like roots spread from a central stalk.

Someone, or perhaps many someones, broke her fall, and she joggled between bodies, her descent to the root dock halted.

The crowd grew up around Kindred, bodies like swaying trees, blocking out light and sound. Little Wing disappeared behind this wall of people, falling down and through them, and Kindred screamed then, sure that Little Wing had fallen off the dock, off the edge, into the Sea. For a moment, she was back at the Arcadian dock, crawling along one of the cradle chains with Little Wing, seeing terror in this mountainous woman for the first time in her life.

Kindred screamed for Little Wing who, she feared, had fallen into the only darkness her fury and fire could not light.

She felt collisions around her body, a constellation of pain describing her fall. Shoulder and rib. Elbow and wrist. Knee and hip.

Those she had landed on and among shrugged her off, and the flows of Once-City peoples surged around her, some tripping over Kindred in their haste to get to the tree or get inside or get to the other side of the docks. She was buffeted from all sides, her vision circumscribed by bodies moving past her.

Kindred let her head loll to the side, and through the thinned thicket of legs passing by, she saw Little Wing, body crumpled on the ground not far away. Relief flooded through her, and then fear as Little Wing lifted her head, eyes open, and found Kindred.

Her look was one of total hatred. Bloodied, broken, betrayed: she was rage, burning.

More bodies pressed around her, and Kindred pulled her arms up to protect her head, pulled her knees up to protect her abdomen.

And though pain screamed through her whole body and though darkness threatened to overwhelm her, Kindred stayed conscious, watching through the gap between her arms as Little Wing was lifted and bound, as fists collided with her face over and over, enough to drag her into unconsciousness, as she was hauled away.

Even as the movement around her calmed, Kindred stayed where she was, stilled by Little Wing, frozen by the memory of those eyes.

Guards climbed the great tree above and wrapped the burning branches in the sopping-wet material – a set of much-worn old sails, a few of them the color of Arcadian sheets.

Kindred heard the sounds of the Once-City saved, cries of relief and cheer sounding from those around her. Captain Caraway knelt beside her, apparently released from wartime responsibilities. Ragged Sarah appeared a moment later, and the two of them helped Kindred to her feet, though they had to support her. One leg refused to take any weight. Long Quixa and Cora the Wraith appeared through the crowd.

Little Wing was nowhere to be seen.

'I guess you made your choice,' Captain Caraway said, her arm around Kindred, staring at the wreckage around them.

Silent, Kindred surveyed the remains of the battlefield.

Vessels listed and burned, like strangers wandering the beauty of the Roughs. An Arcadian schooner, sails burned to nothing, mizzenmast a broken splinter angling sickeningly to port, devoid of crew save two sailors racing about, trying to right the vessel. A pirate ship, one of Morrow Laze's, Kindred thought, approached from behind, the boarding bridges prepped.

Everywhere, the story was the same: Arcadian vessels were isolated and boarded, harried away from one another with precise magical attacks and then, with little fanfare, captured.

I pushed her. I pushed her and I didn't mean for her to fall and get taken but I'm not done with this place yet. I couldn't let her destroy it; I couldn't let it burn. Not yet.

'Ebb!' Captain Caraway shouted, shocking Kindred out of her thoughts. She looked to see Ebb-La-Kem, swarmed by his usual retinue, walking by, snapping out orders. Seraph and a few of the other councillors walked nearby.

'Ah! Jane. Very good. Just the person I was hoping to see.' Ebb-La-Kem turned and approached them, his smile wide, his eyes mean. Next to him, Seraph was frowning.

'What have you done with Little Wing, Ebb?'

'Your quartermaster, Jane, tried to block our guards from scaling the tree and putting out the blaze. Your quartermaster, Jane, tried to kill every person in this city – including you and your crew. Your quartermaster, Jane, is *mine* now.' Ebb-La-Kem's voice dropped as he spoke, getting harder and lower, anger dripping from every syllable.

'Without the interference of Kindred,' he said, favoring her with a nod and a smile, 'we would all be burning. Little Wing tried to destroy this place, Jane. We're putting her to death.'

He spoke as if it were a simple thing. Little Wing acted, and here is her consequence. The sun rises, and so the world becomes brighter.

Shock and anger rippled around the crew of The Errant. Despite her own act – despite being the one who had interfered – Kindred still felt like Ebb's words were a knife in her gut.

Little Wing, put to death, her fire extinguished.

'When?' Captain Caraway asked, her voice quiet.

'As soon as I can manage it,' Ebb-La-Kem said, already beginning to walk away. 'I have vessels to see to and a council meeting first. I need to take care of the citizens who aren't trying to kill one another.'

And with that, he was gone. Seraph made to follow but then stopped and turned around, stepping into the circle of Kindred and the crew.

'I'm so sorry,' he said, looking around at each of them, his eyes lingering on Kindred for a long moment. 'I tried to persuade him to just hold her, perhaps an extended time in prison or more menial labor, but he's set, and he's already gotten a majority council vote. I . . .'

He trailed off, looking down at his grubby hands.

'I'm sorry,' he said again, wincing at the inadequacy of those words.

He looked around again, his eyes lingering on Kindred's, as if he wanted to say more but couldn't.

'Fuck that,' Captain Caraway said. She turned to her crew.

'Sarah, get Kindred down for healing. The rest of you get back to Cruel House and wait for me. I'm not letting this happen. Little Wing may have lost her mind, but she's still one of ours, and I'm not leaving her to their justice.' She walked off, following Ebb-La-Kem and the swarm of people around him.

They watched her go, and Seraph shook his head.

'She can protest until her voice dissolves. When Ebb-La-Kem wants something, he gets it, one way or another.'

'And so, they'll just kill her?' Cora asked, disgusted. 'How?'

Seraph looked down, unable to meet her eyes.

'The Sea. They'll push her out into the Sea.'

Here was the Once-City belief, Kindred thought, played out in its most twisted way. Living in accordance with the Sea and dying in accordance with it, too.

'Maybe the captain can – ' Cora began, but stopped as Seraph shook his head.

'It's done,' he said. 'Ebb didn't say this, but his guards were going to do it right now. If it hasn't happened yet, it will soon. They won't hold her for long.'

Cora's mouth hung open as she looked around, complete disbelief. Sarah, her body aligned with Kindred's, one arm threaded around Kindred's waist, dropped her head.

Long Quixa, moving slowly, covered her mouth with an open hand.

'Little Wing,' she said, memorializing the quartermaster, closing her fingers around all that remained of her. Cora and Sarah did the same, and after a breath, Kindred did, too.

'I'm sorry,' Kindred added, and she didn't realize she was speaking in the language of the hearthfire until the words came out, language like a litany.

And though it was a tongue unknown to the others, they all seemed to understand the sentiment, Kindred saw. They all seemed to understand the feeling. *Language*, the Marchess once told her, *is simply the shaping of what we all know to be true*, and Kindred witnessed that now.

As one, they raised their hands into the prairie wind and loosed Little Wing's name to the sky and Sea. It was a burial at Sea, the only true farewell for a true sailor.

It took Kindred a moment to realize she'd used her burned hand for the memorial, that her fingers had closed around Little Wing's name, that they'd opened again when she asked them, too. She looked down and was surprised to see that each of the curled golden shoots had extended into very small tufts of grass the color of a fading sunset.

Her hand was back – a gift from the Once-City and the prairie Sea in which it floated – but she couldn't find joy in it, couldn't see it as anything more than the container that had held Little Wing's name a moment before.

Silence fell between them, and Kindred was suddenly reminded of her grandmother's crew on the shores of Arcadia, the rough clutch of their bodies as they remembered and celebrated their captain, speaking truths hard and happy through smiles and tears. As she clenched and unclenched her hand, Kindred thought of goodbyes.

'What are they doing?' Cora asked, her voice empty of its usual jocularity. She pointed toward a fleet of smaller vessels out in the harbor, each one little more than hull, mast, and hearthfire, crewed by two people each. The tiny ships raced out into the bay, spreading like dried leaves blown by the wind.

'Putting out the fires,' Seraph said, squinting to see.

Kindred watched the tiny ships, seeing them as if from a great and impossible distance, her half-formed confession curdling in her chest as the world moved on, as the Sea continued to sway and sing.

The vessels were like the little catboats new sailors learned on around Arcadia, and they sped toward the captured vessels and promptly tossed great bags of sand or thick mats of cloth on any fire not dealt with by the pirate conquerors.

'Most of those ships aren't worth salvaging,' Long Quixa said, her deep voice somber, resentful somehow.

'We don't want the ships,' Seraph said, his eyes following the movement of the little vessels. 'We have enough of those. They're protecting the Sea.'

Of course, Kindred thought, seeing the ships anew, not as more wartime vessels, not as part of the constant urge to conquer and fight and war and own.

No. They were stewards. They skimmed over the surface of the Roughs, navigating the dips and rises perfectly, racing for any traces of fire, protecting the fragile balance of the Sea.

Kindred felt a sudden revulsion at the notion of a prairie burn here and now. The Marchess was down there. Little Wing, maybe, was already down there.

Perhaps falling. Perhaps flying.

'You still have burns out here, don't you? Yearly burns where you char the whole Sea and burn it down to the deeps?' Cora the Wraith asked.

'We should get you back so I can look at you,' Ragged Sarah said to Kindred, nudging her along. Kindred followed, listening to Seraph over the victorious voices on the docks, many who had begun singing their odes to the Once-City's valiant defenders.

Seraph nodded at Cora and looked at her as if she were particularly stupid.

'Of course we still burn out here. Once every few years, if the storms haven't already started the fires, we do. It keeps the Sea healthy, brings some of the bigger creatures from below up to the surface to feed on the new growth. And it's the right way of things. I always forget that you Arcadians don't let the Sea around your island burn.'

Kindred thought back to the magically leveled Sea surrounding Arcadia, a buffer between it and the Roughs. For so long, her work sailing had been to find and harvest the handful of plants that still grew among the ubiquitous prairie grasses surrounding the island, their growth never hampered by a burn, by fires racing like the wind through the Sea, devouring and charring the grasses, making sailing impossible until the new growth began again.

She had heard stories of sailors voyaging out to the edge of the Roughs after a burn, sailing up to where the Sea dropped off, leagues deep, a blackened, twisted pit right next to the even, leveled grasses maintained and protected by Arcadian magic.

Or, perhaps, not protected but stifled.

'But burning means a good part of the year you can't harvest,' Cora said, keeping the conversation alive even as those around her kept silent, thinking, Kindred assumed, of Little Wing. 'And with the Once-City no longer able to move, isn't burning dangerous?'

Seraph bobbed his head from side to side.

'I suppose so. In the past, we would simply sail ahead of the burn, into an area of new-enough growth that the fire wouldn't take. And when we first saw signs of the Greys, many citizens thought the burns would take care of them, but sadly, they seem immune to everything; they just stay around, smoking but never burning. Now, as you pointed out, we're stuck, so we've had to follow in your wake and magically protect the grasses just around the City from burning; otherwise, we would be burned up ourselves or dropped to the bottom as the Sea burned away to nothing beneath the City. It's an interesting problem, actually.'

Kindred saw Cora and Quixa shiver at this fate. But Kindred felt a kinship with that darkness. It called to her in a voice that moved through the dull haze surrounding her mind, and she saw herself falling with Little Wing, the two of them like noise and silence twinned and twined together, falling into darkness toward a mystery unmastered.

'But we still burn regularly. It's good for the Sea,' Seraph said, reciting the words as if he had learned them by rote. 'Good for the sky. Good for the spirit. Not even the pirate majority on the council could change that tradition, though that doesn't mean they aren't trying.'

They had reached the central staircase now, and Kindred leaned heavily on Ragged Sarah, the pain surging and pulsing, her leg swelling up. Everything felt so dull and fuzzy, so distant. Only the darkness of the Sea was close, that and the betrayal in Little Wing's eyes as she fell.

The thought of her woven-grass mattress on the top floor of Cruel House spiked a sudden need in Kindred for rest, for the oblivion of sleep.

'I need to go,' Seraph said as they reached the landing and stepped out into Breach. 'The council will need to have a follow-up meeting. I will do what I can to help your captain and your quartermaster. If . . .' He trailed off, silent for a moment. 'If there is any help left to give.'

Kindred nodded, feeling as if she were moving her head through the thick honey of inevitable sleep.

'I'll come by in the next few days to get you, Kindred,' he said, waving goodbye.

Kindred watched Seraph walk away, heading toward the rise of the Council's great grass tower.

'Come on; let's go,' Cora said, moving toward Cruel House.

'I need to get Kindred to the healers; if her leg is broken, I can't do anything to help it,' Sarah said.

Quixa and Cora nodded, and Scindapse, silent since the battle began, said, 'I'll help you.'

She slipped her shoulder under Kindred's free arm.

'I'll come back up once we get her there,' she said.

'You don't have to . . .' Ragged Sarah began.

'I want to,' Scindapse said, and her voice had the iron of a decision made, so that was that.

As they walked down the stairs and then stepped off toward the Forest, Kindred felt her thoughts falling, dropping down as pain and exhaustion threatened her consciousness.

Yllstra was there, and she and another guard strapped Kindred onto a wide board they could use to carry her through the Forest.

She waved a goodbye to Sarah and Scindapse as the darkness took her, and when Yllstra told her to close her eyes, Kindred followed her advice this time.

Her last thought was of sailing *down*, away from this world and its petty squabbles, its martyrs and heroes.

Diving down and falling into the waiting arms of the Sea, into the arms of those waiting for her there.

KINDRED swam through dreams.

She saw herself as if from a distance sailing a two-crewed vessel deep into the Sea, down and down, grasses at first gossamer-thin and then thick as pillars holding up the sky. Songs for hoping, songs for despairing, songs for ecstatic sunrises and joyful rainfall – all of them joined together in that darkness into a symphony for the deeps.

She flew on wings of bone across the surface of the Sea, skimming grasses and flowers and vines and bushes.

'FORTY-SEVEN GOLD COINS PER BUNDLE,' a patch of night-sky-black flowers said as she flew over them, loud enough to shake the Sea and sky, speaking in Little Wing's voice. More plants spoke their market values as Kindred climbed higher into the sky, away from the Sea, angling for the sun.

She woke long enough to find herself being carried out of the Healing Glade, her leg now a tracery of vines pebbled with tiny, hard fruits. Yllstra was there, and Sarah, too.

'She just needs to sleep,' Sarah was saying.

'Too many injured from the attack,' Yllstra was saying. 'No room.'

And then the darkness overtook Kindred again.

She was a blade of grass, leaving her central stalk, joining the Sea.

She fell, a raindrop smudged by dust and infected by sky, down and down through the air into a mass of roiling green.

She was sight.

She was song.

She woke.

Her room was dark, ghostly, silent. On the mattress next to her, Ragged Sarah slept deeply.

And on Kindred's own bed, sitting next to her, was Little Wing, legs folded beneath her, a knife in her hand.

'I'm sorry,' Kindred said after a time, not knowing if this was a dream, not caring either way.

The knife in Little Wing's hand caught whatever stray wisps of light ghosted through the room, caught and held them. It was a spectral shard in the darkness, a splinter of something real in this dream world.

Little Wing's face held no more of its fire. Kindred saw in the slump of her shoulders and the slack in her jaw that Little Wing had been broken. Her cheeks and eyes were sunken, her face an oft-rewritten tale of swooping scars.

'Don't be. I understand now.' Little Wing's voice had been emptied of its passion. It was a whisper in the darkness, a sound that invited silence instead of dispelling it. 'We were never getting out. A ship? No. A life on the Sea? No.'

A stillness held Little Wing that began to frighten Kindred. She had never seen the quartermaster so sedate and calm. She moved not at all, breathed slowly, blinked rarely.

Kindred wanted to wake from this dream.

'Are you all right?' Kindred asked, knowing she wasn't but needing to push at the quiet that yawned like a chasm between them, needing to throw language at Little Wing's strange stillness. She could not sit still with Little Wing, could not accept this terrible silence she now contained.

'I was going to be a captain,' Little Wing said into the darkness, her voice dead. 'I had a ship, a crew, a life, all mine. It was all done, all ready. I was going to be a captain.'

Silence, and the movement of the world.

'I see now,' Little Wing said, emotionless, void. 'We were never a crew; even the captain betrayed our purpose, our futures.'

She stood, silent and stealthy. The knife ghosted in the air between her and Kindred.

'I should kill you now. But you're still part of my crew, still after all of this; I can't let go of it.'

She dropped the knife onto the mattress, the blade burying itself in the coils of looped grass.

'I was going to be a captain, Kindred.'

Eyes spilling tears – the first time Kindred could remember – Little Wing turned and walked out of the room, her footsteps silent on the stairs, as if she floated above this place.

Kindred woke to an empty room, sunlight filling her little space at the top of Cruel House, the shields attached to the ceiling high above burning like little suns.

She pushed herself up slowly, feeling the complaint of what felt like every muscle in her body. The dream was vivid in her mind, and she felt her heart break at it.

And then her hand caught on something solid, something nestled in her mattress.

Slowly, slowly she pulled it out.

A knife.

Kindred tried to breathe but couldn't. Not a dream, not an illusion, not the fantastical work of a breaking heart and an exhausted body.

Little Wing had been there, in her room. Kindred tried and failed to imagine how Little Wing could have survived, how she could have come back from the execution, the fall.

Who cares, Kindred thought. *She did. That's all that matters. She's alive.*

With more pain than she would have liked, Kindred stood and made her way downstairs, finding no one, and then out the front door.

She found Ragged Sarah sitting just outside of Cruel House, braiding a few strands of prairie grass.

'Ahoy there, sailor,' Sarah said, patting the ground next to her. 'How are you feeling?'

Kindred raised her shoulders, or tried to, feeling the pull of muscles not ready to be used all along her back.

'I'm all right. I . . .'

How could she say it?

Sarah let the braid of grass in her hands fall as she stood, her brow pulling together in concern as she read Kindred's expression.

'What is it?'

I was going to be a captain, Kindred heard, feeling the well of tears in her eyes. Shame burned through her as she thought again of slamming her body into Little Wing's, of ending one dream in favor of another.

'Little Wing,' Kindred finally choked out. 'She's alive.'

They found Captain Caraway in the council's chambers. Only a few of the councillors were present – Ebb-La-Kem, Morrow Laze, Seraph, and The Word – which gave the open, rising room a sense of hollowness.

And they all knew, it turned out, that Little Wing was alive.

'That witch-weed somehow broke out of her cell, killed two of my guards, and stole one of our outrigged catboats,' Ebb-La-Kem shouted after Kindred told Captain Caraway and the rest what she knew. 'Killed two more citizens on patrol, stole a sackful of bones, and took our fucking boat.' Gone was the carefully put-together, reserved man Kindred had seen previously leading the Hanged Council. Ebb-La-Kem screamed, spittle clouding the air as he spoke, blood coloring his face in vivid points, as if every bit of effort he could muster was channeled purely into *rage*.

'My boat,' Morrow Laze said. Unlike Ebb-La-Kem, Morrow Laze seemed mostly at ease. He still scowled, though Kindred had yet to see him do anything else, but if it was his boat, as he said, he seemed relatively unperturbed by it. 'She'll never make it on the open Sea with a boat like that. I don't care if she's sailing back through the pass toward Arcadia or out into the unmapped plains in search of Endling's Barony; she won't make it. The Sea will take your revenge, Ebb.'

Ebb-La-Kem sputtered and spit, incoherent in his rage.

'*Though less a craft, our numbers still will hold. This thief will not make weak or steal our course,*' The Word said, twin voices twining together. Kindred saw her own confusion mirrored in Captain Caraway's face. Ebb-La-Kem, though, nodded, as did Seraph, and even Morrow Laze seemed to understand. Perhaps after however many years they had been together on the council, they had grown to make sense of The Word's riddles.

'Why did she visit you and no one else?' Captain Caraway asked. 'Why didn't she tell us what she was doing?'

Behind Captain Caraway, Kindred saw the councillors mostly continuing their conversation, though Seraph was not paying attention to them. Instead, he was watching Kindred carefully, intensely.

She had not told the captain – or Ragged Sarah – about what Little Wing had said, nothing about the content of their conversation. Just that she'd woken to see Little Wing in her room, that they exchanged only a few words in what Kindred thought was a dream, and then woke to Little Wing gone and one of her knives left behind – a sure sign that it wasn't a dream.

'She blames me,' Kindred said, lowering her eyes. *I was going to be a captain.* 'I caused this and she knows it.'

'Little Wing was going to kill everyone here, and that includes our crew,' Captain Caraway said. 'Whatever reason you had for stopping her, it saved us and any hope we have of leaving. We all have dreams, and some of us have monstrous dreams.'

Little Wing escaped and gone. *The Errant* sunk, her crew shattered and broken.

'This place has been poison for our crew,' Captain Caraway said, quietly, for just Sarah and Kindred. 'I should never have pushed us so far. This is just as much my fault as anyone else's.'

As mine, Kindred thought.

Seraph stepped into their circle, followed by the other councillors.

'Kindred, we have work to do!' Seraph's voice was the same bounding, excited thing it always was, but Kindred felt an urgency beneath it. 'Let's let these others discuss the finer points of your quartermaster's madness and get on with it.'

Ebb-La-Kem had already engaged Captain Caraway in conversation, the other councillors leaning in close. Kindred heard the phrases 'your debt' and 'increasing your time here.'

Sarah nudged Kindred toward Seraph.

'You should go. And stop beating yourself up.' She leaned in and kissed Kindred's cheek. 'I'll see you tonight.'

Lingering doubt for paths not taken clung to Kindred as she followed Seraph away from the council's chambers, down the stairs, and out into the open air of Breach.

As they walked down the road, heading toward the central staircase, Seraph didn't speak, and his steps were just a little ahead of Kindred's. About halfway to the stairs, Seraph turned right, looking over his shoulder to make sure Kindred was following him.

She was, and soon they came upon a great gathering of people, citizens old and young milling about in one of the markets Kindred had seen, although it seemed much more than just people buying and selling goods. At a wide, low table set just off the road, a man painted what looked like a map, dipping a brush into pots of inks – each a barely distinct shade of green.

Before him, a troop of children watched in silent awe. Each clutched their own brush, as if waiting for a turn.

Kindred saw jugglers and singers, weavers and artists, sellers and buyers. It was a cacophony of activity and noise, and the area burst with citizens.

'They're celebrating,' Seraph said. 'Celebrating still being alive after the attack, still having a home. And they're celebrating and mourning the lives of those lost.'

To one side of the road, a trio of women recited poetry from memory, turned inward in a rough circle, their voices at times blending together and at times working at odds. One might speak alone for a time, or two, or all three. The effect was like nothing Kindred had ever experienced – a shifting, moving rollick that entranced her.

But what stopped Kindred's steps and slowed her breath, what Seraph pointed at without a word, was the flickering light around which the women formed a circle. At first, she thought it a casting fire and assumed them to be weaving spells from plants burning there. But, as she stepped closer, Kindred saw no basin set into the ground, no fire at all.

Instead, she saw a landscape suspended in the air between the women, like a drawing set into motion, illuminated by some impossible light, blue-green and shifting as if seen through a film of water. Orb-like, it was as if someone had contained a miniature model of a place within a bubble of soap, a shell of glass. And yet the whole of it shifted and moved, almost alive, lit with that strange shine, and Kindred knew it was magic, pure and complete.

The landscape was the Sea, smaller and shifting, and tiny ships cut across its surface, appearing at the blurred edges of the illusion, sailing across the length of it, and then disappearing as they hit the other blurred edge. It was as if imagination had been given form somehow, as if these poets, their words in some arcane language Kindred had never heard, had called into being an imagining.

Kindred looked around for the fire that supported this spell but could see nothing.

'This isn't a casting-fire spell,' Seraph said, following her eyes around, smiling.

'But how?' Kindred asked, her eyes returning again to what these poets had created.

'Exactly,' Seraph said, nodding. 'Some think the poem draws from the tree's magic.' He gestured around at the Once-City itself, carved as it was into the body of the great tree. 'Some think it's the language itself – one of the old tongues we don't understand anymore. Some think its the air on Breach, that it's somehow rife with magic.

'Some even think – and me, too – that there's magic in *speaking*, and if we do it with enough intent and care, that we don't even *need* bones and plants burning in a fire. Can you imagine, Kindred?! The implications are extraordinary! This would suggest that the songs we offer to the fire do more than any fuel tossed in! Oh, yes, certainly, a keeper without any skill in song can supplement their work with the brute strength of bones, but what if that were unnecessary? Imagine it: a keeper so skilled as to *not need* bones! No more captains harvested to fuel a ship; no more bones stored in neat rows; no more death needed to power our lives! Magic in the mere act of song; power in a word spoken or sung perfectly!'

It was insane. It went against everything ever known about keeping the hearthfire, about casting from a fire.

An errant memory pulled at Kindred – standing before the raging fire on Arcadia, watching the Trade burn, and speaking to the fire, giving it leave to break away, to roar and run.

And what of the times aboard *The Errant* when a calming melody had settled the hearthfire, when a tune in its own tongue had offered control or, at the very least, harmony of purpose.

'Wonderful, yes?' Seraph asked, his joy palpable. 'But I wanted to show you this not to give you more theories and speculation, exciting as that might be. All these people, Kindred, all of them, still have a home because of you.'

Seraph spoke more quietly now, and his expression had become serious, thoughtful.

'I know what happened on the branch – I saw it. And I see that you feel horrible, like you've done some terrible act.'

I was going to be a captain.

'But you stopped someone from taking away all of this,' Seraph said, spreading his arms wide, encompassing everything. 'A city full of people – old and young – each one deserving of a full, big life.'

Kindred didn't know how to respond – couldn't. Seraph's words made sense, even if she could still hear Little Wing's voice in her head, and even as she thought of her own, more personal, more selfish reasons for doing what she had done.

I am not done with this place, she had thought. Nothing about the people living inside, nothing about a greater, more communal purpose.

'It's your life, Kindred,' Seraph said. 'And thanks to you, it's all of these people's lives, too.'

It gets easier, the Marchess from the Forest had said. Kindred saw herself betraying everything around her – Captain Caraway, *The Errant*, the crew, Arcadia, even the Once-City – but perhaps she did it all to stay true to something within herself. And maybe that got easier.

'I go to lose myself in it,' she whispered to herself as she turned back to the poets singing into existence their little world.

She toured hearthfires with Seraph again, letting the slow rhythm of the work occupy her mind and distract from everything else. By the time they quit for the day, she had found a new peace, temporary perhaps, but there all the same.

And when she was finished and had walked back to Cruel House, she found Ragged Sarah waiting for her, a grass-braided bag of food in hand.

'Hello.' Kindred arched an eyebrow at the food.

'Hello.' Sarah leaned up and gave Kindred a kiss.

'What do you have there?'

Sarah looked down at the bag and then back up at Kindred, a mischievous smile on her face.

'An invitation.'

'Oh?'

'Here we are, trapped in this floating midden heap, surrounded by enemies on all sides, but the sun is still shining and we both have the evening free and there's no one coming to kill us this moment and *we're alive*. Let's act like it.'

Barque stepped out of Cruel House at that moment, his eyes on them, his whole presence a dark cloud, gloomy and heavy.

Kindred thought again what injury he must have sustained to have blooms across so much of his body.

'Only the first level for today,' he said, brusque. 'The others are off-limits – damage from the battle.'

Ragged Sarah kept smiling and shrugged, ignoring Barque as best she could.

'Fine! The first level it is. Let's go!'

And they did.

Kindred followed Ragged Sarah all over Breach, listening to her tell stories of her childhood there. And after a time, Kindred began to tell her own stories, and they moved this way, talking of little nothings and simple pasts, edging their way toward the bigger tales stalking below.

And though they walked randomly, at times stopping for long moments to look at a house or talk with a few parents walking along with their children, they seemed to keep running into Barque.

At one point, while she and Sarah leaned in close to peer in the windows of an old, abandoned shop of some kind, its walls a mix of uneven stone and threaded grasses, Kindred heard someone muttering to himself and turned to find Barque coming around a corner, his expression indecipherable as he saw them. A few of the buds encircling his neck fluttered open and closed, a necklace blooming in and out of life.

They were caught, both looking at the other, surprised, for the space of several breaths – *In the prairie wind, out the prairie wind* – before Barque turned from them, his eyes more than a little unfocused, the blooms stuttering, juddering closed. He walked away.

Kindred and Ragged Sarah moved on, too, but Kindred found herself trying to leave behind the look in Barque's eyes, the same one she kept seeing that night, each time she saw him.

The look of a man barely in control of himself.

'When I was just five years old, I got lost in one of the breaches,' Ragged Sarah said, pointing toward just one of the several enormous tears in the city wall, the fullness of the prairie Sea spilling through it. 'None of these had grown in so far back then, but they were still pretty thick, and I ran away from home into the one closest to where we lived, right over there.'

She pointed toward a row of long, all-grass homes, many of which looked abandoned.

'I ran and I ran, all the way back to the wall – I had it in my head I was going to crawl out through the breach and throw myself into the Sea, but of course, I got all tangled up in the plants and turned around. A few bug catchers found me as they combed through the breach for a harvest, and they brought me back to my parents.'

Ragged Sarah laughed, lost in memory.

'My parents were so mad. Father the uptight weaver; Mother the brusque ship-builder. They didn't let me out sailing for days and days. "You don't deserve the Sea, Rah-Rah."'

Sarah pitched her voice low, approximating, Kindred guessed, her mother.

'Rah-Rah?' Kindred asked, smirking a little.

'My parents' little name for me,' she said, rolling her eyes and chuckling. 'Gods, I haven't thought of that in years and years.' Her smile faded then, and they continued walking.

'You said they still live here?' Kindred asked gently.

'Yes,' Sarah said before going silent.

'You don't want to seek them out?' Kindred asked, though gently. She had lost her parents so long before; she rarely thought of them anymore. That knobby-kneed girl who left the Mainland had long since been burnished by the Sea into someone else.

'They're part of who I used to be,' Sarah said, shaking her head. 'I closed that part of my life when I left, and I said things I probably shouldn't have. Things I wouldn't know how to take back.'

She turned to Kindred, looking fully into her eyes.

'I don't want to be defined by where I came from, and they're part of that.'

Kindred grabbed Sarah's hand, threading their fingers together.

'When I came over from the Mainland, after Mom and Dad died, I was the little orphan girl. Everything I did was because of that, according to most people. I sailed with my grandmother because I had nowhere else to go. I kept the fire because it gave me control over my shattered life.'

Kindred shook her head.

'It was all bullshit. But when I left *Revenger*, I do think it was because I wanted to define my life outside of my grandmother and outside of that shadow.'

She kissed the back of Sarah's hand and said, 'Let's leave all of it behind and find something impossible and perfect. Together.'

Sarah's smile lit her eyes and dimpled her cheeks in exactly the way Kindred often found herself thinking about in quiet moments.

'Together,' Sarah said, pulling Kindred into a kiss.

Kindred got to see the variety of wards that Breach was broken up into, though many of them had been renamed time and time again, their boundaries rethought and redrawn, until every part of Breach was at once itself and a hundred shadows of what it had been.

'My grandmother always used to say that renaming something makes it easier to destroy,' Kindred said as they walked through the prophets' ward, assailed from time to time by the prophetic utterances and proclamations of the inhabitants. The prophets' guild hadn't existed when Ragged Sarah had lived in the Once-City, and so she had been curious to see this place in its new iteration.

'I suppose that's true,' Sarah said, nodding as she watched a few prophets, eyes covered by thick bands of cloth, leaning out the same second-story opening, offering conflicting prophecies about the sun's lifetime.

They lapsed into silence for a little while as they walked, Kindred thinking of her grandmother again.

'You sailed with the Marchess for a while before joining *The Errant*, didn't you?' Ragged Sarah asked.

'I did. I grew up on *Revenger* basically, learned everything I know about sailing on that ship.'

'She seems like she was an amazing person, your grandmother. I only ever saw her a few times, but I remember thinking no one had ever looked taller or stronger standing on the deck of a ship.'

Kindred laughed.

'I remember we were out once on a harvesting voyage that seemed to never end, and the crew was getting restless, and the harvests were these tiny, pitiful things. We found a few streaks of coneflowers, which sold for huge sums then, but it wasn't enough and we kept chasing them. Water rations were small, and we were on the ninth or tenth day of eating yellow beetle paste.'

'Yuck,' Ragged Sarah said, laughing.

Kindred nodded.

'It was terrible, yeah. But we had gotten to the point where everyone was complaining – senior and junior crew both, and we still had nowhere near enough coneflowers to return and make the trip worthwhile. So, one evening, my grandmother said she was going to cook the meal and sent everyone else abovedeck – she forbade us all from going below to the kitchen.'

Smiling now, Kindred saw that night perfectly in her mind – Red Alay stomping across the deck, Three-Hearts composing a song to her hunger, Felorna and Maggie the Tall whispering about the Marchess's last attempt at cooking a meal – a disaster by all accounts.

'They weren't mutinous,' Kindred said. 'They complained and whispered and shouted – they were all fury and displeasure – but it was somehow all part of what it meant to be a community.'

A burr rankled her memory for just a moment: Little Wing pushing against the captain's orders to sail for the Once-City; Little Wing's unspoken suggestion of mutiny.

And just as concerning, as confusing: Kindred's own mutiny in tackling Little Wing, in preventing her from giving up her life, all of their lives, to destroy the Once-City and everyone inside.

Could a person commit mutiny with her ship gone, the crew shattered and broken, her captain turned into a husk of herself?

Could a person commit mutiny if she offered allegiance not to a ship or a captain but to herself?

Kindred shook her head, returning to her memory.

'My grandmother took all night – the sun was long set, the moon high by the time she came up on deck with food, which turned out to be bowls of stew. She called it a captain's secret when we asked what it was, but gods, did it smell good. I don't know if it was our hunger or how sick we were of the bitter smell of yellow beetle or if it was really the food itself, but I still have never smelled anything so good as those bowls of stew.'

Kindred fell silent for a moment, dazed, floating on the latent joy of memory.

'Well? What was it?' Ragged Sarah asked, leaning toward her, sharing her space for that moment.

'It was the coneflowers,' Kindred said, chuckling. 'She had taken most of the coneflowers we had harvested up to then and made a stew from them and a few other plants she had found in the kitchen.'

'No!'

'She let us eat and eat – some of us had thirds and fourths – all the while saying it was a captain's secret, that she couldn't tell us. But on her fourth bowl, Red Alay found a petal that hadn't been mashed up completely, and she put it together.'

Ragged Sarah was laughing now, too, and Kindred waited a joyous moment before continuing.

'They raged, all of them. Oh, were they mad. Cursing and spitting and shouting, but the Marchess was calm through it all, just finishing her stew and smiling. And when the crew had finally calmed down enough to listen, she just said, 'Tomorrow we find our windfall.'

They walked down the street together, and Kindred let herself be moved by the great pleasure in sharing stories. Even Barque's gloomy presence as he appeared at a crossroads ahead of them couldn't dim her happiness.

'If he's trying to keep watch on us secretly, he's doing a shit-poor job,' Sarah said, laughing. And Kindred laughed, too.

She threaded her fingers through Ragged Sarah's and matched their steps so that they truly walked together, and continued her story.

'I woke up early that next morning – we rotated the hearthfire duties between a few of us and it was my turn. I walked up onto the deck just as the sun was coming up. The sky was shot through with it, new light catching in the clouds, and for a breath – gods, I remember it so clearly – for just a breath, I thought the Sea was on fire.

'I know it sounds mad, and I couldn't explain it then or now, but I was so sure that somehow, the Arcadian magics had failed and the sun had caught on the edge of the world as it rose and set the whole Forever Sea ablaze.

'I thought I was alone on the deck, but the Marchess was there, halfway up the mainmast, hanging from the shroud. I turned around, ready to run back below and get someone, but I saw her there, and her face and hair were caught with that same fiery light.

'She looked down at me and said, "Here we are, my girl, on the edge of everything."'

The sound of their steps filled the space between Kindred's words, and she cut a look toward Ragged Sarah, who waited, smiling and entranced.

'It was a field of lilies, each one opening to the sun's fire and answering in kind. I've never in my life seen so much color, so much life all in one place.'

Ragged Sarah laughed, pure joy.

'You must have had the best haul ever! The trade prices on lilies are some of the best, far better than coneflowers,' Ragged Sarah said. 'Even with a ship as small as *Revenger*, you all must have been rich after a harvest like that. You filled the hull, didn't you? Did you get it all or did you have to leave some behind?'

'We filled the hull, yes, and that payday was enough for several years' worth of bad harvests. But for a while – I don't know how long, but it felt like it lasted all morning – my grandmother and I stood there on the dock, just watching the sun rise over a field of fire.'

As they continued to walk together that morning, Kindred thought on her grandmother's words: *Here we are, my girl, on the edge of everything.*

All her life, she had thought her grandmother meant the great vastness of the Sea, its forever always stretching toward and beyond the horizon.

But now, with everything that had happened, she wondered if the Marchess had been instead talking about a different edge – the edge not of a field but of a cliff.

An edge for teetering over, for tiptoeing along.

For falling.

Seraph found them while Kindred and Ragged Sarah were looking at a row of grass houses.

'Kindred!' His shout was jarring amid their quiet talk. 'I was just over at Cruel House to deliver some excitement for you!'

He looked between the two of them for a moment, nearly exploding with the pent-up secret he held. Finally, he spoke.

'I've decided you're ready to see the Once-City's hearthfires!'

When Kindred tipped her head aside in confusion, Seraph laughed.

'Sorry – I know you've been looking at the hearthfires in our boats. I mean, I think you're ready to see that *other* hearthfire issue you guessed at.'

Seraph tipped his head to the side, too, as he said this last. Kindred had been wondering when they would get around to that, her confirmed suspicion during their first meeting with the council.

'I have some other hearthfires to tend to tonight, so I won't be able to show you now, but tomorrow morning I should be ready to take you down.'

Down? Kindred wondered where a hearthfire that powered a whole city could be kept. Had she somehow missed it that first day as she walked out of her cell? Was it in the Forest somewhere?

'Unless, of course, you want to help with the hearthfires now?' he asked, as if realizing he had very nearly insulted Kindred by not asking her. 'I have to say, it's quite . . . *bare-bones* work.'

He grinned with wide eyes, letting his words sink in.

When neither responded, he nodded quickly and said, 'Bare *bones*? Because I'm fiddling with hearthfires, but it will be simple stuff?'

He laughed, his wide eyes inviting them into his joy.

Kindred laughed, feeling her cheeks grow hot as Ragged Sarah looked on in wry amusement.

'Well, I'm off. We'll get to it tomorrow morning – I'll stop by and get you from Cruel House beforehand!' He patted Kindred on the shoulder before wandering off, his head moving around constantly, looking here and there, never resting, never satisfied.

'I can't believe he's on the council,' Kindred said, watching Seraph walk off toward the central stairs.

'There's always someone from the hearthfire keepers on the council; it's one of the rules. And since he seems to be the only one in charge, I guess it's him. Everyone else is elected.'

'And you said you've never known there to be a pirate majority before?'

Sarah nodded, squinting her eyes up into the light reflecting down from the shields above.

'It's rare, at least I remember it being rare, to have a pirate majority. I heard about it when I was a kid but never knew there to be one. Some here might benefit from the thieving and killing, but most of these people are interested in doing what everyone everywhere is: just living. Water and food – important, yes – were never too hard to come by – not as hard as they are now, for some reason – and most people found lives working as healers or teachers or weavers. The pirates were a part of this place, and some kids got in with them early and then never got out, but they were never the whole of the Once-City.'

'I guess you were one of the kids that got in with them early?' Kindred eyed Ragged Sarah's tattoos, tracing their inky paths. She had only seen those tattoos on the pirates of the Once-City.

'Just a few years, and then I left.'

They began to walk back toward Cruel House, winding their way among the streets, threading their progress between that of the others on the paths, talking and listening.

'Where's the captain?' Kindred asked when they had returned to Cruel House and found it empty.

'Ebb-La-Kem keeps her close,' Sarah said, taking a small cup of water from the rations in the kitchen. 'She's been spending most days with him or one of the other council members, answering questions about Arcadian strategies and resources, defenses and offenses, all of that. Everyone here thinks Arcadia must be hiding some enormous fleet of battleships, and so I think Ebb-La-Kem and the rest keep trying to crack the captain, get her to reveal something secret.'

Kindred thought back to the docks at Arcadia.

'But there's nothing like that. The forces that attacked were most of what I can remember.'

'Yeah, me too,' Sarah said, nodding. 'If only the captain could convince them of that. But it's all for the good. The captain will work, as we all are, and we'll get to sail away from this place afterward. And I thought nothing could be sweeter than leaving the first time.'

And yet Kindred felt the sting of doubt.

Ragged Sarah sat at the table in the kitchen, pulling toward her one of the grass-made stools – one of only two in the house. An edge of the seat had begun to fray, spilling strands of grass out like pinions splayed in flight.

'Gods, I'd forgotten how much of this place is made of grass. Parents teach their kids to braid and plait right along with walking and talking.'

Kindred looked down at the blades of grass in Sarah's hands as she worked them back into the seat – a gentle weave of six individual strands. It made her think of the circlet she had made for Kindred.

'I'm out of practice,' Sarah said, shrugging and pushing the stool away, but Kindred knelt next to it, running her hands over the braidwork.

'No, this is incredible,' she said, examining the swoop of greens, the strange strengthening that occurred. 'I don't think you're out of practice at all.'

Ragged Sarah shrugged again, but Kindred saw a peak of color high on her cheeks.

'I don't know if you would want to,' Kindred said, looking back down at the stool, 'but I'd love to learn if you ever wanted to teach me.'

Sarah smiled and took the stool back, continuing her work without even really looking down.

'Of course I'll teach you.'

A happy quiet grew between them then, and Kindred felt it working like a balm against the harsh hurt of her betrayal of the person she used to be. She thought of bringing it up with Sarah, but it was too near, too painful. She didn't know if it was guilt or anger she felt, or something else, something like purpose, but Kindred wasn't ready to talk about it, and so she spoke instead of smaller things.

'Why do they build so much out of grass here?' Kindred asked, wanting to change the topic, looking around. Cruel House was one of the few completely brick buildings she had seen – a few others were at least an amalgam of brick and grass, and most, especially closer toward the central staircase, were completely grass. 'Is it just too much to get the materials for brick or wood buildings?'

Sarah quirked an eyebrow at her and laughed.

'No, no, if they don't have something here, they have no problem stealing it from elsewhere.'

'Right, *pirates*,' Kindred said, nodding. 'I was a little surprised, though, that they gave us a place like this.' She nodded toward Cruel House. 'I know it needs work, but it was strange to go from those cells to one of the biggest buildings on the whole level, and one made entirely out of brick. I know it's no Arcadian palace or Mainland castle, but it's nice.'

Ragged Sarah grinned at her, eyes sparkling.

'You don't get this place at all, do you?' She put a hand on Kindred's shoulder, softening the blow of her words. 'Kindred, you still think this place is full of wonder and wonderful people. But the Once-City doesn't love us. It's like a piece of fruit, still perfect on the surface but rotting inside, waiting for someone to be fooled enough to bite.'

Sarah gestured around at the level, the nearby houses.

'To build something out of the Sea is honorable, enviable. The Sea is everything to the people of the Once-City, and so to live in a house made entirely of the Sea's gifts? The fundamental belief here is that a person should bend herself to the natural world – to live in and with it. It's a sign of status and enlightenment. Hence the council's chambers. I remember my father saying it took one hundred weavers over three years to build and shape the council's chambers. They wove the creation stories of our people into the walls of that place so that none would forget where we came from and what mysteries lay all around us. But this place?'

She put a hand on the outer wall of Cruel House.

'To be housed here – in a house made of brick and stone – is a mark of shame beyond all else. To them, we're unnatural creatures, bastards who have betrayed the world that gave us life. Putting us in Cruel House is their way of signifying just how little they think of us.'

Kindred spent the night under Ragged Sarah's tutelage, learning to braid and plait grass, watching Sarah's nimble fingers work like a loom against the green, struggling to reproduce even the simplest weave herself.

It was difficult to weave one-handed. The hearthfire burn on her right hand no longer hurt like it had – Sarah's ointments had seen to that – but Kindred continued to keep it wrapped up, and even if she hadn't, her fingers could no more shuttle in this delicate dance than they could build a new hearthfire.

And so she learned slowly. She plodded through Sarah's lessons with the steadiness that had always been her companion. Perhaps not the quickest study, her grandmother used to say about her, but always the surest.

And when it was late and the Once-City seemed to sleep, Kindred followed Ragged Sarah up the stairs to their room, where they abandoned Kindred's old, unwound mattress in favor of the other. So close to one another, braiding their bodies together, Kindred found her worries too distant to really matter, at least for then and there.

The clanging of bells out in the darkness pops the bubble of comfort and warmth the storyteller has worked to create.

A moment later, a shout.

'Enemy at the rocks! To arms!'

The storyteller has sensed all of this coming, has felt the approach of the small band of raiders – four or five of them – from a nearby community, a place called Bale.

Most people died in the events that drew a line between Before and After, especially those who were at Sea, but a few walked the bright line of luck and were spared, and Bale is one such community. A group of people living on the suspended husks of old sailing vessels pierced and held up in the darkness by great green lances of grass.

If the people of Twist think they have it hard, they know nothing. On each of his visits to Bale, the storyteller has choked on the shreds of astonishment he is still capable of feeling at the perseverance of the survivors of Bale.

The storyteller does not move or speak as shouts and cries of rage and terror fill the space. Weapons are produced for those not already carrying them, and a group runs off in the direction of the rocks, led by the First, who gives him an angry, accusatory look as she goes.

Those who remain gather together by the larger of the two fires, their own weapons held tightly. Even the children hold sharpened sticks, fist-sized rocks, or, in the case of one girl who could not have been more than ten, a well-rusted sword.

'I thought the storyteller's presence offered protection,' Praise says, climbing the dais to stand next to the storyteller. He holds a heavy wooden club.

'Only from the beasts in the darkness,' he says, turning to look at Praise. 'I can do nothing about human monstrosity.'

The fighting is close enough that they should be able to hear it, but in the darkness, noise invites trouble, and so these people have learned to fight their battles in near-silence.

When it is over, the warriors of Twist return, bearing their wounded and carrying the spoils of their victory. On a regular day, the people of Twist would have been more dispersed, each person working at whatever job they have been given, and a raid like this might have been successful.

Instead, three of Bale's people are dead, dropped off the rocky edge of Twist and into the darkness below, falling to join Praise's fictional sister.

The remaining raider has fled, the First assures her people. She is wounded: a great gash on one shoulder and a cut along her leg. She smiles at the assembled population and promises she will be all right and that the storyteller must continue his story.

She is right that neither the gash nor the cut will kill her, but the storyteller smells the sharp stench of death on her all the same. The bruise that will bloom on her neck and head – the one brought about by her collision with one of the Bale raiders – will be the cause, a creeping, unfeeling thing that whispers the end before it happens.

Praise scuttles over to the First before she goes, and the two whisper together for a furious moment, neither able to keep their eyes from flicking in the storyteller's direction.

After they finish, the First limps off toward the medicker's home, and Praise takes his seat at the fire, just as most others have started to do. He speaks quickly to the men sitting on either side of him, both of whom furrow their brows and nod as Praise speaks.

'Let us escape again,' the storyteller says, clapping his hands to gather their attention, 'to a story of senseless violence and distrust, a story of love and hope, a story of our worst natures and the devastation a few might wreak.

'Let us follow Kindred further out and further down.'

21

'WE just need to do a walkthrough of the ships above before we can get to the fun,' Seraph said the next morning after stopping by Cruel House to get Kindred. He was nearly vibrating with excitement as they left the house, and he smiled back at her now as they walked up the central staircase. 'It's a daily need, especially after a battle, but we'll be quick.'

Above, in the harbor, she and Seraph examined every single Once-City vessel – both those that had been involved in the battle and those that had sat out. It was tedious work, checking hearthfires for any flaws, listening to their songs for any discord.

She mentioned what Ragged Sarah had said – about how being put in Cruel House was meant to be an insult – but Seraph shook his head, frowning.

'I won't deny that there are those on the Council who might like to give insult to any from Arcadia, but the truth is we thought it might be a softer landing for you all to be housed in a place that was more recognizable. I wanted to put you in one of the woven districts – there are a few wonderful grass homes there that have sat empty for years – but even I was convinced in the end that you lot would be happier in Cruel House.'

Kindred nodded, seeing the sense in that and not wanting to pick a fight where there didn't seem to be one.

Once they had seen to all of the vessels in what Seraph called 'the active harbor,' the one facing the reef pass, they moved to the other side of the Once-City and walked through the vessels facing the rest of the Forever Sea. There were only a handful, with some ships deemed unfit for battle just yet, others still being slowly built or repaired, still others used primarily to skim the dew from the Sea grasses each morning.

Kindred saw Talent up in the rigging on one of the dew-skimming ships. Quell appeared on the deck of another skimmer, lugging a barrel. Both asked after the rest of the crew and the captain, their words freighted with blunted animosity. They had been deemed failures and separated from the rest of their crew, forced into lives of drudgery with only the barest hope of escape, given no information other than what they could scavenge.

And their ship was gone, their crew fractured and broken, because of her.

Kindred offered them what she could, and they went back to their work, jaws set, eyes hard.

It was strange, Kindred thought with the now-familiar swirl of guilt and purpose, talking like this, calling back into being the old alliances and communities. In only a few span, the world had changed decisively, creating new communities and identities, eroding old ones.

She bid her farewells to their backs, promising to pass along their greetings to those living in Cruel House.

'It's where most of our water comes from these days, what with the City no longer mobile,' Seraph said after they had stepped off the last dew-skimming ship and moving back inside.

'All of the water?' Kindred asked, surprised. 'For the entire City and everyone in it?'

Seraph bobbed his head.

'That's impossible,' Kindred said, thinking back to the dew-skimming *The Errant* had been capable of each morning at dawn – barely a barrel's worth caught, barely enough for a tenth of the crew. 'There's no way that many ships could skim enough for the whole city.'

Seraph shrugged and continued walking back inside.

'They don't skim an abundance, and no one is swimming in extra water; I'll grant you that. But they get enough between this and our stores below. Our skimmers are excellent at their jobs.'

Kindred followed him under the archway leading back into the City, her confusion and skepticism pulling at her brow, thinning her lips.

At the central staircase, they went down to the Forest where Kindred saw Yllstra, the guard who had guided her to the Grove.

But Seraph continued down to the third level, Wisdom. There were a few guards there, too, four or five standing around, a mixture of young and old, looking bored and tired.

'Councilman,' one of them said, nodding at Seraph, who waved in return before walking right past.

The staircase ended on Wisdom, the last step flattening into the rough floor of the level, and Kindred followed Seraph off as he moved with confidence between the low-humped buildings. Quickly, the path grew labyrinthine, and the buildings seemed to grow closer together. As she walked behind him, that broken song she had heard just before her first meeting with the council sounded in her head again, doubling and tripling and rounding back on itself, confused and confusing. Whatever was wrong with the Once-City's hearthfire, it was something big.

Kindred looked around, trying to see the entrance to the cells, but her memories of this place were scattered and partial, and she couldn't remember which edge of Wisdom the cells were on.

'Almost there,' Seraph said, his voice quiet now, matching the somber silence of this place and the low light managing to filter down through the Sea and in through the apertures cut into the walls. 'The builders of the Once-City wanted the hearthfires out of the way, but I'm convinced they get harder to reach each day – the path through these buildings seems to be always changing!'

'Did you say hearthfires?' Kindred said. '*Multiple* hearthfires?'

'Of course!' Seraph said, offering a distracted smile back at her. 'You don't think something this large could be held up by just one, do you?'

That explained the strange plurality of the hearthfires' music in her head: not just one broken voice but many. But how many? Five? Ten? She would know soon.

The buildings all looked the same to Kindred, and after no time at all, she found herself lost. She remembered the eeriness in the watcher's words after Kindred had gotten out of the cells: *Sometimes, they whisper. We've cracked open a few, but they're always empty.*

And she could hear them whispering now, words in languages she couldn't identify, languages that sounded strangely similar to the tongue of the poets Seraph had shown her. But they were moving, and Kindred didn't have time to investigate.

Twice, Seraph led them in circles, and somehow, what had once seemed a field of short, rounded buildings had become structures tall enough to block her view of the central staircase, its rise lost amid the near-darkness and crowding buildings.

Seraph muttered as they walked, always something like 'nearly, nearly' or 'getting there.'

The structures, after a time, began to take a strange shape in Kindred's mind, as if they weren't external walls at all, not breaks between exterior and interior. Not walls holding anything; instead, the buildings became the fabric of the world, a thin curtain between this place and *something* else, perhaps many somethings, like hands reaching from a land of eternal night, pushing at the boundary between that world and this one.

Buildings became monstrous fingers pushing at this reality; domed structures became faces and fists stretching ever outward; peaked buildings were claws and swords nearly torn through.

With each step deeper into Wisdom, Kindred grew more unsettled. This was a place she did not belong, a space of curves that stretched too far, of darkness descending into abysses. She began to imagine eyes watching her from shadows, bodies following her own just out of sight. The eeriness of Wisdom culled every bit of self-possession she had; this was a place for fear.

The music in her head had grown, too, louder and stranger and more unsettling, beating behind her eyes and edging toward painful.

'Aha!' Seraph said, startling Kindred. 'Here!'

He had stopped before a building no different from any other, perhaps bigger or smaller than some but still made of darkness, still curving toward insanity.

Except for the door.

A green door, plaited grass resonating in the low light, offered reassuring angles and purpose in this strange place. Kindred had seen rotted wooden doors on a few of the other buildings, doors that looked to never have been opened, but this was something else.

'Are you ready?' Seraph asked, smiling back at her, his hand on the handle of the door, as if this place had no effect on him.

'I . . . don't know,' Kindred said, language strange in her mouth, strange in this place. At first, she thought herself scared, lured into fear by this place, but that wasn't quite right. She felt . . . alien. Wrong. A person living in a place that cared nothing for her.

Somehow, it was deeply exciting.

'That's the right answer,' Seraph said, pushing open the door and stepping inside, revealing a well-lit passageway. Kindred followed, at once relieved and surprised to be out of the darkness.

It was a staircase, descending.

'I thought there were only three levels in the Once-City,' she said, standing on the top stair.

Here we are, my girl, on the edge of everything.

'Not quite,' came Seraph's voice as he descended, his words framed by a smile she couldn't quite see. 'There's a fourth level below, and even the remnants of more below that. Anyone with the right permissions is allowed down here. It's not so much a secret as just a place most people don't go or aren't allowed to. But *you* are special, Kindred! You get to see how it all works!'

Kindred teetered on the edge and then stepped down.

And down.

And down.

At the bottom of the staircase was another door, braided again, and Kindred found herself admiring the craft of it, her recent lessons with Ragged Sarah fresh in her mind, the fear of the darkness gone like a dream.

A sudden pressure bloomed in her mind as the music of the hearthfires swelled.

Seraph stepped through.

So did Kindred.

'Welcome to the Gone Ways,' he said, gesturing out, giggling the tiniest bit.

It had once been a level like any of the others, Kindred could see. The floor on which they stood extended in each direction, unencumbered by more than a handful of small buildings, reaching out toward the remnants of a wall.

But if the walls on Breach had begun to lose their fight against the Sea's encroaching, then this place had long since given up the ghost.

Fragments of a wall reached up from the floor and down from the ceiling, but they were only bare shards, cracked and broken teeth forming an imperfect smile, a mouth filled and choked by the Sea rushing in and through.

As she looked around, the pressure increased in her mind, taking shape, the memory resolving itself into a song, memory into melody. Kindred looked around for the source of the music but couldn't place it.

Plants of all kinds formed an impenetrable wall around this place, bristling and curling upon one another over and over, pushing in and in, toward the center of the level. Kindred saw where these plants had been cut back, forming a large central space, open and circled by an impenetrable barrier of prairie grasses.

And guards.

Guards stood all around, not the too-young or too-bored guards Kindred had seen about the Once-City, the wardens and night watchers who seemed to be going through the motions. These were warriors, tall and short, young and old, but fit and foreboding all.

Kindred saw groups of them clustered all around the central space enclosed by the wall of encroaching Sea plants, but she only managed a short glance before a group of them nearby approached, their shoulders pulling together to form a wall, eyes hard.

'Seraph Three-Twist of the Hanged Council and Kindred Greyreach, citizen,' Seraph said, holding out his empty hands and looking at Kindred until she did the same. That music continued unabated, growing with each step she took.

'Councilman,' one of the guards, a woman with a nose that looked to have been broken and reset more than a few times, stepped forward and looked over both of them before turning to Seraph and nodding her head.

Seraph tugged down on his ratty, dirty robe, pulling at the cloth up near his chin until he had exposed his neck.

Kindred nearly recoiled from what she saw there.

A marbled ring of purpled flesh circled Seraph's neck, deepening to points of black at places, spawning root systems of red veins disappearing down toward his chest. Sores punctuated the bruising, puckering and breaking through the skin at points – sores that looked old, the pusses having long dried, the ruptured skin turned flaky and dead, and yet many remained open.

It hurt just to look at, but Kindred couldn't look away, and she felt a sigh of relief escape her lips when Seraph pulled his robe back up around his neck.

'Thank you, Councilman,' the guard said, smirking at Kindred's discomfort. 'Please proceed.'

The guards split, a few still chuckling. Kindred looked back out into the space, anything to forget about the curve of that ring, a circle of purple and blue and black that begged terrifying questions of her mind, that asked what might unite those on the Hanged Council.

Looking out, Kindred saw what she had seen before: guards moving about the wide, flat space, in small groups or as individuals. It looked much as it had when she'd stepped through.

And yet Kindred couldn't shake the feeling that somehow, something had changed in the few moments between walking through the grass door and now, that she had missed something, that the guards allowing them inside – guards who apparently had authority above and beyond members of the Hanged Council – had blocked her vision of this space intentionally.

Fewer, she realized, the thought straying through her mind. *There are fewer guards here.* She had no idea how she knew, could not have said how many there had been or what evidence there was for her sudden suspicion, but the thought held nevertheless. Fewer.

'Come on,' Seraph said, walking off, free now that he and Kindred had made it through the initial blockade. She followed, the music a wail, a cacophony in her mind.

Seraph stepped around a small clutch of guards circled up and talking, and as Kindred followed him, the center of the Gone Ways was revealed to her.

And the music became a wave crashing over her.

'Here we are,' Seraph said, sweeping one arm across the empty space in the center of this level.

Not five. Not ten. Not twenty. *Hundreds*.

Hundreds of them, spread out along the floor like lesions roaming across a body. Kindred sipped a quick slip of air as song and sight twined in her mind, and she listened to their chorus.

The Marchess had long before taught her how to diagnose a hearthfire's needs based on its song. A low-slung dirge begged for fuel just as clearly as a cracked, high melody asked for guidance. *The path is in the music*, the Marchess used to say.

But Kindred had never heard this many hearthfires singing all at once, their melody a constant barrage in her mind.

'Isn't it wonderful?' Seraph asked, his voice inconsequential next to the chorus of flame and bone before Kindred.

'How can you stand it?' Kindred asked, shouting to hear her own voice over the tumult. The pressure of the hearthfires' song had pushed at her mind like a bad headache upon entering the Gone Ways, but this was something entirely new. She felt as if her mind were sludge, thick and nigh impossible to move through. Thinking was trudging, one solitary thought at a time.

Seraph patted her on the back and smiled pityingly.

'You get used to it,' he said, leaning in close so she could better hear him. 'Most of these brutes' – he gestured toward the guards all around the level – 'can't hear anything. I envy them at times.'

But Kindred wasn't listening to him. She had clamped her

hands over her ears – which dampened the song of the hearthfire, if only just – and had moved closer to one of the blazes, her brow pulling together in confusion.

The flames were frozen. Tongues of solidly grey flames reached up from the metal bowl set into the floor, but they moved not at all, flickered not at all. It was as if the hearthfire were instead a painting of itself, a representation of the truth.

Kindred had seen grey flames before – she could think of a dozen builds that would turn the fire this shade of grey – but to freeze the hearthfire, to stop its motion, to give a strange body to a fire that was only ever spirit, Kindred had never heard of anything that might do that.

'Why is it so loud?' she shouted, if only to hear her voice over the tumult. This close to the hearthfire, the music was cacophonous, like a thousand voices shouting and whispering and speaking in just as many languages.

The path is in the music, Kindred heard amid the tumult, her grandmother's voice reasserting itself as it seemed to do more and more in recent days, but Kindred could see no path, or worse, she could see too many paths, too many needs.

For a moment, Seraph only stared at Kindred, openly astonished, but her distress finally cut through and he moved.

Seraph leaned down and reached into the fire, singing a song Kindred could see on his lips but not hear. His hand, she noticed, pushed with some effort through the thickness of the flames.

He reached down toward the bed ash, pinching some of the blackened dust in his fingers before bringing it out. He took some and rubbed it inside his lower lip before pointing first at his ear and then the fire. The ash was a small pull of black in his fingers as he held it out to her.

Kindred took the pinch of ash and, after a moment's hesitation, rubbed it along the inside of her lower lip. The bitterness flashed against her tongue and teeth, drying out her mouth and filling it with the taste of smoke and age.

And just as quickly, the melody of the hearthfires fell away in her mind, fading to nothing more than a gentle hum tripping along her horizon. Memories of these hearthfires' past journeys moved through her mind: sailing through the Forever Sea, farther out than any map could understand; grinding to a horrifying halt there; the slow creep of age pulling at the Once-City, breaking down walls and slowly hardening the hearthfires; wyrms and other deep-Sea creatures moving about the stalled city, creeping closer.

All of this and more Kindred saw in a flash as the ash touched her tongue and the song of the hearthfires quieted.

'. . . a moment to work. I'm sure you'll be able to hear me in just a little bit,' Seraph was saying, his voice loud and harsh next to her. Kindred stumbled back, still working her mouth to alleviate the dryness.

'Ah. There we are, I guess. So sorry to not warn you – to be honest, I've never met another hearthfire keeper who could hear them as well as I can!'

Kindred shook her head, still letting the chaos of the music disappear.

'The other keepers here can't hear the fires?'

Seraph laughed and leaned in close, as if sharing a private joke.

'Not like that, Kindred. They hear something, of course, but only little whispers from the fires. But you – you can actually hear and understand them, can't you? You know what the fires sing of, don't you?'

Kindred could only nod, and Seraph let out a mighty laugh, all joy and excitement.

'Kindred! You're like me! I've never met another hearthfire keeper who could truly sing with and understand the fire. I suspected you might be different from the start, but I never hoped for this. Oh, my, Kindred!'

Kindred found herself smiling, too, despite the continued echoes of the chaos in her mind. She thought back to Rhabdus, to the school-trained keepers from Arcadia, all of those who treated the hearthfire like an animal to be broken, an animal they couldn't understand and could only shout nonsense orders at. The Marchess had understood the hearthfire, but she was the only other Kindred had ever met. Until now. Until Seraph.

He stood before her, a goofy smile on his face, eyes wide, hands clasped together in excitement.

'What happened to them?' Kindred asked. She looked out over the field of hearthfires, each one host to its own unmoving grey flames, each another voice in the dulled cacophony still moving at the back of Kindred's mind, lessened but not gone.

'Age,' Seraph said, shaking his head. 'These hearthfires have been burning since the Once-City was built. Which, based on the few histories the really old citizens can remember, is somewhere beyond eleven hundred years.'

'Eleven hundred . . .' Kindred said, trying to think of the longest voyage she'd ever been on. Certainly, during her time aboard *Revenger*; the Marchess was infamous among Arcadian captains for being absent from port for huge swaths of time. But even on their longest hauls, skirting the edge of the Roughs and living off of skimmed-up dew and caught bugs and going mad with time away from port, time away from cooked food and firm ground – even then they hadn't lasted more than twenty or thirty days, and after sailing so long, a ship's hearthfire, even one well-tended as Kindred's always were, its flames would be sluggish, the fire slower to respond to changes in build or song.

And to sail for a year? Ten years? A hundred? More? Kindred looked down at the viscous, grey sludge of the flames and found herself at once horrified and unsurprised.

'Don't worry,' Seraph said, seeing the recognition and shock run across her face. 'They're still steady. We're in no danger of diving.'

'How long have they been like this?' She let her eyes drift up and over the field of hearthfires before her.

'Hard to say,' Seraph said, some of the excitement coming back into his voice now that they were talking specifics again. 'Thirty years. Maybe a bit more. But certainly no fewer.'

'Stuck in this place for thirty years,' she said, mostly to herself.

'Without the stories about the Once-City always moving, I suspect those like your Cantrev would have spent time looking and found us long ago.'

Kindred nodded, her mind whirring with possibilities, falling back into old patterns. Questions rose like ghosts: What kind of builds? Age of bones? Changes in the flames based on time of the year? Quality of grass?

And then there were all the new questions, those she had only recently begun to consider: What happened if you burned twists of grass? Strands of hoar flower or thrice-root? She thought of

Seraph's builds on the ships above, his strange and mysterious and exciting and dangerous and horrifying experiments.

'Can I . . .' Kindred finally asked, gesturing at the nearest first.

Seraph nodded, his eyes alive with joy.

'Bones?'

'Just a few fragments – they take very little in the way of fuel to keep their current state.'

Kindred nodded, studying the slow-fire as closely as she could, kneeling before it, shifting from side to side. The lazy arc of the flames was mesmerizing, like nothing she had ever seen.

'That's good,' she said. 'I imagine if they needed more, the Once-City would have sunk years ago.'

Seraph laughed.

'Exactly right! We only need a very few bones each year to stay afloat – I fragment them myself and mete them out when needed.'

'Builds?'

'I've tried it all – more bones, fewer, plants only, plants and bones, braids, everything I could think of. But perhaps not everything you can think of!'

Seraph beamed at her from across the hearthfire.

'We've never had anyone with Arcadian knowledge down here, Kindred! It was a chore to convince the rest of the council to grant you access, but I pushed and pushed because, well, we *need* some fresh ideas. You can help me figure out how to unlock these fires, to rejuvenate them and get us moving again – efficiently, effectively, to escape before Cantrev returns. Or before, well . . .' Seraph trailed off, looking around, and Kindred imagined she knew the end of that sentence. *Before it sinks.*

'How much longer do the hearthfires have, do you think?' she asked quietly, looking around at the scattering of grey blazes.

'I don't know,' Seraph said, his voice almost a whisper.

'And what would happen if you pushed them and tried to move anyway?'

Seraph just shook his head for a moment, and Kindred understood. It was impossible – without a willing hearthfire, a vessel simply would not move.

In the silence that followed, Kindred saw the precariousness of her situation: Cantrev almost certainly approached from the west. The ships of his that escaped would return to Arcadia with the news: the Once-City sits where it was. And then it would not be just the collection of raiding ships that had attacked the Once-City before. This time, Cantrev would sail with the remainder of Arcadia's war fleet, every ship he had remaining.

In the Once-City, the Hanged Council moved to defend themselves and their citizens. Stolen ships built for peaceful purposes – harvest or cargo – outfitted to slide into battle; it was a tactic both sides seemed to have adopted.

And now this hearthfire work, a peaceful solution, one that would leave the battlefield as only another patch of the Roughs. No more boats plunged into the deeps by silent assassins dropping from trees. No more vicious magics burning the air and tearing bodies apart.

Little Wing gone, the crew fractured and broken, her old life only a memory, Kindred thought of *now*. Ragged Sarah's lesson still moved through her mind, and she flicked her fingers in the way she'd been taught, interleaving imaginary grasses as she considered this moment, this place, all of this. Conflicts rose and fell around her, pushed by maniacs wanting power, by misery wanting release, by men and women wanting life, water, a place to exist.

The Marchess's words moved through Kindred's mind, though it was no longer in the Marchess's voice that they sounded. It was Kindred now, speaking to herself, for herself.

Remember, the prairie holds worlds.

An idea took shape in Kindred's mind, barely formed, vague, like a sail barely seen through heavy fog. It was the suggestion of something more, but Kindred held on to it, thinking all the while of a memory, her and Little Wing crawling along the Cradle, looking down on two worlds.

For Little Wing, nothing. An absence of purpose and action and light; an absence of herself in the world and all the fear and worry that came with it.

And for Kindred, everything. A world to be discovered, a mystery to be loved, a darkness to be lit up. And maybe, just maybe, a grandmother to be found.

Kindred's fingers kept their shuttling, and her mind kept its fascination with that sail slowly appearing through the mist.

Seraph had said something about below-boats near the hearthfire supplies. Something tried before by those brave and wild enough to see a world below the waves.

'Do you keep all of your supplies nearby? The stuff you need for the fires, I mean,' Kindred said, looking around.

'Yes, I'll show you!' Seraph said, his smile reappearing. He talked excitedly as they walked. 'There are exactly one hundred and eleven hearthfires on this level. Although each has its own wonderful peculiarities, I've found a certain amount of similarity in each. To begin, the quality of . . .'

She listened as he spoke, but let her eyes drift around to the jagged remains of the wall, the ever-present reach of the dark Sea beyond. Off to the side, Seraph showed her the stores of plants and bones, more than Kindred had ever seen in one place – a treasure vault that he seemed only a bit bashful to show her.

'I've been saving for some time, hoping someone might come along to help me,' he said, excited and sheepish all at once.

'It's incredible,' she said, and though it was, she was interested in more. She looked around and at first saw nothing but more emptiness, more hearthfires, a few buildings, but there, beside a massive morass of plants that had grown in from the Sea, she spied them.

Boats, though like nothing she had ever seen above. Not the sturdy wood that she was used to, and lacking the upright masts boasting sails.

No, they were made of *grass*. Braided, plaited grass that made up the hull and extended all the way above, creating a ceiling above the deck, with windows fashioned into the sides. Sails that looked more like retractable fins extended off the sides of the boats, operated by what looked like pulley systems a sailor could work from inside.

There were only a few of the boats, and only one or two looked remotely finished, but Kindred felt her breath stop up in her chest all the same when she saw them.

'Ah, yes,' Seraph said, following her gaze. 'The boats. Marvels, aren't they?'

'Did they ever sail?'

'No, not really. They have hearthfire basins inside them, but no one could ever figure out how to make it work. Every build ever tried gave too much lift. And none had the skill to try anything more creative.'

Seraph shook his head.

'No, like much here, they became an abandoned project.'

'Could I look at them sometime?' She tried to keep the sudden hope and nervousness from surfacing in her voice, hoping that her question came out casual, only vaguely interested.

'Of course!' Seraph said, nodding. 'So long as you get done with your work here with the hearthfires, you can fiddle with the boats!'

Kindred stared off after them for another moment before turning back to the wonders of Seraph's hearthfire stores. As she grabbed several handfuls of plants totally strange to her, she smiled at Seraph.

'Let's work.'

They settled in front of a large hearthfire, its metal basin as far across as Kindred was tall. She thought suddenly about how strange it was to not know the time of day by the light. The Gone Ways, she realized, were too far down for the sun's light to filter past so much grass and in through the tears and holes and rips in the walls. No shields hung from the ceiling there.

Instead, the whole level was lit by torches thrust upward on stands all around. They pushed back the darkness so much that Kindred had barely noticed right away, but it also meant the passage of time was marked by no diminishment of light.

And so, she had no idea how late it had gotten, whether it was only evening or if they had moved into night. Or perhaps it was even the next morning.

They began experimenting, singing to the flames, asking for permission to enjoin the blaze with their hands. Kindred heard in Seraph's songs not the fumbling Sea shanties of other hearthfire keepers but honest, real messages of entreaty and communion. She smiled and focused on the flames.

Kindred studied the build – a simple, dilapidated thing – with her eyes and then with her hands, testing for places of tension and weakness, searching for a rationale. She flexed her burned hand in the flame, worried suddenly about the tight furls of golden shoots dotting her skin, but they were just fine. One or two even opened slightly, swaying in and with the movement of the fire. For just a moment, Kindred thought she saw an echo in the sway of the golden grasses and the slow-sludge movement of the fire, as if they danced together, moved by the same music.

But Kindred's excitement was too great, and she pushed the thought away, focused on the strangeness of the conundrum at hand.

Seraph, too, began a series of tests on the coal dust filling the basin, checking its consistency and thickness, taste and color, against other nearby fires.

One by one, Kindred held up the plants, asking specific questions about them, which Seraph was only too happy to answer.

'That's wild feverfew.'

'Properties?'

'Some medical. Functioning hearthfire properties that I've noted include heightened fires, white-gold flames; on a mono-fired vessel, a strange nimbus of power at the grass line.'

Kindred stared at him.

Seraph held up his hands, soot-stained, and smiled.

'I know! Totally bizarre.'

Seraph chuckled but then stopped, his face suddenly serious.

'But don't mix it with new bone!' he said, eyes wide. 'Most of these plants don't interact much with these hearthfires down here, and you can use it with that hearthfire since the bones inside are well burned, but I once tried a three-stranded braid of feverfew wrapped around a bone and . . .' He ran a hand through his hair and shook his head. 'It was the strangest thing; the fire grew in size – ten or twenty times – and began lashing out, burning the ground and people nearby, dipping into other hearthfires and coaxing them up, until most of the Gone Ways was filled with these burning archways formed by the fire, each one flashing out and incinerating anything they could . . . except me.'

Seraph shook his head again, and a flash of pain moved across his face.

'I had the strangest sense that because *I* had called it into being, it wasn't burning me . . . but several people – friends of mine – were burned, badly. And others, well, died.'

Kindred watched as sadness broke over Seraph, the memory consuming him for a moment.

'The other councillors were sure it was a breakthrough, and they made me try it again – this time with no one else down here – but it accomplished nothing. No change in mobility, no change in anything really. Just an inferno of grey flames, burning everything it could touch.'

Kindred shivered, and considered the plant in her hand, suddenly cautious. Cantrev would have waged war for such a plant – perhaps he had – but here she was, wary of its mystery and using it to simply know more, to know differently.

Kindred set about her work.

That experiment didn't work. And neither did the one after. Or the one after that.

It was a day full of failures, and Kindred enjoyed every bit of it.

And as she worked, behind the theory and strangeness and possibility, she let a fantasy float along the back of her mind, imagining a boat, braided by her own hand, diving down.

'Now, now!' Seraph slapped his knees as he squatted before an enormous flame, grey and viscous, just as the others had been. His energy seemed undiminished by repetition. 'This is a particularly interesting case. I – '

Two voices, rubbing against one another like dried leaves or jagged stones, interrupted him.

'*A lovely pair of empty minds here found.*'

Kindred's skin flashed with cold as she turned to find The Word looking down on her work with Seraph. She had not heard them approach. Perhaps Seraph's voice had smothered their footsteps; perhaps the boredom and repetition had slowed her senses. Whatever the cause, she felt shock at their sudden appearance, and it was a shock heightened as she watched the two of them straighten their clothing, pulling identical brown robes back up against their chins, hiding again those purpled necklaces hung forever around their throats.

'Oh, hello,' Seraph said, coming out of his analytical reverie to smile vaguely up at The Word. Kindred looked up at and then immediately away from The Word's green eyes.

'*A keyless lock once tried, twice tried. No end.*'

Seraph chuckled and shook his head, and Kindred recognized the comfort in a long-held, oft-visited conversation.

'It's not so impossible. And now with a fresh mind to help me, I know we can unlock them.' He gestured to the hearthfires.

The Word laughed, both voices entwined and uncanny, nearing laughter Kindred had heard and known her whole life. Nearing but never reaching it.

'*If one, a fool. But two? Pair mirrors crack'd. Poor light rebounded endlessly between.*'

Kindred still had no sense of who these people were, why they spoke as they did, or what their odd relationship was. But she could recognize insult even in the singsong verse of The Word's speech.

'A fool?' she asked, some of the old fire she remembered hearing in Little Wing's voice lighting in her own. 'I'm pressed into service to help *your* City and *your* people; I'm one of two, as far as I can see, actually doing anything to save this place, and *I'm* the fool?'

Kindred finished all in a rush, breathing hard, red in the face.

She was tensed and ready for a fight. Her eyes on The Word, flicking between them, Kindred rose and stood, trying to hold herself up, wishing despite everything that had happened that Little Wing were there. Her bravado might have been reckless, but it had always lent a sense of purpose to a conflict.

The silence strained and pulled between Kindred and The Word. No guards approached this time, perhaps too busy or too bored to interfere, perhaps aware of what The Word could do and unwilling to get in the way.

Seraph sat quietly for once, waiting for the storm to blow over.

The Word chortled.

The sounds of mirth dribbled from their lips like dollops of sludge, slick and wet, spittle shining in the unnatural light as their laughter grew, echoing and reflecting off of each other's.

'Pair mirrors crack'd,' Kindred muttered, low enough to be unheard beneath their laughter.

As one, they each reached out and put hands on Kindred's shoulders, green eyes identical and angled in happiness.

'Such words dredged up from fire and dark of deep. To laugh 'midst this is water on dry lips.'

That said, The Word walked away, still chuckling, their strides perfectly the same, weaving between the hearthfires as one, walking the path opened for them by guards who parted before their approach. They walked out to where the prairie plants had formed the wall and then suddenly, by some trick of light or magic, The Word was gone, one moment on this side of the plant wall, the next gone.

'Did you see that?' Kindred asked, turning back to Seraph, who had long since gotten back to working on the hearthfire and had even begun murmuring to himself again.

'Don't worry about them,' he said, shaking his head and looking after The Word, his face full of an emotion Kindred couldn't read. 'We all have our own projects down here, and you're only cleared for the hearthfires. The Gone Ways extend far beyond this space, but our interest is just here.'

'What's back there?' she asked, knowing the question went against the caution Seraph had just offered but unable to help herself in the face of a mystery. She thought back to the breaches on the first level – she had only been able to think of them as eternally open doors, a hole in a wall meant to separate inside from out.

Kindred suddenly saw The Word in her mind, their symmetrical steps taking them through the plant wall and out into the dark Sea, their feet finding nothing and yet still walking, their strange forms insinuating themselves into the sway of the prairie.

'Extra water and food storage, that kind of stuff. It's honestly quite boring – at least I assume. Only a few of the councillors have the authority to go back there. Water and food are scarce things here, so we like to keep them mostly protected and secure.'

Seraph gestured over to one wall, opposite where The Word had just gone.

Barrels were lined up there, a seemingly endless row of them stretching all the way across the Gone Ways – at least, the part of the Gone Ways Kindred could see.

'Those are all filled with dew skimmed by our sailors, and we ration from them, but Ebb-La-Kem, the water master, has more stores back there, apparently – the reservoir to collect rainwater filtered down from the branches, that sort of thing. And The Word are always working on some scheme or another in their own private areas.'

It was a huge amount of trust that Seraph offered to his fellow councillors, and for a moment, Kindred heard Sarah's cynicism, her certainty that the Once-City was rotten, was full of liars and crooks. Full of pirates.

And hadn't she said that both Ebb-La-Kem and The Word were part of the pirate majority on the council?

Kindred bent her head to the hearthfire, accepting the situation for the moment, but doubt crept up on her, reaching cold fingers into the fire of her confidence in this place.

And still her mind wandered back to the boats sitting unused next to the Sea, cast off and ignored.

Waiting, perhaps, for the right hand to bring them to life.

THE next morning, Kindred found the rest of the crew waiting for her when she descended.

'Crew meeting,' Sarah said, lacing her fingers through Kindred's and pulling Kindred into a seat next to her. 'I was going to wake you up soon if you didn't show up.'

Everyone was present, even the captain, who was normally gone by the time Kindred awoke, summoned by Ebb-La-Kem for this or that reason.

On Kindred's other side sat Scindapse, who had gained some of her confidence and life back in the last few days. Kindred watched the young girl, thinking of herself around that age. At fifteen years old, she'd still sailed aboard *Revenger*. Her life became a constant fight to define herself as someone other than 'the Marchess's granddaughter,' and so she had put her head down and become a part of the crew, another pair of carrying arms, another voice for song.

To be part of the whole had meant so much to Kindred then, and she felt no guilt or shame for that. It gave her purpose and place in the world when she needed it.

Kindred saw herself in Scindapse, and in doing so felt more clearly the distance between her heart and those of the crew. She did not seek purpose or place in the world anymore.

Yllstra's voice echoed in her head, her certainty that Kindred was not like the rest, that she felt curiosity when others felt fear, that she looked down as others looked up and out.

'We don't have much time, so hear me,' Captain Caraway said, looking around at the shattered remains of her crew.

Kindred felt that old loyalty stirring inside her, the woman who would have followed Captain Jane Caraway anywhere, fought anyone for her. That old command of the captain's – hear me – pulled again at the person Kindred had been. Though it had only been days since she sailed under Captain Caraway's lead, so much had changed.

But not this.

'We're getting out. The next time Cantrev attacks, we're going to steal a boat from the backside of the City, one of those not fit for battle. I don't give a green damn who wins; by the time it's over, we can be gone in the chaos, on our way to the Mainland.'

The captain spoke with her old certainty. She took care of her crew, saw them ahead to safety.

'What about our fifty days of service?' Kindred asked. 'Why not just wait?'

Captain Caraway shook her head.

'Those councillors have been plying me for information every day, studying me, watching me – but I've been studying them, too. And there's no chance they are planning on following through with their end.'

Nods from the other crew members – especially Sarah – pushed the captain on.

'More than once I've overheard them talking when they assumed I couldn't hear or wasn't listening – they're planning something. I don't know what, and I don't know what it has to do with us, but it doesn't bode well. Something is wrong here. Our water rations have begun to shrink, guards seem to follow us everywhere despite our status as citizens, and they all seem too calm about another attack from Cantrev. I can feel it, certain as sunlight: they mean to fuck us. And I plan to fuck them first.'

'Are any of those vessels capable of making the voyage?' Long Quixa asked.

'I've seen them all a few times and think so. But Kindred, you've worked on them,' the captain said, looking at her. 'What's your assessment?'

Kindred nodded.

'Aye, captain. I've seen to their hearthfires myself. They may not be suitable for battle, but they could make a voyage. Most of them . . .'

Kindred trailed off, remembering the dew-skimmers lined up next to the other vessels. Dew-skimmers that provided water for the entire Once-City.

'Exactly,' the captain said, her whisper pulling the conversation forward. Plans were sketched: during the next attack, each of them would pull away from the crowds – however they could, though less conspicuous violence was better – and meet on the far side of the City. With everyone focused on the attack, they could hop aboard a vessel and be out of the harbor before anyone knew what was wrong. Quixa, Cora, and Sarah would steal as many supplies as possible; Kindred would steal as many bones as possible, preferably a few every day she worked by the fires; the captain and Scindapse would steal what weapons they could. If they were lucky, they could get a dew-skimmer. If not, they could make do with another vessel.

But Kindred's mind pulled around the dew-skimmers, and she realized she'd never really gotten a satisfactory answer about the water stores. There was no way those ships could pull in enough dew – enough water – for everyone in the City, even if the number of citizens had gone down in recent years, even if the stores below were massive. Skimming the dew, stealing from Arcadian vessels, plundering their own stores – it was simply not sustainable, not for as many years as the Once-City had been stopped.

And yet there was the daily ration of water, every day, downstairs. Diminished, yes, but there.

Some piece was missing here, something she couldn't see. But it was too big, too complicated to understand.

'Well?' The captain's voice jarred Kindred out of her thoughts. 'I need to know, Kindred. Are you in?'

Kindred looked around at the other crew members, seeing the resolve in their faces.

Cora the Wraith, grinning, sure of their success even after everything that had happened, everything that was sure to happen.

Long Quixa, remote, nodding at the captain, steady.

Scindapse, young and hopeful.

Ragged Sarah, smiling down at Kindred, her love fierce, and Kindred's love for her fierce in return.

And the captain, a woman Kindred had admired and feared and loved in her own way, ready to lead her crew out of danger yet again.

They planned and sailed for a life together on the seas.

And even though she held a different future in her heart, even though her mind still wandered to those boats below, even though.

Even though.

'Aye,' Kindred said, looking around at her old crew, holding Sarah's eyes with her own.

'Then it's done,' Captain Caraway said. 'At the next attack, we make our escape.'

Kindred found Seraph above, bouncing about and ready to start on their work. They moved among the ships again at the start, stepping from deck to deck, examining hearthfires, and Kindred tried to pay closer attention to those boats left on the eastern side.

But try as she might, she couldn't imagine a life on any one of them. The captain, certainly. Quixa and Cora, absolutely. Scindapse? Maybe. But Kindred knew her path was different, deeper.

She found herself thinking how well Little Wing would have done in this situation. The quartermaster had always been at her best when the world was against her, when hope was a slim shaft of light to be chased.

Kindred shook her head and pushed the thought away. She couldn't go there.

'Are you all right? You seem distracted.' Seraph looked across one of the hearthfires at her, concerned.

'Just a lot on my mind,' she said, 'but I'm okay.' Which was true, and enough to mollify Seraph's worry.

They got back to it, and after the ships, it was back down to the hearthfires.

Kindred moved among them like a ghost, haunting this place

but not really there, her mind elsewhere, her spirit longing for more, for the deeps, for her grandmother, for Little Wing, for a world that was always there but that everyone forgot about.

As she worked, she looked at the rows and rows of barrels lined up against one of the walls. The water stores Seraph had pointed out previously.

Kindred tried counting them, but there were too many. Maybe she had been wrong in her suspicions – with stores that massive, the Once-City would be fine for a long time, especially if they could be replenished by the occasional heavy dews skimmed and the occasional captured rainfall.

Perhaps she and the rest of *The Errant*'s crew were just having their rations limited and diminished because they were still seen as enemies of the Once-City. Kindred pushed the thoughts away and got back to work.

They had nearly reached the end of the day when a shriek behind the plant wall startled Kindred out of her thoughts.

It was there and gone, a piercing shriek that was immediately muffled, pummeled into nothing by shouts from men and women.

And then nothing.

'What was that?' Kindred asked Seraph, leaving the hearthfire she had been experimenting on and walking over to where he crouched next to a trio of hearthfires. 'Did you hear that?'

Seraph nodded, whispering a calculation for himself and holding up a hand. Kindred let her eyes roam the Gone Ways, searching for the source, for the rent in the wall, for the body burrowing through toward them.

She recognized that shriek, would know it anywhere. She could even picture the great hulking body, sinuous and slithering, curling in and around itself. A mouth wide as the world and hungry as anything, opening toward her, ready to devour her.

A wyrm.

'Okay, what was it you wanted?' Seraph set down bones he'd been manipulating and looked up at her, an absent-minded smile on his face.

'Did you hear that shriek? There's a wyrm somewhere near.' Already Kindred was imagining the run toward the stairs, thinking of whether it was safer to stay in the confines of the stairwell or if she should race up to the Forest or even Breach.

'Loud, aren't they?' Seraph asked, shaking his head. He seemed totally unperturbed. Still sitting beside the hearthfires, he was the picture of calm. 'We always have wyrms moving around the Once-City, but they don't cause us any trouble. They live a bit too low for us, and their vines can't do anything on something as large as the Once-City. But the Gone Ways are low enough in the Sea that I can hear them most times I work down here.'

Seraph's expression shifted, toward something more conspiratorial, and he arched an eyebrow as he peered around for a moment.

'Between you and me, I've heard that some of the councillors who have space down here have been experimenting with trapping wyrms. How they're going to manage it, I have no idea. And only the gods know why. Those buffoons, always looking for a bigger, more brutish enemy than themselves to defeat.'

He shook his head, and Kindred marveled at him. On the one

hand, he could say all that as if it were banal gossip instead of a story of terrible possibility. A wyrm *trapped?* On this level? *In the Once-City?* Seraph had already continued his work, numbers spilling from his mouth as he closed one eye, cocked his head to the side, and calculated braid strength and plant width.

But on the other hand, his estimation of his colleagues on the council was too accurate to be accidental, and Kindred was reminded that while Seraph looked the part of a madman, he possessed a gift for seeing. In that way, he was much like the Marchess.

Shrieks sounded twice more while they worked down there, and by the last one, Kindred had pinpointed the source to behind one of the walls. She had assumed them to be little back rooms, nothing more than small storage spaces, but if they had a wyrm back there, and if there were as many people back there as it seemed based on the shouts that accompanied each shriek, it would have to be an enormous chamber, easily the size of the one in which Kindred worked now.

She thought of Captain Caraway worrying away at some plan happening amid the council, some secret design to betray their deal with the crew of *The Errant.*

As Kindred watched The Word and several of their guards appear from behind that wall – the one between Kindred and the shrieks – she thought perhaps the captain was right.

When they were finished for the day, Seraph offered to walk her up to Cruel House, but Kindred begged off. She wanted to look at the grass boats.

'Have fun!' Seraph said before walking off.

There were seven in all, five of them in various states of frayed and coming apart, braids half-done or half-undone.

But two of them were finished, or near enough to be finished as to not matter.

Kindred walked all around them, running her hands along the hard, smooth sides, the grass shiny in the light of the Gone Ways. After a moment of sheepishly looking around to make sure no one was watching her, she climbed in through one of the windows and dropped into the cabin, the space bare and empty and still.

Light cut in through the windows in thin patches, enough to illuminate the outline of a door Kindred had missed and the rope system for managing the side sails she had noticed before.

And there, set into the only piece of wood in the entire ship, the board running from one side of the space to the other, was the hearthfire basin, its metal glinting dully in the light.

She stayed there for a long time, not moving, barely breathing, her eyes opened or closed – it was all the same. Kindred floated in dreams, in hopes, along a path she would take, had already taken. The only sound was the slow movement of grass against the City, like the lungs of the world.

'You're perfect,' she whispered in the near-darkness, her breath already returning to the sway of the Sea.

23

KINDRED didn't get a chance to talk with Ragged Sarah until later the next day. Sarah was sleeping when Kindred slipped up to their room, and by the time she woke up, Sarah was gone to work. She left a note for Kindred that simply said, Soon, love.

Seraph was waiting for Kindred right when she woke, and the two of them immediately set out to the Gone Ways, ignoring the boats above for the day.

They talked of their increasingly wild theories about the hearthfires, and Kindred let herself drift off into the comfort of that conversation, buoyed up by the thought of a ship made of grass, built for the grass, one that might spring to life under her hand. A small smile played across her lips as Seraph spoke, as she worked, as they went about their day.

And so it was that she nearly missed it.

She was kneeling before one of the smaller hearthfires, her hands moving about inside it, her mind wandering, when her fingers brushed over a knob of bone, some product of too many years burning in the same slow-dying hearthfire. As she touched it, Kindred heard a slight shift in the hearthfire – in *all* of the hearthfires – a movement in the key of their songs. It was there and then gone, so small a change that she would've missed it had anything else been going on. In fact, Kindred thought she might have missed it even had she been paying attention, but because she was so lost in thought, her active mind elsewhere, some other, deeper part of her could pay attention to the spirit of the flames.

She looked over to Seraph, who was working on a few fires nearby, but he showed no sign of having noticed anything.

Kindred turned back to her fire and looked closer, singing softly to the flames until they parted enough for her to see the structure of bone. Like the others, it was sturdy and unwilling to change, joints fused into blocky, unwieldy masses. For a moment, Kindred thought she wouldn't be able to find whatever it was that she'd touched, but it was there, waiting for her, a spur of bone extending into the heart of the structure. A strange growth too articulate and distinct to be accidental.

Running her finger over it again, Kindred listened to the shift in the song, from steady to slipping, from a constant buzz to – for just a breath – a melody fit for the fire. It took five times for Seraph to notice.

'What's that?' he asked, cocking his head to the side and looking around before noticing Kindred grinning at him.

'A clue,' she said, before waving him over and showing what she'd found.

Seraph cried big, wet tears as he laughed and hugged her.

'I knew it! I knew you were the one to help us! But keep going – keep going! What does it mean? What effect?'

Kindred was smiling, too, thrilled with the discovery, but she focused again as she turned back to the fire, singing her soft song, reaching it. The spur of bone was tough, unyielding even beyond what the rest of the slow-burning structure was. Her song rose, cutting into faster melodies, harder syllables, the beats thundering out of her, and Seraph was singing, too, his voice twining with hers, providing an intuitive counterpoint, buoying her efforts.

Kindred pushed and pried at the bone spur, feeling the wail of the fire's song as she did so, but it wouldn't budge. It held firm. She pulled at it, squeezed it, but it would not move – until she reached with her burned hand, pulling with all her strength. The golden shoots dotting her hand unfurled as one, swaying not in the movement of the fire but with the rhythm of Kindred's song, as if they, too, had joined the chorus, and it was as if Kindred had new strength – or at least new-found strength that had always been there. She grasped the bone spur and peeled it from the structure, feeling the pebbled mass in her hand as she removed it from the fire.

The hearthfire's song changed now, moving in a way it hadn't before, and Kindred understood as she had always understood – intuitively, abstractly. The piece of bone she held in her hand had long since turned to stone; it was the hearthfire's attempt to remove the sickness of time from itself, but it couldn't push it far enough away, couldn't contain the sickness. Instead, the death and decay of this long, slow rot had only been focused, had only further taken over the flames.

'Do you hear it?' Kindred asked, and Seraph could only nod. She felt a sharp spike of kinship then with Seraph. Never could she have explained the song of the hearthfire to another, save the Marchess. Not to Rhabdus or any of the other keepers from Arcadia – to them, this would have been impossible magic or strange insanity.

Even Scindapse, who some day might have enough experience to understand, was not yet there. But Seraph understood just as she did.

The fire had been trying to save itself. And thanks to Kindred, it finally had.

Kindred sang again to the fire and pushed her hands back in, feeling for those essential forces – push and pull, movement forward and back. And yes, she could feel them . . . almost.

'I think the Once-City might move now, Seraph,' Kindred whispered, speaking quietly. 'That bone spur was a lock, and once we find the others – because I think there might be others scattered throughout the fires – we should be able to guarantee some movement at least. They still need time to heal – sailing now would almost certainly cause too much damage to the fires and the City itself – but with some time, I think the Once-City might sail again.'

Seraph was nodding beside her, hearing the double of what she said in the fire's song.

'Oh, yes,' he said. 'Oh, yes.'

Soon enough, the day was over. Kindred and Seraph had spent the rest of the time seeking out more of the bone spurs, which was a task made much easier now that they knew what to listen for. They found four more and estimated another ten were still out there, waiting to be discovered. Seraph bid her a happy farewell – embracing her again once more – and then Kindred raced back to Cruel House to find Ragged Sarah, who had also recently returned from her own work with the callers above.

'The work is always the same,' Sarah said, taking a sip from the meager water rations at the table. They had diminished again, Kindred noticed. Perhaps a not-so-subtle message from the Hanged Council that they were in control. 'Rebuilding crow's nests and refitting calling-fire basins in them. I don't know how much more mindless drudgery I can take.'

Ragged Sarah ran callused hands over her shoulders, and Kindred moved to stand behind her, helping to massage away the pains.

'Oh, and the reef! Always monitoring the thistle pass.' Sarah shook her head. 'I've been having my birds watch the reef every day, and some – those who can fly further – pushing out toward Arcadia a bit, and there's no movement. And yet still, they tell me to call the birds, to monitor the pass, to record my findings, to do the whole damn thing again.

'Anyway, I'm just complaining, and I don't even have to deal with that fool Seraph all day,' Sarah said, her head lolling back in pleasure. 'How was it down among the hearthfires today?'

'It was amazing,' Kindred said, before leaping into an explanation of their work that day. She ended by saying, 'And Seraph's not so bad. I actually like him.'

Kindred didn't know why she felt so strange defending Seraph, but she did, and she could feel the tension building suddenly in Sarah's shoulders.

Slowly, Sarah detached herself from Kindred's massaging hands and turned to face her.

'Kindred, he's part of the council that forced you to spend time in a prison before giving you the gift of working for your freedom. He's exactly what's wrong with this place – wild and wonderful on the surface and crooked and rotten inside.'

'He's really not.' Kindred's voice rose to match the elevated tone in Sarah's. 'He's a good person. And he's actually trying to help this place and the people here without resorting to violence. You should have seen how excited he was today, Sarah! He was crying! He just wants to find a way to solve the Once-City's problems without any more violence.'

She thought of their work on the hearthfires below, of seeking to get the Once-City moving again without killing anyone, without waging war against Cantrev, without stealing bones or plants or resources or *anything*.

And she thought of him, seeing what had happened with Little Wing and telling no one, of offering her understanding when she feared none would, could.

'There are no good people here, Kindred.' Sarah kept using her name, speaking it sharply, air hissing against her teeth. 'There are only pirates, looking to steal. Maybe not bones or ships, but they all steal something. Everyone is a pirate, Kindred; everyone takes *something*. Especially the people here. They're no different than Cantrev. The only difference is, Cantrev is at least an asshole to your face.'

Kindred shook her head, closing her eyes and letting all of this fall away as much as she could.

'This is stupid. I don't know why we're fighting about this. And . . .' Kindred extended her hand, a gesture of peace. 'I have something to tell you, something more important than whether some old man is good or not.'

A tense moment passed in which she half-expected Ragged Sarah to stoke the fire of their fight, but she didn't; she nodded.

'Let's go to our room,' Kindred said after a moment, and they did, sneaking up to their mattresses, pulled together.

There, in the low light of that open-air room, Kindred told Sarah about the Gone Ways, about the boats, about what they might do.

Ragged Sarah stared at her in the silence, skepticism still written across her face, as if trying to decide if this whole thing was a joke.

'You're going to sail a ship made of braided grasses?' Ragged Sarah said. 'Wait. No, first you're going to steal a ship. And then sail a ship. A ship made out of prairie grasses. And sail it away from the Once-City?'

'Yes,' Kindred said, holding back the most important bit, at once desperate to speak it aloud and make it true, and yet terrified of what Ragged Sarah would say. If she was worried about the plan so far, then she would never sign on for the rest.

'What about the plan? The captain's plan?'

Kindred waited in the silence, wondering if she could say it. For so long, she had been part of a crew, and now?

'I'm not going with the captain. Scindapse can keep the fire on whatever vessel the captain and the others steal; she'll be able to do it. But I'm not going. I'm striking out on my own. Or, hopefully, not on my own, if you'll come with me.'

Kindred cringed at it, the silliness of what she was saying, but Ragged Sarah seemed to actually be considering it. Her brow squeezed into thought lines, and her eyes had gone soft, seeing Kindred's plan out there, out in the distance, something to be caught and held.

'It's possible. Maybe,' she said finally. 'But I don't know that a ship like that could make it back to Arcadia, much less the Mainland. And who knows what's further east in the Forever Sea. I suppose they have better maps here of the Eastern grasses than we did in Arcadia, but I don't know. My father used to tell me about a great port city out on the horizon, one where the magic of plants had spilled out into the buildings and streets and the very air itself, where the Supplicant Few went. But none of the outfitted ships sent out that way ever made it back.'

Kindred nodded, thinking of the Marchess's letter, seeing the Sea in her mind not as a plane to be traversed but a thin layer of the known hiding mysteries. This wasn't the looking-out that so many believed in, not the need for mystery elsewhere, the need to conquer mysteries on the horizon.

No.

This was a looking-in, Kindred knew, a finding of mystery within herself and in what she had known all her life. How strange and wonderful, she thought, to see mystery beneath her feet rather than in a world not her own.

'I'm not sailing toward Arcadia or the Mainland,' Kindred said. 'And I have no plans to sail east.'

'Where then?'

'Down,' Kindred said.

Sarah stared at her, confusion and uncertainty moving through her eyes and across the slant of her mouth. After a moment, she spoke.

'Kindred, I know losing the Marchess hurt. She – '

'I'm doing this,' Kindred said, feeling a strange thrill at the sound of her voice, which rang out stronger than she had ever heard it. 'This is where my wind is blowing, and I have to let it take me.'

She *was* doing this, and that gave every thought weight and significance in a way none ever had before. Her feet were already on the path; all that remained was the stepping.

'I've been paying attention in my work with Seraph, and I

think I can build a fire to control a dive without too many bones. There's enough of the plants I'll need in Seraph's stores to do it, and even if he won't give them to me, I'll just take them.' *Everyone is a pirate*, Sarah had said, and apparently, she was right. 'I can make this work; I know it.'

Kindred waited for a moment, waiting to say the thing that was hardest.

'And even if you won't come with me, I'm going to do this.' A breath. 'But I still hope you will.'

Silence fell between them, and Kindred watched Ragged Sarah's eyes, noticing again how green they were, how much they called to mind the forever of the Sea. Kindred's fear was gone, and in its place she found a strange peace. This was her path, and though it would be difficult and treacherous and filled with unknowns, it was hers, and that made all the difference.

Listen for me in the grasses and listen for me below.

She felt closer to her grandmother now than she ever had. She remembered all of those days spent sailing their tiny path of the Forever Sea, crewing her grandmother's ship, listening to her give orders, her smile as big as the world when it appeared, her frown like the most terrible storm, capable of rending sails and slashing hopes.

And yet Kindred thought the image of her grandmother in the Forest, the one she had nearly left the path for – this was the picture she held in her mind, as if somehow seeing her grandmother underneath it all, floating in darkness and yet smiling just a little, as if that were somehow truer to who the Marchess had always been.

'You're absolutely serious, aren't you?' Ragged Sarah asked, and Kindred nodded. She really was.

Sarah squinted at her before breaking into one of her smiles that made Kindred feel it in the soles of her feet.

'Then fuck it. I'm going, too.'

Before Sarah could say anything else, before she could pull Kindred into an embrace or take the lead some other way, Kindred moved forward and kissed her, hard, her lips dry and Sarah's lips dry and yet who cared?

'When? When should we go?' Kindred asked, caught in the web of her excitement.

'I . . .' Sarah said, trailing off. 'I just need some time to get ready. But soon. We'll tell the captain at least before we go, right?'

'Absolutely,' Kindred said.

They were going, the two of them, going to find a new forever. Soon.

And so, life began to take a strange and new shape for Kindred. She stole what time she could around her work with Seraph to spend time among the grass boats, sketching them out so Sarah could see how they worked. She grew comfortable in the bare space inside the grassy shells, grew familiar with the way the sails extended and folded up when she pulled on this grass rope or that one.

During the day, she would follow Seraph around, working on a hearthfire together or working in parallel on two near each other. Seraph would talk, and Kindred would half-listen, her thoughts mostly on her boat, on the Sea, on the terrifying thrill of what was to come.

Kindred was surprised to see other members of the Hanged Council frequenting the Gone Ways. As the days passed, she saw all of them, some even appearing a few times a day, passing through the space and walking among the guards, who seemed to perpetually fulfill the role of simply existing.

Seraph had told her once that they needed this many guards to protect the hearthfires and the water stores.

The Word was the most common presence down there, but no matter how hard she tried to follow their movements, Kindred was never able to see exactly where they moved through the plant wall.

And then there were the shrieks, which continued, one or two a day, always frightening.

'What are the other levels below this one like? The fragments, I mean, the ones you mentioned before,' Kindred asked one day as they worked.

Seraph tipped his head from side to side, thinking.

'I've only ever seen a tiny bit. No one really goes down there anymore,' he said. 'The whole thing is just rough fragments slowly falling away into the Sea.'

'But what were they used for? Back when they were whole, I mean.'

'Homes, I think, though of course, that was when our population was much greater. Probably food collection, too – easier to capture bugs and harvest plants when you're that far down, I suspect.'

He spoke without much conviction, and it was clear he didn't find the question particularly interesting.

When Kindred had asked him where the steps were, he had shrugged and gestured vaguely toward one of the areas of the seemingly monolithic wall of prairie plants.

But Kindred had learned something about monoliths in the days since her grandmother disappeared.

'The prairie holds worlds,' she whispered to herself one day, her hand working deep in the sludgy viscosity of a hearthfire, her eyes tracking The Word and Ebb-La-Kem as they walked together among the guards, offering a few words here or there.

But Kindred lost track of them as they wandered farther and farther out. She was kneeling beside the hearthfire, trying to peer between the legs of the guards standing nearby, all of them pointless, she thought. Obstructions. Distractions.

'Good! I think we're making real progress,' Seraph said, cutting into her stultifying fear. Kindred took the opportunity to stand and look after the councillors, but they were already gone into whatever back room existed. Or perhaps they had taken the stairs, wherever they were, and even now stood farther below the Sea than Kindred and Seraph.

'It's getting late,' Seraph said, 'but why don't we squeeze just a few more in. I have some new theories about tensile strength in aged grass and thrice-root twists that may prove fruitful for us. And you only have a half-span left here! I need to get all the help from you I can while you're still here!'

The thought was a jarring one for Kindred. Amid all the twisting plans: the captain's, the speculations about the council's, and her own, Kindred had forgotten about their sham deal – fifty days of work and the reward of a ship, fully stocked, ready to make the long voyage to the Mainland.

Seraph, she realized, must be the only one on the council who actually believed that fifty-day nonsense, the only one innocent and trusting enough to think such a thing would happen, was ever going to happen.

She laughed along with Seraph and set about the work but

without any real focus. Instead, she thought of plans coming to fruition, of a race in which only one could win.

'There's still no sign of a mounting attack,' Ragged Sarah said one night, the two of them flopped next to each other in bed.

Kindred frowned, staring down at the spare strands of grass she was braiding and rebraiding. She enjoyed the feel of weaving the blades together, but it was also good practice for her healing hand, good training to return some of its nimbleness and strength.

'None?' Kindred asked.

'None. A raiding party sailing on one of The Word's ships just returned yesterday. Captain Norn was talking with Ebb-La-Kem and Morrow Laze and saying something about how they were able to get within visible distance of Arcadia. No sign of a growing navy, apparently. No signs of Cantrev's next attack.'

'That can't be,' Kindred said, thinking back to Cantrev's slick smile, his calculating eyes. 'He wouldn't let this go.'

Ragged Sarah shrugged and snuggled in to Kindred, burrowing her face into the curve of Kindred's neck.

'Captain Norn said, if anything, there seemed to be fewer ships than ever at port. He could only count three. Ebb-La-Kem all but claimed victory. He thinks that last attack was everything Cantrev had.'

'Idiocy,' Kindred said, shaking her head.

Ragged Sarah laughed.

'Morrow Laze said the exact same thing. Called them all a pack of idiots and walked away to continue preparing defenses.'

Kindred nodded and the two of them fell again into a comfortable silence.

'Funny thing is,' Sarah said after a time, picking up the conversation, 'I'm not sure who I'd like to win if another fight does happen.'

Kindred nodded but didn't respond.

Images of those people and places she had come to know – both in the Once-City and on Arcadia – rose in her mind.

Mick, his wheezing and scheming and good heart.

The Forest, the kindred strangeness of it.

Legate, his broad shoulders taking on the weight of resisting Cantrev at home.

Ragged Sarah, who had somehow become Kindred's person on the way to the Once-City.

Yllstra, walking along the paths in the ever-encroaching Forest.

Red Alay and the other crew members of *Revenger*, keeping the Marchess's memory alive with their every breath.

'I'm not sure either,' Kindred finally said, working at the grass in her hands.

After another moment of silence, Kindred spoke, venturing into what had been worrying her.

'Maybe it's time to think about leaving.' After the excitement of telling Sarah and their agreement to go, they hadn't talked much about it, not in any real way. Sarah looked at Kindred's sketches, and they talked about stealing away some food and water rations, but when Kindred pushed Sarah to think about a day to leave, the conversations always seemed to die away.

Sarah was too tired to talk. Or too busy. Or she needed to really think about it.

'Maybe,' Sarah said, her breath hot on Kindred's neck.

'You still want to, don't you?' Kindred asked, voice small.

'I . . .' Sarah said. She pushed herself up on one elbow and looked down at Kindred. 'I do, Kindred. I'm just – scared. What if something goes wrong? What if you can't get the hearthfire to burn right in the boat and we drop to the bottom and die? What if we don't find anything down there? Or what if we find something terrible?

'I know,' she said, holding up a hand against Kindred's protestations. 'Seraph told you about the bits of evidence that there are people down there, and you have your intuition that the Marchess is still alive down there.

'It's just *thin*, Kindred. It's not much to go on, and I still don't really understand what you want down there, and I don't know if we're going to be okay. You want to take this leap, but you don't even know if there's anything to catch you.'

'Are you saying no?' Kindred asked. Everything Sarah had said, all of her doubts, hurt, not because Kindred felt some betrayal in them, but because they were the doubts that reached for her in the quiet moments, in the moments when her confidence flagged and a more reasonable, more rational part of her wondered if any of this was a good idea.

'No, I'm not saying that,' Sarah said, though she didn't look up to meet Kindred's eyes. 'I'm just saying I want to think about it more. And I want to understand why you're so set on going below.'

Kindred searched for the words, for the reasoning, but it was late, and she was tired, and she had lost the lift of Sarah's confidence.

'I just . . .' she began, closing her eyes and thinking of her grandmother's letter. 'The Sea is dying, and all anyone can do up here is squabble after power. I want to leave this place behind. Maybe I won't find the Marchess down there, but I have to try. And maybe I won't figure out what's been happening to the Sea, but I have to try.

'Boats have never been my home, Sarah, not really.' She opened her eyes and looked into Sarah's, falling into the green there. 'The Sea has been my home, the wind and the grasses and the way it's always moving in some dance that seems too profound and too beautiful for this world. If there are worlds below, and some answer to this sickness can be found in them, I want to be there. And if no answer can be found, I want to be there anyway.'

Kindred rolled over onto her side.

'I can't explain it better than that. I don't know why I'm pulled into the unknown, but I am.'

24

THE prairie burned in the sunlight of early morning.

Expanding out from where Kindred stood on the root dock, the prairie became itself in that early morning light, the sun peeking over a horizon onto a clear day. It was as if every bloom, every leaf, every strand of green and red and yellow and purple hoped to catch the sunlight as it streamed by, each plant lifting seeking fingers high. Feather grass moved in a gentle sway of impossibly fine yellow-white strands caught in the wind; plants Kindred had not even known existed before her time in the Once-City jigged and bobbed and danced their joy to that early morning. She whispered their names like a prairie litany, calling to the Sea in names at once true and false, names that somehow both captured and freed the prairie. On Kindred's face, the sun and wind played, healing the worry and pain of her conversation with Ragged Sarah the night before.

Kindred had woken before Sarah and sneaked out, not wanting to face the fallout.

'Prairie palimpsest. Wyldwort. Meadow sweet. Queen of the

prairie. Rachel's joy. Lousewort. Blue-eyed grass.'

On and on the names spilled out of Kindred as she watched the prairie unfold into a sheet of light and flame, creased and riffled by the wind's touch. This was the Forever Sea at its truest – baronies of color and texture and growth in every square length, an explosion of difference and sameness all bending in the same breeze, all joying in the same sun. Even the patches fallen to the Greys were glorified in this light, burnished and brightened.

Kindred breathed in the prairie air, letting it expand in her lungs and still her spirit. Seraph's excitement in recent days had reached a peak, and he had been starting their work days earlier and earlier, but this – cool, pure wind stirring in her lungs; a prairie Sea aflame with light – was enough to calm her.

They moved through the fleet, checking and correcting as they went, twisting bone and plant to keep hearthfires burning or ready to be lit.

As they walked around the trunk, Kindred saw the dew-skimmers coming in, their long, thin hulls cutting lines in the fiery Sea. One by one the boats docked, and burly Once-City pirates carried barrels of freshly skimmed dew into the Once-City. Kindred watched as they moved, trying to count the barrels and translate that number to water rations, but she eventually lost track. Still, she thought, it wasn't enough. Not nearly enough.

She and Seraph began moving through the defender boats on this side and then through the dew-skimmers. They had just a few recently emptied boats left when another dew-skimmer cut into port. It was *The Quisling*, Kindred saw. She'd been spending so much time aboard these vessels that they had begun to look familiar.

It was the last vessel to come in, and she worked on the other

hearthfires while the crew moved back into the Once-City.
Kindred waved at them as they moved by, but none returned her
greeting, burdened as they were with various sacks and bags of
supplies. Their hoods pulled up against the sun's early light, she
couldn't even make out most of them.

'Can you get *The Quisling*'s blaze?' Seraph called over from
where he huddled on the deck of another skimmer. 'And then we
can head down to the Gone Ways.'

Kindred nodded and hopped aboard *The Quisling*, her eyes on
the remnants of light playing across the plane of the prairie. The
sun had moved high enough that most of the fire was gone, but
bits remained, and Kindred let her mind wander.

She had nearly completed her work on the hearthfire when
she noticed it.

The build was strange to her at first, orderly and compact, even
and linear. No grasses or plants wound through the fire – only the
clean white of bones angled around and against one another. She
had begun to teach the hearthfire keepers of the Once-City how
to better manage their fires, but none of them had reached the
point of building a fire like this.

The clean white of bones, Kindred repeated to herself, cocking
her head to the side. Clean white bones meant *fresh* bones.

She looked again at the hearthfire, studying the order of it.
Something was off there. Something she couldn't quite grasp. The
earliness of the morning and the silence in which they worked
had dulled Kindred's mind, allowing it to wander, and it was
taking effort to pull herself back to the present.

All in a rush she saw.

The Quisling coming in late.

Crew members moving quickly, ignoring her greeting.

A hearthfire built with new bones, orderly and even.

No reports of Cantrev from the west.

She stood quickly and rushed belowdecks. Water barrels, each one full or mostly so, tied up and ready to be brought in. Beside them, half-filled bags of sand leaned against one another, and more sand spilled out around them. On the ground she saw a few large leaves covered in scrawled diagrams. Kindred leaned in and saw they were drawings of the Once-City, with various points labeled. On one in particular, arrows had been drawn to show the path through Wisdom, the path to the Gone Ways.

And there, back behind the water barrels and up against the hull, puddled in shadow and blood, were the bodies of *The Quisling*'s crew, evidence that some of them had been tortured, broken, perhaps for exactly the information in those drawings. Among them, Kindred could see Talent, her body contorted and bloodied.

But why impersonate the crew? What could eight or nine do in the Once-City? Where had they gone?

She ran back up to the deck, leapt from the ship, and rushed to where Seraph knelt beside the hearthfire.

'The attack has begun,' she said, breathless, her mind racing with the possibilities. 'Seraph, Cantrev's attack has begun. The crew of *The Quisling*, they're dead.'

'What?' Seraph said. 'I just saw them, didn't I?'

'That wasn't the crew!' Kindred shouted, but Seraph was looking past her, his eyes focusing on beyond, out into the harbor, to the east. Kindred turned and gasped.

Sails crowded the Sea, approaching at pace, emerging out of the fiery glare of the sun's ascending rays.

Kindred raced inside with Seraph close behind, moving through the archway and down the stairs fast enough that she nearly tripped. Down to the first level, where the City still slept. Kindred wondered why no one was awake, why no sentries had seen the attack, how she and Seraph could be the only two people aware of what was going on.

But they all thought Cantrev would come from the west, through the pass in the thorn reef. It would take spans to sail around it, to find another way in.

Spans he'd had.

Kindred stepped off onto the first level and was suddenly unsure of what to do.

'The Hanged Council's chambers!' Seraph shouted from behind her, winded by that short run. 'I'll begin the tolling!'

And Kindred took off.

As she arrived, she saw five or six wardens walking out the front door, probably just given their assignments for the day, and Kindred felt some sort of relief that Barque was one of them.

'Barque!' she shouted, her lungs pained, no longer moved by the same easy, steady in and out. 'Cantrev's attack. It's happening. Now. He has people in the City. Eight or nine. Maybe more. Dressed like dew-skimmers. Ships on the horizon.'

Barque stared his confusion at her, the buds decorating his skin tightly furled today. The other wardens he was with laughed at Kindred.

'Our callers scouted last night and found no collections of

ships between here and Arcadia,' he said after a moment, his voice gruff, dismissive.

'No,' Kindred said, coughing out the word. 'He's not coming from the west.'

The guards continued to laugh, and Barque continued to simply stare at her, anger and annoyance beginning to move over his face.

'The crew of *The Quisling* is dead! The attack is happening now!'

'You're lying,' Barque said, but something in Kindred's voice had finally caught him.

Seraph finally did his part, and that great tolling rolled again – the same sound Kindred had heard during the last attack – echoing through the City, filling the entirety of the space.

As the City came to life around them, and as wardens and sailors and citizens raced about, shouting orders, Barque grabbed hold of Kindred, his eyes wild, the buds on his skin beginning to flutter open.

'What did you do?' he asked, his voice hard, his eyes searching her face. 'How did you do it?'

Kindred recoiled as if she'd been slapped.

'What? What are you talking about?'

'Did you sneak them in? Or send messages to Cantrev somehow? I know it was you, you and your old crew. All that fucking plotting you've been doing. I knew you were up to something. Now, how did you do it?' He was shouting by the end, his voice rising above the tumult around them.

The buds on his face and arms opened now, blue limned by white, and Kindred found their perfume intoxicating. She'd never been this close to Barque when the flowers were open, and she found herself pulled in by the smell, and even with the chaos, even with the realization of the impending attack, it took everything she had to stay sane and present.

'I didn't do this,' she shouted back. 'Why would I come and tell you about it if I had? How would I even communicate with them?'

'I don't know!' Barque shouted back. 'I don't know how your mind works! But I know you did this. Somehow, you and the other Arcadians have fucked us all over.'

Kindred ground her teeth, but she saw it was pointless. Barque's eyes were mad, and there would be no convincing him.

And if he thought her so guilty, she didn't have long to act.

She looked around him, angling her body away from his, pulling at the grip of his hands on her arms. Boots were all she could see, a wave of them moving around her, people fleeing the fight or running to it.

Barque's anger rolled off of him in waves, pulsing through his hands, creating a tide of the aroma coming from his flowers. He was frantic, out of his mind.

Stillness, Kindred thought. She breathed, feeling the prairie wind moving through her again, in and out, and with every bit of strength she had, she brought her knee up between his legs at the same time that she rammed her head straight into his face. She was aiming for his nose, hoping to break it or at least hit it hard enough to get him to release her.

Instead, she felt something soft and realized she had hit the flower blooming just below his eye.

Barque roared in pain, and suddenly he was off of her, his hands gone, and as Kindred rose, she saw him not clutching at his groin but rolling about on the ground, his hands to his face, to the wrecked flower now pasted limply to his cheek.

But Kindred couldn't spare the time for him, and she raced off, not up to the battle but to Cruel House, hoping to catch the crew there, to warn them of the folly of their plan.

'Kindred!'

She felt her breath catch and hitch in her chest as Ragged Sarah ran toward her from the doorway of Cruel House. Kindred wrapped her in an embrace and realized how worried she'd been about Sarah, how anxious she'd been for her safety without even realizing it. Here, with Sarah in her arms, things were better. Not good, but better.

'What's going on?' Sarah asked. 'Cantrev? How could he get past the birds?'

'He came from the east.'

Sarah shook her head.

'That asshole. Of course he did.'

'Is everyone else inside?' Kindred asked, moving toward the door, but Sarah stopped her.

'No, they all went up except Scindapse. The captain got pulled up by Ebb-La-Kem, and Quixa and Cora went up, too. They all think the plan is going to work.'

'Dammit,' Kindred said, slapping her hand against her leg. She turned back to Ragged Sarah. 'We have to go for it. There are too many ships out there, Sarah. No one is going to win this battle. We have to go for it.'

'But you just said Cantrev's coming from the east. We won't be able to steal one of the ships, especially not if Cantrev's fleet is what you're saying it is. They'll need every available vessel.'

'I'm not talking about that plan,' Kindred said, shaking her head.

Ragged Sarah frowned, and then, a moment later, recognition shot across her face.

'Kindred . . .' Sarah began.

'I'm going,' Kindred said. 'I'm sailing it today.'

Sarah let out a breath and then said, very quietly, 'To the unknown?'

And Kindred found she loved her all the more in that moment. She'd never met anyone who so easily moved with changes in the wind.

'What do we do?' Sarah asked.

Kindred thought for a moment.

'We need to get everyone else. I never told them about our plan; I thought we would have more time. But we can't just let them die here, either from Cantrev's attack or from some foolhardy plan. I'll get Scindapse; you go get the captain and the others. Meet at the stairs. We should be able to fit.'

'Should?' Sarah said, skeptical, but she was smiling, and Kindred felt confidence buoy her up.

'Aye, should. See you soon.' Kindred leaned in to kiss Sarah, wishing it could last longer and knowing it couldn't.

'Soon,' Sarah said, and then she was gone, one of many running for hope and sanity in the chaos.

Inside Cruel House, Kindred found Scindapse sitting up on her mattress.

'What's going on?' Scindapse asked, her voice small, so young.

'Cantrev's attack,' Kindred said. 'We have to go.'

'Go where? What's happening, Kindred?' Scindapse shrunk back on her mattress.

Kindred thought back to the curious, energetic girl who had taken to keeping the fire, who had joyed at finding her place among the crew. So like Kindred had been. Still held rapt by the delicate machine of this surface world.

Kindred did her best to speak as Captain Caraway did, mimicking the power and authority in the captain's voice.

'Get up, Scindapse. The crew needs you, and so do I. Get up.'

It was as if a different person had spoken, one who had not spent her life merely part of a crew, one who had not spent her life in service but instead in power.

Scindapse moved, nodding her head. She followed Kindred down the stairs and out of Cruel House, and then they were running through Breach, dodging around citizens. Above, Kindred could hear the beginnings of the battle. She could feel the sear and crack of magic, the pull of hearthfires burning, of casting fires releasing huge amounts of magical power – all of it shivered through her bones, but she ignored the call and continued to move.

As they ran, Kindred shouted bits of explanation back to Scindapse.

'Have you figured anything out with the hearthfires? Can the Once-City move away yet?' Scindapse asked.

'Not without major structural damage,' Kindred called.

As they ran, Kindred was surprised to find fewer people out in the streets than she had expected. It was still chaotic, but this first level of the Once-City had the feeling of watchful silence, waiting for the victor to emerge. Waiting to see if it would survive this battle or sink to the dark deeps.

'If we can't steal one of the boats, what are we going to do?'

shouted Scindapse as they came into view of the staircase, where Kindred saw the others already waiting.

But Kindred didn't hear her, not really.

Horror moved through her, quick and fast, a lightning strike of realization.

Where had the fake crew of *The Quisling* gone? They had docked with enough ease that Kindred assumed they knew something of the Once-City, and they wouldn't go for anything on the first level, where they were sure to be caught and killed before doing much damage. And there was nothing to steal or destroy on the second level.

'No no no,' Kindred whispered. It was martyrs again, she saw. Always fucking martyrs, a great contest to see whose life could be used for the greatest impact, the most efficient and effective extinguishing of a flame.

Half-filled bags of sand. Kindred knew this game, had seen it already.

They were going to the Gone Ways. They were going to do to the Once-City precisely what the pirates had done to Cantrev's vessels during that first battle.

A gang of assassins striking at the heart of the Once-City, going to extinguish its hearthfires and pull it down to the deeps.

'They're going to sink it,' Kindred whispered.

'Kindred, what – ' Captain Caraway said as Kindred and Scindapse approached. They were all there: Cora the Wraith, carrying an already-bloodied axe; Long Quixa, with a stout shield covering one arm; Ragged Sarah, wielding two long knives; and Captain Caraway, sword in hand, alert and ready.

'We have to go! Follow me and stay close!' Kindred shouted, as she plunged down and down, past the Forest and its odd stillness, seemingly untouched by the battle being fought above.

She looked back, just once, suddenly afraid that captain and crew would not have followed her, that she had lost or broken too much of their trust. But they were there, flying down the steps behind her.

Down on the third level, she stepped off and plunged into the maze of small buildings, happy that she'd been given a few span to memorize the path to get down to the Gone Ways.

She moved through darkness with speed, and at the entrance to the Gone Ways, she found the plaited grass door broken apart and a few guards on the ground dead, killed quickly, efficiently. Cantrev's killers moved with purpose.

'I think there are eight or nine,' she said, turning to the others. 'The hearthfires are down here, and I think Cantrev's people are coming to put them out. But back beyond them, I have a ship that can take us out of here. It won't look like much, I know, but . . .'

'Kindred,' Captain Caraway said. 'We need to move.'

Kindred nodded, and pushed through the doorway and down the stairs, unsure of what they would find. Had all of those guards who normally occupied the Gone Ways rushed up at the sound of the central column tolling?

Or did some stay? Was there a perpetual guard down there?

Down they walked, down and down, and then they were at the bottom of the staircase.

This door had not been torn apart; the plaited grass remained intact, and Kindred peered through the sliver between the slightly open door and the frame.

A small skirmish filled the space with sound and movement. Kindred counted at least eight soldiers, still wearing their stolen dew-skimmer uniforms, their blades out and flashing in the light.

Against them, desperately trying to hold their ground, four Once-City guards fought, defending one another and moving as a unit. They were good but outnumbered and unprepared, and Kindred saw the fight would not last much longer.

Around them, the hearthfires burned in sludgy grey – or most of them did. Kindred saw a few of the fires had already been extinguished, reduced to tortured piles of bone and plant braids choked with sand.

'Okay, I think we can skirt around the battle and . . .'

Kindred trailed off, about to move through the door, but stopped when another figure entered the fray, and Kindred felt the air rush out of her as if she'd been punched in the stomach.

Little Wing leapt into the battle, her robes in tatters, her once-powerful frame now angular and taut, muscle evaporated into stark lines and emptiness.

Little Wing, former quartermaster of *The Errant*.

Little Wing, Kindred's ghost haunting her dreams.

25

KINDRED watched, knowing she should move, knowing she *had* to move, but suddenly unable to think anything other than *Little Wing is here.*

'Kindred?' Sarah whispered.

The former quartermaster moved in battle as if she were born for it. She carried a naked blade in each hand, and they sang through the air as she parried and blocked and cut. As she had always been, Little Wing was a force all her own, though Kindred noticed she sang no song during this fight. She moved her body to no melody, no rhythm.

'Kindred!' someone, Cora or Quixa or the captain, said.

'Move, Kindred,' she whispered to herself. '*Move.*'

She slipped the door open and moved, keeping an eye on the battle, edging immediately to the right, away from the battle. She hugged close to the wall, gesturing for the others to do the same, and they began creeping along, moving as quickly as they could without drawing attention.

And as they did, the Once-City guards steadily lost ground,

taking injuries as they parried and thrust slower and slower.

'Is that Little Wing?' Captain Caraway hissed from beside Kindred, her eye locked on the battle. 'What's she doing?'

The battle would soon be lost, and Kindred cast about for anything that might help.

For so long, she had operated at the periphery of action as the hearthfire keeper – working the hearthfire in the center of a ship while her crew fought or sailed or harvested, singing for others, always the heart and so rarely the hand.

'Come on,' Kindred said to the others. 'I need the supplies for the boat's hearthfire.' She rushed along the wall, toward Seraph's collection of bones and plants. She flicked her eyes over the plants, fear and panic making her hands shake, her breath come in labored stitches.

'Bluestem,' she whispered, seeing the blue-red stalks, thinking of the way the casters could shape it into a shield. But that was on a working casting fire – not the sludgy grey these had become. And it was with an experienced caster.

'Let's go, Kindred,' Cora whispered from where she hid behind the storage containers holding the hearthfire supplies. 'That battle isn't going to last much longer.'

'Prairie smoke. Echinacea. Thrice-root.' On and on she moved through the plants, ignoring the growing worry in those around her. Never having done more than imagining taking the boat out, than theorizing how the hearthfire might burn – *what* it might burn – she had no idea now what she might need.

So, she filled her pockets with everything she could think of, plants she had known her whole life and plants she had only recently met.

Behind her, the sounds of battle, bright and sharp, and of dying, abrupt and awful, filled the space.

She was nearly at the end of the plants when one caught her eye, thin green stalks ending in perfect white flowers.

'Feverfew . . .' she mumbled, memory reaching back through the fog of this day to something – *something* – Seraph had said.

But it was too far, and the battle behind her was too near. She scooped up a handful and dropped it in a pocket.

And finally, she grabbed a few smaller bones and one of the longer leg bones in the collection, a hefty thing that looked and felt like a club. It was disrespectful, a bastardization of purpose and meaning and value and everything else. But it would have to do.

Kindred turned to the battle.

Little Wing and the other Arcadians fought the Once-City guards, their battles spread out across the level into small skirmishes. Bodies littered the walkways between hearthfires, Arcadians and citizens mixed together, the same in death.

'The boats are just there,' Kindred said, pointing. They would have to cross some open area to reach them, but it was the only way.

'Sorry, not those big grass messes, right?' Cora said, her voice rising in disbelief. 'We're not escaping this pirate city on half-formed grass sculptures, are we?'

'Shut up, Cora,' Sarah hissed.

'They're not all half-done,' Kindred said. 'But . . . yes, our boat is made of grass.'

'Oh, good,' Cora said. 'We're all going to die.'

'Enough, Cora,' Captain Caraway said, her eye still trained on Little Wing.

'Get ready to run for it,' Kindred said, steeling herself against the fear. She breathed for just a moment – *In the prairie wind, out the prairie wind* – and then she moved, a heart become a hand.

'Go,' she whispered. And they went.

Her feet felt light beneath her as she pelted along paths she had been walking for many days, past fires she had begun to know as friends. The others took parallel paths, all racing for the hopeful green on the other side.

She ran, feeling the air change as she neared a skirmish. One Arcadian, his back to Kindred, filled the air before him with sword cuts, pushing back the two citizens who looked for any way in. Behind them, one of the larger hearthfires, waiting, hungry.

As she approached, Kindred heard the Arcadian's laughter, high and haughty, and Kindred was reminded of Cantrev, his self-satisfied smirk, his chortle as the Trade behind him burned.

Kindred cut her own swath through the air, the bone in her hand a flashing arc of white for just a moment before it collided with the man's head, shattering at the end with a bright *snap*.

The man dropped, slack and empty, to the ground.

One of the citizens, a woman Kindred had seen before in the Gone Ways, nodded her thanks.

The other, though, was looking over Kindred's shoulder, eyes wide.

Kindred turned and immediately dropped to the ground, falling under the cut of the blade from one of the two Arcadians who had come to join the fight. The bone in her hand, almost as long as her arm and fractured to a wicked point at the end, skittered away as she fell, and Kindred could only scuttle back, crawling awkwardly but desperately needing to *move*.

The woman pursued, a vicious smile on her face, and it took

a moment for Kindred to realize it was Rhabdus. She carried two swords, like Little Wing, and they moved in her hands as if they belonged there. A laugh brimmed up from her chest, wicked and gleeful.

'Oh, I hoped for this moment, girl. Hoped and prayed for it.' She sliced at the air, cutting closer and closer to Kindred.

The other Arcadian warrior engaged the two citizens, pressing in far enough to effectively cut them off from Kindred. And beyond, Kindred saw her friends caught up, too, tangled in this petty, sprawling, all-consuming conflict. The captain's blade flashed into a fight, and Ragged Sarah's shouts echoed above the battle sounds.

Back and back Kindred moved, crawling and scampering as fast as she could, but she tripped and fell into a sprawl.

'This was always where your wild ways would lead you,' Rhabdus said, looking down at Kindred with a sneer. 'The end of a blade. You were always a traitor, girl – I just saw it before everyone else.'

Rhabdus closed, her swords gleaming in the low light, and Kindred pushed herself back one more time, every bit of strength she had just to fall back a bit farther. Her arms and legs splayed in exhaustion as she hit the hard floor, and one hand fell into a hearthfire.

As if by instinct, Kindred began to sing, letting the language of the hearthfire spill out of her in breaths short and pained. The sluggish grey of the flames answered, flexing around her hand in a kind of hello, viscous and oily.

Rise, Kindred, pleaded, begged. *Rise and consume this place.*

'Die, girl,' Rhabdus said, and Kindred heard her blades cutting through the air.

Rise, Kindred sang, feeling the fire moving about her hand.

And it did.

Grey flames like grease and oil and sand, hot and thick, flared from the hearthfire basin, not the mighty reach of a clean blaze on a fresh ship but instead the hoary grasp of a hearthfire too old, too tired to burn in colors beyond the grey of an overcast day. The flames did not consume the woman, did not even reach her – instead, they formed a thick shield, a protective layer over Kindred that lasted just a moment, but long enough to startle Rhabdus and pause her sword cut.

Long enough for Kindred to reach into the heart of the blaze and grab a shard of bone, long ago grown hard in the slow death of the fire.

Kindred rose through the vanishing trails of grey flame disappearing from the air like veins emptying of blood. With a shout, her voice still shaping the language of the hearthfire – a language Rhabdus would never understand – Kindred drove the bone into Rhabdus's chest, hard and fast. She felt it break inside, shattering into pieces, but the work was done.

Rhabdus fell, her swords angling without purpose through the air around her. One cut a line along Kindred's arm, eliciting a hiss, but Rhabdus was dead, and her swords fell next to her, still.

Next to Kindred, the hearthfire returned to its usual size, though it had begun to shudder and quake, the movements subtle but clear. Kindred had asked much of it, and its surge of power was taking a toll.

Kindred knelt next to it, listening for any change to its quiet song, and it was only then that she heard the shouting.

It was Little Wing and Captain Caraway, their blades clashing together over and over again, their words lashing out.

'You didn't believe in us, Jane!'

'You didn't trust me!'

'I gave my life to our ship and to you!'

'We were going to be okay!'

Accusations like whips cracked the air between them. It was the only battle remaining; the others had dispatched the remaining Arcadians, but though they circled Captain Caraway and Little Wing, there was no way to interfere and help. The fighting was too fierce.

A great shriek from one of the walls broke the hypnotic movement of the fight, and they all turned to see one of the false walls that Kindred had noticed before suddenly fall away, torn back to reveal a huge open space.

And there, coiled and flicking its muzzled, roped head back and forth, was a wyrm.

It was a prisoner, surrounded by citizens holding it captive. At first, Kindred thought they had been caught by the vines growing from the wyrm's body, but then she saw the truth – they were ropes, tied around the beast and coming off it in every direction, each one held by a citizen. Slightly smaller than the one that had nearly destroyed *The Errant*, the wyrm was still far bigger than anything inside should be. Its white, mottled skin was sallow and sickly in the light of the Gone Ways, and its eyes rolled and glared madly.

Some of its arms, Kindred could see, had been chopped away to make space for the ropes – all of them braided grass – that held it. Others, though, were free and clawed at the air and the ground, seeking anything to gain some control.

It looked sick. And angry.

Its captors were moving forward, pulling it forth from the space it had occupied – based on the state of it – for some time.

And walking before it, twin smiles lighting up twin faces, was The Word.

'A *slave returned to seek her own revenge*.' They moved forward, but Kindred and the others were too shocked to do anything. One and all, they stared at The Word.

And one and all, they stared at the wyrm, pulled forward bit by bit into the central area of the Gone Ways.

'Aye,' Little Wing said, recovering enough to spit and sneer at The Word. 'Me and every bit of the Arcadian fleet have come back to end you and everyone here. Shame you couldn't kill me when you had the chance.'

She took advantage of the moment and rammed her shoulder into Captain Caraway, sending her sprawling, before turning to The Word.

She advanced on them, undaunted even then, a fire unquenched, unquenchable. A blade in either hand, Little Wing advanced.

But The Word did not ready their weapons – him a tall, carved staff, her a great hammer carried as if it weighed nothing at all. They did not signal any of their guards to attack or defend or move.

They did not advance on Little Wing or shrink back.

Instead, they laughed.

It was a sickly, peeling laugh, discordant and cacophonous, two voices near enough to harmony to make Kindred long for it and far enough away from it to make her feel ill. It was wrong, that laugh, and even Little Wing stopped as she heard it.

'*Bravado in a fool is twice as sweet. Your strength is **ours**,*' they said, biting down on the word with savage glee. '*A tool you have become.*'

'What?' Kindred asked, stepping forward and feeling a slight shock of fear as The Word turned their gaze onto her. 'You want

Arcadia to destroy the Once-City? What are you talking about?'

That laugh again, high and wrong.

And this time, when The Word spoke, they did not do so in that singsong way, voices rubbing together. Instead, they traded words, one for him, one for her, and so on, each one like a great rock breaking, a sound to make teeth grind together and bones shift uncomfortably. In voices unlike any Kindred had heard from them, they said.

'We. Let. Her. Go.'

Silence.

'We. Wanted. Cantrev's. Attack.'

Silence.

'The. Whole. Fleet.'

Silence.

'Arcadia. Its. Water. Undefended.'

Tremors shook through the Once-City, and Kindred saw the hearthfires, so staid and unchanging until then, *shift*. Some grew, their flames reaching viscous hands toward the ceiling and the sky beyond it; others dropped low and wide, the grey grounding out to the absolute black of a starless night.

Kindred knew that movement, that shift of light and heat, but it couldn't be. It was the dance of a hearthfire being pushed, of a blaze offering speed to a ship.

But that *couldn't* be.

The tremors rumbled through the Gone Ways, and Kindred saw the barrels holding the water stores topple and fall, rolling about, spilling . . . nothing. No water splashed out as more and more of the barrels jostled about and fell over.

The water stores were empty.

And suddenly Kindred understood, felt the threads snap together in her mind, each one part of a larger, more sinister whole.

The Once-City, dilapidated, dead in the grass, falling apart and slowly being reclaimed by the Sea. The Forest encroached on the second level, taking up more and more of the Once-City, taking it back for the Forever Sea. Breaches above, like hands reaching in to take back what was once the prairie's.

Even Barque, his skin taken over by plants, becoming the Sea. Her own hand and leg, too, becoming plant, grass, flower.

And their water rations, smaller and smaller. A punishment? Or smaller fractions of a smaller whole?

'You had this planned?' Kindred said, staring at The Word with astonishment. 'You wanted the attack so you could occupy Arcadia, take over the water stores? All of this – *all of it* – was about *water?*' Underneath her surprise and shock, Kindred felt disgust welling up inside her. The Once-City had been a place that lived *with* the world, that moved and bent and swayed with the world's wind, but this? This was the work of people determined to break the world and everything in it to their wills.

'Without. Water. Our. People. Will. Die.' The Word's voices ground into Kindred's skull, too low and rough to hear without pain.

'But you can't sail the Once-City to Arcadia!' Kindred shouted through the throbbing in her head. 'The whole thing will fall apart! Even if you make it, you won't be able to sail it away!'

But even as she said it, Kindred heard the problem in her logic, and Little Wing turned to her, a sad smile on her face.

'They don't want to live on the Once-City anymore,' she said, broken. 'That's why they've been stealing so many ships. They have enough for their people.'

She turned back to The Word, and as she did, Kindred took a step nearer the hearthfire beside her and put a hand in her pocket.

'That's what the wyrm is for, isn't it? The only thing Arcadian magic can do nothing against. What are you going to do, let it loose on Arcadia? Let it clean out the island for you? The only people still there apart from the guards in the towers will be *children*! *Elders*!'

The Word smiled together, sharing a glance between themselves. They nodded.

The absence of people on Breach suddenly made sense to Kindred – they would have been loaded onto their boats – the ones constantly loaded with supplies, waiting for this moment. They were abandoning their city, which had begun to abandon them long before. With each new Breach, each new push from the Forest, each day of decreased water stores, the council must have gotten more desperate. And so they turned to pirates, a majority who could scheme and plan something this terrible, this awful.

Kindred wondered idly if Seraph had known. Their work together in getting the hearthfires going again, all of it making this possible. Had he known? Had he been using her just as everyone else on the council had been using *The Errant*'s crew? Was he up on one of the ships right now, waiting to sail to his new home? Somehow, she couldn't imagine that.

'Fuck that. And fuck you,' Little Wing said, and she rushed them, her swords out, her battle cry ringing in the air.

But Kindred was faster.

'Get to the ship!' she shouted, as she pulled the handful of wild feverfew from her pocket along with a few of the bones – her mind now singing with the memory of Seraph describing what had happened to him, his warning to never mix feverfew with new bones

– and thrust them into the hearthfire, her voice rising in a terrified shout of song, a single word, held even as the fire recoiled from and then devoured the plants she dropped onto the bones at its heart.

Burn.

With a great sigh, the hearthfire rose, a pillar of grey swaying and writhing and reaching, arcing this way and that until it touched down in another hearthfire. Heat filled the space, pressing in close, and Kindred heard screams, but she could not see who they belonged to, and she could only hope that it wasn't Sarah or any of the others burning – her eyes were for the fire, and she watched as it spread, leaping from basin to basin, forming an interconnected web of fiery grey archways, dripping and bleeding flames, nowhere safe, nowhere calm. It was an inferno, and it spread.

Through the archways Kindred could see the chaos her action had caused. Bodies passed through the gaps in the flames, some on fire themselves, and behind it all, the wyrm shrieked and roared and pulled free. Too many of its captors had abandoned their charge in the face of the flames sprouting before them, an ever-growing barony of fire.

Before she turned to run, Kindred saw The Word, their twin faces ashen, wiped clean of their usual smirk, empty of anything other than shock as a great column of flame arched over them and dropped, consuming their bodies and leaving little behind.

Kindred ran for the boats but found herself stopped, blocked by Little Wing, who forced her back, swords flicking forward, cutting the air where Kindred had just been.

Back and back, away from the green chance of her boat, until she reached the doorway. Maybe she could lead Little Wing away and double back. There was no way forward, and the flames effectively cut her off from the rest of the crew.

Through the door and up the stairs she ran, hearing steps behind her but unwilling to look behind. Only when she got to the central column did she look back.

'Stop, Kindred!' Little Wing shouted, but Kindred was moving, climbing the stairs, thinking of her grass ship waiting, a chance to escape this – all of this.

But it was no good, she realized. She would never outrun Little Wing, and even if she could loop around and get back to her ship first, she would only succeed in leading Little Wing to her ship, to the crew. It was too much of a risk, Kindred thought as she climbed.

And so, she did the only thing she could think to do.

On the second level, Kindred leapt from the central staircase and raced into the Forest.

Little Wing followed.

26

KINDRED plunged into the darkness of the Forest, and suddenly, the world and the battle and every hope and frustration swirling about in the chaos above were gone. The trees around her offered only silence, watchful and waiting.

Great tremors continued to move through the Once-City, rippling in this place, too. The trees, strangers in the shadows, shivered in time, as if shaken by a great heartbeat racing in response to the danger.

The path was thinner than she remembered, the trees reaching in closer than before. The darkness between the branches was thick, oily, and it swirled with Kindred's movement. Each step left a trail of inky black washing away from her.

As she pushed farther in, keeping ahead of Little Wing, Kindred saw the effects of the tremors worsening. Trees shook in the darkness like naked bodies in the cold, uncontrolled and wild. And around the trees, reacting in their own way to the chaos that had infiltrated this place of deadly peace, were the lantern bearers.

They lined the path, articulating its end and the Forest's

beginning. Some lay along the path, paralleling it, while others hung from trees or floated above, their eyes and smiles lit from behind by a ghost light, their lanterns – some whole, others shattered and floating in place in the darkness – dripping white-silver radiance into the darkness.

It was a cacophony of light and presence, and yet not a single lantern bearer spoke or sang, and the Forest devoured even the sound of Kindred's pelting steps.

She'd stumbled at first upon seeing them crowding the path, but Little Wing was close behind, and she had no choice. She threaded her body through the hollow light of the lantern bearers, trying to ignore their smiles, their knowing looks. Though the quakes moving through the Once-City continued to shake the trees, the lantern bearers moved not at all, shook not at all.

At once, they began whispering, each voice speaking with a different cadence and tone but saying the same words.

Come, see, they whispered. *Come, know*.

Kindred kept her eyes ahead, remembering Yllstra's words from their trek along the path before.

The path is safe so long as its sanctity is never broken.

But something had broken it, Kindred saw, at least enough to leave cracks in the barrier between path and Forest. The light from the lantern bearers snaked curling fingers in toward the path, and Kindred moved carefully. A few lantern bearers had even put hands and fingers through, reaching out from the darkness of the trees, reaching for Kindred.

The world shook again, and Kindred saw the cracks in the barrier light up for a brief moment, brought into sharp relief by the tremor.

Whatever was happening with the battle above, whatever

magical attacks Cantrev's forces were launching against the Once-City, it was beginning to break things down.

Kindred ran as fast as she was able, dodging around intruding sprays of light and the reach of claws rimed in silvers and whites coruscating in the darkness.

Kindred ran past faces familiar and strange to her, through the miasma of their voices, cloying and pleading and grinning, all of them whispering the same words, inviting her in to see, to know. Inviting her precisely as she hoped to be invited and for precisely the right reason.

'Go,' she said to herself, voice hoarse as she puffed for air and strained for more speed. 'Go, dammit.'

Along the path they wound, and Kindred knew it was only Little Wing's bare existence over the last several span that was allowing her to stay ahead. The Little Wing with a half-decent meal in her stomach, the Little Wing who hadn't had to bear the horrors of a solo journey back across the Roughs before turning around and coming back – that Little Wing would long since have caught and killed Kindred.

Kindred ran.

No plan formed in her mind as she dodged lantern bearers and stuck to the increasingly narrow path. Only a vague idea, something unclear and intuitive.

'I go to lose myself,' she whispered to the Forest, thinking back to the last time she'd seen her grandmother here, the last sorrowful look the Marchess had given her before fading back into the darkness. 'I'm coming, Grandmother. I just need your help first.'

Kindred rounded a curve and there she was.

Other lantern bearers had gone wild with the tumult and tremors, raging against the failing barrier like animals, but the Marchess was serenity and calm embodied. She did not blaze with reckless light like the others, and she did not press herself to the barrier.

She stood in darkness and watched Kindred approach.

Kindred, for her part, slowed her steps, thinking it was because she intended it and wondering if it was because her muscles and lungs were giving up. Before her, the Marchess smiled and nodded.

'I go to lose myself,' Kindred whispered, and so, too, did the Marchess, echoing Kindred's words.

Behind her, Little Wing closed the distance, and Kindred could hear the impending victory in Little Wing's gasps, the surety that this was it.

And it was.

Kindred neared the Marchess, and Little Wing closed behind, and the Marchess watched all of it, serene and implacable.

'Now,' the Marchess said, her voice floating out from eternity, and Kindred didn't know if she jumped before the Marchess spoke or if she jumped because the Marchess spoke. But she jumped, leaping into the darkness, taking the leap she had meant to so many days before in her prison cell.

She leapt toward her grandmother, or the thing that looked and spoke like her grandmother, and she leapt toward a darker, deeper forever.

A buzz of light and pressure passed over her skin as she moved through the barrier, and then she was free, flying or falling through darkness, out and away from the path, toward the Marchess, who opened her arms and somehow caught Kindred.

In the weightlessness of that jump, Kindred saw the shape of this place, caught a glimpse of its form. It was not a Forest, not truly, not simply another level in the Once-City. The trees were not trees but great lengths of plants, bigger and stronger and wilder than anything Kindred had ever seen, growing up from somewhere, somewhen else. Any illusion that this was merely a flat space being crowded by an impossible army of trees was shattered. The Once-City had been invaded by the Sea, had been reclaimed by the true wilderness of the prairie, which longed to correct the mistakes of those who lived there. This was not a room in a house holding monsters; it was a doorway through which another world, a truer world, was creeping through.

Despite the surety she'd felt only a moment before, Kindred winced and closed her eyes, knowing she had misjudged, knowing she had only been fooled by a particularly clever lantern bearer.

But the strike never came, and no claws cut into her body.

She opened her eyes to find the Marchess looking down at her, the Marchess's smile kind and sad and somehow far away.

'Oh, child,' the Marchess said, her voice pure melody and music, a voice that gave purpose to song. 'So brave. And so foolish.'

Kindred looked past the Marchess, above – for she had fallen, down into darkness removed from the path – to where Little Wing stood on the edge of the path.

But Little Wing no longer hungered for Kindred. Instead, she stood at the break in the barrier that Kindred had created, face to face with her own lantern bearer, a figure of cutting contrasts between dark and light. Her lantern bearer's body shone with pinpricks like stars and then rippled as if playing host to a night that had never known light. She was a storm of opposites, and she stood before Little Wing, nodding and speaking words Kindred could not hear.

Tears coursed down Little Wing's cheeks, and Kindred saw a smile on her face. It was a smile not for callous victory or bitter defeat, but a smile of pure, childlike joy, the smile of one who knows herself and rejoices in that knowledge.

Kindred felt tears on her own face as she saw Little Wing laugh, just for herself and the lantern bearer, and it was enough to wash away the strain and pain in Little Wing's face, the trials she had endured, all of it. She laughed and reclaimed some part of herself that had been missing, had perhaps never been there at all.

The lantern bearer didn't attack, and Kindred was surprised to see other lantern bearers holding back, as if they didn't dare invade such a solemn and important moment.

'We long only for harmony,' the Marchess whispered, as if she knew Kindred's thoughts, could read her frustration in the tension of her shoulders, the catch of her breath. 'We are agents of the deep, come to wreak peace, come to sow order.'

Kindred shook her head, confusion and exhaustion slowing her thoughts.

'But the bearers are so . . . monstrous,' she said, waving her hand at a group of them lingering off in the darkness, their ghostly smiles etched in flickering lights, their clawed hands cutting air.

'For those who live in a monstrous world and call it home, any creature of order is a monster,' the Marchess said, smiling down at Kindred. 'The bearers, all of us, are only reflections, child. Shadows of the whole, desires and fears and hopes and power and weakness – all of it made manifest in shadow and light. For the woman who hopes to grow big and strong enough to protect those around her, a bearer taller than the trees. For the child wishing to see his parents one day, a two-voiced, two-faced bearer capable of showing the child's greatest fears and desires.

'For the woman who cannot decide if she ought to follow the path before her or the path behind,' the Marchess whispered, looking intently at Kindred, 'two bearers, one showing her the way forward and one showing her the person she once was, left behind.'

Off in the distance, Kindred could see her own lantern bearer, watching carefully, watching as a predator might watch its prey.

'We are made by the Sea, child, and the Sea seeks only balance. Just as you walk above, the Sea moves below, strange enemies in a fight neither asked for. The lantern bearers are the Sea's imaginings of you, and in their reach, they show only the need for harmony, peace, equilibrium.'

The Marchess pointed up, to where Little Wing stood, face to face with her own reflection, the Sea's reaching hand.

'And for one who has lived chaos in search of peace, who has walked every path in search of her place, a bearer who knows the cut of light against darkness and who has found calm.'

Little Wing's lantern bearer held out a hand and Little Wing took it.

A thrum of energy – song and light and heat and power – raced out from that contact, and Kindred was momentarily unable to breathe. Her eyes squeezed shut and her body curled upon itself, leaning into the steady strength of the Marchess.

And when she opened her eyes and looked, Little Wing was gone, and so was her lantern bearer. The path once again held only dim light.

'Where did she go?' Kindred asked. The Marchess had begun

carrying Kindred – walking or floating or flying, Kindred didn't know – back toward the path.

'That is a question wrongly asked,' the Marchess said, a phrase she had often invoked when trying to teach Kindred a lesson.

A streak of light from nearby pulled Kindred's attention away from the approaching path.

Her own lantern bearer approached, in figure and form exactly like Kindred herself, her lantern recently shattered and now only a bare flame dancing in the space around her hand. She neared, moving through the darkness with speed and poise, smiling at Kindred, her eyes wide and knowing.

Without thinking of it, Kindred began to push against the Marchess's arms, pushing herself toward her lantern bearer, thinking of Little Wing and the joy on her face. Harmony.

'No,' the Marchess said, and she spoke a word then that Kindred had never heard before, could not truly comprehend, and from the Marchess a rush of light emanated that engulfed Kindred's lantern bearer, throwing her back into the darkness, carrying her away on a wave of the Marchess's power. 'Not yet.'

'Why?' Kindred asked, feeling the intoxication of the lantern bearer's thrall wearing off but still confused.

'It's not your time,' the Marchess said, shaking her head and smiling down at Kindred. 'Not with so much left undone.'

They reached the path and the Marchess dumped Kindred gently back onto her feet. Out in the darkness of the Forest, more and more lantern bearers were moving, racing in chaotic loops toward the path and the cracks in the barrier.

'Go,' the Marchess said, favoring Kindred with one final smile. 'This is not how you rejoin the Sea.'

Kindred opened her mouth to respond, to ask more questions that were perhaps wrongly asked, but the Marchess cut her off with a slash of her hand.

'Go.'

Kindred went, racing back toward the central staircase as the path collapsed to nothing around her and the Forest reclaimed the second level of the Once-City.

27

CRACKS ran through the central staircase as Kindred reached it, and she had to leap over several to climb up. As she did, another tremor ran through the Once-City.

Kindred descended, though the way was treacherous. The central column bore great tears and scratches, and many of the stairs were cracked or broken entirely.

All the way down she ran, racing and leaping over the broken path, and when she heard the scream of the wyrm above, so tortured and mad with hunger and fear and the wrongness of it all, she knew what had done this damage. It had climbed above, probably racing to escape the fires Kindred had given power to below.

When she reached the Gone Ways, she stumbled into stillness at the change.

The hearthfires swayed as one, their movements hypnotic and mesmerizing, as they channeled whatever power they had left into speed for the Once-City.

And beyond them, where walls jagged as broken teeth once closed on the reach of the Sea moving in on the Gone Ways, now the steady movement of grass pulling by could be seen.

Every stretch of plant that had grown over the years into the Gone Ways was . . . gone.

The Once-City sailed again, and beyond the rips and tears in the wall, the mostly dark Sea was a moving image, plants sliding by as the Once-City moved through the Sea.

Kindred watched legions of plants, baronies and kingdoms of rising plant stalks – all of them passing by the Once-City.

The Once-City was sailing again.

'Kindred!' Ragged Sarah shouted from where she stood by the boats. 'We have to go!'

Kindred ran through the paths between the hearthfires, trying to ignore the dead and burned bodies lying so still. When she reached the boats, she felt a gulp of relief when she saw everyone still there, a few nursing wounds, but nothing deathly, nothing mortal.

'Where's Little Wing?' the captain asked. When Kindred gave her head a slight shake, she understood.

'We need to move,' Kindred said, looking around at them all. 'They're insane to push the Once-City into sailing. Seraph and I only started to fix the hearthfires, but they're not well enough to sail, not really. They're going to destroy this whole place, and I bet this level will go first.'

As if her words needed proof, a huge crack sounded as an enormous chunk of the wall was ripped away.

'Help me move this boat to the edge,' Kindred said, gesturing at one of the two completed vessels. They all set to, and as they did, the captain explained what they had seen on the battlefield.

'We all thought they were unprepared for the battle, but we

were wrong. A few ships went out to defend, but it was a stall tactic. Ebb-La-Kem and the other Hanged Council members were herding their people onto boats as fast as they could, all of them stacked with supplies. There was no way for us to steal a ship – they used every damn one of them.'

Kindred shook her head, wanting to find it unbelievable, but after everything that had happened so far that day, it all seemed right.

'Ebb-La-Kem offered the captain a spot on one of the vessels,' Cora the Wraith said.

'Aye,' the captain said, spitting once on the ground. 'Just me. He said my crew could ride their way down in their new City.'

She sighed, weary suddenly, and Kindred wondered for just a moment what rest for Captain Jane Caraway would look like. What would it take for tears of joy and the finality of peace to be writ on her face?

'But what about the battle? They just gave up the city?' Kindred asked. Their plan to hold the wyrm there, to sail the city up to Arcadia, wouldn't work if they handed it over to Cantrev.

'Prairie fire,' Ragged Sarah called down from where she was working on the ship.

'What?' Kindred asked.

'The defense boats Ebb-La-Kem and the others sent out were just meant to slow Cantrev's forces,' the captain said. 'Once the City began to move, the remaining boats lit a fire among the plants, and since it's so late in the season, they caught immediately. I saw Cantrev's forces trying to flee, but. . . but . . .'

Captain Caraway broke off, shaking her head. Long Quixa finished her thought.

'They couldn't get away fast enough. The fires overtook them, and they burned. All of them.'

'Gods,' Kindred whispered, horrified.

'I don't understand why they're doing this,' Cora said, angry and afraid.

'Water,' Kindred said, her voice a grunt as they shifted the boat along the ground bit by bit. She explained what she could.

'They're going to take Arcadia. Cantrev's forces are depleted, and there can't be much of a guard left around the island. The Once-City has been running out of water for a long time, and this is their solution: take control of Arcadia, the island with more wells than anyone would ever need. Who cares if the City starts falling apart on the way; none of them intend to live here ever again. They're going to take Arcadia.'

'But the mages in the towers,' Cora the Wraith said. 'What about the lighthouses and their defense? No ship can get close to the island if they don't wish it.'

'And why sail the City there?' the captain asked, skeptical. 'They have the ships, and they had enough supplies to make it all the way to the Mainland, it looked like. What do they need the Once-City for?'

'The wyrm,' came a voice behind them, and they turned to find Seraph, out of breath, his usually unkempt robes now ripped.

'They're going to sail the City right into Arcadia, run it aground and let the wyrm loose to clean out the city.'

Cora the Wraith leapt away from the boat and picked up a sword from the ground nearby, a piece of detritus from the battle.

'Please!' Seraph cried, holding up his hands, empty of anything but soot stains from working the hearthfire. 'I didn't know about the plan! None of them told me until it was too late to stop it. I escaped and didn't know where else to go. And I knew you would be down here.'

He said this last to Kindred, his eyes on her, on the boat.

'I've seen how you look at those boats. If anyone can work the hearthfire in one of them, it's you, Kindred. Please take me with you. Please.'

'What do you all think?' Kindred asked, looking around at the rest of them, but another section of wall tore away, and great cracks tore their way along the floor. The Gone Ways were going.

'If he can help push, I say yes!' Cora said, dropping the sword and returning to the boat. A chorus of agreement sounded, and then they were pushing, straining at the weight of the boat.

Would it sail? Was she crazy? Had she gathered enough supplies? Was she about to kill every one of her new crew, her old captain, the woman she loved?

Close. Closer. Closer.

Escape, the green of the Sea whispered to her.

Belief, the dark of the deeps said.

The nose of the ship passed through the great absence where the wall had once been and was immediately pulled hard, and the rest of the ship began to follow, moving of its own accord, shifting to join the motion of the Sea.

'Everyone aboard!' Kindred shouted. 'Get in!'

They began leaping in through the door, falling in a muddled mess inside but not caring. Kindred was last, and she vaulted inside just as the boat pulled free of the Gone Ways.

Down.

'Oh, gods,' Scindapse shouted as she lost her footing and slid back. The others clung to what they could, but the boat began to fall, and fast.

The flame.

Kindred leapt forward to the hearthfire basin, glimpsing it for just a moment before the light was gone. As others clung to whatever they could, she held herself close to the basin and worked in the dark.

Her purposes, her lives up to this point lined up for this one moment: building the hearthfire, keeping and tending it, all to the beat of the deeps, all with the dark in mind.

She pulled two bones from her pocket and wound them together with a three-part braid of prairie grass, bluestem, and echinacea she had braided a few nights before in preparation for her voyage. When she was finished, it was a rough circle, a structure meant to at once circumscribe the fire and give it breath. It was a build for the deeps.

This, Kindred set into the basin and held down.

The song came easily to her. It was the first song any hearthfire keeper learns: a melody to start a fire. She let the viscous syllables rub against one another as they slid from her tongue. Harsh and heavy, the song required strength to sing, not strength of muscle but of will, something that Kindred might once have struggled to find but no more.

Her song gave a thickness to the air, and although the craft still spun, still fell, the air around Kindred stilled and condensed as she sang.

A fire, blue-green and hungry, bloomed atop and around the bone structure, and the effect was almost immediate.

The ship slowed and then stopped its fall, and with a few changes and a slower, lower-pitched song, Kindred was able to stop the spin.

Beside her, Ragged Sarah knelt, unable – like everyone else – to do anything, but her hand on Kindred's arm was a note of confidence and a reminder of her love.

'Let's get back up to the surface,' Kindred said. 'Cora, pull those braided ropes there. Quixa, pull those on the other side.'

'What do they do?' Cora asked as she moved to do as Kindred said.

'They release the sails,' Kindred said.

How long had she spent watching the Sea, Kindred wondered, watching it and seeing the currents that moved through it? Not the wind that stirred its surface but something more significant, a wind for the dark and deeps.

She felt it in the fire when the sails opened, their curved expanse meant to blend with the Sea as it cut forward and displaced the subsea wind to give them momentum, speed, stability.

'Cora, stay there and pull when I tell you. Quixa, the same. You're both our way to change course horizontally.'

'There's no wheel?' Captain Caraway asked from where she huddled near the prow's forward jut.

'No wheel,' Kindred said, shaking her head. 'Just the fire and the ropes for the sails.'

Captain Caraway nodded in the near-darkness, the only light from the hearthfire. She smiled.

'Hold on to something,' Kindred said to those who hadn't been given a job. She leaned into the hearthfire and, slowly at first, pushed both hands into the flames, watching as the golden shoots on the one unfurled, waving lazily about in the fire.

The flames curled and moved around her hands evenly, and

Kindred smiled. Though different, they were both her hands, one the unblemished hand of the woman she'd been, the other the changed, healed hand of the woman who she had become. Kindred worked the bones, adding a few more from the bag at her hip.

And she sang.

A song of leavings and new beginnings, of friends lost and lives changed.

The ship leapt forward, faster by far than anything Kindred had ever sailed in or seen. It cut through the Sea with ease, as if it belonged. Kindred smiled.

She sang. She sailed.

28

THE Once-City, by the time they got their bearings and gave chase, was well ahead of them. But Kindred's ship moved without frozen hearthfires dragging it down, and soon enough, they sailed just behind the City, its great mass leaving behind an enormous wake that took Kindred a few attempts to navigate.

As they sailed, Kindred explored her new vessel, feeling its response to her urgings, moving tentatively at first and then with greater confidence, growing to understand and love the green, braided confines of it. As other crew members bandaged themselves up or rested themselves, Kindred spent the voyage getting to know this new friend.

And Seraph explained what had happened above.

'Ebb-La-Kem and the other pirate councillors began loading citizens onto boats, ward after ward, moving far more efficiently than it seemed possible. Clearly, the councillors had been practicing. A few of the pirates remained behind on the City to pilot it, but the rest got out. And most of the citizens went, too, though some refused, and they were killed. Morrow Laze tried to raise a rebellion – him and several of his sailors fought back, and for a bit, I thought they might actually stop it all. Morrow was a fierce warrior, and he fought all the way to the end. But finally, they cut him down. I couldn't watch.'

Seraph shivered, and Kindred thought again of Little Wing, of a warrior who believed so strongly in a certain view of the world, who fought and would keep fighting for it no matter what. She shook her head, disgusted at all the lives lost, the damage done – all for control over the world and its gifts.

'I was lucky that they needed me for the hearthfires – Ebb had one of his lackeys toss me in the hold of one of the ships instead of killing me. But I know those vessels better than any of those monsters. I made it out and escaped.'

'Did every other citizen know?' Kindred asked, her voice quiet. She was remembering those poets, their voices so beautiful, calling into existence their shimmering scene. Did they know all along? Had they lived their lives in joy and anticipation for the day when such destruction would happen?

'No,' Seraph said, shaking his head, and Kindred felt some strange relief. 'It was only the majority of them on the council, I believe, and a few of their trusted friends. Even as they were loading people onto the boats, Ebb and the others were lying to them, saying that the City was falling apart, that they had to evacuate, that they would find somewhere else to go.'

Seraph looked down at his hands.

'It was . . . awful.'

Kindred could think of nothing to say to that, and so she stayed silent, as did everyone else aboard.

The ship cut through the grasses as if they were nothing, friendly whispers on the hull, and though the voyage began to grow long and uncomfortable without the steady rush of air and light from above, Kindred found herself growing accustomed to it.

After what could have been a day or five, the Once-City began to change course slightly and pick up speed, its wake shifting enough to draw Kindred's notice.

'I'm going to bring us up, captain,' Kindred said. 'Will you pop the top hatch and get a look around?'

The captain climbed the short rope ladder that hung from the hatch, and when Kindred nodded at her, she opened the hatch and stuck her head out into a beautiful prairie evening.

The effect of real sunlight on those inside was immediate. Smiles, still tentative, showed on faces, and a few spots of conversation and even laughter broke out. The surface still existed, and for everyone, that was a relief.

'Arcadia just in sight,' the captain said as she dropped back down. 'The entire armada of the Once-City is keeping pace with the City itself. Probably forty ships in all. Maybe more. Everything from the dreadnoughts to hoppers being pulled behind bigger ships.'

Kindred nodded at this.

Arcadia wouldn't have been so close on a normal voyage, couldn't have been, but the Once-City sailed at a dangerous pace for something so large, and Kindred couldn't imagine the structural damage being done to the City. What would be left when it crashed ashore on Arcadia? What sad remnant of the lives lived there would still be around to see?

'Should we try to take out the City? Stop the attack?' Cora the Wraith asked. 'Or, should we help them attack and try to gain back their favor?'

'We can't stop the City,' the captain said. 'That's impossible.'

'It's too big,' Seraph agreed. 'It's repelled more attacks throughout the years than any can count.'

'And they don't need us anymore,' Kindred said. 'There's no winning back their favor. We never had it in the first place.'

'The best bet is to run,' the captain said.

'But where?' Ragged Sarah asked. 'We have no stores here, not anything that would last more than a few days.'

They all fell silent, mulling this over, searching for a way.

'We don't have any stores,' the captain said slowly, thinking her way through her words as she spoke them aloud, 'but each one of those ships in the armada is packed full, stores enough to last spans and spans. Who's to say how long the sacking of Arcadia will take? Who's to say how long they'll have to wait for the wyrm to do its work?'

The captain let her words fall into silence before she continued. 'Why don't we steal one of their ships?'

No one spoke for a moment, and then Kindred laughed.

'Aye, captain,' she said. 'I'm up for it. Let's be pirates.'

The planning took no time at all, because it turned out they had no equipment and almost no weapons save for a few lengths of wood.

What they did have were the plants Kindred had stolen from the Once-City. These she pressed into Scindapse's hands with brief explanations for what effect they might have on a hearthfire. With a boat as small as the one they were looking to steal, it would be easy enough to leap aboard, toss the plants in the fire, and make use of the panic that would ensue.

'Kindred, can you bring us up behind one of the last ships in their fleet? Just close enough to climb aboard. We're sailing over even grass now, so I think we should be able to make it. After that, we take them by surprise.'

The captain spoke to the crew as Kindred piloted the ship as close as she could get to one of the trailing vessels in the armada. It wouldn't be precise until someone looked out the hatch again, but she thought she could tell roughly where the ships were based on the wakes they were leaving.

'We aren't likely to be dealing with hardened sailors on every vessel, and our chances are best with one of the cutters trailing at the end. Smaller crew, easier to overwhelm, faster and more maneuverable than others. We'll be sailing off and away to the Mainland by the time anyone realizes what's happened.'

'And what about the island?' Cora the Wraith asked. 'I have family there. My dad still keeps a house in the Twist District.'

The captain said nothing, which said everything.

'We'll burn hard to get to the Mainland and rustle up what help we can find there,' the captain said finally. It was thin, and Kindred could see the dissatisfaction on Cora's face, hers and others', but there was nothing else to do.

Maybe.

A plan, wild as the wind on a dark night, had begun to move

in Kindred's mind, shaping itself into something impossible and just strange enough to warrant immediate dismissal.

And yet.

'Approaching,' Kindred said, nodding at Captain Caraway and Seraph, gesturing them near. Privacy didn't exist in a boat like this one, Kindred realized, but the others around them looked away or shuffled fore or aft slightly, giving them some space.

Except Ragged Sarah, who stood by Kindred's side, as if she already knew.

'Are you sure?' Kindred whispered to Sarah.

'Into the unknown,' Sarah whispered back, as the captain neared.

'Can you keep it steady long enough to climb aboard with us, Kindred?' The captain kept her voice low. 'Or do you want to sail behind? We could pull you once we're away from the armada – I know you couldn't get many bones, so you can judge whether you have enough to make the Mainland or not. Or . . .'

The words died away as the captain looked, really looked, into Kindred's face. Seraph, too, was watching her with interest.

'What is it, Kindred? What do you have?'

Kindred brought the vessel just up behind a clipper, its sails huge and bloated with wind. The hull was enormous, at least from what she could see of it through the hatch and from the captain's descriptions; it would certainly be the kind of ship to make it to the Mainland.

'Everyone ready?'

One by one, the ship emptied out as Kindred focused on keeping them steady.

And one by one, the people who had been her family for so long said goodbye.

Cora laughed and told Kindred she was crazy, but there were tears in her eyes as she hugged Kindred and Ragged Sarah goodbye.

Long Quixa said only, 'I will remember you,' before touching her forehead to Kindred's and then Sarah's.

Scindapse still didn't understand what Kindred was doing and why, but she had given up trying. Instead, she thanked Kindred, gave Ragged Sarah a big hug, and then moved toward the rope ladder, the plants Kindred had given her clutched tightly in her hand, the song Kindred had told her to sing playing over and over on her lips as she practiced.

'You're going to be great,' Kindred whispered to Scindapse, giving the girl a wink.

The last was Captain Jane Caraway.

'Are you sure you want to take him with you?' she asked, gesturing toward Seraph, who knelt before the hearthfire. 'We could tip him over the edge and not a soul in the world would care.'

Kindred shook her head.

'I would.'

'Fair enough. You always did have a soft heart,' the captain said, laying a hand on Kindred's shoulder. 'I hope you keep it that way.'

'Aye, captain.'

'Oh, no. You're the captain now. captain of your own vessel,' Captain Caraway said, gesturing around.

Kindred laughed.

'I suppose that's true. But you'll always be my captain, Jane,' Kindred said, hugging Captain Jane Caraway, wanting to say so much and knowing so little about how to do it. So, she simply held her captain close one last time.

The captain tightened the cloth around her bad eye.

'And you're sure about this?' the captain said for the fourth or fifth time as they pulled away from one another. 'You know you don't have to do this, Kindred.'

'I know, captain,' she said, tears coursing down her cheeks now. This was the end, she knew. A person can only follow two paths for so long, and to cut one away, even to follow yourself – this, too, was loss, Kindred understood.

'And you, Sarah? You're sure?'

Sarah nodded, her jaw set, and Kindred felt love, fierce and bright, inside her chest. Sarah shook the captain's hand.

'Very well. Good luck to each of you.'

She touched her mouth, her forehead, and then offered Kindred her hand.

Kindred did the same.

'Thank you, captain. Safe seas,' Kindred said.

'Aye. And you, too, captain,' Jane said, and then she, too, was at the ladder, moving among her remaining crew. Up they went, one by one, ready to leap.

Kindred piloted the vessel close behind the pirate ship, held it as steady as she could, until they were all gone, lost to the sounds of Sea and wind. She heard no alarms or shouts of violence, only the soft sounds of Scindapse's singing, getting quieter and quieter until they were gone.

They had their own battles to fight, Kindred thought, and so, too, did she.

And for the moment, that was enough.

She turned to Ragged Sarah and Seraph.

'Let's do it.'

Kindred settled herself in front of the hearthfire and pushed the ship below the waves again, feeling the comforting embrace of the Sea close around her, and then they were off, sailing faster than she had ever managed above the waves, the current pushing them along, flowing like a ghost wind through the grass.

They overtook the Once-City, and Kindred dove down deep under it, deeper than the scraggly remains of the Gone Ways, until they were past it.

They rose then, up and up, pushing out in front of and away from the Once-City.

'Sarah,' she said.

Ragged Sarah let the ropes she had been using to control the sails fall and instead scurried up the rope ladder and pushed open the hatch.

'Nearly there. Arcadia is close.'

'Good. Now the doors.'

'Aye,' Sarah said, dropping down and moving to each main door on either side of the cabin. These she pulled open, exposing the inside of the ship to the slipping song of the prairie grasses sliding by. Sarah lashed the doors open so they would stay that way before climbing back up to the open hatch.

'Seraph, get ready.'

'Aye,' he said, kneeling down on the other side of the hearthfire, opposite Kindred, beginning to sing in his quiet voice.

'Nearly there. Nearly,' Sarah said, looking back and forth between Arcadia and the Once-City. Finally, she dropped down into the cabin and said, 'Now.'

Kindred reached deep into the hearthfire, calling the flames as she had so long ago on Arcadia, remembering the blaze that she had unlocked, the deep hunger of the fire she had been only too happy to aid. She did not beg and she did not order; she spoke to the flames as a friend, as kin, asking for aid and justice.

And the fire poured out in response.

Gouts of flame, too big for any one person to control or shape, exploded from the hearthfire. But it wasn't just Kindred – Seraph too reached in, his voice twisting with Kindred's as they both called to the fire, both called to its mystery, their twin litanies rising like prayers.

The hearthfire split and sent tendrils out in either direction, Seraph guiding one and Kindred the other, ropes of blue and gold and green and grey flame extending out the doors of Kindred's vessel and spreading among the prairie grasses – untouched by flame for so long, protected against the natural spread of it.

But the Sea longed for the flames just as the flames longed for the Sea, and Kindred was only too happy to oblige. Too long had the Sea surrounding Arcadia been denied the burn, too long had it been kept even and monolithic, flat and still and contained.

Kindred left her place at the fire as her vessel continued to slide forward, leaving twin trails of flame behind it, Seraph nodding when she asked if he could hold both for a moment. The fire was doing its work now, and he only had to watch and shape in small ways. It wanted to burn, and there was plenty to burn.

And Kindred wanted to see her work, to be present for this instead of trapped behind as had so often been her wont in life.

She climbed the ladder and emerged from the hatch, craning around, seeing as much of the surface world as she could.

Seeing it while she could.

Her vessel cut a line between Arcadia and the approaching Once-City, its bulk followed by the outfitted pirate vessels. The blaze she left behind devoured grasses with the hunger of one kept away too long – although it skirted around the swaths of grasses affected by the Greys, their ashen masses remaining like tiny, dying islands. Flames leapt and scurried and ran and roared and plunged, widening the line between the Once-City and Arcadia into a gulf, a blackening chasm that threatened to devour any who would enter it, to send them down to darker depths than any thought possible.

Kindred laughed, her mouth and throat filled with a prairie wind dancing with smoke and heat. *In*, she breathed the wind; *out*, she exhaled.

As her vessel sailed, it left behind destruction and, if the legends were true, rejuvenation, the return of beasts and plants impossible to fathom and control.

'Sarah! Come up and see!'

The vessel continued its fast circle around Arcadia, and as her love joined her, Kindred saw the few Arcadian defenders who had rallied suddenly cut off from the Once-City and the ships beyond it. Instead, their massing sails pulled to turn back, away from the waves of flame running toward them, fast on the wind.

'It's working,' Sarah said. 'I can't believe it's working.'

Kindred shook her head, just as surprised.

It wasn't a perfect solution, she knew, but it was something, and that would have to do for now. As she thought of the people living in Arcadia – Mick, Red Alay, and the rest of the Marchess's crew, Legate, all of them – and those aboard the Once-City vessels, she knew she couldn't tip the scales toward one side or the other. Was it a crime to want for something so natural as water? Was it evil to want to help your people, to make sure they had enough food to eat, enough water to drink, enough safety from those who would harm them?

Kindred didn't know, couldn't think of people and communities with such simple calculations as good and bad.

She was sure the Arcadians would scheme to get around this, just as she was sure the Hanged Council would soon be working on some way to continue with their plan.

But for today, Kindred knew, she had stopped them both. No more killing today; no more good and bad today.

As she watched, the Once-City raced headlong into the widening chasm of the burn as the ships of the armada cut hard away, angling to get clear of the oncoming flames. The Once-City broke apart as it fell, dropping as fast as the fire burned, collapsing through charred plants to descend to the deeps.

'You were right about them,' Kindred said to Sarah, feeling the heaviness of everything ending. 'You said they were rotten, and I didn't believe you, and now all of this.'

Sarah frowned and leaned close to Kindred, catching her downturned eyes.

'It's all right now. It doesn't matter anymore. We're here, and there's a whole world ahead.'

Kindred nodded and looked up.

'Ahead. And below.'

Sarah nodded, then smiled.

'Hey! You never named the ship! It's bad luck to sail a ship without a name!'

'Indeed!' Seraph said from where he sat before the fire, a wild smile on his face. 'What will it be, captain?'

And Kindred realized they were right. In the push to finish it, and in the complicated chaos of the last few days, she hadn't even considered a name – a bad omen for her first journey unless she fixed it.

She felt too caught in this moment, the juxtaposition of destruction and beauty, growth and death colliding violently, powerfully, significantly.

I go to lose myself in it, Kindred thought, her grandmother's words become her own.

'*The Lost*,' she said finally. 'Its name is *The Lost*.'

'Aye, captain,' Sarah said, grinning, and from below, Kindred could see Seraph nodding in appreciation. 'And what is our destination?'

Kindred eyed the flames. *The Lost* approached the point where it had started her burn, nearly completing the circle around Arcadia. It would do.

The Sea was burned away, but Kindred's eyes snagged on the patches of the Greys left behind, and her mind leapt suddenly back to a day not so long before, standing with Seraph on the docks of the Once-City and looking out across the Forever Sea. Stories of what lay below had been his explanation for the Greys – impossible stories the world had long since discounted as fanciful, imaginative nonsense for children.

She wanted impossible stories. She wanted the imaginative nonsense. Those stories everyone knew but few believed? Kindred wanted those.

She dropped back down, followed quickly by Sarah. Kindred kissed her then, fierce and quick.

'The deeps,' she said, pulling back and looking Sarah in the eye. 'We sail for the deeps. Aye?'

Ragged Sarah grinned back, her eyebrows rising.

'Aye.'

And with that, Kindred knelt before the fire, nodding to Seraph, who sat back, face wet with sweat and exhaustion. Kindred plunged her hands into the hearthfire once more, pulling it back and into the vessel. She sang her melody, a lilting hymn of exploration and discovery, of dark spaces hiding wonders, of a world beneath the world, of a life unlived until that very moment.

The Lost dove for the deeps.

The storyteller stops, letting the last words fall from his mouth in slow, heavy drips.

'That's it!?' comes a shout, the tone caught somewhere between disbelief and anger. Its owner, one of the men sitting beside Praise, stands up. 'That can't be the end of the story!'

'Yeah!' says the man on Praise's other side, standing, too. 'You promised to tell us our history! You haven't explained any of *this*!' He gestures around: at the broken bones of the world that was, at the ever-present darkness, at the pillar, grey-green in the firelight, rising from the ground and reaching above.

Others are nodding along, a few beginning to stand, all angry or confused, and then the questions come, shouted at him. What happened to Kindred? Did the pirates make it to Arcadia? Did Kindred ever find the Marchess?

And yet they never ask the one that so weighed in Kindred's mind: What is below the waves?

And why should they ask it? They know the answer, have been born into it. Their fantasy is not to dive below but to live above. For people born in the darkness below the Forever Sea, their dream, their *only* dream, is sun on grass, open sky above, the darkness below their feet.

The storyteller ignores them. They will get their answers.

Instead, he watches Praise, who stands, flanked by the two men, and approaches the dais. He puts one foot up and then pauses, and the storyteller wonders with the thinnest flicker of hope whether this time will be different.

But no, of course not. Praise hauls himself up after a moment of indecision, and then the two men join him. There was only one the last time, but Praise was younger then, fitter, less an old man gnawing at the last few bones of his life.

'Storyteller,' he says, turning out so that those assembled might hear him. 'We don't have much in our small community, but what we do have, we have offered to you freely and without payment. You have come here, you say, to tell us our history, our story, but instead you drink our water, eat our food, and mock us with a story half-told. You have taken advantage of our hospitality.'

The storyteller gave up being surprised by this sentiment long ago, the words rehearsed and wooden.

'I have given you enough of your history,' the storyteller says, his eyes locked on Praise's. 'And some of your present, too.'

'It is not enough,' Praise says, again to the crowd. 'You owe everyone here more, much more.'

The two men take their cue from Praise and leap forward, each one grabbing one of the storyteller's arms. He does not fight them, except when one tries to take his pack.

To this man, the storyteller whispers a word in a language not spoken in ages, and the man releases the bag with a start.

'I will go with you,' the storyteller says to Praise. 'But you will not take my things.'

'Fine,' Praise says. 'Keep the bag.'

'My friends,' comes a voice from the edge of the firelight, and the crowd turns to find the First there, her wounds bandaged, her face pale and pained. The headaches have already begun. She will not last the night.

'The storyteller will extend his stay – and his protection – until he has finished the story to our liking. Let us thank him,' she says, clapping her hands quietly.

The sound of laughter and cheering accompanies the storyteller as he is led away from the light of the fires, back to Praise's home, to the only room in Twist with a door that locks.

The hammock is still there, but now a set of rusty chains hangs from the wall, and the feel of them against his skin as he is locked in for the night is a comfort to the storyteller. Familiar and honest. This was the truth all along – now it is simply out in the open air for all to see.

'I'm sorry it has to be this way,' the First says, standing in the doorway with Praise as the men chain him up. 'I wanted to do it without all of this, but when you turned down our offer to stay, well . . .'

The First trails off, shaking her head to clear the sudden throb of pain.

'I have my people to think about,' she finishes.

For a time, he sits in the idyllic silence, letting those old words tumble out from his memory: 'I'll see you after.' Five simple syllables, each one a weight on the storyteller's still, still heart.

They leave him, with one man outside the door. The chains are tight, but not so tight that he can't get his bag open.

He reaches inside and pulls out a book and a stub of coal, the only items inside. He flips past pages and pages filled with an archaic script – the same language he spoke earlier when the man tried to take his pack.

On and on the book goes, far too long, far too many pages, more than the binding seems to hold from the outside. And yet there they are, a seemingly infinite fan of pages.

Finally, though, the storyteller reaches a page half-filled with the script, and he traces one finger along the last line, whispering the words to himself and the walls of his cell.

'Let them forget us. Only this matters. Only this.'

For a long time, the storyteller reads and rereads these words, thinking of hands held in the darkness, a blade of grass clutched between them.

He flips forward again. Gone is the packed, precise script now. Instead, these pages are filled with an untidy scrawl, the hand uneven, the text often smudged to the point of being illegible, just a series of cloudy, coal-black shapes.

It takes him some time, but finally, the storyteller finds a blank page, as yet untouched by his messy hand.

With morning on the way, and the next chapter of the story with it, the storyteller pushes the coal across the page, mouthing the words as he writes them, the same ones he has been writing since Before became After, filling page after page of this endless book with the same question.

Kindred, are you there?

He stares at the words for the rest of the night, waiting in the stillness for a miracle.

ABOUT THE AUTHOR

Joshua Johnson lives in Minnesota, in the Prairie Pothole Region of the United States (which was an inspiration for the environment of the novel) and teaches classes about writing, literature, and the environment at a small university. His work has been published in *Metaphorosis Magazine*, *The Future Fire*, and *Syntax & Salt*, among others.